KOOTENAY
Justice

A Novel

By David Crouse

donated to BEMC Library May 6, 2014 by:
Ken & Wendy
Thanks for your
friendship & love

David Crouse

Produced by:

FriesenPress
Suite 300 – 852 Fort Street
Victoria, BC, Canada V8W 1H8

www.friesenpress.com

Distributed to the trade by The Ingram Book Company

DEDICATION

I am dedicating this book to the love of my life,
Karen Arlene Crouse

Her support and never ending encouragement have made this book possible.

ONE

Excitement stirred Cody as the first hints of dawn began to give shape to their campsite, nestled in the gorge of the Blaeberry River, on the west slopes of the Rocky Mountains. As his mind climbed out of a deep sleep, he savoured the major milestone that he and his three friends would achieve today. Even Quinn rolled out at dawn without being dragged from his blankets. Darcy and Jed were also more eager to get this new day rolling than usual.

As Cody splashed his face with the icy, glacier fed river water, he marvelled at how far he and his friends, The Pards, as they had come to be called, had come. They were rough and tumble young guys back in Montreal but they had changed dramatically in the course of their journey this far. They were now trail hardened. The long days of paddling the huge cargo canoes, the innumerable portages where every man was expected to carry at least seventy-five pounds, some carried two hundred, at a time had hardened their bodies to a strength that surprised themselves. Not only had they travelled from Montreal across the vast wilderness of the prairies, and now over the passes to the western slopes of the incredible Rocky Mountains by canoe and horse, they had also gained an education in the ways of the Hudson Bay Company as it continued its domination of this huge reach of territory, larger than most kingdoms of the world.

After battling snow, mud, insects and ornery pack horses as they crossed the Rocky Mountains for what seemed too long, they were more than ready to follow a wide valley instead of climbing up and down treacherous mountain trails. The Columbia Valley should open up before them before this day closed. That was their immediate objective.

"Come on slow pokes!" taunted Jed, "I'll be so far ahead of you I'll have Columbia River fish caught and fried by the time you get yourselves to the bottom of this miserable Blaeberry River."

A sudden snort and piercing whinny signalled a problem from the horse herd. Each man had his own mount plus two pack horses. Somehow Darcy, who was the least skilled horseman, had drawn the worst knuckle-headed beast any of them had ever seen. In fact they had named him Knucklehead. While the others had been happy to let Darcy struggle with the rebel packer and offered plenty of jibes about his lack of horse sense, the problem had grown worse as the days wore on.

This time the ruckus continued with a mix of Darcy's curses, the rattle of rigging, hooves pounding, loud snorts, and now shrill neighing. Suddenly Quinn bellowed over the noise "He's caught up on the pack saddle!"

Instantly, the three dropped whatever they were doing and tore to the scene of struggle. Darcy was being flung up and down. His heavy coat had hooked on one of the cross pieces of the pack saddle. In the grey dawn, he looked for all the world like a rag doll being tossed by a puppy as the enraged horse strained against the lead rope that kept him tied to a tree.

Cody yelled, "Hang on, we're coming!" not that Darcy would want to hang on any longer at all!

Quinn and Cody converged towards the head of the enraged beast. Cody stripped off his own jacket as he ran. Quinn lunged for the neck of the horse, wrapping his huge arms around as he rode the tosses of the horse's head to a standstill with his immense strength and weight. Cody managed to throw his coat over the eyes of the struggling horse as Quinn bit down on the beast's ear. The struggle slowed, giving Jed a chance to close in to Darcy's rescue.

Jed's heart lept to his throat in the instant he realized that Darcy was not moving.

"He's out cold! Doesn't look good!" yelled Jed.

Cody jabbed the edge of the coat into Quinn's hands under the horse's neck and rushed to help lift Darcy free of the pack saddle.

With two of them lifting, it took only a moment and they had Darcy laid down, away from danger.

"OK Quinn. Let him go!" called Cody.

The horse reared and spun as far from Quinn as the rope would let him.

To their great relief, Darcy began to stir. He went to sit up but his eyes rolled back and he immediately passed out again. Jed got a canteen and spilled a little water into Darcy's mouth. This time as he came to, the others kept him from trying to get up.

"That horse is wolf-bait!! I'm never going near it again except with a gun" spluttered Darcy.

He sounded surprisingly strong for someone just rescued from near death. But they assured him that Jed, their most experienced horseman, would take Knuckle-head and Darcy would get the most placid packer of the herd.

Once they got Darcy back to the campfire, seated with his back against a big fir tree, Cody stirred the coals, adding some twigs so they could make a new pot of coffee.

Darcy was looking beat up with one eye swelling badly and a deep scrape oozing blood by his left ear. Those wounds signalled lots of bruises on the rest of Darcy's body as well, yet, fortunately, nothing seemed broken.

"We'll hold up for a while and see how Darcy is doing" said Cody.

Jed nodded, "Anybody would have the shakes after a ride like that!"

"I'll be fine" protested Darcy, "This is the day we get to the Columbia and I'm not going to be the drag that keeps that from happening."

"If you wouldn't talk so much you might get your strength back quicker" chimed in Quinn who was also showing marks from the battle with the renegade horse. He kept wiping some blood from a split lip where he had collided with the rearing horse's head.

"The Columbia will still be there tomorrow if we don't make it today" Cody offered, trying to take pressure off Darcy.

Jed jumped up, "I'll go check the pack saddle on Knuckle-head"

"Better tie it on a real short rope while you do" Cody advised.

"It's nose will be snubbed right against a tree trunk with a blindfold over it's eyes!" assured Jed. He and Quinn wandered over to the picket rope to busy themselves with checking all their gear and supplies.

As the coffee started to boil, Cody fought down a sense of doom and gloom. His grandfather, David Thompson, the renowned explorer of this area, had assured Cody that even though he was only nineteen, he was more than ready to lead an expedition that would take care of some issues concerning Hudson Bay Company business. Was his grandfather too old now to have a clear understanding of Cody's ability and what it would take to accomplish this secret mission? Sure – his grandfather had been an orphan of only fourteen when he had been apprenticed to the Company and shipped from England to the desolate shores of Hudson Bay. But just because Grampa had had an unusual ability to adapt and flourish under extreme conditions didn't mean that it would be true for his grandson. Cody had done lots of short hauls into the Quebec wilderness but nothing that compared with this Howse Pass crossing and being so far from assistance by Company crews or other people using the pack routes.

Darcy was shivering now and Cody pulled a blanket off the back of his saddle to put around him. After pouring a steaming mug of coffee he dug a flask from his saddle bag and added a good slug of "medicinal" whiskey. Giving it to Darcy, he then poured a mug for himself minus the medicine.

The aroma sifting up to his nostrils reminded him of coffee times with his Grampa back in Montreal hearing stories of this very trail. Having just struggled over the Pass, Cody unconsciously shook his head as he tried to picture his Gramma Charlotte making this trek with 3 small children, one of them an infant on her back carried papoose style!! Plus, they had done it earlier in the season when there was not only deep snow clogging the route but the temperatures were much more severe. Gramma's half Cree Indian heritage had served her well in the life she had married into, given the exploring career to which Thompson was committed.

The fire shifted, sending a shower of sparks skyward. Darcy had slumped into a restless snooze. Cody could hear Jed and Quinn working with the horses and, as usual, Jed was getting Quinn to do all the heavy lifting.

Cody mentally reviewed the meeting he had been in at the Hudson Bay headquarters. The Howse Pass would be officially abandoned as a supply route to the Kootenay/Columbia posts. Goods were now coming in from the Pacific and from the south at much less cost. They needed one more trip to pick up cached supplies that over the years had been strategically placed along the Pass to give emergency help to Company workers making the trans-mountain trip.

Cody's ears burned as he recalled the debate that erupted once he was introduced to the directors. One director had even accused David Thompson of being senile that he would want to turn this mission over to a mere boy given the dangers involved! That was all Cody learned before he was asked to leave the room.

Cody could hear the raised voices behind the closed doors but could not make out the words as the debate continued. The concern among the directors was not only the young age of the proposed leader but also the serious peril that would be included through the secret commission that the Pards would only learn once the expedition reached the Columbia Valley.

The full purpose of the trip was to remain a secret even from the team that was to be assembled given that on previous efforts information had leaked that lead to disaster for the welfare of the Company's business and personnel in the Columbia/ Kootenay region. This time the leader would carry a sealed pouch containing full details of the mission that was only to be opened if and when they reached the Columbia Valley. Cody had been full of bravado at that meeting as he assured the senior partners that he could handle whatever might happen in the far west. Especially as the proposal would let him employ his three friends with whom he had grown up and with whom he had trekked on local supply expeditions. Cody had to admit that it was only his Grandfather's reputation and strong words of support that had tipped the scales and now had him and his friends on the edge of finding the valley. But right now, with his one friend narrowly escaping death, the bravado was leaking and he gave a silent prayer that Darcy would recover well.

A couple of hours passed before Darcy began to stir. During those hours, as Cody's gaze kept returning to Darcy's face, Cody reflected on the unlikely make-up of their foursome. Right now Darcy's half Chinese features were pretty much hidden by the abrasions and swollen eye. Cody remembered the first time he had seen Darcy when they were just five or six. He was being chased down an alley by rock-throwing kids much bigger than him. The bullies were yelling taunting slurs that always included "chink." That immediately enraged Cody who consistently took the side of the underdog. The little ruffians scattered quickly when Cody challenged them. Eventually Cody learned that Darcy' mother, Zheng, was from a Chinese family that had been rescued from the Opium War by the crew of a Quaker- owned trading ship. One of the young sailors had been entranced by the petite young daughter of the family and eventually married her. They had come to Montreal thinking that the mix of people from different backgrounds would hold far less prejudice against their mixed marriage than the rigid British snobbery they had endured while living in London.

They soon found out that they would face a myriad of obstacles in their new land as well. Darcy had found sanctuary in the group of four buddies and had jumped at the chance to head to the vast western wilderness with them.

He groaned as he sat up. Weakly making it to his feet, he staggered, having to grab the tree for support.

Jed, very relieved to see him looking like he would recover, was quick to suggest that just maybe he'd had more than enough "medicine"! Darcy winced and promised to pound Jed for that remark – but at some later date.

The tension that had Cody's stomach in a knot eased a little as he heard the two of them start to quip at each other. His memory flashed back to their young school days when the four of them would go at each other as much as they got picked on by other kids. Gradually they had intuitively come to realize that each of them had to battle disadvantages in life. Jed had been the thirteenth child in a poverty stricken family and had been pretty much on his own to run the streets. Often stealing food to survive, he came to school in tattered clothing. His small size was made up for by very fast feet. Quinn was from an Irish family in a French district. He carried a big chip on his

shoulders,coming from the fact that his Dad had a major drinking problem and would regularly beat him and his mom. It was
completely natural that, when he grew so big so fast, he tried to
solve everything with his fists even while he was feeling so alone
inside. On top of that, Cody had his own war with the world.
His half breed mother had died giving birth to him and when
his father became overwhelmed at having a baby to care for and
had abandoned him, he was taken in by the McVeigh family
who raised him as their own. He only learned of his adoption
through the teasing of other school children when he was six.
Suddenly he had a hole in his life that he didn't understand but
it left him angry and empty. He started a life-long fight against
unfairness and authority. He was a square peg in every round
hole. His one great connection turned out to be his grandfather,
David Thompson, who was his adoptive mother's father.

These boys began to stick up for each other against those that
would taunt and bully them individually. While fighting his own
battles, Cody formed what would be a life long compulsion to
stand up for the underdog even though it would often mean his
own detriment. Through that he had become the natural leader
of this foursome from junior school days on. What had formed
them into a brotherhood on the school ground, carried over into
the streets where they fought battles against other toughs who
would make the mistake of thinking they could take advantage
of one of them. One of the good things about this journey to the
wilderness was that it got them far away from all the baggage
of that fighting environment and opened up a new future for all
of them.

"What's everyone standing around for?" Darcy said, with
more energy than he felt. "We've got a date with a river!!"

TWO

Jed and Quinn already had the horses ready for the trail. Darcy's two pack horses were divided between Jed and Quinn, with Jed having Knuckle-head. He had tied a rope from that horse's bridle to it's belly cinch so that it couldn't get its head up to rear back. Every horse was fully loaded because of all the extra cached supplies they had recovered through the Pass. Cody gave Darcy a leg up into the saddle. Even with the help, it was agony as Darcy managed to get his right leg over the horse's back. Although Darcy said he would be fine, he didn't look it. Cody reminded himself to keep a close eye on him as the day wore on.

A couple hours later, Cody's spirits were lifting because they had made some steady progress. The sun was strong, the birds were singing, the pine trees smelled good and the mountain peaks were majestic. The Blaeberry River was running strong and adding its music to the environment. A much easier trail lay ahead. Best of all, Darcy was doing OK if not, in fact, a little better as time slipped by. Soon they would see a gap before the next mountain range indicating a broad valley below.

When they stopped for a lunch break Cody said,

"We need to start watching for signs of game. It would be a big help if we could add some fresh meat to our diet. A grouse or rabbit or even a small deer wouldn't add too much weight."

Quinn responded that he would get his gun off the pack horse and be ready if someone spotted an animal. No one noticed Jed picking up a handful of small rocks.

Quinn said, "I'll pull in ahead of Jed so that if we see some fresh sign, I'll jump off and my horses will simply stay in line and I'll catch up."

After the pack train had once again settled into its steady plodding rhythm, Jed took three of his rocks and pegged them, in quick succession into the bush off to the left. Everyone turned to look in that direction.

"Quinn!" Jed called in a forced whisper, "I think I saw something move over there."

As Quinn looked down to pull his rifle out of the saddle boot on his right side, Jed pegged five more rocks, one after another to make it sound like an animal moving quickly though the undergrowth. Quinn vaulted to the ground and was running as he landed. After he was safely away from the rest, Jed let out a cackle and told the others what he had done.

They couldn't help joining in Jed's infectious laughter.

"I wouldn't want to be you if he figures out what you've done!" commented Cody with a knowing smile.

"Here," said Jed, "I'll move him over even farther to the left."

With that he threw another few rocks in the direction he had indicated.

"Hey Quinn! I think it's moving east," Jed shouted.

There was no response other than Jed's ongoing chuckle.

The pack-train continued its steady plod. The guys began to wonder when Quinn was going to show up.

Suddenly there was a burst of noise as powerful arms wrapped around Jed, dragging him from his horse, and Quinn hissing through gritted teeth,

"You skunk, you're going to pay for this!"

Quinn had circled around and crept up from behind to catch Jed unaware. He was fuming! Red in the face from both exertion and anger, he was tussling Jed out of the saddle, as he spat out

"I saw you throw those last rocks! I had already seen that there was no sign of any animals and I had turned to come back. Your voice let me know where to look through the trees and I saw you. You've gone too far trying to make a fool out of me!"

Jed caught one glance of that fearsome face and knew that if he couldn't sprint away he was in serious trouble.

The two men went to the ground in a ball of fury. Arms and legs flailed as Jed tried to twist out of Quinn's grasp and Quinn tried to hold Jed so he could land the blows that were all pent up in his mind and body. In that instant, Cody knew this was beyond the ordinary wrestling spat that these friends occasionally got into. Jed had been riding Quinn for days probably as much to amuse himself as anything just to break up the tedium of so many days on the trail. Cody had noticed though that it wasn't sitting well with Quinn and, although they were all fast friends, every once in a while some things boiled over and needed to be sorted out on a physical basis. This looked to be one of those times. Yet with the slow burn that had been smouldering inside Quinn for a few days, Cody wasn't sure that Quinn would know when enough was enough. He had come close to being jailed several times because of beatings he had laid on cocky young toughs who had taunted him for his Irish accent and huge size. Cody dismounted and walked back to be close by.

They were rolling from side to side, causing the horses to snort and side-step. Grunts and groans rose as fists found their target. Dust blossomed up as they each tried to get on top. Quinn's size and strength were taking their toll. Jed was desperately squirming to escape the hammer blows that Quinn was landing on his body. Quinn rolled on top once more. Jed winced and let down his guard for just a brief moment. Smack, smack!

Quinn threw a two punch combination that found its mark on Jed's jaw and rolled his eyes back. As Quinn cocked his arm for another punch, Cody lowered his right shoulder and dove at Quinn. He knocked him sprawling away from Jed. Quinn came up instantly in a fighter's stance. Cody came up with his hands out front with palms facing Quinn.

"Whoa, it's over! That's enough! You've got your pay back!"

The fire visibly drained from Quinn's eyes and he slumped to the ground breathing heavily. Cody turned to check on Jed who was writhing and groaning, then gave Jed a hand up where he stood leaning against his horse, gingerly checking out his jaw to make sure it was still working.

Then Jed, between panting breaths said,

"OK big guy, I get your message. I went too far!"

Darcy, from his ring-side seat on his horse, piped up.

"You guys gonna kiss and make-up? Let's get going!"

That was the catalyst everyone needed and with no more words, rigging was checked and horses mounted. The journey to the Columbia Valley resumed.

THREE

The sun was just a ways past its zenith when the pack train emerged from heavy forest onto an exposed knoll that formed the south edge of an alpine meadow. This could be their first view of the valley they had been heading towards for so many weeks. Cody led the pack train to the right up to the top of the open rise of land. Below them was a magnificent view of a lush green valley with a bright ribbon of river meandering from south to north and another range of mountains on the far side. All four men rode up beside each other and sat in silence as they drank in the view. There was an unspoken but real sense of shared accomplishment that they had overcome all the challenges and obstacles of canoe and horse travel all the way from Montreal.

In those moments of inspired stillness a healing peace seemed to come from the majesty of mountains and valley and settle into Cody's soul. He had a sense of belonging beyond anything he had ever felt before. In all the turmoil and searching, both conscious and unconscious, since the day the taunts of other children had taught him that he was adopted and that he was a "breed" he had never felt peace within. It was more than just being far away from the background that had pummelled his spirit and left him feeling unwanted. As he looked out over this incredible scene, he somehow knew that he had arrived at a significant new place. What it would mean for him he really had no idea but now there was a compelling draw towards the future. He wondered if his three friends were sensing any of this grandness, of this pivot of life path, that was happening to them in these moments. Though they hadn't talked a lot about it, each of them had struggled with their life circumstances which had obviously drawn them to each other – them against the world – and now they were all stepping into brand new possibilities that never would have been available if they had stayed in Montreal. Cody hoped that some day they would be able to put it all into words for one another.

There were big challenges of a different kind ahead but he felt much more confident about taking those on now that they had conquered this huge step.

"I sure wish I had both eyes to drink in all of that beauty!" offered Darcy. "What I see with one eye is plenty big but two eyes would be quite the painting! Cody, you're trying to tell us that this Columbia is flowing north but empties into the ocean a long ways south. That's kind of hard to conjure."

"Yep, I saw it on the big map my Grandfather made. In fact, he started using a mountain pass way up north that came out just where this river starts its big turn west and then south. He called his camp "Boat Encampment" cause they built canoes there if there wasn't one stashed that was useable."

"But why so far north when his Kootenay House Trading post is south even from here?" Darcy queried?

"Indians"

"Indians? But didn't he come here to trade with the Indians south of here and get them to do more trapping? Why would he cross the mountains so far away from them?" puzzled Darcy.

"Well," Cody said thoughtfully, wondering if he could make this make sense. "He came to trade with the Kootenay Indians but a tribe from east of the mountains and south of where we travelled didn't want the Kootenays getting guns. They are called the Peigans; part of the Blackfeet Tribes out on the Prairie. They had been enemies of the Kootenay for a long time. They liked to sneak through the passes and steal horses and they didn't mind if some Kootenays got killed in the process. Grampa had his own run-ins with them and sometimes they would even steal horses in broad daylight. So they harassed Traders to keep them away so they could continue to bully the Kootenays."

Quinn growled, "I'd like to see them try to bully us and steal our horses!!"

"Be careful what you wish for!!" Cody responded as he jigged his horse back towards the trail. "Let's go get our camp set up and get these horses onto some good graze."

Another hour brought them to the valley floor. What had looked like a sea of grass from high up turned out to be a mix of marsh and occasional rock outcrop. It took some searching to find the right combination of dry ground, shade trees and abundant pasture. They also found evidence of past campers that had taken advantage of the excellent natural provision on this spot , although it looked like it had been some years since it had been used.

They all set to work stripping saddles and packs from their horses. Cody noticed that Darcy was having a hard time even taking the tack off his own riding horse.

"Darcy," Cody said, "It sure would be good to have a change of diet tonight. Why don't you see if you can catch enough fish for our supper by the time we've finished hauling off all these packs?"

Jed quickly spoke up, "Hey, I was injured by a mule today. I think I should do some fishing as well!"

Quinn happened to be out of hearing range at the time. Cody grinned and said,

"I suggest you keep working at these packs or that mule is likely to turn into a mean & hungry bear fresh out of its den! I wouldn't want to be you!"

They had set their camp in the shadow of a cliff face and stacked all the cargo at the base of the cliff. That left a spacious gentle slope down to the river, mostly shaded by huge cottonwood trees. To the south a low ridge of rock, only three or four feet high, separated the camp from a large meadow where the horses would have rich pasture. As they stripped the gear from the horses, Jed took the horses out onto this pasture area and turned them free. Some of them bucked a little, some of them rolled over but all of them settled down to munching the belly high grass within a few minutes. Jed kept his own horse on a long tether just in case the herd decided to wander farther than it should. He was pretty sure that rattling the pail of oats would bring them all back but - just in case.

The warm summer evening felt like a bit of paradise. Everyone relished the feast of fresh fish and were glad to laze around and talk as the evening quiet settled over the marsh and the loons and geese were nestling in for the night as well.

Quinn mentioned that he had noticed a lot of wear and tear on the pack saddles.

"Maybe we should take a day or two to repair harnesses"

Cody responded, "Might be a good idea! That would also give us a chance to find that soap and do a little scrubbing down of our own!"

"Who-eee! Chortled Darcy, "We must be getting close to some pretty Indian maidens for Cody to want to get all gussied up!!

"Hey," said Cody, "If I could find an Indian maiden that is half the woman my Gramma Charlotte is, she would be well worth a little work with a bar of soap! But, that is definitely not the reason right now. Until this afternoon, I just blamed the horses for the odour. Now I can't do that when they're out on the grass. Guys – we all stink! Tomorrow we all take a bath!! AND THEN...we'll break open that sealed pouch. Finally, we'll know what this big secret assignment is."

They went about their usual chores as they settled their camp for the night. Jed and Quinn moved the tether for Jed's horse and hobbled all the other horses so they could graze close by, re-assuring one another that if a mountain lion or bear came looking for an easy kill, the horses would make enough noise to waken them.

Darcy cleaned up from the evening meal and Cody gathered wood for their morning fire. They were all glad to hit the sack after making sure their firearms were within easy reach.

FOUR

The next morning, after a huge breakfast of flapjacks, when they were on their second pot of coffee, Cody dug the sealed pouch out of his saddlebags. Everyone was eager to find out what was so important that it had been kept secret until now. These next minutes were going to shape their future.

Cody broke the seal and pulled out the folded sheets of expensive linen paper embossed at the top with the insignia of the Hudson Bay Company. He started to read.

By Authority Of The Directors Of The Hudson Bay Company. We hereby commission Cody McVeigh of Montreal, and a team of 3 men of his choosing, to conduct an expedition west for the following objectives

1. To close the Howse Pass as a Hudson Bay route of trade with the Indians of the Kootenay River and Columbia River regions. This shall be done by traversing this route once more and collecting the cached supplies to the advantage of the Hudson Bay Company.

2. To search out and apprehend Louis Leblanc and George Lagasse regarding their misappropriation of Hudson Bay

Company trade goods. Be advised that previous attempts to bring these villains to justice has resulted in bodily harm to Company agents. There has been evidence that they have had advance knowledge via spies inside the Company regarding previous secret plans to achieve reparation to the satisfaction of the Hudson Bay. Thus the need of secrecy to this extent.

3. The public objective of your expedition, which will serve as a cover for your continued presence in the region, will be to provide the means to move Fort Kokanee, operated by John Linklater, which, because of a recent decision by the International Boundary Commission , finds itself located on American soil. Such Fort is to be relocated to the area known as Joseph's Prairie by which to provide convenient access for Kootenay Indians to continue bringing furs for trade. The goods collected crossing the Howse Pass will help re-provision the relocated Post. After this move is completed you are to serve as agents of the Hudson Bay Company in whatever ways best serve the Company until further directions are sent to you from the head office.

There was a pause as Cody finished reading, then everyone erupted with questions at once.

"Can you believe we get to chase the bad guys for real?"

"Should we start wearing those pistols?"

"How do we find John Linklater?"

"Did they include police badges in the packet?"

"What do we do with them if we capture them?"

"Did they give any clue where to find the thieves?"

When the excitement settled down a little, Cody said,

"First of all we have to keep our lips tight. Can't talk to anyone about what we're really doing. Understood?!"

There was a chorus of "you bet, not a word."

Cody continued, "For now, we just carry on with getting to Kootenay House and from there get directions to Fort Kokanee. All the while we'll keep our ears open for hints about these two guys without being too clumsy about digging for information. So let's get everything ready for getting back on the trail tomorrow."

The day passed quickly with Cody and Quinn sorting and organizing the goods they brought with them and that they had picked up crossing the mountains. Darcy focused on food supplies. Jed spent the day grooming the horses, checking shoes (adding a nail here and there) and carefully finding the weak spots in the harness. In the evening they all worked on harness and saddle repairs and as they talked, the seriousness of their commission continued to settle down on them. However, with the optimism of youth, there was a counter balance of excitement and challenge along with huge confidence that the bad guys were as good as captured.

Darcy asked, "How dangerous are these guys really?"

Cody chose his words carefully. "Well, I do remember my Grandfather describing something about them in the stories he told. Nothing has been known for sure beyond their theft of the trade goods. They took a full amount that a trader would need for a big haul of furs in return. But - - I seem to remember more recent stories that there have been some serious injuries and several fatal 'accidents' that took out people who happened to spend some time on the trail of Leblanc and Lagasse. Nothing tied these incidents directly to them. Apparently they've wormed their way into some bands of Kootenays and, by one means or another they've got a whole network of people that will spy for them. I think we have to assume that they are ready to do whatever it takes to keep from being caught."

"Well, with four of us scouting them out they'll have a hard time slipping away or doing us in. It will be a pleasure bringing them to a stop." Jed sounded eager!

Quinn added, "I think they've given us a pretty good cover and most people will think we're too young to be working on an old crime that most people probably don't even know about, let alone care about."

"Yeah maybe we can even get to know them without them having any idea of what we're really doing," chimed in Darcy. "I'd love to watch their faces when they realize that we have actually caught them!"

With that said they made their final preparations for the night. Jed and Quinn hobbled all the horses this time given how content they had been on this meadow and how close they had stayed to the one horse they had kept on a tether.

Several hours later, Cody came awake. His sixth sense stirred him to listen to the night sounds. The moon gave enough light that he could make out some features of his surroundings. He heard a knicker from a horse and a little shuffling of hooves. His first thought was that it was probably the knuckle-head horse stirring things up and that they would settle down. When the shuffling continued, Cody wondered about a wild cat or other animal on the prowl. It was enough for him to decide to check it out. He picked up his rifle and headed over the low ridge to the field. The herd was moving away from him and at a pace that hobbles would make impossible. Cody couldn't believe his eyes and ears. The herd was actually galloping!! He could just faintly make out a couple shadowy figures on the horses closest to him but there was not enough light to see any details.

Cody fired a shot into the air at the same time he yelled for the others. This couldn't be happening. Instinctively he started running after the horses but soon realized the futility of it.

The others came racing over the low ridge hollering their questions and Cody hollering back that the horses were stolen. Jed, the fastest of the four, started running after them just as Cody had. Cody called him back and he eventually turned and walked back with his head hanging.

"I'm sure we hobbled all of them! What did I do wrong? Horses can't get out of those ropes."

"Look here," said Quinn, "I just stumbled over this."

He held both ends of a short hank of rope that had been on the front legs of one of their horses just a short time before. The men could feel the ends of it and could tell that a sharp knife had cut right through it. Someone, or maybe several, had been able to creep in among the herd so silently so as to cause little disturbance and slice off all the hobbles. Then they rode bareback to herd the horses south away from the camp. Disbelief held the men standing in the dark with nothing to say.

Eventually they made their way back to their camp and made coffee.

Darcy shook his head and said, "I can't believe that Knucklehead didn't raise a ruckus cause he hated any human coming close to him."

"It was probably him that I heard that woke me up. It just wasn't soon enough," said Cody. "They sure were slick horse wranglers. When it's daylight we'll have a look to see what the tracks of their own horses look like, if we can find any. Stealing them right from under our noses like that sure suggests Indians. Maybe the Peigans are still making raids."

"What do we do without horses?" asked Quinn. "There's way too many supplies here to pack ourselves. Do we follow those horses until we get them back? Do we send someone to buy horses?"

Cody shook his head. "That herd can keep moving a lot faster than we can on foot and there is no guarantee that you could take them back. We don't know how far someone would have to hike to buy horses and whether there are horses available when you find a camp. On top of that it doesn't look as though any one might come by so we could find out who is camping in the whole valley. Let's think about it and see if we can figure something out later."

Cody wanted to get off by himself away from the questions. He didn't begrudge them having questions. He had plenty of his own. He just couldn't think clearly with all the talk. He left the

22

others to get their breakfast and walked up the easy side of the cliff that was behind their camp. Sitting there, he watched the dawn grow brighter and the colours on the mountains on the far side of the valley grow bright and clear as the sun touched the far peaks. The peacefulness of the river valley almost mocked Cody because the landscape just sat there as if nothing big had just happened. His thoughts went back to the serenity he had seen in David Thompson, his grandfather, when things had seemed to go wrong in every plan or investment he had to provide for them in their old age. Cody knew that his Grampa found peace from God and that in a tight spot like this he would read the Bible and pray. His practise of Bible reading every Sunday for everyone in his crew regardless of where he was in the wilderness was legendary among those that worked with Thompson.

As Cody thought about those memories, the peacefulness of the valley seemed to creep inside his own feelings. He prayed, somewhat awkwardly, for a solution to their problem. After sitting for a while longer, a plan formed in his mind and he got up with renewed energy and headed down to the camp with long purposeful strides.

FIVE

"

Canoes!!!" choked Jed. "In case you haven't noticed, there are fewer canoes here than there are horses. I suppose they are just going to fall from the sky?!"

"No," chuckled Cody, knowing what kind of reaction was going to come when he finished, "We are going to build them!!"

Darcy groaned, "Have you ever built one before? Do you have any idea how much work is involved? This is going to take forever!!!"

"As a matter of fact I watched my Grandfather build a canoe a few years ago, plus we travelled in those voyager canoes so we know that they can carry huge loads."

"But they were built by canoe builders, not by four guys whose greatest skill is eating!!" Darcy lamented.

Quinn spoke up, "I lived close to a shop where they were building some of those transport canoes that could carry up to 20 people along with cargo. They let me help once in a while because they liked to have me there when they were lifting them out of the warehouse. We can build them. It's just going to take a while when we haven't done it before."

"It will probably take us a couple weeks by the time we gather material and figure out how to put it together so it will float," Cody looked at each man in turn and asked, "Are you OK with this?"

Jed responded, "I don't see any other way that would be any faster. If somebody comes along with horses we can always change our plans. But from what we can tell there haven't been any horses here before ours for months."

Darcy shrugged, "This is a rotten turn of events so it looks like we don't have any alternative."

Quinn stood up and said, "Let's get at it. What do we do first?"

"Hang on a bit Quinn," Cody responded, "Let's talk over what needs to happen. We are going to need fresh meat and we can use the fat to mix with the pine pitch to seal the seams. We will need to make thin cedar planks so some big straight cedar trees will be needed for the wood. Quinn and I will sketch out some plans to follow."

Jed offered to go hunting with Quinn and scout for cedar trees at the same time. Darcy agreed to search out pine pitch from the ponderosa pines that were quite plentiful as well as organizing the camp for the longer stay. Cody sorted through the trade goods for the tools they would need and set out a work area. All of them were grateful to be busy as the cloud of the stolen horses kept looming in their thoughts.

What a set-back! What a shock! There had been no warning that would have alerted them even if they had expected some trouble. Was it a native raiding party that just happened to be in the area? Was it trappers down on their luck and fell onto a way to put some money in their pockets? It was a lesson for sure. They would have to sharpen their attention to all kinds of possibilities and dangers if they were to ever be successful in tracking down their quarry.

Cody mulled all of this over as he inventoried the tools and materials that they would use. When he finished doing what he could, he walked over to the meadow where the horses had been. He picked up all the pieces of rope the hobbles had been made from. In one sandy spot he saw a clear footprint that looked like it had been made by a moccasin. He found a few more human tracks, all flat like a moccasin print and all looking the same without any distinctive markings. As he walked back towards the camp, a quick glint in the grass made him stop. He stepped back and forth until he saw the tiny flash again. Then he spotted the source. A button. A metal button! When he picked it up, he saw that it had a distinctive crest embossed on it. Definitely not of Indian origin. But then again, it could have been traded to an Indian from a European source. He would show the others so they could all be on the alert for something matching this one. However, it really left them with the possibility that the thieves could have been either Indian or white. Cody turned to walk up to the far edge of the meadow scouting for the right kind of cedar. He tried to process the clash of an exciting mission that had been given to this young band of adventurers along with the harsh reality that they could be in well over their heads in this huge wilderness. It trimmed a man down to size in his own eyes.

Every one had somewhat come to terms with their new reality by the time they were together for supper.

Quinn reported, "Didn't see any game but saw lots of fresh sign. There's a well used game trail to a stream where I plan to be waiting before daylight. We'll have fresh meat tomorrow. But, there's not likely much fat on any animals this early in the year."

Jed commented, "Lots of tall straight cedar in a grove back of this knoll. Quinn says it will be more than enough for two big canoes."

After Darcy reported on finding pine pitch, Cody pulled the button he had found from his pocket. He told them what he had seen by way of footprints as well as the button. Lots of specu-lation was offered but in the end they all agreed that they had no way to identify the thieves they would be looking for. What they did know now was that they really couldn't trust anyone but one another.

Canoe construction started the next day. It began with a couple of huge trees being chopped down and cut into lengths that they could drag back to the camp. Everyone took their turn with broad axes, with each one trying to get the longest, thinnest, but widest, cedar strip. Advice flew thicker than the chips from the axes. Cody and Quinn were arguing and planning the design. Cody wanted to make it with style and Quinn argued for function. It would have to be wide and flat bottomed to carry the amount of cargo. They could agree on that. Quinn would have settled for "a raft with sides." But Cody declared that just because they had lost their horses, they didn't have to arrive at Kootenay House in a pig of a boat!

Through lots of trial and error, the first canoe gradually took shape. Cody insisted on doing some parts of it over and over until it "looked good" which drove Quinn crazy. Then Quinn would go for a walk and often come back with a suggestion that both could agree on. Small trees, tall and slim, were used for some of the main structure with the thin planks being bent and nailed or lashed to the skeleton. Darcy, also through trial and error and advice from the others, managed the caulking with a brew of pitch and fat.

The second canoe went much faster. By the end of the second week, both boats had been thoroughly water tested and sealed. The paddles were carved and ready for use. In fact, they carved several extra knowing that they would be used as poles to push them off sandbars and around rocks as the river would get smaller as they got closer to its source.

As they loaded the cargo they were all very satisfied at how stable the canoes proved to be and at how little water they drew. As they shoved off, they let loose with some cheers to celebrate overcoming a major setback. They were very glad to bend their backs to the new challenge of paddling upstream.

"Kootenay House, here we come!"

SIX

They fell into a new routine as the days slipped by and they worked their way south. Muscles that hadn't had the strain of paddling for some time were sore for a couple days and then hardened to the demands of fighting the current. For the most part, the river was more than deep enough for these primitive, heavily loaded cargo canoes. Only twice did they have to use a tow line with three of them on shore pulling one of the boats at a time up a rapids. One man stayed in the boat to pole away from boulders.

On the morning of the fourth day of working their way up the Columbia a persistent light rain fell. All of them were soaked through but found that the exertion of paddling kept them warm enough that they didn't get out the canvas coats that would have made them too warm. It was when they were stopping for their lunch break that day that Cody was surprised when he noticed a thin column of smoke farther upstream.

"Look ahead, just above the trees on the left. Smoke! We must have company."

They decided on a cold lunch so they didn't announce their presence to the other party by making their own column of smoke. That's when the rain became a misery to them. They would like to have made it a brief lunch but discussing the possibilities of who was ahead kept them from moving out right away.

"I wonder who it might be," mused Jed. "What do you think, friend or foe?"

"Well, the horse thieves would be long gone by now" said Quinn, "and no one else is supposed to know that we're here so it shouldn't be anyone hostile to us."

Cody agreed, "As far as I know the Traders have had a good relationship with natives that live in this area. So I would expect that whoever made that fire will be glad to see us."

"Well I think we're crazy to just blunder into their camp with all this cargo," said Darcy. "We have no idea who is there! It could be bad guys as easily as good guys. I think we should scout them out before we paddle into their space. Remember, we thought everything was OK and then we lost all our horses."

Cody argued for the friendly approach but Darcy's words had sent a chill through the others. After a little more debate Cody realized the guys were determined to take the cautious approach so he agreed. They chose Jed, who was the quickest and lightest on his feet, for the scouting trip.

He left immediately. By following the river-side trail he was able to keep the smoke in view which let him know when he was close enough that he needed to fade back into the forest to avoid being seen. The pine needles that covered the forest floor plus the softening from the rain allowed Jed to creep very close to the camp without being noticed.

Strange sounds were coming from a crude shelter that he spied through the brush. It sounded like moaning and crying all mixed together. At first he could see only one elderly man at the fire feeding it sticks. Then a young girl joined him. As they conversed they were both shaking their heads. They looked bedraggled and miserable in the rain as they huddled under some wraps. An elderly woman slumped over to the fire. She said a few words as she also shook her head. Jed could hear misery and discouragement in their voices even though he couldn't understand their language. She scooped something from a pot and returned to the lean-to that was made of boughs. There was obviously nothing threatening here.

Suddenly there was a voice behind Jed!

"Stop where you are or I'll shoot! What are you doing here? What do you want?"

Jed froze and then turned slowly to see an arrow pointing right at him and the bow string fully drawn back. It was held by a young teenage boy who had fired the questions and now looked very nervous and excited. Jed put out his hands with palms forward.

"Don't do anything. I'm a friend. I mean no harm!" choked out Jed as his heart pounded in his chest."

"Pierre, what is it? What's going on?

It was the old man's voice speaking Kootenay and Jed could hear him moving towards them.

"Well you certainly got something bigger than a squirrel this time! Who is he?"

"He's a spy! I found this guy spying on our camp!"

Although Jed couldn't understand their words, he could see that Pierre's arm was tiring from holding the bow ready to shoot and it was starting to waver which was making Jed very nervous that his grip might slip.

"I mean no harm," Jed repeated. "I'll explain, if that arrow could be pointed some place else.!"

The boy named Pierre spoke some rapid words to the old man who replied, "OK Pierre, we won't shoot him for now. You can put the bow down. Let's hear what he has to say."

Jed saw the arrow lower to aim at the ground and then the bow string being relaxed. He took a deep breath.

"Thank you! My name is Jed, Yours is Pierre?"

Pierre nodded and motioned toward the fire although he kept the arrow nocked and the bow in a position that he could rapidly use it on Jed.

"Grandfather is willing to talk. He can understand quite a bit of your language but he has a hard time speaking it."

"Will you translate for us then?"

Pierre nodded, his expression still very guarded, as he followed Jed to the fire. The crying had stopped although Jed could still hear loud moans.

"I'll translate for you, and Pierre will guard you!" The young girl, who must have been about 12 or 13 years, had watched what had happened and wanted to be part of the excitement now that she was sure there was no threat. She had understood Jed's words and felt the truth of them. But she was also proud of her brother for standing up to this stranger.

"Who are you and why did you come in secret to spy on us?" the grandfather asked.

Jed quickly and briefly explained,

"My name is Jed. I am a trader with the Hudson Bay and I have three friends just downstream. We are headed to Kootenay House but all our horses were stolen. We have had to build canoes. So when we saw your smoke we didn't know if you were friend or enemy. I came to find out and I have found friends."

Grandfather responded, "I am called Grey Owl and my granddaughter is Maria. We came to this area to hunt and fish. We had not been successful in finding game. And then two days ago my son, Little Bear, slipped on the rocks and broke his leg. It is a very bad break. Now he is out of his head with fever and only lays there and moans. We have only Balsam tea to treat his fever. He is the hunter in the family and the rest of us do the skinning and drying of the meat. Instead of stocking up on food we have eaten up our supplies. When the rain started making everyone miserable this morning, we had given up hope that my son would live through this and that we would get back to our people at Kootenay House."

Jed broke in, "We can help. We have lots of supplies."

"I fear that we will be too much of a burden for you."

Jed managed a smile as he noted that Pierre had laid his bow and arrows against a tree.

"We'll figure things out as we go."

With that, Grey Owl called to the people in the shelter to come and meet their new friend. The elderly woman Jed had seen before came first and was introduced as Yellow Sun. Behind her came Bright Star, the daughter-in-law. It was obvious that she was the one who had been crying so loudly. Her face was swollen and showed tear tracks which made her look very sad. Jed was invited to step into the shelter to meet Little Bear. The sight of him alarmed Jed. He was racked with fever and reached out to clutch at Jed, jabbering in meaningless words which seemed to be a combination of English and Kootenay. The fracture in the leg showed clearly at the same place there was an open gash which must have happened at the same time as the break.

Jed wasn't so sure about their ability to help once he saw the injured man. He wondered if he had been a little over zealous in his assurance of their assistance. However, they couldn't just leave this bedraggled family in their dire circumstances. He and his friends would have to do what they could.

Jed's insides gave a lurch as he thought about the gruesome task of setting Little Bear's leg.

After assuring them that he would return with his three friends, Jed jogged back to meet the others. They were growing concerned at the amount of time he had been gone and were beginning to wonder if they should be following him up the path. They were glad to see that he was in one piece when he appeared through the bushes.

Jed gave them the details including his promise to help. The others backed that promise without hesitation and quickly got the canoes ready to move. As they bent to paddling against the current they speculated about the best help they could give. Could they set the broken leg? Jed was emphatic that the man would be a cripple if they didn't. Was the infection so advanced that he would die of it anyway? What about the open wound? Would gangrene set in and the leg have to be amputated?

Darcy reacted, "I'm getting sick just thinking about it! Let's hope we can move the poor guy so that we can get him to more experienced people than us! By the way, Jed, how old did you say this Maria was?"

SEVEN

Pierre and Maria were waiting at the edge of the river as the ponderous canoes swung into view. They quickly tried to help bring them up onto the gravel.

"Easy! Cautioned Cody. "We'll tie them to that tree so we don't damage the bottom. You must be Maria and Pierre. I'm Cody." The others of the family came up to meet them and names were given all around.

Grey Owl was saying thank you over and over. Jed showed the others into the lean-to and all their faces became grim as they saw for themselves how badly the leg was swollen and disfigured both by the break and the infection. Cody was sure that the bone was showing through the flesh of the open wound. The obvious agony and moaning of Little Bear made them all want to get back out by the open campfire even though the miserable drizzle of rain kept a sense of gloom hanging over this huddle of humanity.

All the Pards had to go on was the primitive treatments they had seen given in previous wilderness expeditions and the stories told around campfires and fireplaces. None of them had seen anything this serious.

"The bone has to be pulled straight as much as it can if he is to ever walk at all," Cody was stating the obvious but they all grimaced at the reality of what would have to happen. They talked over the rest of the treatment they would give while they made a meal to share with Grey Owl and his family.

Darcy offered to find some tree branches to cut for splints as much to get away from the moaning and the agony that would come with setting the bone. Maria offered to help him. Pierre turned down the invitation to go as well, declaring that he would stand strong for his father.

Cody quickly retrieved their medicine bag including the whiskey flask and the small bottle of laudanum that had been entrusted to him for emergencies. Cody and Quinn took on the direct treatment of Little Bear's leg. They managed to get several swallows of whiskey into him before they touched the break. Jed was assigned to hold Little Bear while they cleaned the wound of the obvious debris that had stuck to it. They did as much cleaning as possible with water. When they were done that Cody said,

"OK, hold on tight Jed. I'm going to pour some whiskey over this wound. He's not going to enjoy this."

Indeed, Little Bear's whole body convulsed as the fire of the alcohol on the wound shot through him. Jed almost lost hold on his shoulders and Quinn had to lay his weight across Little Bear's waist. Once the patient had calmed from that step, Quinn and Cody gave each other a knowing look and prepared for the most difficult and most important step for this brave's future. Quinn's face had become a mask betraying none of the anxiousness he felt about what he was about to do. Cody took Jed's place behind Little Bear's head. He lifted him a little and put his arms under Little Bear's arms and laced this hands together across the patient's chest. Quinn took a death grip on

Little Bear's ankle. With a quick nod at Cody to brace, Quinn put his huge weight and strength into the pull on the injured leg. Little Bear screamed a long continuous scream for a few moments and then passed out. Quinn kept the pressure on and could feel the grating as the bone and flesh began to yield. Then there was a sudden little give and snap as the bone cleared the last spot of overlap. Quinn immediately released the pressure. The quiet hung over them in such contrast that Jed stepped back into the lean-to to check that Little Bear was actually breathing. Both Cody and Quinn took some moments to recover their own breathing which had been suspended during the agony of setting that bone. The others of the family waited as well after enduring the trauma of Little Bear's screams. When Cody assured them that the bone was aligned and that now the battle was infection and fever, there was a definite lifting of spirits. The rain also ended and patches of blue began to show above the mountain range on the west. They couldn't help but feel like the clouds were lifting on more than one level. A battle had been fought and won.

This was familiar ground for the two women now. They had no way of dealing with the fracture but they had cared for fevers and infections. When they heard Little Bear beginning to stir and call to them, they took their ingredients for making a poultice - clay and crushed Balsam — and began their tender administering on the leg wound. While the boys weren't too pleased with mud being put on a wound, Yellow Sun assured them that this was clean clay and that they had used this combination many times before.

Cody shrugged in agreement for them to go ahead and said to the others, "I'm glad they are so confident about their poultice. It's their kin so it takes the responsibility off of us."

Darcy had returned with several good sturdy splints which were gently and carefully tied into place on the broken leg.

"Let's make sure we leave enough space to change the dressing on the wound?" Cody said. "We will have to adjust the tension on the splints as the swelling goes down."

Cody noticed Bright Star dipping out a liquid from the pot over the fire. When she told him that it was Balsam tea for her husband, he asked that they let him add medicine to it.

"Make it a small amount of tea so that he will drink all of it."

Cody added a dose of the precious pain-killer to the tea and Bright Star took it in to her husband. It was not long until the moaning ended and Little Bear was deep in an exhausted and drugged sleep.

"Now all we can do is hope and pray that the fever will break overnight." Cody went on to explain that they could fix a bed on top of the cargo in one of the canoes for Little Bear and that the rest of the family would have to walk along the trail at the river's edge.

Grey Owl nodded in agreement, "That trail is how we got here so we know that we can make our way back. We can help pull the canoes up the spots where the current is too strong or the river is too shallow."

"We'll gladly put the tow lines in your hands, Grandfather!" chirped Jed. Grey Owl smiled at the friendly gesture of being called grandfather by Jed.

"Can I ride in the canoe?" Maria addressed the question to Darcy. Darcy blushed, but answered,

"Sorry, all the space is taken with cargo. Besides we need you to carry your own pack and help on the tow lines." Maria pouted briefly but soon brightened as she watched the men adjusting the containers in the canoe in order to make a pallet for her dad. They cut two small trees to make poles and then tied canvas to them as a way to transfer Little Bear to the boat.

Next morning, as the sun touched the western peaks, Bright Star was already getting food ready. She was obviously energized by the renewed hope that the help that had been given to her husband offered them. The fever had subsided during the night. Although it was not entirely gone, there was definite improvement. Everyone was more than eager to get on the move.

EIGHT

They made steady but slow progress over the next several days. The stops for meals and overnight gave opportunity for story telling. Grey Owl took full advantage of the curiosity of his new friends to tell something of the history of the Kootenay people as well as stories from his own years of growing up in this region. He was especially excited when he discovered that Cody was the grandson of David Thompson.

"I remember the excitement we all had when some of our braves returned from the plains and told us that white people were planning to come to us so that we could trade our furs right here in our own valley. I was just a young boy, maybe Pierre's age. What we wanted most from the traders was guns. The Peigans had guns so we couldn't stand up to them when they came raiding from across the big mountains for horses. We thought guns would make us powerful and solve our problems. There were lots of improvements for us because of Kootenay House but it also turned out that when the men were paid for hunting and for their furs they just stayed and gambled with each other. Sometimes Mr. Thompson had a hard time getting them to get out on their trap lines so that the Company would make a profit."

The comments about the Peigans raiding for horses touched a sore spot for Cody so he asked Grey Owl.

"Do the Peigans still steal horses from this valley? Do you think they could be the ones that stole ours?"

Grey Owl was thoughtful, "Now that I'm convinced that you boys are trustworthy, I'll tell you more. There is bad medicine around Kootenay House. We wouldn't go there if we could avoid it. When your grandfather built the trading place, we were important to him. He gave fair value for our furs. He gave protection to families. The lazy gamblers and the troublemakers were kept back from the compound and from the gates where they tried to take stuff from us. Now they seem to run the place. They claim there is no place that wants our furs. The goods they have on the shelves fall apart when we use them. Food is spoiled when we get it. But more than that, we are accused of things we don't do. If we complain, we are threatened with losing what we already have. When some have started making noise about how they are treated, accidents have happened in the dark. We are even afraid to talk about it because people know about what has been said when we are away from Kootenay House. No one knows who is spying and who is causing the accidents. Sometimes we hear that Peigans are around. Sometimes someone sees traders from the south but we never get to know them. They hide from the Kootenays. This is part of the reason that we came so far north on our hunting trip. We try to supply our own fresh meat away from the trouble, and have some nice peaceful spring days to ourselves."

Steady progress was made day after day in a rhythm of paddling the canoes upstream, the family hiking the shoreline path, the tow line being thrown out when the current was too strong, making camp each afternoon, and getting Little Bear trying out his crutches that Darcy had carved for him. After the camp was readied for the night and dusk was falling, it was story time. Cody noticed that Grey Owl seemed to lose his ability to speak English in the evening compared to the times Cody had talked to him alone. When Cody asked him about this, the cagey grandfather winked at Cody and said,

"If one of the grandchildren have to interpret then they learn our history. They aren't very interested at their age otherwise."

While Grandfather did most of the story telling, Little Bear was able to add a little more information about the troubles at Kootenay House. He had joined in on some of the games the braves used for gambling. At first it was just putting in time and everyone would lose some and win some. After awhile he was approached by one man, Wolfleg, who asked him to help cause one particular player to lose big. At first Little bear was non-committal but he began to see that the one who had approached him was often in the trading house.

"One day I stopped in to get some small item from the trader and there was Wolfleg back in the fur room where only the store workers can go. When I got their attention, they stopped what they were saying and the Trader accused me of sneaking in. He was much more angry than what the situation should have caused. It looked like trouble so I stayed away from them and the gambling all together."

Each evening one of the crew would eventually raise some question related to the changes that had happened at Kootenay House. They were trying to learn everything that might help them find Leblanc and Legasse and their inner senses were responding to these troubles as somehow connected to the two renegades.

One evening Little Bear was telling of a time when three Peigans had stolen his horse.

"It was very early morning, just after dawn. I had a bad stomach and couldn't sleep. I heard shuffling and a nicker from my horse. When I got out of my robes, I could just make out the three thieves running off with my horse. I was pretty sure that their head bands were Peigan. A couple days later Pierre was out squirrel hunting west of Kootenay House when he heard voices. He is becoming a good Indian hunter and he got close enough to see them without being seen. There were two big white guys and three Peigans. Some money passed from the whites to the Indians. Was it just a coincidence? Were they being paid for stealing my horse. But not all was happy either. There was a big argument when they saw how much money. One of the Peigans pulled his knife and the white guys pulled guns. That made the Indians back away. We keep hearing about these 'big bosses' but no one sees them anymore. They come and go at night. We think these two were the bosses"

Pierre added, "Those guys were really mean and angry. I sure didn't want them to see me so I got away fast."

"Can you tell us what they looked like, Pierre? Just in case we come across them. We'll know to be on our guard if we see them." Cody asked, trying to sound casual, not wanting to give away the fact that these were probably the two they were looking for.

"Well, they were tall. They had lot's of black hair. One of them had a scar by his eye that was big enough that I could see it through the bushes."

When they were off by themselves the young traders reviewed what they were learning.

Darcy said, "Looks like these guys are willing to do damage to people that don't cooperate. They sound like bullies."

"They must expect trouble from people if they are carrying pistols," added Jed.

"I'm afraid our arrival is going to be seen as a threat to their little power kingdom," Cody observed. "That comment that they operate in the dark says to me that they are sneaks and back-stabbers. We'll have to be very alert when we get into their territory, and make sure everyone knows that we are just passing through on our way to Linklater's Post."

One day, at their lunch break, Grey Owl informed them that they were now back in familiar territory and that he thought they were about two days from Kootenay House. Cody noticed that the closer they got the more somber the Indian family became. The chatter among the women walking the trail lessened considerably. Even young Maria, who was usually full of giggles and nonsense, became subdued. Clearly, this family was not looking forward to getting home.

Later that afternoon, Pierre urgently beckoned for the lead canoe to come close to the river bank. In a very excited voice he said to Cody,

"Don't look now but I'm sure I saw a flash of light at the top of that next knoll to the left! I think we are being watched!"

The hair on Cody's arms stood up. He knew this kind of thing would pro' ɪy happen but now that it was being reported in words, it ᴗent a tingle through his whole body.

"Aw, it was probably an animal – maybe a mountain goat – that kicked a smooth rock over and it showed a white side." Cody tried to downplay it for his own sake as well as for Pierre and the others.

"It was too bright for a rock. Grampa says I've got really good eyes, you know!!"

By this time the other canoe had pulled alongside and the others were all informed of Pierre's sighting. Little Bear had no hesitation that the report would be true.

"It seems that everyone knows everyone else's doings since the troubles started. I hear that the Big Bosses have lots of spies."

It was all disturbing information, but everyone agreed that they had no reason to not move ahead. They would simply have to be extra alert and watch for any other signs of people being around and especially watch for unusual behaviour if they did see anyone.

They camped that night almost directly below the knoll where Pierre had seen the flash of light. Cody and Jed decided to hike up to see if there was any evidence to verify what Pierre had said. They actually welcomed the change from so much time in the canoes. In about twenty minutes they came out of the undergrowth at a spot that gave a complete view of their whole day of canoeing. There was no doubt that people had been at this spot but nothing was distinctive about the scuffs in the bare ground. Neither were there any rocks that could have produced what appeared to be a flash of light.

After carefully looking around for a few minutes, they were about to leave when Jed's eyes caught something unusual by some rocks that formed a natural place to sit.

"Wait a minute. What's this?" he exclaimed to Cody. He pointed to a small crevasse at the side of the flat boulder. Trapped in the rock were three small strands of leather. Cody pried them out with his knife and laid them on Jed's hand.

"Looks like buckskin fringes from a leather shirt," said Jed.

"And look at the ends," replied Cody, "On everyone of them one end is almost white and the other end is almost black. These have been torn off very recently, probably even today, and haven't had time to darken from exposure to the weather! I think we have just proved Pierre to be right!"

Cody frowned as he collected the small strips and put them in his shirt pocket. "Why would someone watch us and not come and speak to us when there are so few people out in this wilderness? It is only basic courtesy to connect with people in the wilds. You never know when you might need their help or need to help them. It certainly makes you think that there is someone unfriendly out there.

Jed nodded agreement. "It looks like we are going to have to watch our backs for sure!"

NINE

Late that night when it was fully dark, a lone figure slipped through the forest a half mile south and west of Kootenay House. The sureness of his steps showed that he had been here many times before. The cabin he was approaching was only a darker smudge in the setting of the forest. No light showed from inside so either they were sound asleep or not even there. Wolfleg knew that he carried information that would be important to the two Big Bosses so he had to risk rousing them. They were harsh men at the best of times and very unpredictable when wakened in the middle of the night.

Wolfleg gave the usual signal – the hoot of an owl. He tried this several times with no response from the cabin. However he did hear some shuffling off to the right and back of the cabin. He knew this was where they kept their horses, so he was fairly sure that they were asleep in the cabin. He pondered his approach. If they had drunk themselves into a stupor which was often their pattern lately, they would be hard to rouse at all and would be meaner than a she bear in spring. He could shout from a distance, he could throw rocks at the cabin or he could pound on the door. He decided on pounding on the door but standing to the side where the thickness of the logs would protect him from bullets that might come right through the slab door.

His pounding eventually brought some groans and some curses as one man grumbled at the other to quieten down or else his hide would be nailed to the cabin wall. Wolfleg pounded some more. Finally one of the men shouted into the darkness for the troublemaker to go away or else. Wolfleg could tell that his knocking was gradually penetrating the booze haze in their heads.

Now he called softly and identified himself. More curses now directed at Wolfleg and what was about to happen to him.

"I have very important news. You'll be glad I've come when you hear it. Open up so I don't have to shout it to the whole world," persisted Wolfleg.

He could hear stumbling and a crash as something fell but someone was getting close to the door. Wolfleg stepped back a little as the door swung open. The sour stench hit him even before he could make out the figure swaying just inside the doorway.

"This better be good or you're dog meat," slurred Louis Leblanc.

"That rumour from the Peigans that there were traders far to the north...??!! Turns out it's true! And they are only a couple of days out from Kootenay House." The news poured out of Wolfleg.

"Aw whose been stirring you up? You get more excited than an old woman over nothing. You been smoking that funny weed again? How do you know this stuff?" This from deeper in the cabin from George Lagasse.

"I saw them with my own eyes. Panther was with me. There are four young guys. They have hooked up with Little Bear and his family. Little Bear is on crutches, must have broken a leg. Listen, they have a huge load of cargo in two of the ugliest canoes you'll ever see." Wolfleg tried to spit out what he thought would be important to the Bosses as quickly as he could. He knew that the amount of trade goods that was on those canoes would create a problem for the monopoly the Bosses had built up. The gouging that they were doing to the area bands would quickly be exposed, and Wolfleg would lose his share of the take. He didn't know all of the reasons why the Bosses hated outsiders. They had created loads of trouble for any newcomers thinking they had some authority and rights when they came into this region. If they didn't simply leave or give in to the Bosses, they faced more trouble than anyone could handle. One way or another, any opposition eventually disappeared.

"OK," growled Leblanc, "Get a crew and meet us at Birch Creek at noon. We'll have a plan by then."

Wolfleg slipped away into the dark, glad that he hadn't had to go into the cabin.

The Bosses stumbled their way back to their cots, grumbling about the dumb Hudson Bay Company sending more trade goods over the Rocky Mountains. They couldn't believe they would send kids into their territory considering the trouble they had given to full grown men over the past few years.

Leblanc snorted, "This is going to be like taking candy from babies. And that's what we'll do. We will just take their trade goods, spank them and send them back to their Mommies!!!"

Lagasse hooted, "Yeah, like who's going to stop us?!! We're the Bosses!"

With that they let themselves slide back into their troubled dreams.

TEN

F or the next couple of days the Traders made steady progress even though it was interrupted several times by meeting family groups of Kootenays camped along the river. These families were also taking advantage of the spring to keep their distance from Kootenay House. More than once the Traders noticed plenty of shaking heads and somber talk. Later Grey Owl told them that people were complaining about how little they were being given for their furs from this past winter when they needed to trade them for essential supplies. The head trader claimed that the furs were poor quality but the Indians knew better. When they argued for better exchange they were threatened that they had better be glad they could get anything or else they would not be allowed to trade here at all.

Grey Owl said, "Kootenay House used to be a good place and it gave a sense of belonging where people could not only trade their furs at a fair price but could also look forward to visiting with friends from other bands. Now some families are going a different direction even through it is much farther to other Posts. I think the trouble is going to grow until there is a big fight. I am afraid for my family. We may have to move to another area. It is sad because this has been our home base now for three generations."

The four young men absorbed all of this. They each knew that they would be part of trying to stop the deterioration of a Post that had a great history. It had been the first Trading Post established on this whole Columbia/ Kootenay watershed and had brought great benefit to the natives of the area as well as profit to the Hudson Bay Company. How would they be able to turn around an entrenched system of cheating and abuse? As they talked among themselves, they determined that all they could do was move straight ahead and deal with situations as they arose. They reminded each other that their cover story was that they were on their way to help move Linklater's Post and John Linklater himself to Joseph's Prairie and then resupply it. They needed to stick to their story.

The last stretch to Kootenay House should have been all pleasure for the team. The waters of Windermere Lake were like glass. The towering mountains to the east created a panorama of majesty. Everything in the valley was covered in lush green. Waterfowl called to their chicks as the canoes slid along.

Instead there was a rising tension as their first encounter with the personnel of the Trading House was just ahead. Kootenay House hove into view. It sat on a prominence on the first bench of land rising from the lake. It was like a terrace which would provide unobstructed view of a large swath of the lake. Soon they could see the landing at the water's edge below the Post.

News of their approach had obviously arrived well ahead of them. There was a cluster of people standing on the shore beside the wharf where they would tie up. As they closed in on the dock, Cody picked out the head trader by the colours of his clothing. He knew that his name was Sam Ogilvie. It was tradition for the Head Trader to be present and give a formal welcome to a crew of voyageurs. There were several other workers from Kootenay

House identified by their European clothes. Most of the others were Indians.

Cody could see that Ogilvie was slovenly in his appearance. That was disappointing as the Hudson Bay Company workers were representatives of the British Empire, especially the leader of each Post. They were the civilizing, law and order, people who would bring all the benefit of centuries of culture to this vast territory that had been granted to the Hudson Bay Company when they first established their toehold on the west edge of the Hudson Bay. While these young traders didn't hold with a whole lot of ceremony, they did look for certain things from leaders. The unkempt appearance of this leader was definitely out of place and didn't fit their expectations.

As they floated closer to the wharf, they noticed the dark expressions on the faces of the braves who were lounging about.

"Heads up everyone. Looks like we have a welcoming party and they aren't going to be serving cake!"

muttered Jed.

"Looks more like an un-welcoming party to me," Quinn responded.

Cody gave some directions. "Quinn and Jed looks like you should stay with the canoes. If you have any trouble give a shout. Darcy, you come with me for a little chat with Mr. Ogilvie. I have some mail to pass on to him."

Several people helped tie up the canoes at the wharf. Some reached out to help Little Bear off his seat on the cargo. There was some goodnatured jesting with Little Bear as they teased him about riding when the rest of the family had to walk. Those friends helped him go off to meet up with his relatives who were eager to see the whole family.

Cody jumped on to the dock and walked up to the Head Trader, "Mr. Ogilvie, I'm Cody McVeigh. I bring greetings from the Directors of The Hudson Bay Company. My companions are Darcy, Quinn and Jed."

"So! The rumours were true," responded Sam Ogilvie with a huff.

"Rumours, Sir?" questioned Cody, wondering what rumours could have gotten here ahead of them and what the source could possibly be that might have blown their cover.

"We thought it was just some Peigans trying to stir the pot. They claimed that one of their scouts was at Rocky Mountain House and saw a party leave for Howse Pass headed here. He reported back south and when some of them came here through the south pass to make trouble they brought that story with them. We didn't believe it, but here you are. What possible business could the Directors have dreamed up that sent four kids out into the western wilderness and especially over the Howse Pass?"

Cody was taken aback by the brusqueness and lack of welcome given by Ogilvie. "Perhaps we could spend a little time in your office and I will explain what I can of the Directors wishes, sir."

Ogilvie continued his rudeness. "I don't much care what the Directors wish anymore. They don't know the realities that I deal with. But come if you insist, you probably have some mail for me."

Cody and Darcy followed Ogilvie and a couple other employees of the Trading House as they started up the quarter mile path to Kootenay House.

At the boats Quinn and Jed were adjusting some of the cargo to a better arrangement now that Little Bear wouldn't be riding anymore. Quietly Jed warned Quinn, "Looks like these guys are spoiling for trouble! See those others moving toward the dock? I saw what looked like some signals passing back and forth. Maybe they have some plans for us."

Quinn muttered, "Just maybe we have some surprises for them."

Three of the braves had gone to the other canoe on the opposite side of the long narrow dock and were loosening the ropes holding the covering canvass in place. When Quinn and Jed looked up from the knots they had just finished, to their amazement, they saw one man hand up a carton to another who then turned to walk to shore. Others were waiting for more goods to be handed over. Quinn and Jed were momentarily stunned to see broad daylight theft going on.

Jed yelled, "Stop, that's not for here!!" Both of them strode toward the gang that had assembled. The man with the parcel set it down and braced himself to look as menacing as possible.

"What do you think you're doing!" Amazement was still in Jed's voice at the audacity of these ruffians just starting to help themselves.

The man lifting the cartons out of the canoe seemed to be the leader. He sneered at Quinn and Jed, "Well we heard that these were gifts for the nice Indians at Kootenay House. Now that you've delivered them you can turn around and go back where you came from!!" Some of the other men laughed out loud and egged on their spokesman, Bighorn.

Quinn's face had formed into a deep scowl, "Put the package back and all of you clear off this dock before we throw you off!"

Bighorn laughed at Quinn, "You better take a careful look at how many of us are here. Be smart and just run along." The rest of the gang stepped back to leave a clear space as they anticipated the fight that Bighorn was initiating. They were all enjoying the confidence that their overwhelming numbers gave to them.

In a sudden blur of action, Quinn seized Bighorn by the front of his buckskin shirt and threw him into the lake. Shouts rose from the rest of the gang. When Bighorn surfaced he spluttered and screamed out to them, "Take them!! Don't just stand there!"

The two closest to Quinn rushed him, but Jed took a step into their path and dropped to all fours giving a neat block causing them to somersault and lay tangled on the boards. Jed was instantly back on his feet. He dodged a punch which landed on his shoulder then he jabbed in return finding his intended target. Blood immediately gushed from the victim's nose. Quinn blocked some blows and banged two heads together but the gang was starting to pressure them back. Even though they blocked lot's of punches, there were enough getting through that they had to give some ground.

The shouting when Bighorn went into the lake reached the ears of Cody and Darcy before they went inside. As soon as he heard Bighorn yell at the gang to charge, Cody turned around and said to Darcy, "Let's go! Now!"

Both men raced back down the path. By the time they reached the melee Quinn and Jed were almost backed to the end of the dock. Cody let out a blood curdling yell and waded into the back of the gang throwing bodies left and right. Darcy followed in his wake and when several turned to challenge Cody, Darcy's martial arts training instincts took over. Two open handed chops from behind dropped two men larger than himself. Cody's fists were taking their toll with several bucks dropping out of the fight while holding various body parts that were bleeding or sprained. With the distraction of Cody and Darcy joining the fight, Quinn and Jed were making progress toward their partners and the ranks of the gang were seriously thinning down.

Bighorn had rejoined the brawl and when he saw the tide turning, he became desperate to save face. With a snarl he said to Panther, "Use your knife!" Panther immediately reached down to his legging and pulled out a hunting knife. With the dagger in hand, he turned toward Quinn and through clenched teeth said, "Let's see how brave you are now Mr. Big Man!"

Quinn crouched to face the new menace, fully ready to battle him, but before any contact was made, there was a sudden "Hieyah" from Darcy that caught everyone by surprise. At the same time Darcy spun and delivered a kick to Panther's wrist. The knife flew into the lake and Panther let out a howl as he grabbed his wrist. That immediately ended the fight. The gang members froze for a moment in shock at the combination of the unnerving yell and the faster-than-the-eye-can follow kick from Darcy. A loud curse from Bighorn brought everyone back to action with the gang members mumbling and retreating as they kept looking over their shoulders at Darcy. Bighorn was the last to leave. He faced Darcy and the others behind him and snarled, "You'll pay for this!

Darcy raised his right hand as if to chop at Bighorn's neck. That sent him scurrying after the rest of the gang.

Once the gangsters were gone, the foursome started checking each other over for wounds. All of them had some trophies from the brawl but beyond some minor cuts over eyes, some bruises and one bloody nose they were relatively unscathed.

Jed focused in on Darcy, "Where did you come up with that move? I've never seen anything like it. That knife was shoulder high and your foot sent the knife off like a gunshot! It sure took the fight out of what was left of those guys."

"Aw, it wasn't the kick that scared off those scrappers, it was Darcy's yell! My gosh, it made my stomach hit my throat. Indian war whoops have nothing on a Chinese battle cry, if that's what it was." Quinn was teasing when he wanted to let Darcy know how grateful he was. The words got tied up in emotion that was foreign to Quinn and he couldn't quite choke it out so he settled for the teasing.

Cody pursued Jed's question. "Seriously, Darcy, where did you learn that? Quinn was in a tough spot against that knife."

Darcy quietly responded, "My mother knew that I was going to run into lots of rough stuff being half Chinese in Montreal. She insisted that my Dad find someone to teach me Chinese martial arts because she didn't think my father's pub brawling techniques as a sailor would be adequate. It wasn't easy because there aren't very many Chinese in Montreal but my mom wouldn't let it go and Dad finally found a cook who was awesome at it. He had had to flee China because he had killed someone during the Opium War and that family was determined to get revenge. He insisted that I keep my training secret so he wouldn't be found out and that no one would think of him as anything but a cook."

"Here we thought you were learning to cook Chinese food!! Well, I'm glad we know now," Jed said, "because, all of a sudden, we have a secret weapon we can turn loose if we need it!"

Jed wiped at the corner of his mouth where a trickle of blood was still oozing from a split on his lip. He addressed the others, "Did any of you see what I saw on the sleeve of the one with the broken wrist? There was a gap in the fringes on his buckskin shirt. It would just match with those little strips we found at that lookout and the colour was white so they were fresh rips. This wasn't the first time Mr. Broken Wrist has had his eyes on us. He obviously helped prepare a welcome party for us."

"Well guys," Cody said to bring them back to their problem circumstances, "Looks like we're going to have to have a constant guard on our goods. We'll take turns. Jed you take first watch. We'll trade off every few hours, no longer than four hours at a time. Quinn, dig out the guns for the guard. It's ridiculous that we have to stand guard with guns at our own Hudson Bay Post. No wonder Grey Owl wants to get his family away from here. I've got some serious issues to take up with Mr. Ogilvie. Darcy I'd still like you to come with me. My guess is you'll be getting some big respect from people around here. No more "Chink" slurs here!"

Cody and Darcy headed for the store where the Chief Trader had his quarters.

ELEVEN

Sam Ogilvie didn't even offer them a seat when they entered his backroom. Instead he began to berate them for causing trouble for him.

"You haven't even been here an hour and you've created a brawl. Now I'll have to try to patch things up with those Indians so that we can have some peace around here."

Cody's anger showed on his face. "Mr. Ogilvie, the least we could expect from you would surely be safety for Hudson Bay goods. Surely on one of our own Posts, we would be given safety from local thugs who think they can simply walk away with property that is not their own! Then they had the nerve to start a war when we simply stopped them from stealing in broad daylight!! What kind of operation are you running here? This place looks like a garbage dump. It looks like you're running it into the ground." Cody was trembling with anger as the litany of offences had mounted.

Ogilvie's face was purple with rage and his eyes were bugging out!! "Who do you think you are, you young pup, to land in here with no notice given and in an hour start trying to tell me what I should be doing. You know nothing of the realities of operating a Post in this god-forsaken wilderness as well as trying to please every last savage that thinks he's owed a favour."

Darcy tried to calm things down. "Sir, maybe we got off to a bad start, so if we can just start over...."

"Shut up!! No Chinese kid has got anything to say to me!! Now get out of here and leave me alone!!"

Cody yelled back as he blocked Darcy from going after the Trader,

"Ogilvie, you are way over the line! No one insults my friend and gets away with it. If you weren't the head of this Post I would take that out of your hide. We'll go now, but we'll be back when you've found your senses and are ready to apologize to Darcy."

Cody threw the mail pouch on the table and stormed out, pushing Darcy ahead of him.

"I'll never apologize to a chink!" Ogilvie yelled at the closing door.

Darcy tried to turn around and go back at Ogilvie. Cody held him as he said, "We'll get him one way or the other but right now is not the time. There is something really strange here. Let's get some fresh air and take our time to sort out what is going on."

Now that he was away from the scene of their humiliation, Wolfleg dreaded the meeting he would have to have with the Bosses. As he approached the small draw that cut back from the river just south of Kootenay House he seethed with resentment that these two men had taken such control of his life. He felt like he was a prisoner to their demands just as he was a prisoner to the liquor that he craved. Leblanc and Lagasse had gradually taken control of all available supplies of alcohol coming into the valley and were like puppet masters to those whose thirst constantly burned for more. Wolfleg knew that even though the Bosses lived like pigs they were growing rich on their bully tactics that kept everyone in fear. They would not be safe to be around when they heard what had happened at the dock.

As he turned into the narrow gap that led to a box canyon, he smelled the smoke of their cigarettes before he spotted them. A shiver of fear ran up Wolfleg's spine. He gave the owl hoot just to make sure he didn't startle them and risk a knife in return.

The Bosses stood up without speaking. They were looking behind Wolfleg expecting to see other men coming in with all the packets of cargo from the canoes. As the moments ticked off and no one else appeared the expressions on their faces began to darken.

"What have you done with all the goods, Wolfleg? You're not going to be foolish enough to try to hold on to it for a bigger share, are you?!!"

Wolfleg couldn't lift his eyes to look in their faces. Fear gripped his stomach. Still looking down, he mumbled,

"We didn't get it."

Incredulous, Leblanc said, "What did you say?"

Wolfleg forced his words out a little louder, "We didn't get anything!"

Leblanc's hand went to the knife at his hip as he took steps toward Wolfleg. He backed Wolfleg against a tree and put the tip of the knife against his throat. Terror registered in his wide eyes. He knew the savagery of these men and knew that his life hung by a thread.

Words spilled out of Wolfleg. "They were way stronger than they looked. We almost had them but the two with Ogilvie got back faster than we figured. They threw people around. The chink did some magic – kicked a knife out of Panther's hand, ruined his wrist."

"You mean that ten of you couldn't handle four of them? Now they are going to think they are somebody big and that means trouble for us. You're not getting any more liquor until those four are chased out of here. Don't come back unless you have something helpful. Get lost!" raged Leblanc.

He pulled the knife away from Wolfleg's throat and gave him a shove back in the direction he had come. He ran fast hoping he wouldn't go down with that knife in his back. He craved more liquor. Desperation gripped him at the thought of being denied it. He blamed the newcomers for his fiery thirst. They would have to be taken care of. Wolfleg vowed to himself that somehow he would get back into favour with the Bosses and get back his supply line of booze.

The Bosses were stung. Instead of counting their new wealth and storing it in the shelter at the back of the small canyon, they were walking out with nothing in their hands. This failed attempt to take the cargo and the surprising strength of the young traders was putting their little empire in jeopardy. If Wolfleg's band of thugs couldn't keep everyone under control it could mean that they would have to get directly involved which they had determined not to do. The more shadowy and mysterious they could remain the easier it was to keep people out of the way through threats and fear. Their "tax" on the business of the Trading Post, the low values for furs, and the inflated prices on goods was building a good nest egg for them. At the same time it kept them abundantly supplied with drink.

They decided to go back to their cabin, get roaring drunk, pass out for the night and see what the next day would bring. It certainly would include a visit to Ogilvie to make sure he didn't get big ideas about what he could do just because there were some young and foolish new Hudson Bay people on site.

TWELVE

Cody and Darcy were still steaming mad when they got back to the canoes.

Cody spewed out his version of what had happened in Ogilvie's office. Then Darcy poured out his account as well.

"I've never been so tempted to land a kick on someone's mouth. I probably would have if Cody hadn't been in my way," finished Darcy.

"We didn't even have any chance to talk about our plans to help Linklater at Fort Kokanee or get any directions from Ogilvie for finding the place. Maybe things will cool down a bit overnight. This has been so intense that we haven't sorted out anything yet. I suggest we go back downstream to make camp. If we don't do it now darkness will make setting up pretty difficult." Cody continued to explain his view of the mess their arrival had turned out to be as they untied the canoes and turned them downstream.

"There's no doubt the attack by that gang today had been planned ahead. They knew that if they tried stealing so brazenly it would provoke a fight. Then the others that had looked like they were just hanging around out of curiosity would join in. I'm sure they had simply assumed that their large numbers would easily overpower us. Even though Ogilvie is a skunk, I can't believe that he would organize something like that."

"Are you thinking that it is Leblanc and Lagasse that are behind it?" queried Jed.

"It could easily be if what we've learned so far is accurate," replied Cody. "If they are behind it they will be upset that today was a failure and they will be very determined to get their hands on this cargo. Looks like we'll have to continue the constant guard."

Ogilvie was still shaking from his yelling match with Cody and Darcy. He had slumped into his chair as he heard the outer door slam shut. With his head buried in his hands he felt completely trapped. Those boys had no idea of the pressures he was under. Why, oh why, had they shown up now to add pressure to the precarious trap that could snap shut on him at any time.

He reached for the jug that was behind his desk and poured a generous amount into the tin cup always within reach. "The Bosses would be out of control over this. Who could guess what ridiculous demands they would make now?"

Ogilvie groaned out loud. How could things have deteriorated so far that even he was thinking of Leblanc and Lagasse as the Bosses. He had only let himself get a little involved with them at first. It looked like he could add to his own profits which made sense given the meagre salary the Hudson Bay was giving him. After all, he was making lots of profit for the Company. What thanks would he ever receive that would come close to giving him what he deserved? If it meant a little commission for the Frenchmen – well – that was only fair.

How he regretted those first steps now! It hadn't taken long before Leblanc and Lagasse were turning up the pressure. Their threat to expose him had shocked him into quickly agreeing to another step of fraud. Now he was in so deep there was no possibility of walking away from this web of scamming every one who had any dealings with the Trading Post. That didn't stop him from wishing with all his heart that he could simply start over and keep himself from ever letting someone else take power over him. His despair grew darker the more he mulled over his situation because there seemed no path or seam of escape. Tomorrow would be horrendous – even worse than today.

As he poured another cup of spirits his eyes caught on the mail pouch Cody had slammed down on his desk. With nothing else for him to do for the evening he thought he might as well read through the usual drivel that head office sent out trying to tell him how to run his post even though they could never understand what he faced.

Ogilvie broke the seal on the flap of the leather pouch and pulled out quite a stack of envelopes. He pulled the lamp closer and settled in to work through this pile. The only good thing was that it gave him something else to focus on. After several lengthy letters containing reports and instructions on values of furs because of sales in England, Sam's mind was growing numb. He was ready to crawl over to the cot that was against the north wall of his office, rather than going to his quarters, when the words on the next envelope changed his mind. "Regarding The Assignment Of Cody McVeigh, Hudson Bay Trader."

Ogilvie said to himself, "Well, I've nothing to lose by reading how the Directors think they can stick this young know-it-all into my affairs. At least I will know what I have to contend with."

As he read, a little crack of light started to pierce through his gloom. Just maybe there was a way to side-step a major showdown. These instructions from the Directors sparked an unexpected glimmer of hope.

"Robert! Robert! Get your lazy bones in here!" Ogilvie yelled to rouse his assistant whose quarters were in one of the side rooms of the trading house.

"Sir?" Robert appeared as he was still pulling up his suspenders.

"Find Wolfleg right away. I need him tonight. Understand? Tonight! I have to get a message to Leblanc and Lagasse. Have him come to the corral and give me the signal when he is there. And don't forget – keep it away from the eyes of people hanging around. People aren't to see regular connection between us and the Frenchmen or we'll lose those bonuses. Understand Robert?"

Robert slipped out into the night. Sam Ogilvie took the top off his inkwell, sharpened a quill, and laid a scrap of wrapping paper on his desk. All he wrote was "See me first." The Bosses would know what he was referring to but if it fell into the wrong hands it wouldn't be too revealing of their plotting together. After passing the note into Wolfleg's hand, and wringing a promise from him that he would actually place the note in one of the Bosses' hands, Ogilvie felt a slight lifting of the cloud hanging over him. He had a plan to act on in the morning! With that fixed in his mind he retired and was able to drift off to sleep.

THIRTEEN

Quinn had the last shift of the night. He liked it. Liked the peace and the sense that he was experiencing a new life. Just as the dawn brought a fresh new day, he had a new dawn to live for. No more drunken harangues from his father. No more episodes of him beating his mother and him until he was big enough to stand up for himself. But he couldn't be there all day and all night everyday to protect his Mom. He had watched her health go down hill. There had been no peace for her like Quinn was experiencing now. She hadn't died directly from a beating but Quinn knew that it was the abuse that had taken her will to live.

As the birds and waterfowl started their own greetings to the new day, Quinn thought about the new things in his life. Amazed that he was in this totally new environment. Excited that a man was accepted for what he could do with his own hands. That here everyone came with a fresh page. You could write your own life without being discounted because you were Irish in a French community, or because you were dirt poor, or because your drunken Dad was the laughing stock of the street.

Now Quinn looked back with amazement that he had become buddies with these three. He had only attended school for three years and that was where he had met these guys. Quinn grinned as he remembered that they had connected through fighting. Every boy eventually measured himself and learned his place in the pecking order by scrapping. Both Quinn and Cody had taken on every kid that dared to try them and had come out on top – until they took on each other. What a crowd that one had drawn just on the edge of the school grounds right after school! Quinn was a loner and was feared by the boys that knew him. Cody was a leader who had a following of kids that just liked to be around him because he was always doing crazy stuff. They tussled and grunted and groaned with the onlookers yelling and cheering. Quinn's size kept him in the battle and would get him on top for a time. Cody was not quite as big but was faster and just as strong and that would get him on top at other times. The boys finally exhausted themselves with no clear winner. Between huge pants for air while their arms and legs were locked up and neither one could move Cody called "truce?" Quinn puffed out "OK!" From that day Cody had included Quinn. What was especially significant, Cody kept including Quinn even when he had to drop out of school.

Now here he was watching this incredible fiery dawn. The tops of the mountains on the west were just starting to be set ablaze by the rising sun. The shades of grey around him were giving way to the beautiful lush greens of summer and the varied aqua colours of the lake. Time to stir the fire and start the coffee.

A sound caught his attention. He cocked his head to the side to pick up the noise ahead. There it was again – definitely hoof beats. It was too faint to tell if there was one or more horses. What he could tell was that it was fairly rapid.

"Rise and shine guys, we've got company!" Quinn called out to his sleeping mates. They scrambled quickly asking what was going on at the same time.

"Horse or horses coming. It might be nothing, maybe even just passing by. Just being cautious."

They were all standing as a single horse and rider appeared. To their great surprise it was Sam Ogilvie.

"Hello!" he called, "May I come in?" His politeness was a surprise and made the young men wary.

All of them looked at Darcy to see how he felt about it. His face was stoney and unwelcoming. Cody turned back to Ogilvie.

"State your business." barked Cody.

"I've come to apologize and try to start over with you!" he replied.

"If anybody else shows up unannounced Quinn will be keeping that gun pointed in your direction and his first shot will be for you!"

"Come, come lads, that won't be necessary. Just a little misunderstanding!" Ogilvie tried to jolly his way around the events of yesterday.

Cody's face went dark. "Sir, a gang attack of ten against four, a knife pulled that threatened Quinn's life, plus, you insulting one of my team. That's more than a 'little misunderstanding.'"

The air seemed to go out of the head trader as Cody listed these wrongs. He dropped his gaze to the ground. He had no defence to offer back.

"Listen, I do apologize. I jumped to some wrong conclusions when the rumour came that four men were coming. I thought you were coming to take over from me, and that the Company was putting me out in the cold. A man gets strange thoughts after a long time alone in the wilderness, so far from communication with others in the same business. When I read the mail last night I discovered that you are on your way to relocate Linklater. The Directors said that I am to help you on your way. I will do what I can with our limited resources to help you.

One more thing. Darcy, I apologize to you personally. I guess it was a combination of paranoia and drink but that is no excuse. I trust we can try to start over and let bygones be bygones."

Cody looked at each of his mates in turn and took a silent poll. Each one gave a shrug and a slight nod of agreement. Cody addressed Mr. Ogilvie.

"We're willing to try again. But I have to tell you, this whole thing has put us on our guard. We'll do the business we have to do here and then be moving on as soon as we can."

"Understood," replied the Trader, "Now let me offer you the hospitality I should have offered to you yesterday. Please, all of you come for breakfast. I'll have the cook do up some flapjacks, eggs and steak with biscuits that'll tune up your taste buds after weeks on the trail. It'll give us a chance to talk over the needs and plans that you have."

"Well, that's kind of you but we can't all leave our supplies unguarded," said Cody.

"Look, I'll send my Assistant Robert to stand guard while you're enjoying a feast!! I'll send him down here when the food is ready. Shouldn't take more than an hour or so."

With that Ogilvie reined his horse around and was gone.

The boys stood staring at the trail where Ogilvie had just disappeared from sight. They were stunned at this sudden turn around on the Head Trader's part.

Jed hissed out, "Can you believe that? That's the last kind of thing I expected to hear from him today!"

"That blows me away," Quinn added. "Who is the real head trader at this post. This guy this morning or the guy we saw yesterday?"

Darcy said softly, "I don't believe him. There's a lot more to this than that kiss-off we were just given."

"I think you're right," Cody nodded vigorously. "And we'll be checking it out. But our cover story has given us a breather so we can poke into all of this without having direct confrontation.

So, breakfast at Kootenay House will give us a good start to get Ogilvie talking and to learn what resources are around here."

"I'm not going!" Every one turned to look at Darcy. His look was defiant. " I know, he said the words of apology but I don't think they were sincere. He didn't look for a response from me. And besides, having Robert guard our supplies is a little like having the fox guard the chickens. I'll stand guard while you socialize with Mr. Big. I'll rustle up some breakfast for myself and I'll enjoy my own company better than the company you'll have."

An hour later Ogilvie played the congenial host to the hilt. Urging the young men to have second helpings of all the food. It didn't take any extra invitation. The smells and tastes had been lacking from their lives for what seemed an eternity. Within the safe confines of that dining room the Head Trader easily fell back into a comfort groove he had known before the troubles had started. In fact he envied these four who were experiencing so many new and expanding steps in their lives.

As the boys related some of the adventures of their travels Sam picked up on some of the names of other traders he had known over the years. He was genuinely glad to hear news from the outside. The story of their horses being stolen caused a momentary shadow to pass over Ogilvie's face but he quickly recovered and offered his sympathy for the dangers of the wilds.

"Well then, boys," he finally exclaimed, eager to get to the purpose of having the three guests at his table. "How can I help you on your way!?"

They talked about the fresh supplies that could restore what they had used so far. Also, Ogilvie offered directions and some advice about getting to Linklater's Fort Kokanee. He also promised to ask around about horses that might be available for the next stage of their journey, emphasizing to them that he didn't really keep up on the latest sales of horses. It seemed he went somewhat overboard distancing himself from the topic of horses.

Darcy puttered over making his own breakfast while his three friends were in the Trading Post. He had sent Robert back with the them. It was a glorious summer morning and the solitude massaged his spirit. He mulled over the renewal of anger towards his Chinese blood. It was nothing new to him but he supposed he had had a growing hope that it might not be present in his new life in the west. That faint hope was certainly shattered now. The travel out had been a pocket of tranquillity regarding racial matters through the total acceptance given by each of his three friends. Darcy added another layer of gratitude for his three friends on top of the accumulating pile of the treasure his buddies were to him.

A young musical voice calling his name roused him from his reflections. It was Maria. Darcy blushed at how pleased he was to hear her voice and though he would have denied outwardly any special feelings towards her, his faster heart rate gave him away. She had run ahead of the rest of her family who were on the way to the Trading Post for some supplies.

"Hi Maria. Are you all alone?"

"No," she replied. "I ran ahead to surprise you. But where are the others?"

"They are having breakfast with Mr. Ogilvie and I'm guarding our supplies."

"Why are they spending time with that mean old man?" Frowned Maria.

"Well, we need to find some horses so we can get to Joseph's Prairie and on to Fort Kokanee. How's your Dad today?"

Maria's family had arrived, stopping to chat for a few minutes before continuing on to the Trading Post, and heard that last question from Darcy.

Bright Star answered him with a snort. "He is tired of sitting around and he's getting grouchy. He's getting in the way of women's work, trying to tell us how to make pemmican when we've done it forever! Pierre is going to have a bow and arrow contest with him this afternoon to get him out of our way."

"Grampa! Guess what?" Maria was excited to give some news to her elders. "Darcy is going to Joseph's Prairie where Sophie is. They'll be able to meet my cousins!"

Grey Owl responded, "We had wondered what you would be doing. If you stayed here there might be trouble with Ogilvie and his henchmen. But we didn't want to pry into your business."

"Well, it's public information now that we've informed Ogilvie. We'll take this outfit to Joseph's Prairie and then go get Linklater to help him move there. All we need now is a string of horses," offered Darcy.

Grey Owl grimaced, "Horses are in short supply around here. Most families that had a horse have had to trade it in to pay debts at the Post. I don't know how all of this will end. We are being ground down to almost nothing. Pretty soon we'll have to move away from our home area to where there is another Post to trade with. That will mean finding new trapping areas that we're not familiar with. It is hard to think about leaving this valley and mountains that I've known all my life.

Darcy asked, "What happens to the horses once they are traded in?"

"They all seem to get sold to Big Plume who runs horses on the east side of the next lake further south where there's lots of open grazing land. Rumours are that The Bosses really run it and that they work out some deals with the Peigans. We know that the prices are way too high when anyone tries to buy one back from them. They'll try to take all your supplies if you buy from them but I don't know what else you'll do to get horses."

FOURTEEN

As soon as breakfast was finished and the boys were ushered out of the Post, Sam Ogilvie called his assistant. Robert knew what to expect. Another message would go to the Bosses via Wolfleg. He was chaffing at having to be a messenger boy for thieves and bullies rather than looking forward to being a Chief Trader at a post of his own. The Hudson Bay would never promote him when they saw the dwindling profits from Kootenay House. Robert wondered if there was any way out of this tangled web, and if he would ever find the backbone to stand up against the scandal of the Hudson Bay being used as a front for cheating, robbery and murder.

"Robert!" roared Sam.

Robert shrugged and said to himself, "Well, maybe another day."

This time Ogilvie felt he needed to talk directly to the Bosses. He couldn't take a chance that they would ignore or misunderstand messages passed through several hands. So his message arranged a face to face meeting for later in the day.

Leblanc and Lagasse were fuming at having to sit on their hands and wait for the Trader. They were men of action and they wanted to storm these young guys in their camp and eliminate them as a problem. Their impatience with indirect action was growing. They were becoming more arrogant as their loot kept growing. Their dreams of heading to Mexico as wealthy men who could run their own hacienda filled with wine, women and song were growing stronger and stronger. Why should they hang back worrying about four young pups when they could just snuff them out? Ogilvie worried about their escalating violence and knew that it would take some careful talking to keep from losing the benefits from their whole scheme – his own included.

"What's the matter with you Ogilvie, you're acting more like an old woman all the time. We're the brains that run this operation, so you better have a real good explanation about keeping us back from wiping those four young snots out. We aren't just going to sit on our behinds and let other people ruin our plans."

Ogilvie held his hands out in a motion of getting them to calm down.

"That's just it, I've got good news that's going to put us in the clear. They are just passing through rather than being assigned to Kootenay House. All we have to do is let them buy some horses and they will be heading down south to work with John Linklater. This way you don't have any interference and I don't have to make up stories to report back to my Directors. In fact, you'll make huge profit on those horses considering the price you paid for them. Probably double what the Peigans would give you. Make sure you get Big Plume to cooperate. We don't want him putting prices so high that these kids can't buy them and get the heck out of our space."

"You're way too soft, old man, but if you're sure this will clear them out then we'll set up the horse deal. Just remember, we can't baby-sit the Indians and some of them will not be too happy that these kids will get a free pass. If something happens to them we can't help it. They've stuck their noses into it and they'll have to get themselves out of it." growled Leblanc.

Ogilvie retorted, "Believe me, it's for your own good to cool those hotheads down!"

The Bosses shrugged and headed for the back of the Post where they usually found someone to be their messenger. Before long Wolfleg rode out from the paddock behind the buildings, headed to the big horse ranch at the far end of Columbia Lake.

Meanwhile, Darcy was being thoroughly roasted by his mates when they came back to find Maria hovering around like a butterfly although she left quickly when the others showed up.

"No wonder you didn't want to go to the post for breakfast! Must be pretty nice to have a young female helper show up just when you've gotten rid of us!"

Darcy couldn't help a pinkish tinge colouring his face as he warned them to watch their tongues or else!

"Actually, I've been gathering vital information while you've been wasting time with the enemy. I know who to buy horses from. Big Plume runs horses south of here, although Grey Owl thinks he's in cahoots with the Bosses. Apparently he has bought up just about all the horses there are."

Quinn growled, "I wonder if he'll sell us any. I hate to do business with the devil!"

"According to Grey Owl we probably don't have any choice if we really want horses." said Darcy. "Also, some good news. Grey Owl has family in the Joseph's Prairie area. He says he's sure they'll be glad to help us in any way they can."

"Now that really is some valuable information, Darcy, I guess you were doing a little more than flirting with your little butterfly!" laughed Cody. "We'll do some more talking with our friends about what we'll find when we get that far."

It was late afternoon when they heard the sound of a horse approaching. Once again it was Ogilvie. And again he was Mr. Congeniality.

"As I promised, I've made enquiries about horses for sale. I'm told that the only horse operation in the area that has enough horses for your purposes is on the hills above Columbia Lake, the south west end. It's run by a man named Big Plume. Probably two days to hike there and a long day back on horse back. Good luck!"

With that The Trader spun his horse around and loped back the way he had come. As the Pards watched him ride away there were lots of questions in their minds. Cody put some of them into words.

"I wonder what's gone on today that he came with that message so late in the day? Wouldn't he have known that this morning? Somehow he was delaying and I'd give a lot to know why. I have some bad feelings about having only one option for horses and that we are being herded into that option by a man who is obviously on the wrong side of things."

As they chatted over the situation they all agreed that they had to move ahead by trying to buy those horses. They resolved that Quinn and Darcy would stay with the cargo. Cody needed to negotiate the purchase and Jed was their best wrangler so those two would make the trip along the Columbia Lake. Given the hostile atmosphere around Kootenay House, they were concerned for only two men guarding their goods day and night.

Darcy offered a suggestion. "Maybe Little Bear could hobble this far. He and Pierre could help by spelling us off. Just having more people around should discourage any thievery. We could pay them a little for their help. Sounds like their archery skills are up to date."

Jed chortled, "Shame, shame, Darcy!! You sure know how to attract a little butterfly by having her family here!!!"

That almost started a wrestling match but Cody intervened.

"Look you guys, Jed and I will have to leave early! Let's get our backpacks ready.

FIFTEEN

Dawn was just breaking on a foggy, overcast day when Cody and Jed shouldered their packs, hefted their rifles in one hand and headed out of their campsite to the trail that would take them south. Suddenly a voice called softly from the side of the trail. Both Cody and Jed jolted to a stop, instantly ready to fight, their hearts racing, their guns coming up. Through the gloom their eyes made out the form of Grey Owl sitting cross-legged beside the trail.

"Grey Owl, you nearly scared us to death!" whispered Cody, the heavy cloud making whispering a natural reaction.

"I didn't want to risk being shot by coming into your camp and I knew you had to pass here." said the senior man in a voice barely above a whisper. "We had information come to us late last night that you are in danger on this trip. Some of the gang that you threw off the dock are burning with shame and are being laughed at. They want to regain face. I have no other details. Be very careful my friends,"

Cody and Jed, without any further words, turned and continued to the main trail. Both were turning over and over the message Grey Owl had given them but it was some time before either of them spoke.

"Kind'a spoils the start of the day, doesn't it?" commented Jed. "The hair on the back of my neck is already feeling prickly and we haven't even passed the Trading Post."

"Let's just hope we keep our hair attached to our heads!" replied Cody.

"Oh great! You're supposed to be the one that keeps us optimistic. Now my scalp is doing more than prickling!!!! You don't think these Indians still scalp people, do you?"

Cody couldn't help a macabre chuckle. "As long as you can feel those prickles, you know you haven't been scalped yet!! Maybe this mist will keep us covered for the day."

The duo made great time on the well used trail that followed the river as it twisted and turned and then the contours of the lake. Sometimes the trail went up and over ridges that came right to the lake. As the sun burned off the low clouds that had been trapped in the valley, the view from these occasional heights stirred both of them as they marvelled at the contrast to their city backgrounds. Much of the region had only sparse trees with lots of open hillside meadows which would provide no cover for an ambush. In these stretches they could relax and enjoy the new countryside that offered fresh vistas around every turn in the trail. When they did encounter a forested stretch, they paid close attention to be aware of movement or sounds that would let them know someone was following them. For the whole day they only saw an occasional canoe where people were fishing and only met a couple families on the trail. Even the wildlife was sparse. There had been nothing to cause them any alarm.

As dusk was approaching they began to watch for a good campsite. The landmarks that had been described to them by Little Bear indicated that they were more than halfway and that they would reach their destination in good time the next day.

Both knew that by choosing the right kind of setting they could lessen the risk of someone catching them unawares.

They finally agreed on a site that was in a narrow draw that had very steep clay banks. It formed a triangle that opened out toward the lake so that it could only be entered from that one direction. Tall trees provided a natural canopy and a small spring provided water for drinking right where they would have their fire and sleep.

They were both weary from the long day of hiking and ready to settle for the night. As they were savouring their second cups of coffee Jed spoke the question that was on both of their minds.

"What about Grey Owl's warning? This campsite seems pretty secure but if we are both sound asleep what's to prevent someone sneaking up on us?"

Cody responded, "Yeah, I've been wondering about it, too. Grey Owl went to a lot of trouble to warn us so I think there must have been some strong reasons for him to do that."

As they were thinking over what they should do, they heard the piercing cry of a nighthawk and then the whistle of its wings as it bottomed out its dive to capture another insect victim. Cody shivered with the image of night time predators of all kinds beginning their stalking.

"Okay, let's set ourselves up so we can welcome any visitors! Losing a night's sleep is a lot better than the alternatives."

That was the answer Jed had been hoping for although he wasn't going to be the one to say it first. He had become less sleepy as the dusk had thickened to darkness and the creaking of the tall trees in the evening breeze had made it seem like the night was full of activity. They waited until their little cook fire had died to glowing coals and then they got their backpacks and retrieved their bedrolls and rifles.

Bighorn smiled to himself as he saw the two hikers settling their campsite for the night. He had trailed them all day and he knew that they had not been able to spot him even though they had often looked back to see if they were being followed. He had used a little known parallel trail that was several hundred feet higher on the mountain side. Most of the time it was completely out of view from the main track along the lake but he could check when he wanted to see that Cody and Jed were still on the only major path anyone would usually take given their destination. As daylight changed into twilight Bighorn had closed the distance between them and had been able to locate them by the smoke from their fire and then later by the light of their campfire.

As their fire died down, the fire of his hatred burned brighter in his mind. He still couldn't believe that these tenderfeet from across the mountains had beaten up on his gang. They had shamed him and he couldn't let that go on. His grip on the loyalty of his helpers was slipping as they were beginning to challenge his leadership. Panther was being especially critical saying it was Bighorn's fault that he couldn't hunt with the rest because of his broken wrist. Well, he would get his revenge tonight. The laughing would stop when they knew that he had single-handedly eliminated two of these intruders. He settled in to wait for the half-moon that would give enough light to stalk them when they were sleeping and to be accurate with his arrows. He couldn't afford to miss and give them any opportunity to use their rifles.

Bighorn waited until he was sure they would be sound asleep and then waited extra time to be doubly sure. He patiently placed each footstep to be sure he didn't step on a twig or a rock that might roll. As he made a little progress, a pheasant clucked softly. Bighorn froze and gave time for it to settle again and then took the next step away from where the bird was hidden. It shouldn't have been enough to wake the sleepers. As he got closer the light wind in the trees began to give him some noise cover.

It was harder to make out shapes as he came in view of the campsite because the trees were blocking most of the moonlight. Very patiently he moved in close. He wasn't sure if he was hearing the heavy breathing of the men or if it was the wind in the trees making a sighing sound. Gradually he could make out the two bed rolls. He pulled an arrow and nocked it. Moving a couple steps closer, he drew the bowstring. No movement This was going to be easier than he could have hoped. His heart was racing as he steadied his aim.

Twang! Thud! Bighorn reached for the second arrow as the first one found its mark. He was already setting the next arrow as the realization was also setting in that that was a strange sound for an arrow hitting flesh. Continuing on reflex, he sent the second arrow into the other bedroll. Twang! Thuft! More strange sound! And no movement at all.

"Hold still, don't move!!" Cody's voice boomed in the stillness of night. From the opposite side, "I've got you covered! Put your bow on the ground!!"

Cody and Jed closed in on Bighorn from each side with their rifles levelled at him. They were only a few steps on either side of the path Bighorn had chosen. As he dropped his bow his other hand slid up his side in a panic grab for his knife. Cody had stepped right up beside him and heard as much as saw the knife clearing it's sheath. Instinctively Cody swung the butt of his rifle and Bighorn collapsed to the ground in a heap and lay still.

As Cody and Jed stood over their unconscious enemy, the reality of their narrow escape settled in. Jed's voice had a tremor, "Those arrows really would be in us if we hadn't set this up!"

"Exactly! That was too close for comfort! But what do we do now?"

"The only thing I know for sure right now is that we better tie this guy up before he comes to. I'll get some rope," said Jed as he headed to his back pack.

They bound Bighorn hand and foot and dragged his limp body into their camp. Knowing they wouldn't sleep any more, they stirred up the fire and put some coffee into the pot. When the fire gave enough light they recognized their prisoner.

"This was revenge. He was trying to regain face with his fellow renegades after losing the battle at the dock. We sure don't want to drag him around with us but on the other hand we can't kill him or just let him go." Cody kept turning things over in his mind.

Jed spat out, "Why not kill him? He certainly made a direct attempt to kill us. It would be self-defence!"

"If we hadn't taken him alive - killed him to keep him from shooting us - I wouldn't have hesitated. But now that we have him, we can't kill him now!" replied Cody thoughtfully.

"Well, if we just let him go nothing has been accomplished. He'll just come after us tomorrow. Something has to happen to change his mind and I don't think a goose egg on his head will be enough." Jed's frustration made him jump up and start pacing.

"More than a goose egg on his head!" Cody mulled an idea, "I think you've given me an idea that just might take care of this brave for a long time."

Bighorn started to moan. His eyes flickered awhile before he came back to full consciousness. He tried to sit up but the ropes kept him on his side. When he saw Jed whittling shavings into the fire, his expression went from questioning to outright fear as he remembered voices just before everything went black. The pounding in his head made him realize what had happened to him. He struggled against the ropes to test his circumstances. His face became contorted with rage and he spat in the direction of Jed.

"I don't think it's right that after we saved his life he spits at us! "Jed said to Cody at the same time he waved Bighorn's knife in his direction. "Do you Cody?"

"I think we might have to teach this brave a number of hard lessons before we're through with him," Cody added with gritted teeth. "Someone trying to kill us in the middle of the night obviously has some things to learn. Bighorn – you are in for some major changes. And we are going to force those changes on you."

"You can't make me change, White Man! You just got lucky this time." Bighorn snarled.

"Bighorn, you better start letting some things sink into that thick skull of yours. You and your thugs got beat up on the dock even though you had way more guys. Your braves blamed you for it. You lost face with them. Now you thought you could get that all back – get them to do what you tell them again – by putting our lights out. You've failed again, Bighorn!! You're finished, you just don't realize it yet.

"I'll get you some time, some way!" Bighorn tried to sound fierce but fear crept into his voice.

Jed chirped in and said, "See Cody! Whatever it is you have in mind he isn't going to quit until we kill him. Just let me shoot him!"

Now the fear showed plainly on Bighorn's face and he struggled some more against the ropes that bound him securely.

"I think we have something worse than death for Bighorn. If he had killed us he would have taken some trophy from us that proved he had been brave and successful. Have you heard of 'counting coup'? Well, it looks like we get to count coup. To prove that he was defeated and disgraced and that he should now be an outcast from all the people. We get to take something from him that he cannot hide or explain away. And Bighorn, you'll have to disappear or you will be the most shamed brave there is. Your effort to save face has become just the opposite."

"What can accomplish all that?" Jed wondered out loud.

"His braids," replied Cody. "We are going to give him a haircut!"

"Noooooo!" Bighorn wailed. "No you can't do that to me! No, no,no! No one will have anything to do with me! I won't go after you anymore. I promise, I'll leave you alone. Please, not that. I'll have to leave completely. I will lose my power."

"You deserve this for the way you've used your power. Maybe you will learn to treat life with respect." Cody was unrelenting.

The day dawned bright and clear. Cody and Jed walked the newly shorn Bighorn to the main trail and told him to go back north on the path that was visible for a long way.

"We will watch you for as long as you're in sight. We will have a rifle aimed on you all that time. If you stop or turn off the path before you're out of our sight, we will shoot. When you have gone beyond our sight you do whatever you wish, but if you cause any more trouble, we will show your braids and tell what you have done. And if you try anything else, we will shoot to protect ourselves."

By the time Jed had watched Bighorn out of sight, Cody had packed up their camp. They shouldered their back packs, now containing a braid each, and headed on toward the horses.

Jed shook his head, "I've never seen someone so completely changed over a haircut! There was no fight left in him at all!"

"Pretty superstitious, but as long as he believes it so strongly it serves us well," Cody answered. "Just the same we better stay sharp and check our back trail pretty often."

"Aw, you had to say that didn't you. You just made the hair on my neck prickle!!"

SIXTEEN

Cody and Jed set a brisk pace to make up time used to deal with the trouble caused by Bighorn's attempt to kill them. It was mid-afternoon when they came to the lodges of Big Plume's horse ranch.

Three teepees stood out in sharp contrast to the sparsely treed rolling hills that stretched out to the west. There were a number of lean-to shelters scattered on some of the hills giving testimony to the winds that could sweep across the area. Several pole corrals with a few horses held in them were visible as Cody and Jed trudged up the incline to the top of the rise that gave a clear vista from the lodges should anyone unwelcome try to get close to these dwellings.

Several men materialized from around the lodges and the corrals. It was a show of strength intended to put Cody and Jed on the defensive.

"Let's go slow and steady!" breathed Cody to Jed. "If we don't over-react we should be able to convince them that we simply want to do business."

A big man with a weathered round face and a few eagle feathers in his hair which was tied back in a pony tail detached himself from the group at the largest teepee and approached the newcomers.

"You look like you need horses!! I'm Big Plume and I can fix you up so you can ride rather than walk!" Big Plume hooked his thumbs into small pockets of a finely embroidered purple vest which was completely out of character with the buckskin leggings he was also wearing. He gave a big grin that to Jed looked more gloating than welcoming.

Cody and Jed nodded back to him and each gave their names by way of greeting. Big Plume responded as a congenial host.

"Come on up to my lodge. My wife will bring us some food and drink so we can relax and get acquainted! You are new to the area and I have been here forever!" This last was said with a laugh. "What brings you to the valley?"

As they walked to the lodge, Cody explained that they were with the Hudson Bay and that they were just passing through to help Linklater down at Fort Kokanee. Big Plume was full of sympathy when he heard about the theft of their horses. When the conversation led to Cody mentioning that he was the Grandson of David Thompson, their host was excited to tell stories he had heard of the great explorer.

"My father was hired by your grandfather as a hunter to supply meat for the new Kootenay House. It was a great thing to have a trading post right in our community. Thompson also read from his big black book every week. My father passed on some of the stories. Like the very first brothers getting into a fight and one of them got killed So it's just part of who we are to fight. I especially liked the spirits singing when there was a special baby and a special star. I see those bright spirits in the northern sky and sometimes I think I can hear them singing."

Cody found himself telling stories about his grandfather in exchange for Big Plume's stories. When one story would trigger another, Cody was glad because he was hearing bits and pieces about his ancestor that he had never known. It stirred something inside him as he listened to more of his own heritage even though the stories were probably embellished. It told him the view that the Kootenay Indians held of his Grampa and it was a view of high regard. This was the ideal that had stayed on his mental canvas and had pulled Cody forward to be that kind of person. He wanted to fit into that kind of portrait that one day would be him.

Jed had finished the lunch that had been provided for some time and the lack of sleep was catching up with him. He had given up trying to be interested in the stories, some of which he had heard more than once on their long hours crossing the country. Now he was losing the battle with heavy eye lids.

Just as Cody was starting into another story that he had heard before, Jed jumped into the conversation.

"Cody, I know it's a good story, but maybe we should take care of some business!!"

That snapped Cody to attention. He reminded himself that he was sitting with a man who was probably his enemy and would be happy to gouge him over the price of horses. In fact, he was pretty sure he was in the company of one of the men who had stolen their horses.

"Of course," said Big Plume, continuing in the mode of the congenial host, "You wish to get a good deal on some horses! I'm glad to offer very favourable prices for David Thompson's grandson. I'll have my men bring the horses from the south range and you can make a selection." Do you want saddles, halters, pack saddles?"

"We have all of that back at Kootenay House, The thieves didn't take any tack. So we'll ride bareback for one day. We may need some extra rawhide rope for trailing back." responded Jed. Cody could hear hostility in Jed's voice because he felt he was dealing with the very thieves that had robbed them.

Cody and Jed moved their back packs to the side of the pole corral and sorted through the rope that they did bring. Now that they were well away from any listening ears, Jed vented his frustration.

"You sure seemed to take to that slippery character!! I don't trust him at all. He was way too phony in how friendly he was to us. It was like a cat toying with a mouse before moving in for the kill. I'm already mad at the price he's going to ask for the horses and what can we do? We're trapped into paying whatever he asks! I think we ought to face him up with stealing our horses when there aren't any others in the whole valley. It had to be him. At the least he's got stolen horses here whether they are ours or belong to other people."

Jed's voice kept getting louder as he worked himself up into a lather.

"Hold it down Jed! I wish we could but we don't really have anything on him yet. Let's just get some horses and get out of here. If we keep our eyes open, we'll eventually collect enough facts to break up all this evil that's being pushed down on people around here. Did you notice his ridiculous looking vest? The buttons match the button we found on the field where our horses were stolen!! And his vest was missing one." Cody spoke with as much conviction as he could muster to try and keep Jed from bailing out of their plan.

Eventually they heard the thunder of many hooves as the herd crested the ridge behind the lodges. Knowing that it was just a short distance the wranglers had taken the opportunity for the fun of galloping the herd at full speed. The riders were letting out excited "whoops" and "yips" as they pushed the horses into the corral at a run. The twenty or so horses milled around the pole enclosure, as excited from the run from the pasture as the cowboys obviously were.

The herd quieted gradually. A few stopped to drink at the trough but others with ears back and nostrils flared kept checking out the onlookers as they continued to circle. Eventually, two or three came to the poles to sniff the newcomers. As Jed and Cody rubbed their noses, they nickered in return as if they were trying to tell that they would be good purchases.

Once the herd became fully quieted, Jed slipped between the poles to inspect the animals more closely. Horses always accepted him and let him pass his hands over all vital parts, starting from their heads, so that he could gain a good sense of their health and attitude. First he looked for saddle horses and as he discovered one that was suitable he would put a rawhide hackamore on it and lead it to the edge of the corral where he tied it. Then he selected the pack horses that they needed. These he secured with a loop around their necks. Before long he had the twelve that he would work more extensively before making a final decision on their working remuda.

Jed borrowed a riding saddle and a pack saddle so that he could try out each horse. With Cody lifting saddles off and on, Jed carefully worked through the whole string even though it was getting late in the day. Virtually every horse bucked a time or two when it felt the cinch strap tighten. The realization of their loss of wild freedom was striking home at that point. Yet Jed's wrangling skill seemed to work some magic as he calmly talked the horse into quieting along with his hands soothing the neck and muzzle of the horse. Each riding horse was given a turn or two around the corral with one of the two men on its back. It was evident that they were well broken to saddle and quickly became obedient to the usual commands. Jed made one exchange when the horse originally selected would not settle while the pack saddle was on its back.

Cody grabbed his pouch from his backpack and went to negotiate the purchase with Big Plume. A sense of tightness crept into Cody's shoulders as he headed for what he expected to be a difficult session of price bartering. He knew that he had no leverage for bringing the price down from whatever Big

Plume might demand. All he could do would be to simply argue for a reasonable price. There was no alternative plan available. Fortunately the Hudson Bay Directors had supplied them with generous emergency funds so that he should still have money left for other unforeseen situations that might come down the road.

The initial price suggested by the owner was high but not as outrageous as Cody had expected it to be. He carefully masked his inner reaction by keeping his face in a frown. Quick mental calculations gave him a counter figure that would be in a range that would keep the bargaining going. They had almost arrived at a price when the sound of a horse in a furious gallop intruded into the negotiations. The rider was yelling in Kootenay and others were starting to gather around him. There was a rapid fire exchange with Big Plume. He, in turn, issued some orders to all the hands that had gathered and they instantly dispersed.

Turning to Cody he apologized and said he would accept the last price Cody had offered as an emergency matter had arisen.

"We've had a serious problem with wolves killing our horses. Mainly they prey on the colts and we've been losing some choice little ones. The wolf pack has been spotted on the range we brought these horses from. The word is that they have a kill out there that they are feeding on. We had told everyone that the next time the wolves were seen, all hands drop whatever they are doing and we ride out on a wolf hunt until we clean them out. I have to leave right now."

One of the men had come to ask a question. "Do you want me to get the herders from the north pasture?"

Big Plume nodded and spoke a quick "Yes, we said everyone!" With that the man ran to his horse and pounded out of the yard heading the opposite direction.

To Cody he said, "You are welcome to camp close by and keep the horses in the corral overnight. The cook will be here if you need anything. Looks like we'll have some wolf pelts to trade with the Hudson Bay this fall."

The money was exchanged and Cody rejoined Jed. In a few minutes, Big Plume and several more riders galloped out of the yard heading south.

"I think we've been given an opportunity to check out more about these horse thieves", Cody said excitedly to Jed. "Did you hear that rider ask Big Plume about collecting herders from a north pasture. He spoke in English by mistake. But Big Plume agreed. Did you notice the one guy gallop off to the north? There must be a herd over there that they weren't going to show us. With everyone pulled into the wolf hunt, you could check out that north herd and see if we can learn more that will help bring this operation down."

Jed was excited to have some action to help respond to the thefts because it had seemed like they were cut off from doing anything to gain some justice.

"There should be enough light from the moon a little later so that I can take a look around," Jed answered.

Jed slept for a couple of hours while Cody kept watch. When the moon was high Cody wakened him.

"Better watch out for a sentry just in case they held someone back from the wolf hunt. But they seemed so excited about it that they probably took everyone," Cody cautioned.

Jed slipped into the night. He was very light on his feet and soon Cody could hear no sound from him at all. He followed the path north that the rider had taken earlier. It was easy to follow the well worn trail which had obviously been used by many horses over time. An hour later Jed topped a ridge to see a broad valley bathed in the moonlight. It was a natural pasture with only a few ponderosa pines scattered about. The large herd was quietly grazing or standing still. A few were laying down.

Jed was careful to not be silhouetted against the night sky which would make him very visible to a herder keeping guard. He sat still among some boulders for at least an hour while taking stock of every detail that he could separate out in the low light. He saw the stream that provided the needed water. An open lean-to showed where the herders would keep any supplies for caring for the animals. Eventually, he was able to pick out the tethered lead mare that would be the reason the herd didn't wander too far. The fact that she was tethered was a strong indication that everyone had cleared out for the wolf hunt. Jed carefully, patiently, scanned the valley and the hills for any hint of a sentry or sleeping herdsman. There was absolutely no sign of human presence.

Jed slowly worked his way down the hillside to the meadow. First he crept up to the side of the lean-to to double check that no one was there. He listened for sleep sounds – heavy breathing or snoring. Nothing. Then he went inside and felt his way around in the dark interior, identifying various items of tack and tools and a cot. In a very soft voice he began to talk to the horses. At first they became completely still then some nickered and some blew out a breath. Jed continued his soft talk as he walked toward the bunched portion of the herd. There was minimal movement as Jed worked his magical connection with horses. Once he reached them, he stoked their muzzles and necks. Several horses shouldered their way towards him as if they were familiar with this particular man. Jed wondered if he was touching the horses that had carried them over the Howse Pass.

He moved out to the far fringe of the clustered herd. The next horse he reached out to responded with a bite and a tossing head rather than a soft muzzle. Jed shook his hand but also rubbed his other hand the length of the horse's head up to his ears. Then the horse reared as it spun away and then kicked out with its rear hooves. In the instant of feeling between its ears Jed knew he had met up with Knuckle-head and knew what was coming as the horse turned. He had started to duck even before the kick slashed the air where he had been an instant before.

"Well, Knuckle-head, you've finally been a help to us. You leave no doubt that these are the horse thieves."

As he started back through the herd toward the lean-to, a memory of what he had touched inside the shelter came to mind. Now that he knew the stolen horses were here, this item took on greater significance. As he had felt his way along the tack items he had noticed something that was not braided rawhide. It felt like the rope that the Hudson Bay issued for use on its equipment and animals. Hoping that he could find it again, Jed retraced his steps. After a few minutes of fumbling in the dark his hand closed on the rope. It was knotted but came away from the other harness in a clump. Taking it with him he headed over the ridge and back to their camp.

Once he had told Cody about his discoveries, they built up the campfire so they could have a look at the rope.

Jed exclaimed, "See that is the rope that we had and it's still tied in our hobble knot. I'd know that knot anywhere because I'm the only one I know of that ties it just like that."

"Hmmm, I wonder how it got all the way here when the thieves had simply sliced both loops on all the others. This is only sliced open on one end," Cody mused.

Jed let out a laugh, "I bet it was on Knuckle-head. Once he felt the hobble go free from one leg, he would have started rearing and kicking and there would have been no chance of freeing the other side!"

"And he would have worn that flopping on one leg all the way here until it just loosened enough to drop off," added Cody.

Cody took his turn to get a little sleep. At dawn they gathered their belongings, tying their two backpacks across one of the pack horses. Cody put the dominant horse on a rope tied to his riding horse and led the way. Jed brought up the rear so he could make sure all the others followed the leader. As they left the yard, the cook came out into clear view and gave a wave. Both men waved back wondering how much the cook had seen during the night.

The horses were excited and full of energy. Once they were out on the trail, Cody let his horse have its head. Especially because he was riding bareback, he felt the powerful muscles of the horse tighten as it spurted to a full gallop. All the horses leaped into a flat-out run. Jed couldn't resist a "Yahoo" as the herd thundered down the trail causing the wind to whip his face. Both men hung on for dear life, suddenly realizing how precarious their position was without saddles. After a dash of fifteen or twenty minutes the herd settled into a lope that ate up the miles quickly. Their journey would have gone quickly but they needed to stop every once in a while so the men could walk for a stretch to save their sore back-sides.

SEVENTEEN

When they stopped for a lunch break and for the horses to drink, Jed looked at Cody with a mischievous grin.

"How about we liven things up at Kootenay House!! Let's go at a hard gallop right through their yard all the way right in to our camp site. There have been so few horses around there that it'll seem like a big stampede."

Cody chuckled, "That sounds like fun. It'll also send a loud message to everyone at the Post that they shouldn't mess with us. We've been able to deal with everything they have thrown at us."

Later when they spotted the buildings, from the top of a ridge, but well before their presence would be known they pulled up for a break. Jed was so excited about their plan to stampede into camp, he couldn't keep quiet.

"This will be a great uproar! I hope Ogilvie is around to see it. We'll really shake up Quinn and Darcy when they suddenly have twelve horses in the camp!"

"You're as noisy as a blue jay! Why don't you take the lead? Then you can get full credit for making a big hullabaloo!" Cody offered.

"Great idea! Let's get going!" Jed was swinging onto the back of his mount before he finished his words. He pivoted his horse toward the mare that had the lead rope and in seconds was moving out onto the trail with the herd scrambling to catch up.

Jed managed to keep the horses to a lope until they came around a corner that brought the compound into view. Immediately he let out a "Yee Haw!" and kicked his horse into a full gallop. Several horses neighed adding to the thunder of the hooves. Chickens squawked and flapped out of the way. Half a dozen dogs began to bark. People yelled for children to run for cover and for others to come and see. The bedlam was all that Jed had hoped for!

They raced across the whole yard of the trading post and continued on the main trail toward their own camp. Jed was laughing like a maniac and continued his hellbent plunge to thoroughly impress their buddies. Cody knew they were in trouble when Jed didn't start lowering their pace as their camp site neared even though they forced some people to scramble off the trail as they thundered by. When they got to the fork that turned to the camp Jed pulled his horse hard to the left so suddenly that the horse had to lean way over to avoid crashing into trees that were beside the trail. The horses right behind bunched to make the turn with a couple of them going by the fork and then causing more jumble as they tried to turn to follow the leaders.

Darcy and Quinn had to jump back among some trees to avoid being trampled by this onslaught of thunder and mayhem. Suddenly twelve over-excited horses had nowhere to go so they milled around feeling more and more crowded as the last ones crammed into the camp yard outlined by saddles, supplies, cargo, clothes lines and cooking utensils. All of the equipment and supplies were kicked and trampled and strewn about. As the last horse entered this small arena, one of the first ones in got tangled in guy ropes on one of the tents. It flapped wildly as the horse tried to get away sending some of the pack horses back out on the trail. The racket of pots clanging and canvas ripping added to the din of people yelling and horses snorting, stamping, rearing and whinnying!

Cody managed to turn back the ones that would have escaped as he had held up because he had a last second vision of what was going to happen. Then he jumped off and tied his horse to a nearby branch. Whirling around he watched for his opportunity to grab the rope dangling from the lead mare as she continued gyrating in the crush of horses. When he snagged it he set his heels and put all his weight against her direction and managed to get her head turned. He got her out of the whirlpool path of the rest of the herd and tied her to another tree. Darcy and then Quinn picked up some lead ropes that had been scattered by the stampede and managed to get loops over a couple more horses as they were all gradually slowing down. It took a few more minutes for all the horses to be roped and then tied to a picket line that Darcy and Quinn had had ready for the arrival of their pack-train.

Once the horses were secured, the four walked back into the centre of their camp area. It looked like a cyclone had touched down. Nothing was left untouched.

"I can't believe you guys did that!" Darcy spit out through gritted teeth. "Did you leave your brains somewhere on the trail?" His face was contorted in anger.

"Ah, come on!" Jed retorted, "We were just having a little fun!"

It was the wrong thing to say. Darcy exploded, "You just wrecked three days of work and now you've ruined some of the supplies as well. You guys are idiots!"

"Don't get so uppity about it!" Jed yelled back at him.

Jed didn't see the punch coming. Darcy could not contain his fury and landed a glancing blow on Jed's jaw. It sent him stumbling backwards a few feet. He recoiled and dove at Darcy, absorbing a punch to his midsection in the process. Jed took him down and gave a jab to Darcy's face. They locked up grunting and yelling as each tried to roll the other off and get on top.

Cody yelled at them to knock it off. "Come on Darcy, it wasn't that bad."

Cody started forward to try to separate them. Suddenly he was flying sideways and landing with a whoosh of air out of his lungs. Quinn had tackled him from the side. As Cody twisted around he was nose to nose with a very red, very furious Irish face.

"You ruined a lot of work and you're going to pay for that!"

Quinn landed a big fist on Cody's cheek. Cody knew he was in for considerable punishment if he didn't get out from under Quinn's bulk. He sucked in a big breath of air and braced to one side, managing to lever Quinn in the opposite direction. They both scrambled to their feet and stood toe to toe trading blows. Most of the punches were blocked but enough got through that they were both hurting as their battle continued.

By this time a crowd of people had gathered and were cheering the fighting. They had been drawn first by the stampeding horses and now were delighted with this entertainment. It didn't matter to the onlookers which ones were gaining the upper hand. They yelled equally for anyone who got in a solid punch or twisted on top of the other.

"I give, I give!" Jed gasped. Darcy had one of Jed's arms twisted to an unnatural position and was braced to put more pressure on it.

"I'm sorry we messed up all your stuff!"

Jed's yelp of surrender had caused a pause in the pummelling that Quinn and Cody were laying on each other. With fists still ready, Cody croaked out, "Enough?"

Quinn dropped his fists and answered, "Enough!"

All four flopped on the ground gasping air, totally exhausted. The onlookers grumbled because it had ended so suddenly but that was entirely lost on the combatants. All the spectators drifted away when they were sure that there would be no resumption of fighting in the offing.

Still on the ground, Quinn asked, "Can anyone reach a canteen?"

They all slowly felt around where they lay. Jed's hand closed on the strap of a canteen.

"Now that my arm is extra long, I can reach one!"

He proceeded to take a drink and passed it along . All four drank almost as if it was a communion cup, their brotherhood purged and sealed by the shared experience of the fight and the re-affirmation of care for one another by passing the canteen.

When they had somewhat recovered, they found enough food that wasn't mangled so that they could have a meal. They talked over their next steps and agreed that they could start out the next morning even though it might not be early by the time they were ready.

"By the way," said Darcy, "We weren't just sitting on our hands while you were gone. We've arranged for a guide."

Surprised Cody responded, "I didn't think we needed a guide and I'm not sure we want to put out money on someone we don't need."

"Ahh," Darcy answered, "The very things we thought you would say. This guide offered his services for free! It was too good a deal to pass up"

"Just who might this gift of a guide be?"

"Right from Grey Owl's family! It's Pierre. Actually his Dad suggested it. Little Bear says he knows the way to Joseph's Prairie real well. He's been there several times. Plus, he can introduce us to his relatives and put in a good word for us." Darcy was confident as he gave all this reasoning.

Jed asked, "He's a little young isn't he? I think it's more likely that it's his sister that persuaded you."

Darcy's hackles rose. "Don't start, Jed!! Grey Owl vouches for Pierre's ability as a guide and he's sure that we'll be glad for his help in finding the home of his other son, Broken Antler. He knew we wouldn't have a horse for him and he's willing to walk all the way. My guess is that these horses will be loaded so heavy that we won't be going any faster than a walk anyway."

The four spent the evening on all the necessary re-organizing and re-packing needed to get their supplies ready for the pack horses. Jed looked after the pack saddles and riding saddles that hadn't been used for awhile. Some of the adjustments would have to be made as they were actually loaded onto the horses the next morning.

EIGHTEEN

A mist hung in the valley as the young Bay men stirred early. There was promise of a sunny day knowing the fog would burn off by mid morning. The crackle of the campfire competed with the groans from sore bodies - left over reminders of yesterday's dust up. But the smell of the coffee and the need to visit the bushes soon had everyone on their feet. They were eager to get down the trail, away from the toxic atmosphere of Kootenay House. Pierre showed up as promised to be their guide. He was determined to prove himself to be an asset to the team so pitched in with getting the horses saddled.

The progress was slow on their first day. Jed insisted on frequent stops to check on the fit of the saddles on the pack horses.

"Jed, these horses are going to die of old age before we ever get to Linklater's if we keep stopping like this." Quinn complained.

"You'll have to carry the packs yourself if we let sores develop on these ponies," retorted Jed.

By late on the third day they had pushed well beyond Columbia Lake. They were glad that they were on horseback when they crossed the portage to the Kootenay River. The thought of having to unload canoes, carry the cargo the mile and a half through many return treks and then carry the canoes themselves – while not a difficult portage compared to some – made them glad they were on horseback.

About the time they were starting to look for a good campsite, they spied a lone figure leading a mule coming toward them. There had been no one else on the trail that day so they were curious to meet this traveller.

"Howdy boys! Looks like you got serious business with all those pack horses! Name's Findlay, George Findlay. No one uses the last part of that handle so just call me George."

Cody nodded as he swung down from his horse. "I'm Cody, this is Quinn, Darcy, Jed and our young guide is Pierre."

George nodded to each one. He was medium height with a full beard and long hair that looked to be mixed brown and grey. His clothes were baggy and coloured with earth tones, although it was hard to tell whether that was the colour of the cloth or of the layers of earth that looked to be embedded in the material. He wore a slouch hat that had been through many seasons. Cody wondered if maybe George had thrown his hat on the ground and jumped on it when he was upset. He looked like he might do that kind of thing. But what really stood out were his eyes. They twinkled! The boys all felt that they had just met someone who had a lively brain behind all that rough exterior and it would be a pleasure to spend some time with him. Cody guessed his age to be forty or fifty.

"I wonder if you've guessed that I'm a prospector?" Then he laughed a musical enjoyable laugh as if he had just told a very funny story. "By the way, my mule is Henrietta! She isn't near as nice as me but she's a lot smarter!!"

The laugh that followed was infectious. The boys found themselves being drawn in to George's humour.

"George, we were just about to make camp for the night. Why don't you join us? Darcy cooks up a pretty good plate of beans, bacon and flapjacks," offered Cody.

"Why, I'd be mighty pleased to do that. That's right kind of you. It would be good to have somebody besides Henrietta to jaw at for a spell."

Everyone pitched in to get camp set up for the night. It didn't hurt to have both Pierre and George helping Quinn lift down the packs from the horses. Jed was able to be a little more particular in checking the condition of the pack saddles after a full day of jerking along the trail.

The smell of coffee soon mingled with the pine scent of the trees. It was a very pleasant mixture that was a magnet to the whole crew. Dusk was settling down as six men leaned back with very full bellies.

A few questions got George started and with an occasional nod of encouragement from one of the boys he told his story.

"Yep, I been riding the gold trails for a few years now. Always making enough for a grubstake to be able to move on to the next Eldorado. There's one just up ahead here. I can feel it in my bones. I'll be the one to stake the mother lode claim on this next one. Seems like I've been lagging just behind the big ones on some of these big rushes. Over on the Fraser in '58 so many Americans sailed up from San Fran that little guys like me just got pushed aside. They had to make the whole area into a Crown Colony to keep it from exploding into a wild west shootout like they had down south. Yessiree, they appointed this Judge Begbie to crack the law and order whip. Hear tell they're calling him the hangin' judge!!"

"Too crowded for my liking so when the big rush moved north, I started east. Got to Rock Creek in '61 but the rush there had peaked in '60. The troubles there got Governor Douglas to build a pack road right over the mountains. Hired a man by name of Dewdney. They claimed it was to keep law and order but mainly it was to rip off men like me with taxes. Ha! What a joke. Them Americans just slipped back south through the valleys with their gold. It's guys like me got caught by the collectors. So I've headed towards this free country here for a couple years now. Feeling good, too. Just about time for another grubstake but the signs all point to a big find up here. You boys should give up all this hard work and get in on the prospecting and the big find that's up in these creeks. Yessiree, this is the good life!!"

By the time the fire had burned low George had run out of stories and Quinn was snoring.

"Oh, oh! 'fraid I out talked my welcome. Well, this is a special entertainment for me to have a one night audience. Night boys!!"

Next morning George continued north as the pack-train headed downstream along the Kootenay. The boys developed a rhythm to their days that they carried out without much thought. There was lots of open graze for the horses and convenient camp sites for the men. It gave them time to chew over some of the things George had told them.

"Sounds like big changes coming for this territory," commented Darcy. "I thought the Hudson Bay Company was doing just fine in providing all the law-keeping that was needed. Don't the natives provide their own controls for their own people?"

Cody responded, "I had heard that the west coast gold rush was forcing some changes that were beyond the Bay's responsibility. That Governor Douglas that George talked about, he was the head guy for the Bay on the Pacific Coast so it was pretty smooth for him to be made Governor with a whole lot more power."

Quinn put in his thoughts. "It don't seem right that people way over in England get to make decisions that could cost me taxes right out here in this wilderness; wilderness that they will never see!"

"Well, get ready to face into that when we help Linklater move his Post north," Cody added. "There may be American

Border Agents that will try to collect from us. My Grandfather actually surveyed for the International Boundary Commission and he argued for the border to be way south so that it would be at the mouth of the Columbia River. Linklater could have stayed where he is and a huge parcel of land would have been ours instead of the Americans. But people that had never been out here thought that it was just empty territory and that it was no big deal to let the Americans have it. I think Douglas was afraid that because so many Americans flooded up the Fraser River for the gold that the Americans might think they should just take over what is now the British Columbia Colony."

"Wow, that all seems unreal while I'm sitting out here in this incredible wilderness setting of mountains and valleys and freedom!" Jed added.

As the days slipped by, Pierre's excitement grew. He was looking forward to seeing his Uncle and cousins. Besides, he was feeling very grown up that he was the guide that would introduce his four friends with their big cargo. The last time he had seen his cousins they had just spent their time playing tag and wrestling. Now he felt like he would be far too important to play children's games.

NINETEEN

Pierre identified the junction that would turn them away from the Kootenay River to take them to Joseph's Prairie the next day. It was late enough in the day that Cody called a halt to make camp and once again dug out the soap.

Quinn complained, "Cody, you are just way too fond of that soap. It's bad for our skin to have all the natural oils burned off it so often!"

"Give me a break, Quinn. I'm doing you a favour. There's a whole village just ahead of us and who knows what young ladies might appear and you'll thank me for my encouragement!! Hey, Pierre, how old did you say your cousin Sophie is?"

"I'm not sure. All I know is that she's a little older than me and likes to boss me and the other younger kids. Her Mom died a few years ago so she thinks she's in charge of everything."

"But I thought you really liked her!" Cody tried to dig for a little more about this potential friend.

"Oh I do!" responded Pierre. "When she's not being all serious, then she will chase us or go for a swim with us. She gets us all laughing until we can't stand up any more, but when she gets back to the lodge where my uncle is, then she goes back to being bossy."

When they stopped for their lunch break the next day, Darcy raised some questions about how they would secure all the trade goods they were bringing with them.

"Don't you think this is a pretty big burden to lay on a family that we've never met? This cargo has a lot of value and will be a big temptation to thieves. How can this family guard it for us all day and all night?"

"I've been wondering about it myself." came back Cody. "We can't afford to leave any one of us behind when we go to Linklater's."

Darcy spoke up, "Remember that log cabin we helped build south of the St. Lawrence two summers ago? So we know how to do that. What if we build a small one over top of the supplies and put that chain we've been carrying to good use on a heavy door? It could be done in just a few days."

"Well, every trading post needs a storage room that can be locked up tight." nodded Cody. "We'll have the same kind of need when we get back from Fort Kokanee. If we pick the right location, and build it big enough, it will be the first building of the Joseph's Prairie Fur Trading Post! Hopefully, there'll be a good site close to Pierre's family so they can still keep an eye on it."

With that decided, they were quick to finish scrubbing themselves down and get back on the trail. Pierre's excitement had infected all of them and it seemed even the horses had sensed it and upped their pace as well.

"There it is!! There it is!!" Pierre was shouting back at them as they were cresting a rise in the trail.

In a few minutes all of them had come to a stop side by side as they took in the scene of at least a dozen lodges nestled at the far side of a huge stretch of open meadow. There was an occasional ponderosa pine scattered about. While behind the village, was a small mountain that was densely forested but with a line of cottonwood trees that marked a water course. It looked idyllic. After a few moments, they began to pick out an occasional person moving among the teepees. And then to the south, a sizable herd of horses were spread out and contentedly grazing on the excellent pasture of this mountain prairie.

"Whew! That is one of the prettiest scenes I've laid my eyes on in all my days! It makes you think that if you ever wanted to stay in one place for your future this would be it." Quinn surprised his mates with a comment this reflective and with the idea that he might even be thinking of settling down!

"Just don't go settling down too soon. We need your muscle on a few projects yet, my friend" said Cody as he jigged his horse forward and the others fell into their usual place in the pack-train.

The village seemed unusually quiet as they approached it. The few people they had seen from a distance had disappeared. For some reason Pierre had suddenly turned kind of shy as he got close to actually seeing his cousins. He wondered if they would be happy to see him or would they be reserved, so he held back rather than running ahead and yelling to announce their arrival.

Through no fault of the Pards, it seemed like they were sneaking up on these families. Cody was leading the way as they slowly came up to the first lodge. He twisted in his saddle to look back at the others. He shrugged as if to say, "I'm not sure what's going on, so stay alert!!"

Before he could settle back firmly in his saddle, a high pitched squeal tore apart the quiet. A small animal darted around the nearest lodge, still squealing and dancing from side to side. A sudden chorus of shouts and more squeals erupted on top of the pig's noise as half a dozen little children raced around the corner, after the hog, right at the feet of Cody's horse. The mayhem of the pig and the children so sudden and so close sent Cody's horse rearing and spinning away. It's immediate shrill neighing added to the pandemonium. As soon as the horse's front feet recon-nected with the ground it exploded with a powerful buck off all four hooves kicking the air. Cody launched off the horse like he had been on the wrong end of a catapult. For a tiny moment he seemed to float in the air with arms and legs flailing! That ended with a puff of dust as he landed face down, splayed in all four directions.

Momentarily stunned, the first sound he heard as he regained his senses was a giggle. A very feminine giggle! Cody managed to open one eye that was clear of the ground and took in a very pretty young woman looking down on him, with one hand clasped over her mouth. Even from his humiliating prone posi-tion he noticed her sparkling eyes filled with amusement just above her hand.

As his breathing came closer to normal and as he realized that all his limbs had feeling, his embarrassment grew and showed itself by a distinctly red colour creeping over his face. This was not the image of the leader of the Pards that he had planned to present to this village of Kootenay Indians let alone to a beauti-ful princess of the village. There was no graceful way to exit from this so he pushed himself up to a sitting position, letting a grin register on his lips as he said,

"Hi, I'm Cody! I usually just kneel rather than lay on my face when I meet a beautiful woman!"

Sophie, for indeed it was Sophie, giggled some more at this nonsense and then fled after the pig and the children all of which were in her care.

Jed returned with Cody's horse as the others were dismount-ing and gathering around Cody. Jed also dismounted, joining in the teasing that had started as soon as Cody had shown that no serious injury had come to him. While the others were having fits of laughter, Quinn literally picked Cody up and stood him on his feet but kept a hand on him as he steadied himself. Darcy and Jed were holding their stomachs as they tried to find words to describe the sight of Cody sailing through the air and landing on his face. More spasms of laughing would burst out with each attempt.

Three elderly men appeared from among the lodges looking very curious about what was causing so much uproar in the village. Pierre went to talk to them and soon had them laughing over the ridiculous plight of the young white guy. He soon reported back that one of the men was a grandfather to his cousins. Further he learned that the village had set this as the day to pick huckleberries and most were up in the forest. Only the small children and those too elderly to make the hike were present under Sophie's care. The huckleberries and the pig, which was a big novelty because it was the first pig the children had ever seen, were destined to become pemmican the next day.

Dusting himself off to try to regain a leader's dignity, Cody led the way to meet these elders. Introductions were made all around. Cody had Pierre stay right beside him to be the translator. The grandfather that Pierre had mentioned, whose name was Goodfellow, was the chief of this village and the other two men were part of the main council. In the course of getting acquainted, a comment was made about Cody's grandfather having been in this area over 50 years before.

Goodfellow smiled at this and said, "I remember meeting the white stargazer. As a young man I watched him with his magic instruments that told him exactly where he was in the whole world. I remember his words when he said that what he learned from the stars told him more about the Creator on top of the knowledge that was in his black book. He was a very fair man who helped settle some tough disputes among our people. Stargazer's grandson and his friends are welcome in our village."

Cody's heart was filled with pride as he heard this report from a leader of a culture that was so very different from his own family's background and realized again that David Thompson had been a man of amazing wisdom. "If only he could now live up to that heritage that was a gift into his life," Cody thought as he answered Goodfellow with an emotional and simple "Thank you!"

Goodfellow indicated an area where they could set up their camp and invited them to a council fire that evening when the berry pickers were back. They would tell their story to the village at that time.

TWENTY

As dusk descended people began to assemble at the council fire area. There was an excited buzz of chatter as questions and opinions were bounced back and forth about the newcomers. Laughter would erupt here and there, making Cody feel sure that another telling of his ignominious landing had been shared. The village settled itself according to its own scale of standing with Goodfellow and the other two elders that had been with him at their first meeting sitting front and centre. Behind them were other men extending the arc of people most of the way around the council fire circle. Room was provided to the right of the Elders for the guests to be seated. Behind the men were their wives and then closing the circle were other youths both male and female but with the girls behind the males. The young men jostled one another for the best places to be able to size up the outsiders at the same time they were showing off for the young women. Pierre was in the middle of the youth section and seemed to be greatly enjoying himself. It was somewhat of a festive atmosphere as they were anticipating stories from the world beyond the region of the Kootenays of which they were becoming more and more aware.

While people were still milling about, Cody scanned the crowd hoping for a glimpse of Sophie without being obvious about it. As his gaze slid along the faces further to their right his heartbeat quickened when he picked out her face in the crowd. With strong self-control, he forced himself to continue scanning past her to take in more of the circle. Then when he thought it safe, he began roving his eyes back towards her and this time he paused so he could study her features in more detail. At that moment Sophie looked directly at Cody, their eyes connecting. A tingle travelled the length of his spine and his eyebrows raised in the magic of that moment. He was sure she smiled a little before she demurely lowered her gaze and turned to the side.

Goodfellow stood and the tribe gradually quietened. Sitting just behind the Pards, Pierre translated what was being said in a low voice. Goodfellow gave a speech that welcomed the visitors and told something of the history of the Kootenay Bands. There was an open cherishing of his band and their Kootenay region. His experience with David Thompson came into the speech with obvious pride and from that he extolled his village to give every assistance and consideration to Thompson's grandson and his partners. Goodfellow commented that Cody would present his request when it was his turn to speak to the crowd.

Cody gulped when it hit him that he was expected to give a speech and that the level of cooperation they would get from the village would be based on what he said. Nervousness clamped down on his insides and his mind fluttered over a hundred possibilities of what he might say. Goodfellow finished his speech and sat down. Everything went quiet. Darcy jabbed Cody in the ribs and hissed "Your turn! Make it good!"

Cody's mind jarred back to the present. He slowly got to his feet surprised at how weak his knees felt. Cody had been at a number of Indian Council fires in the Quebec wilderness but had never thought about what he would say if he was one of the speech makers. Once he was standing, and he had signalled Pierre to come and stand beside him, he took the time to look around the circle of faces all focused on him. In that moment a life-long nervous reflex took over and he couldn't help giving a little giggle. Surprisingly, it started a chain reaction. Everyone smiled and most gave a giggle in return. The atmosphere around the council fire changed as people relaxed because of the apparent happy demeanour of the guest. There was a buzz of readiness to hear what he had to say. Although the listeners didn't realize that Cody had giggled out of near panic, their positive response settled Cody and what he needed to say was suddenly clear in his mind.

He took his turn giving some history, only his focus was the Hudson Bay Company and the good relationship the Company had with the natives. His emphasis was on the mutual benefit they brought to each other. The Indians had access to the fur bearing animals and the Company in turn brought trade goods that the Kootenays very much desired.

"Now," said Cody, "we can bring all those benefits closer to the Goodfellow band. We would like to establish a Trading Post right here on Joseph's Prairie."

That sent a stir through the onlookers.

Cody went on to explain that John Linklater's Trading Post would be moving to a new location. Again there was a chorus of excited chatter because some of them had been as far as Linklater's and had found him to be a very fair and kind man.

"As part of our planning we would like your permission to bring a trading post here and we would like your advice as to the exact location. You saw the heavily loaded pack horses we came with. We will need to build a storage house right away and then we will go and help Mr. Linklater move his goods here. That will mean adding more buildings when we get back."

When Cody finished, there was a chorus of voices offering their opinion on his offer. Everyone was in agreement that having Linklater's Trading Post locating on Joseph's Prairie was a very good thing. However, the location was a point of hot debate. Some wanted it beside the present location of their village. Others wanted it well away. The discussion eventually began to focus on a trail that was being used when some of the Kootenays wanted to visit bands that were located on the lake that was to the west. They were also seeing occasional prospectors wandering along that trail. Another benefit that surfaced through the extended debate was that less than a mile from the village that path skirted a heavily forested mountain where there would be good logging for the storehouse they wanted to build as well as for the main trading post buildings that would follow.

The next morning the Pards and the Elders surveyed the potential locations for the new trading post. It was a matter of selecting the best from among numerous good possibilities. Eventually they settled on a site, a little closer to the village than what they had hoped, that offered a good sized stream for water, abundant graze close at hand and the low mountain behind it with its dense forest that would provide easy logging as well as an endless supply of firewood.

Goodfellow assured them that the closeness to their village would not be a problem as the band moved its location once or twice a year to find better pasture and better trapping. This would be even more important now as they would be using the same supply of firewood and grazing as the trading post.

When the men returned to the village, Pierre was quick to let the Pards know that they were invited to have lunch with his relatives. Four very happy young men made their way to the teepee of Broken Antler and his family to enjoy a rich venison stew. Cody found himself constantly watching Sophie and enjoying what he saw. Darcy also noticed that Cody couldn't take his eyes off her.

He nudged Cody, " Your eyes are going to fall out if you keep them locked on her all the time!"

"What?" Cody responded vaguely, "Did you say something?"

Darcy laughed, knowing that he had an opportunity that was too good to pass up, "I said there are ants crawling up your legs!"

Cody jumped to his feet, sending his tin plate clattering to the ground, slapping at his pant legs. Sophie rushed over to see what the problem was. She picked up the plate assuring Cody he could have more. Cody stopped his brushing when it dawned on him that there were no ants. His face turned crimson by the time he stood up straight. He mumbled thanks to Sophie but declined more food. As she turned back to the cook fire, Cody glared at Darcy and the other two who were all trying to stifle giggles. They were seeing a whole new side of their leader who was so obviously smitten by this Indian Princess! Cody managed to threaten them with dire consequences which made them laugh even harder.

They spent the rest of the day setting up for construction of their log storage cabin. Cody and Darcy staked out the twenty foot by twelve foot rectangle that had been agreed would be big enough to hold all the pack-train cargo plus some of what they would bring from Linklater's. They also carefully levelled the ground for those important bottom logs. Quinn found the axes and spent a long time using the sharpening stone to put a good edge on all of them. He calculated the approximate number of logs they would need to bring the walls up to five or six feet at the back and at least eight feet at the front. The roof would slope from front down to the back. Jed constructed some harness that would be used to skid the logs out of the forest and chose one of the pack-horses for the skidding work. He gave it a little work out pulling around a large branch. After some initial skittish jumps because of something trailing behind, the horse settled into its harness and pulled steadily.

Next dawn the four were up and eager to get started. After a quick breakfast, they headed up the mountain, chopping a skidding trail right into the thick of a stand of the right size trees for building the cabin. Soon four axes were ringing out a steady rhythm as four strong, healthy, young men bent to their task.

"Timberrrr!" Quinn was the first to call out. He had notched the tree perfectly to bring it down between other trees so that it fell cleanly to the ground. Soon the others were calling out as their trees came down. Jed's tree was hung up in some others and he needed help from Quinn as he came along with the measuring line to mark the length needed. Jed was more than glad when those first logs were trimmed and cut to length so that he could work with the horse rather than with an axe.

By the end of the day, a nice stack of logs was accumulating. In fact they had cut and trimmed more logs than Jed had been able to skid down, even with Quinn and Cody carrying the last log of the day on their shoulders. They were well set for the cabin to start taking shape the next day.

Throughout the day, a number of people had ambled by to satisfy their curiosity about the cabin. The men of the Band had stopped briefly to observe as they headed to the horse corrals where they were breaking horses for riding and as they returned in the late afternoon. As dusk lingered, Pierre and Sophie along with some younger children came by to see what was happening. The fun and laughter of the group made it easy for Cody to get over his jittery feelings when he was close to Sophie. When it was time for the children to head back to the village, Sophie hung back from the group and Cody fell in step with her to walk her back to her lodge. Conversation came more easily with a mixture of Kootenay and English words along with lots of hand motions and pointing. They were glad the children dawdled as they wandered along behind the cluster of little ones. Both of them wished the path was longer. Neither of them noticed the young brave lurking behind the meat drying racks watching them walk close together.

The square of logs grew slowly the next morning. Cody and Darcy were extra careful and were learning by trial and error as they made the first notches where the logs crossed at the corners. They made sure that they didn't notch them too deeply and they would also take a log off to chop down a knot that kept the log from laying flat. By being so careful, their notches virtually locked the logs in place which would lead to this being a very solid, secure building. By late afternoon the building had grown considerably and the builders were starting to plan for sinking a couple of logs into the ground so they could form upright doorposts.

Again, that evening, the group of young people and children visited to see the progress on the building. It was really to spend time with the young adventurers who had stories about people and places that were so very different. Pierre was enjoying being an important person as the interpreter. It also provided Sophie with a reason to spend time getting to know and to enjoy Cody. That enjoyment went both ways. As Cody and Sophie walked at the back of the little troop heading back into the village, they again failed to notice the young man spying on them from the shadows.

Eagle Claw was from a different band of the Kootenays but had joined the Goodfellow band to learn their horse breeding methods. He was the only young man of similar age to Sophie so Eagle Claw and others had come to assume that the two would marry. Right now his face was twisted into a silent snarl. The blood was pounding in his head. He felt rage boiling inside. He could not let this go on. This white boy from far away would find out that he could not simply steal what belonged to Eagle Claw of the Kootenays.

By the next afternoon the Pards were working on the roof. Quinn had found some big cedar trees and he and Jed had split out long shakes that they nailed to the lodge-pole pine cross members. While they were engrossed in their project, they became aware of a high pitched voice yelling and yelling. The sound of the voice grew more distinct. It was Pierre. And he was obviously in major distress.

"Help, help!!! It's Sophie! Eagle Claw has a knife! He' going to kill her!!! Come quick!"

All of them ran to meet Pierre. Cody grabbed him, "Pierre, slow down. Who is Eagle Claw? Why is he threatening Sophie?"

"No, no!" begged Pierre, "Don't slow down. Come with me, I'll tell you on the way!"

They started running together toward the village. Between gasps he blurted out, "Eagle Claw is from the Lower Lake band. He thinks Sophie has to marry him. She has to stay away from you or she'll die!! He says he will kill you.!"

They all skidded to a stop as they rounded the first lodge. There was Sophie sprawled on the ground where Eagle Claw had thrown her. He was standing over her with a knife in his hand, ranting at her in Kootenay! When he saw Cody and friends burst into the circle, he sprang behind Sophie and pulled her to him with one arm while he brandished the knife with the other hand.

"You're the cause of this!" he screamed at Cody. "Everything was just right until you came pushing your way in. You have no right to take Sophie away from me. She's my woman and you have to get out. Leave this village right now or she'll pay for it."

Cody was shocked by how deranged Eagle Claw was in his ranting. Pierre translated some of it but Cody could tell by the manner of words spewing out that this was beyond reasoning. Sophie was in huge peril and Cody knew he had to draw Eagle Claw's focus away from her. He raised his hand with his palm towards Eagle Claw and Sophie and took a couple steps toward them. Eagle Claw shrieked at him to stay back.

"Eagle Claw, put the knife down so we can talk." Cody tried to keep a tremble out of his voice as he saw how frightened Sophie was.

Eagle Claw shouted back, "There's no talking. You leave. That's the only thing! Turn around and take your bunch with you. Right out of the area."

"Do you think I would just give in to a boy that is showing he has the heart of a woman?" Cody raised his voice and yelled this back at Eagle Claw. "You are hiding behind a woman. Anyone with a knife can do that! A true brave that has a man's heart would face me directly, not from behind a skirt!" Pierre quickly put it into Kootenay!

The fire in Eagle Claw's eyes flamed even brighter. He instantly said, "You are going to die now white man. You cannot get away with insulting Eagle Claw on top of trying to take his woman."

He pushed Sophie away and started toward Cody. He was waving his knife in front of him.

"Your blood is going to stain the ground of our council fire. It will be the right use of your deceiving life."

Cody reached for his knife that he wore on his belt. It wasn't there! He had been using it when Pierre came for them and he had left it lying on a timber. A trickle of fear crept in as Cody realized he was going against Eagle Claw bare-handed. Quinn called out "Cody, catch!" With a quick glance and a quicker snatch, Cody had Quinn's knife at the ready. Now he was on equal terms physically but the madness in Eagle Claw's look signalled that this attack would be very unpredictable.

The combatants began to circle each other to the right. Eagle Claw waved the knife back and forth. The menacing flashes of sunlight glinting off the knife made it seem alive. Cody held his knife steady. Every nerve alive to each move of both the body and facial expression of his foe. With a yell Eagle Claw dove toward Cody who blocked the slash of the knife with his forearm. Pain shot through Cody as the weapon contacted flesh before it was pulled back. Cody worked his hand up and down assuring himself that it was not a serious wound. Eagle Claw laughed and danced to his left.

"There will be many more cuts before I finish you white boy. Why don't you just run away and leave us alone?" Eagle Claw darted toward Cody and then back again.

"You're the one who needs to leave, Eagle Claw. Sophie will never want you, especially now!" Cody said as he saw Eagle Claw repeating the same movement over and over. With careful timing as Eagle Claw made another feint and slash, Cody's left fist made a lightening quick jab to his jaw that sent him reeling backwards. Eagle Claw did a backwards somersault and landed in a crouch with the knife still in his hand. He stayed motionless for a moment to clear his head then started forward. Hatred contorted his face. He crept forward with determined steps, much more wary now. There was another flurry of bobbing in and out with glittering blades making fast arcs in the air. A cry of pain marked contact of Cody's knife on Eagle Claw's shoulder. Blood was showing on both men and both men were panting out their draining energy.

Once again Cody blocked a slash but this time grabbed Eagle Claw's arm with his left hand. They strained against each others grip as Eagle Claw brought his free hand to match Cody's hold without either gaining the advantage. Loud grunts came from the life and death struggle. Suddenly Eagle Claw swept his right foot against Cody's left leg spilling him onto his back with Eagle Claw landing on top. As they were landing Cody was already twisting and the two of them rolled over and over. Their hands were still locked, with knives poised to plunge into each other. Cody swung a leg over Eagle Claw and managed to establish a scissor grip that stopped their rolling. As he did this Cody lost his knife to the gasp of onlookers. However, Cody put all his two-handed strength to control the knife in Eagle Claw's hands.

He levered himself backwards so that he could use the strength of his arms as well as wrists to overcome Eagle Claw's lock on his weapon. Cody began slamming his enemy's hands against the ground over and over. Despite Eagle Claw's ferocious struggle to regain ground against Cody, the repeated punishment on his hand forced him to lose the knife and let it skitter away.

Cody scrambled to his feet while grabbing the front of Eagle Claw's shirt and pulling him upright. Cody pounded a right-handed punch against his left eye. Eagle Claw's head snapped back and his legs buckled. Cody held him up by his shirt and cocked his fist again. But Eagle Claw was out cold so Cody simply released his shirt, dropping him to the ground.

The onlookers crowded around Cody congratulating him on his victory, exclaiming over the knock out punch. Sophie immediately examined his bloody arm, concerned that it was a serious wound. She was relieved to find that with a compress and tight wrap it would heal fine. All of this seemed to be happening in a fog for Cody as he gradually calmed from the intensity of a life and death fight. People began to disperse hoping they could find someone to tell about the fight.

Cody turned his attention to Sophie. "Are you alright? Did he hurt you?!

"I'm fortunate, Cody. He only shoved me around and yelled at me. All along, all he wanted was to get to you. I was so afraid for you because he was absolutely committed to killing you. I was hoping you wouldn't come, at the same time I desperately wanted to see you. I'm so glad you beat him down."

"Now what do we do?" Cody said. "Maybe he will just be more crazy and this will happen all over again!"

Sophie quickly responded, "The Elders will decide what should happen so we just bring him to them."

Quinn and Darcy quickly found some rope and trussed Eagle Claw up. After checking to make sure the shoulder wound had pretty much stopped bleeding, they dumped him in the shade of one of the lodges and headed back to their camp.

TWENTY-ONE

T he next day the Pards were able to make the storage house fully secure and move their cargo inside. Jed spent the afternoon inspecting their horses and their tack to ensure that they could get an early start the following morning. Chief Goodfellow came by to check on Cody's condition.

"It is good to see that your wound is healing. We are very sad that you had to fight Eagle Claw while you are a guest in our village. Today he is saying that he sees the wrong that he did. Our council will decide tonight how long he should be banished and where he should be told to live. We need you to be there so the Elders can have full information. The decision of the Council will control Eagle Claw's choices. Our people do not know any way of life beyond our Tribe. So when the decision of one council is made, all the Bands carry it out. Our people do not even think of life outside of Kootenay circles. Even a jealous and angry young brave like Eagle Claw, once he cools down will be bound by the choices of the Council. You will not have further problems with him."

Cody nodded. "Your words are appreciated Chief. We will be there."

The council held a long discussion about Eagle Claw's bad behaviour giving anyone who wished to add comments the opportunity to do so. Cody was asked a few questions but he stayed very quiet otherwise. He respected the fact that he was an outsider who was being given more than fair consideration. Eagle Claw did seem truly contrite and actually thanked the Chief when it was decided that he would be sent to live with the Coloured Horse Band near Libby for a full cycle of the seasons. Only after a full year could he change his location.

When the meeting of the council ended, Cody and Sophie went for a long walk in the lingering twilight. Cody tried to put some words together out of the scrambled feelings that tumbled through his mind. Finally he was able to give a brief version of the many things he was thinking.

"I couldn't believe the pain I had inside when Pierre said that you were in danger yesterday. Sophie, please be very careful. I don't want anything bad to happen to you!"

Her lighthearted laugh set Cody at ease. "Look who is talking about being careful!" She teased. "Between trying to fly from a horse's back and getting into a life and death fight I think you are the one to worry about!"

They were silent for a while and then Sophie took Cody's arm as she quietly said, "I feel safe when I am with you!"

That stirred some feelings in Cody that he had never felt before. It placed a lump in his throat that would have kept him from talking even if he would have known what to say. He walked Sophie back to her lodge and mumbled "See you when we get back from Linklater's Post." There was a pause and then Sophie turned to her lodge. Cody stood frozen in those brief moments, unsure what to do. Then she was gone and all Cody could do was head back to his camp. But his heart was in brand new territory!

As a red dawn spread across Joseph's Prairie, the Pards began to stir. Everyone had their own tasks towards getting underway on their journey down to Linklater's Fort Kokanee. Breakfast, harnesses, provisions for food, and finally locking up the storage cabin. None of the boys were expert builders but they managed to cobble a few upright thin logs which they set down in a trench and had the tops fit against the horizontal log which was a cross piece at the top of the doorway. A second cross piece on the outside which extended from vertical doorpost to vertical doorpost was held in place by a chain. A lock secured the doorway. It wasn't pretty but it would take a huge effort to break through and, besides, Goodfellow had promised to keep an eye on it.

They tried to get past the village without creating too much of a ruckus but the horses were excited and full of energy. Their snorting and neighing started the dogs barking which further excited the horses. The end result was twelve horses thundering right past the lodges. No one was left asleep but no one noticed the flap pulled aside as Sophie waved a secret goodbye to Cody.

The boys felt a thrill as the horses burned off their pent up energy. With no heavy packs on any of the horses, the riders let them gallop as hard as they wanted. The wind flared their hair and rippled their shirts. Clods of dirt sprayed into the air. The early morning smell of the forest was invigorating. An occasional "Yahoo!" could not be held back especially on a flat open area where the boys couldn't resist fanning out and letting the horses race side by side. Gradually the galloping diminished to a steady lope as the horses and riders settled in for an all day ride.

Their first stop came as Jed called out that some of the empty pack saddles were loosening. Everyone checked the rigging on their own horses, dug some pemmican out of their saddle bags, and soon they were on the move again.

The Pards easily fell back into their travel routine that they had honed over the thousands of miles they had travelled. Evening camp was established by habit rather than by thought, and the same with breaking camp in the morning. They were easy with one another like a family that gave both security and freedom to its members.

It was somewhere in the second morning out from the Goodfellow Band that some of this came to the front of Cody's consciousness.

"This is great!" he blurted out before he realized he was speaking out loud.

The other three, not having any context for his exclamation, looked at each other and at Cody. They assumed he was thinking about Sophie. When no more words were forthcoming, they winked and grinned and shrugged to each other but left it at that.

However, Cody was going beyond his usual level of reflection. The feelings that had been stirred up by his attraction to Sophie were crowding into space in his life that was already full; the beauty of the summer morning, the warmth of the sun, the chatter of squirrels, the occasional glimpse of deer, the smell of pine trees, the rippling muscles of the horse, the camaraderie of his pals and the freedom to stop or go as they chose. What a list he could accumulate with very little thought! Now he could understand something of what propelled his grandfather to explore wilderness that was completely unknown to the outside world. So many shook their heads when talking of how David Thompson trekked through unbelievable hardships after a broken leg that healed so slowly and losing sight in one eye when sight was so crucial to mapping locations. This morning Cody felt that compulsion, that need, to see and experience the next curve of the river, the uniqueness of the next valley, the other side of the mountain! This was what brought the greatest pleasure. It was simple.

The trouble was that now he also longed to be with Sophie. She brought out a whole additional realm of desirable components to life that he was finding very powerful.

"Yet, look at what happened within a few days of having a special relationship," he said to himself. "When I was ready to call it a day, she wanted to walk and talk. I wanted to as well but I was so tired the next day I didn't pull my weight with the guys. Jealousy put me in a life and death fight. Every big decision had to be aired at their council. She is comfortable being with the Band all the time and probably couldn't stand being away from her family. I know that I would suffocate being that close to so many people all the time."

Cody did remember his Gramma Charlotte who had actually trekked with her husband through conditions most men couldn't handle. She had completely made her life with Thompson wherever and whenever it suited him, but she was the exception rather than the rule. Sophie seemed so much more rooted in her family than his Grandmother. Maybe the difference was that Gramma Charlotte was half Scottish and Sophie was full Kootenay.

There seemed to be no answers, rather life just looked more complicated the more time Cody spent on trying to see beyond the present. Besides, he was getting a headache!

Relief from all this heavy thinking came in the form of a warning call from Darcy.

"People up ahead!"

The Pards slowed their horses to a walk. Almost all the travellers you met on a wilderness trail were good people but it paid to be cautious because of the few troublemakers. The other party of three men did the same. Words of friendly greeting were exchanged and all agreed to break for lunch together.

The three were prospectors and they were very glad to have people to talk to other than one another and their donkey named Dumbo. They competed for the attention of the Pards and their stories got increasingly wild the more they talked and tried to outdo each other. Once the boys realized that the stories they were hearing had gone into the realm of fantasy, they actually settled back and enjoyed the noon hour entertainment. They loved the story that on one of the lakes to the west, a prospector had discovered a whole boulder of gold clinging to the edge of a cliff. When he and his friends chipped away the rock that held it attached to the cliff, it was so heavy it broke the ropes that were supposed to control its drop. The gold boulder rolled down the cliff, smashed through the bottom of their boat and disappeared into depths of the lake never to be seen again – so far! The stories got so outlandish that the prospectors started berating one another for filling the heads of these fine young men with so much rubbish.

Before the men parted ways they did exchange some valuable information about what lay ahead in each direction. The prospectors were following rumours that there were gold nuggets just laying in creeks further up the Kootenay simply waiting for people to pick them up. They asked about the conditions they would face and how long it would take. The Pards assured them that no one was picking up nuggets of pure gold along the Kootenay and then shared what they could in exchange for the same kind of information downstream to Linklater's Post.

Jocko, who seemed to be the closest any of them were to being the leader, had some serious words of caution to give them.

"Montana Territory is pretty wild. It is becoming the last refuge of all the gangs, gunfighters and general outlaws that are running ahead of the law in the rest of the territories. On top of that there are those that have deserted from the war. You'd better keep a pretty keen eye out. That's why we're here in your territory so the Great Mother Victoria can keep us all safe. Those horses of yours are going to look pretty good to some of those owl hoots. Then once you fill those pack saddles you better have an army to protect it all! Adios, my friends!"

Jocko's words left the boys very thoughtful as they continued south.

"Think we'll have to fight off outlaws?" questioned Jed. "It never crossed my mind until now!"

"Bring'em on," Quinn burst out. "Anybody that thinks they're going to rob us now better think again."

"But that's the problem, we're out of the reach of Hudson Bay people except for Linklater's place. Sounds like it's every man for himself down here. What do you think....maybe we better clean our muskets and do a little target practice this evening." Darcy said thoughtfully.

Cody quietly responded, "Maybe we'll do the same with the pistols we brought. Maybe carry them in our saddle bags so they're easy to get to rather than in the packsaddle."

The Pards rode in silence, pondering the possibilities of the unknown that was waiting for them. In the days it took to get to Linklater's Post the occasional thunderstorm seemed to be a harbinger of things to come. They just prayed that there would be a rainbow at the end of whatever storm was brewing south of the 49th.

TWENTY-TWO

They knew from talking to the occasional traveller on the trail that they were almost in sight of the Trading Post when a powerful thunderstorm blew up that caused them to go off the trail into the shelter of an overhanging cliff. They did a cold lunch of pemmican and water while the storm boomed around them. The sun actually came out while the clouds still clung to the east mountains and the thunder still echoed down the valley.

Quinn noticed it first. "Listen!! That isn't all thunder. That's gunshots that we're hearing now!"

Jed and Darcy jumped up and started running to the horses.

"Wait!" Cody called to them. "We don't know what we'd be riding into. This storm may have saved our lives by getting us to stop off the trail. Let's get to where we can see who is shooting at who without them seeing us. Better carry your rifles."

Quinn added, "I think we can take our riding horses closer. Maybe we should tie up the pack horses here."

They quickly did that and started walking to where the trail topped the ridge that would give them a view of the Post and hopefully show them what the gunfire was about. As they neared the lip they faded off the trail into the forest so that they would blend in to the underbrush. The wet from the thunder storm soon soaked through their clothes but it softened the debris on the ground, giving them greater opportunity to creep closer to the activity ahead without making too much noise. The trees were not dense so it was easy for the horses to be led into cover. The gunfire was continuing, seeming to alternate between heavy and lighter calibre. The boys could only conclude that the fort was under siege.

All four men tied their mounts and crept to the edge of the underbrush. The trading post was sitting in a bowl shaped valley. The trees and brush had been cleared back so that no one could sneak up on the buildings from any direction without being fully exposed. The Trading Post had put up a stockade all around with gates facing west. From those gates you could see the Kootenay River a good five hundred yards to the south west. It looked as though a few men could hold off an attack quite well.

The gun fire had tailed off to just an occasional shot and reply.

In a low voice Cody said, "Let's try to pick out where the attackers are and how many there are before we let anyone know we're here."

Over the next half hour they identified six shooters spread out in pairs in a small arc that focused on the gates. The leader was part of the middle pair. Return fire from the fort came on either side of the gates and through a couple gun holes in the gates themselves.

Jed had a suggestion. "I can drop back of this ridge and circle behind them without them knowing. It would only take me fifteen minutes."

As they were discussing this one of the gang yelled out.

"What will it be Linklater? Come out and we'll let you ride away!"

"Why would I trust you not to shoot us down when you think you can just take whatever you want?! You're going to die trying to rob this Post."

"The dying is going to be inside the fort! If you don't come out we'll wait till dark and burn you out. You won't even see us coming."

The fort answered with a volley of shots at the positions the boys had identified. It only brought a cackle of laughter from the hill.

"Those little guns are a joke, Linklater. You should have got yourselves real guns like these."

The thieves let loose a volley of shots that sounded like cannons by comparison. Quiet settled over the valley. The people in the fort now had to ponder their fate with the gang having declared its intention. The Pards knew that it would be a terrifying time for them. They wished they could signal them that help had arrived but they obviously couldn't do that without alerting the outlaws.

The Pards huddled to lay their plan. There was no need to rush according to what had been said by the leader of the gang. Better to have a good strategy even if it took some time to ensure they could take down the robbers. The position of the leader had been pinpointed. He was well protected from the guns in the fort by big boulders. However it looked like all the shooters were exposed to the high ground behind them.

"We should be able to get in position above them without them even knowing that we're here," said Cody. "

They discussed who would take which bad guys.

Darcy said, "I think if we make sure the leader is taken out the others will probably give it up."

That was generally agreed and they settled on Jed and Darcy each taking one of the side pairs. Cody and Quinn together would take on the leader and his side kick.

"Watch for us to make the first move. Hopefully we'll be able to see each other as we get into positions above them. Those side pairs will be able to see their boss taken out and hopefully they'll lay their guns down."

Quinn looked Cody in the eye, "If they don't drop their guns right away we have to shoot to kill. I know you always want to give an extra chance but these guys have shown that they are scumbag killers."

"Ok, I agree." Cody was reluctant but had no option.

Quinn continued, "So I think we should have pistols in hand. None of us should die out here today!"

Both Jed and Darcy nodded in agreement. Cody thought for a few moments but then pulled the pistol out of his belt. The others did the same. They all double checked that all six chambers were loaded and that the balls and caps were in place. There were some quiet moments as they all looked at each other, each one connecting eyes with each of the others. The bond between them making words unnecessary as they stepped over a new threshold of danger. They had come through many wrecks together but this was the first time they had ever, of their own free choice, stepped into a gunfight where one misstep could take a life.

They moved out by retreating back from the ridge line and then circling to come up behind their assigned spots. Time seemed to crawl as the boys walked through the forest using every stealth technique they had learned and practised in the woods as kids. They had agreed that they would not be pressured by any kind of time goal. Each one was to put quiet ahead of haste. The guns had been quiet for some time as the people in the fort and the bandits waited out the day. As the young men moved closer to their targets they could hear snatches of conversation between the gangsters which let them know the bandits hadn't moved out of their positions.

The final steps were excruciatingly slow for all of them. They battled the blood pounding through their veins and the sweat on their hands as the showdown crept closer. No one wanted to be the one making a mistake that would blow their cover.

Cody and Quinn moved into position by Cody holding a pine bough back to let them through. Quinn, holding the pistol in front, peered around a tree trunk and looked directly down on the backs of the leader and his partner. Cody looked to his left and made eye-contact with Darcy. When he looked to his right there was no sign of Jed. He looked back to Darcy and shook his head.

As he did that, they all heard a horse nicker! Jed must have stumbled on the mounts of the gang. Cody's heart almost stopped. Would the robbers leave their positions to check on the horses? It was good that it was Jed bumping into the horses. If anyone could keep the horses from making more noise it was Jed.

"Think I should check on the horses Jakes?" The question from one of the robbers rippled the quiet.

"Naw, they're OK! We need to stay watching that bunch down there in case one of them tries to make a break for it. Don't forget the order we'll shoot – centre, left, then right. That will make for almost no pause while the first ones reload." The voice of the leader came from right below Cody and Quinn.

The afternoon forest noises returned. The birds flitted around, a squirrel chattered and a magpie called from back in the trees. Nothing moved. Most of the bandits had relaxed a little and laid their long guns aside.

Cody checked to his right several times and eventually, as if appearing out of nothing, Jed was there. He let Jed settle for a few minutes. Then he stood, pointed his pistol to the sky. It was the signal they had agreed on. The others did likewise with their weapon.

They aimed their guns at their targets...

"Freeze!!" came the sudden shout from Cody. "Hands up and not one false move!"

As the leader spun around his right hand slapped to his pistol. Quinn pulled his trigger! Jakes grabbed his chest as he crumpled. His partner dove for his rifle. Cody's gun blasted and the partner landed on his face, crimson immediately blossoming on his shoulder. A gun to their right roared in the same moment. To their left they heard "Don't shoot, don't shoot!

"Darcy, you OK?" Cody yelled.

"Yeah, they've both got their hands in the air.!"

"Jed, what about you?"

"One wounded bad, the other has his hands up and pleading!"

"Well, their leader is dead, and the other one here wounded. Quinn will come and help you collect the guns and bring these lowlifes together over here. Shoot if any of them make a false move."

In minutes Quinn had collected the guns and the bandits had all been brought together. Seeing their leader laying dead and two of them leaking a lot of blood took the last of the fight out of them. One of them, that the others called Shorty, spoke up.

"Hey we weren't part of planning to burn them out. We were just going to get some supplies from the fort and they shut the gates and started shooting at us for no reason. We had to defend ourselves here. Jakes got carried away in the excitement saying we were going to burn the fort and kill them. We'll just go away."

"Shut up, you weasel!" Quinn glowered at him and raised his pistol in his direction. Shorty backed away.

Cody was pondering this new problem. What do you do with gangsters that you've captured alive? They had no idea if there was any kind of official lawmen in this wilderness. From what they had heard it wasn't likely. So far, the head trader of the Hudson Bay posts, according to their charter, had been as much of a law system as there was where ever they happened to be located. But now this fort was going to move so they couldn't keep any prisoners for very long. Officially they were in another country since that 49th parallel had been set as the border, so they wouldn't make any friends by taking the law into their own hands.

"What do we do now?" Jed broke the silence.

"I'm not sure," Cody's puzzlement sounded in his voice.

"If they made a break for it we could shoot them!" Quinn offered as his solution. Which made Shorty start to babble again. Quinn silenced him with a scowl and a wave of the pistol.

"I think we better talk this over with Mr. Linklater. After all, they were the ones being shot at, not us!

With that, Cody stepped to the edge of the rocks that hid them from the fort and hailed the Trader.

"Hello the Fort!! Mr. Linklater!"

In a moment the response was shouted back, "This is Linklater. Who are you?"

"I'm Cody McVeigh, we're here from the Hudson Bay. There's four of us. We've captured the bandits. Can we bring them in?"

"Come ahead!"

They made two of the gang help the one Jed had shot. The ball had hit him in the side and it had gone right through. His partners had to almost carry him. Shorty helped the one Cody had clipped in the shoulder. He was weak but not nearly so bad as the other one. They were a sorry looking remnant of a gang that, the Pards learned later, had carried out many raids to the south and had been working their way north. Cody led the way with the prisoners following and the others behind them with pistols in hand.

As they slowly approached the Fort the gates opened a little and a tall burly man stepped out and made his way toward the approaching party. He was neatly dressed in the clothes of the frontier. His stride was firm and confident. The smile on his face was definitely welcoming of these rescuers who had changed his day from terror to victory. He held his hand out to Cody and gave a hearty handshake.

"You are a very welcome party to our Fort. I'm John Linklater. You solved a nasty business for us. Our deepest thanks."

"Glad to be of some help. Although we can't take any credit for the timing of our arrival."

"Well, we'll give thanks to the Good Lord for that part of it!"

"These grim looking fellows are my partners, Darcy, Jed and Quinn!" Each one stepped forward and shook Linklater's hand sensing a kindred spirit behind the firm grip and the direct eye contact.

Linklater's face clouded as he looked at the rest of the party. "These sorry looking excuses for men must be what's left of the Jakes Gang! Where's Jakes himself?"

Cody reported that Jakes was dead and went on to give a brief description of what had transpired on the ridge overlooking the Fort. Again John Linklater expressed the gratitude of everyone in the fort for risking themselves by taking on these cutthroat outlaws and invited them inside the stockade.

"We surely would like to do that but maybe we can take care of a few things first," Cody said. "Having these bandits on our hands is not something we want. With what we need to do in the next days I doubt you want them on your hands either. Would you have some remedy you could suggest?"

Linklater scratched his chin while he turned some thoughts over in his mind. After a bit he said, "You're right, we really don't have any way to keep them. The first lawman we could find is a long ways south and we can't afford the manpower to escort them that far. Even though the stories we've heard make out that this gang has done enough evil that they deserve hanging, I don't feel that we could be right being judge and jury and finishing them off. Thanks to you fellas they didn't actually kill anyone here. With Jakes dead I think the head of the snake is cut off and these guys will disappear. I'm of a mind to take all their weapons, put them on their horses and send them south. I would be glad to hear your opinion of my thoughts."

"Sounds about right to me," offered Cody. Turning to his mates, "What's your minds on this?"

"I can go with that." Jed agreed. Darcy and Quinn nodded their agreement as well.

"What about the knife in Shorty's boot?" asked Darcy. That caused Quinn to immediately swing his pistol in line with Shorty who raised his hands and started vigorously shaking his head. The captives were all searched and a knife was found somewhere on each of them. When one of them started to protest that it wasn't fair to turn them loose in the wilderness with no means of defending themselves Linklater rounded on him with anger.

"You deserve to be shot right here, right now!! Don't give me any whine about fairness when you planned to kill all of us!"

Turning away, he said, "Let's get these lowlifes out of here before I change my mind!"

Between them, Cody and John organized Jed to take several men who were hunters for the fort to bring all the horses in to the fort corral. Quinn and a couple other freighters went to dig a grave. Darcy and a cook and a blacksmith guarded the prisoners. They put some ointment and bandages on the wounds as well as giving them some water and food. The odds of the most seriously wounded man surviving were pretty slim but the first aid would better his chances. When Jed and the others returned with the horses, each of the bandits claimed his own, mounted up and headed south.

In the meantime, John Linklater showed Cody around the fort while discussing the huge job of moving this operation north of the border.

TWENTY-THREE

A couple of hours later Quinn came looking for Cody.

"We've got the grave dug and the body in it. I'm just checking to see if you want to say some words over the body before we fill it in."

Quinn's question caught Cody off guard. In all the turmoil of the past hours this item hadn't come to mind.

Linklater said, "Ah, he was a murderer and a thief! Just an animal! Worse than an animal because he made choices to rape and pillage. I say just throw the dirt on him and let it be."

Cody was quiet as he faced this dilemma. But Quinn was standing there waiting for an answer.

"Part of me agrees, but he was still a human being. One of God's creation and the image of God was in there somewhere although buried over by the evil. That image of God makes him different than the animals and we have to treat that difference with respect or we can all become like him. I'm not sure how much sense I'm making but I'll say something at his grave."

"Thanks Cody," Quinn responded quietly. "I hoped you would. Somehow that will help when it was my bullet that killed him." Quinn's voice had turned husky. He quickly averted his face and walked away.

The word went around the Fort of the fact that they would have a kind of funeral late in the afternoon. As the time approached Cody was wishing he hadn't gotten himself into this. His first thought had been to read what he had heard at several burials. The Shepherd Psalm. But when he pondered the opening words "The Lord is my Shepherd" it just wasn't true for this man and Cody couldn't be false just for the sake of sounding pious. It would have to be something else.

As he walked to the grave the only other ones who had come besides himself and Quinn were Darcy and Jed. They were only there to show their solidarity with Quinn. Then Cody knew what he would do. He simply prayed the "Our Father." "It was truth," Cody thought. " It was the prayer Jesus taught His disciples to pray and it was never out of order."

They each threw a clod on to the corpse and walked away. Quinn stayed to fill in the grave. It gave closure for him. These young men had taken another significant step in maturing into the rugged frontiersmen they were destined to be.

That evening John Linklater and his two trusted assistant traders had a long talk with the Pards. There was news to share about the Hudson Bay Company, news and rumours about the war between the States, and news about the developments of the still new Colony of British Columbia and the spreading gold rushes. Eventually, as the hour grew late and the activities of the Fort dwindled to silence, these men huddled closer to talk strategy for defeating the marauders, like the Jakes gang, who would do all they could to capture all these goods as they were moved north. Linklater had given a lot of thought to how this could be accomplished and shared his ideas with the circle of men gathered in the lamp light on condition of strict secrecy. The Pards headed to their beds feeling new optimism about accomplishing the big move north now that Linklater had divulged his plan.

Preparations for the big transfer of this prosperous trading post began in earnest the next day. Linklater was a very organized leader and he had been preparing for this move for several months. Over the years Indians and Trappers from a wide territory had made this their base for getting the supplies they needed. John gave fair value for the fur they brought in and reasonable prices for the goods they took in trade. Fort Kokanee, under John's leadership always added to the profit columns of the Hudson Bay via the piles of eighty pound bales of fur that got transported all the way to the warehouses in Montreal each year. From there whole ship loads of furs were transported to Europe where some of these pelts would be made into the grandest fashions of the day for the rich and famous.

Its prosperity became the problem. Kokanee was drawing customers from so far south that they were draining business from trading posts in territory that had first been claimed by the Lewis and Clark expedition. Their complaints forced the hand of customs agents to threaten Fort Kokanee with such high taxes that they would be driven out of business. In fact, the border agents had threatened to seize the whole trading post for doing business in United States territory since the Oregon Treaty in 1846 when the manifest destiny campaign in the States had pushed the British claims north to the 49th Parallel. Linklater was sure that these agents were going way beyond their true authority and were really common thieves with only a veneer of legality. Because of all these accumulated problems, this enormous move north was necessary. Now, if only they could actually get the cargo safely into the new colony of British Columbia.

By lunch time, Jed was excited to tell his buddies about his new experiences of that morning.

"Hey guys," he chortled, "you should see me drive a six mule team! That makes for a whole lot of pulling power when they are working together."

His enthusiasm was so infectious that the Pards took their tin cups of coffee out to the corral to see what all the fuss was about. Jed darted through the parallel poles of the corral to untie the team that had been left harnessed over the noon break. He also grabbed up a coiled bull whip from the tie rail and settled it on a hook that was now hanging from his belt.

"You wouldn't believe what it takes to get all the harness sorted out for six animals at a time." Jed called over to them as he climbed up to the high seat on the big freight wagon. "Now, watch this!"

He then took the reins behind the six and clucked them into motion, driving them through a number of manoeuvres. At one end of the corral the two lead mules tried to go opposite directions nearly causing a pile up of the team. Jed grabbed the bull whip, slipped all the reins into his left hand, and gave a mighty yell and heave of the whip. Something misfired and the whip settled gently across the backs of the first two mules on the right. At the same time the whole team was bunching up in a corner. At this point the driver, who had been keeping an eye on the proceedings came up along side Jed and talked him through what he needed to do in voice commands and in working the reins. In a few moments the six were all going the same direction. Jed got them back to their tie post no worse for wear.

His buddies were all over him! "Jed, how did you manage that special trick in the corner!" "What is your secret to good mule driving?!" "Can you teach me how to use a bull whip?"

Red faced, Jed took the ribbing in good stride. It had looked so easy when the experienced driver had given them a workout this morning and had been sitting right beside Jed when he took over the reins for a couple turns around the big coral.

Cody noticed that they were out of earshot of anyone as everyone went back to their tasks.

"What did you think of Linklater's ideas of how to escape the border gang that wants to claim all of this for taxes?"

After a moment Quinn commented, "Well, I guess anything is better than just sitting here like ducks on a pond."

"I'm wondering about this phony Rendezvous party that he is going to use to make people think that we're not leaving for two weeks," offered Darcy. "Can we trust so many people to keep the secret that we're actually going to leave a week before that?"

"Well, John seems pretty sure of his men." Cody commented. " By the way, he told me this morning that only very few will know ahead of time that we are leaving early. Most of the crew going north with us will only be told the morning that we actually leave. Anything else?"

Jed had been surprisingly quiet. "That new road that he's been carving out in the valley to the east is a great idea to hide us from across the Kootenay, but the pass we'll have to go over at the far end sounds like it could be a big problem. It will be steep both up and down. It could take several days to unload and load the freight waggons let alone winching them up and down. That's where the bandits could catch us. I think we'll have to have some full time armed guards at that point. Once we get beyond that pass we're back in the Colony and there will be a lot more traffic. That gang won't come north of there."

"Well it will be a great campfire story if we can pull it off," said Cody. "Jed, now that you've had a look at the stock, do you think we have enough animals to move everything?"

Jed laughed, "According to Linklater whatever we don't move will get trashed or hauled away at that big party we're going to miss. Can you imagine how ripped up those border agents will be when they find out they've been duped, especially after they've found the whiskey we're leaving behind. I'd love to be a fly on the wall to see that!! But, yeah, there's enough stock that we'll be able to haul pretty much everything we want to."

As the Pards started drifting back to their packing there was a burst of galloping horses heading out of the gates, leaving a cloud of dust behind.

"Well, there go the guys taking the invitations to the party. Word will spread a long ways in a couple of weeks. Two weeks from now every kind of trapper, freighter, prospector and hard-case will start drifting in. Let's hope we can pull this off." Apprehension thickened in Cody's voice.

TWENTY-FOUR

A week later every single item in the fort had been identified as stay or go. Everyone knew the fort was closing so nothing about all the sorting raised suspicions that a big deception was underway. All the residents and hangers-on were making their own choices about moving north with Linklater or setting out to the south to find new opportunities and a new life. The trading post on the Flathead Lake seemed a favourite choice of those planning to drift south. "Party Packs" were also being made up for the rendezvous as the gifts that were being promised in the invitations. Again, everyone knew about the party that was a couple of weeks away so every one was in high spirits anticipating seeing friends and acquaintances that were often crossing paths only once or twice a year. It would be a rip-roaring time! Little did the majority imagine however, how truly "rip-roaring" but totally in a different way than they expected!!

The fateful day arrived. A day after the regular pay day. The inner circle agreed that it was now or never for the best possible outcome. On the morning that the big move would start, Linklater started ringing the big bell that was used to call everyone together in an emergency while it was still dark. He kept ringing and ringing. Men started showing up from all directions, still pulling their clothes on. Bleary eyed and stumbling, they moved into the light of torches being held by the Pards. A murmur swelled as they asked what was going on. "Was there an attack coming? Had someone died?"

Linklater called for quiet. "None of us want to move – but we have to! We don't want all of this to fall into the hands of the Border Patrol gang. Thanks to all your hard work we can get a head start on that gang. Everyone planning to go north, WE ARE PULLING OUT TODAY!"

Cheers interrupted Linklater. After a few moments he continued. "The party planned for another week from now is still on. Anyone not going north can stay as long as you want. You can host the rendezvous! Pass out the gifts! Look after yourselves. We know that this fort will be ransacked when the whiskey runs out. You can leave any time you want. Thank you for making this a great Trading Post. Give my greetings to all my friends that show up for the rendezvous."

Another round of cheering started after someone yelled out "Let's hear it for Linklater!"

Linklater was a little embarrassed by the good wishes. He felt like he was abandoning all the men heading south but knew that he had no choice. When the cheering quietened to a buzz of conversations he called out "Let's get breakfast and let's get loaded up!"

Daylight had come as the men finished their hasty meal. In spite of the impending demise of Fort Kokanee that overshadowed all of them, there was a surprising enthusiasm to join in the grand deception of out-witting the menace of the Border Patrol gang.

No one noticed the shadowy figure at the back of the crowd that slipped away rather than coming in for breakfast. Newt James had recently shown up as a freelance hunter. His ability to regularly bring in an elk or a deer gave him a place in the mix of people living in and around the Fort but he kept to himself so that no one really knew him. This in itself was not unusual out on the frontier where many people were escaping from something in their past. People learned not to probe or to get too personal unless the other party volunteered information. Everyone was given a chance to show who they were by their actions rather than by anything in their past.

Newt, it turned out, was an old friend of Joe Morgan, the leader of the Border Patrol, and owed him some favours. They had crossed paths a while back in Billings. During a long night of drinking, Joe had reminded Newt that he would either have been shot by a firing squad or still be in a military prison for punching a Union Sargent if Joe hadn't helped him escape. Now there was a way that he could pay back that favour.

Joe had said to him, "There's a trading post up near the border that's going to be packing up and moving north. Once they have everything loaded up we are simply going to claim it for government taxes and bring it all south instead. You know how the government needs those taxes!! We have some other business to the west of Linklater's place but we need someone to let us know when they actually start the move. Newt, you're my man aren't you?" This was said with a force that showed there was only one answer possible.

Now, as Newt rode away from Fort Linklater he struggled with the obligation that Morgan had laid on him. The men at the trading post had been decent with him and didn't really deserve the mayhem that the Border Patrol gang would bring down on them. "Oh well," he thought, "he would do this one favour and then move on again to be as far from his past as possible. Mind you, he didn't need to particularly rush to find the gang and if he just happened to use up some extra time that might let Linklater cross the border first, Morgan wouldn't know it until he was long gone beyond Morgan's reach."

Fort Linklater was busier than a kicked over ant-hill. The men who would have been working away for the day gave a hand. The wood-cutters, the hay makers, the hunters, the traders and even the cooks joined the wranglers in making up this huge pack train. It was mid-morning by the time all the pack-horses and waggons were loaded, the mules harnessed, and personal mounts saddled.

Finally, Linklater mounted his horse and with a wave of his hat yelled, "Let's move 'em on out!!"

Everyone cheered. Many called out "good luck"! Dogs barked. It had the atmosphere of a carnival to have that many people and animals heading out at the same time. A big plume of dust hung in the air as the last of the train moved beyond the fort.

Linklater had another surprise up his sleeve. As he had explained to the Pards, there was a hidden valley one low mountain range to the east that ran parallel to the Kootenay Valley. Very few people knew that it existed, mainly hunters and wranglers. John had had a few guys do a little bit of trail development during off seasons from other essential work. He had kept the work on the alternate trail very low key. For those he had asked to occasionally work on it, it had been described as a convenience trail along the hidden valley floor for hunters and livestock. Wranglers would graze their livestock on some of the meadows that formed somewhat of a chain along the floor of the valley and would sometimes lend a hand to clear a little more of the trail. Access was only by a twisting route that went up and over several rocky ridges directly behind the Fort that could only be navigated by animals that could scamper over out-croppings of rock. In fact some wranglers shied away from using the hidden valley grazing simply because there was too much risk of injury to the animals getting in and out. This all seemed normal for the everyday activities that it took to keep a thriv-ing fort humming along. No one even considered the possibility that waggons could ever get into this long boxed in valley. Plus, it was simply common knowledge to those few that had been there that there was a rocky pass at the north end that boxed in the valley from the north as well. Absolutely none of the men leaving that morning had any idea that they were going to do anything different than use the usual riverside trail that followed the Kootenay River.

It had seemed a very slow day for the train. There had been frequent stops to check on the pack saddles of the many horses. The drivers of the pair of six-mule teams had to repair some of the harness that gave way, so there had been no official lunch stop as everyone just chewed on the jerky that had been issued and drank from their canteens as they wanted. Those that had ridden a ways with them just for fun had dropped away hours ago as the stops and starts became boring.

Mid afternoon, Linklater who was riding lead of this whole caravan turned right towards what looked like a dead end ravine. They had already passed innumerable gorges and box canyon ravines that day. They all had steep banks suited only to mountain sheep and goats. Most were choked with trees and brush especially on the north facing slopes. At most they ran back a couple hundred feet where some had a small stream bed that ran only in spring. A murmur of voices raised questions as drivers and wranglers further back saw where he had turned.

"Are we stopping already?" "We won't be able to turn our teams around if we head into a draw like that"

In fact this was Linklater's trump card in the gamble that they could escape the Border Patrol. Over the past few years since starting the trading post in Montana Territory, John had spent many days on horseback exploring much of the vast region along the Kootenay River at the same time as he hunted to keep a good supply of meat. He had poked around in many of these ravines hoping to flush a deer or elk that found these places excellent refuges. What he had accidentally discovered, by following an elk on a game trail, was that this particular gorge did not end a few hundred feet back but continued through a maze of twists and turns as well as a continuous up-slope eventually opening out into the parallel valley. Some inner prompting had caused him to keep the existence of this unknown access to himself.

As the pressure had mounted from the Border Patrol gang, Linklater had paid another visit to this possible escape route.

"Could we possibly get the whole pack train through?" he pondered to himself. "The pack horses could make it by the crew chopping just a few trees to clear the path wide enough for the loads the horses would have. But what about the waggons?"

After careful scrutiny, Linklater was sure that by cutting about a dozen trees close to the ground there would be a route through.

Now he called the men together to explain his plan. There were many murmurs of surprise as he revealed that this was no ordinary clay bank gulley. A new excitement rippled through their voices as they all felt drawn into this unexpected twist in their journey. Linklater explained that they were to trample as little as possible as they pushed through the underbrush on the apron of the ravine so they could try to camouflage the existence of the pass.

There were more than enough volunteers when John asked for men who would take axes to the trees that stood in their way. Some of the men were designated to be sawyers who would cut the felled trees back once they were down. Soon the rhythmic music of axes and saws filled the narrow draw. It was pleasant to the ears of Linklater and the Pards as they saw this advantage against the Border Patrol opening up. The caravan moved slowly forward. The men actually cheered when the axles of the first wagon to go over the stump of a tree that would have prevented progress cleared with inches to spare.

The floor of this ravine was so narrow in some places that the sides sloped up on both sides of the game trail that formed the bottom. The drivers of the waggons had to choose which side of the path they drove on according to the clearance for the top of the wagon. In one spot that threatened to halt their progress because of a cliff overhang the loggers traded their axes for shovels. By shovelling the mixed gravel and clay from the bank opposite the cliff to the side of the trail almost directly under the cliff they caused the wagon to lean away from the overhang. They barely made it past with nothing more than light scrapes along the sides of several waggons. Once again there were cheers from the men. They had taken on this challenge as if they were battling a huge enemy and every obstacle overcome was like a major blow against a villain.

When Linklater saw that they were most of the way through the gorge and was certain that they would make it past the rest of the tight spots he called together a few of his most trusted men.

"I want you men to go back to the entrance to this pass and wipe out our tracks as much as you can. We might gain some extra hours, even days, if the Border Patrol misses our turn and gallops right on past. Then as you are coming back fell a tree or two at the narrowest spots so that even a single horse will have trouble getting through. Matt, I'd like you to take charge of this."

It was turning to dusk as the last of the caravan cleared the east mouth of the ravine. The open meadow that spilled down the gentle slope in front of them was a welcome sight to the whole crew. The stream at the bottom immediately drew the animals' attention and hastened them clear of the trail they had followed.

The men made a hasty camp in the gathering darkness. Everyone was bone weary at the close of this very long and demanding day. But it was a good tiredness that comes when you know that important steps have been accomplished towards the goal that you share. These men had the added satisfaction that they were part of a giant deception that looked like it was going to outwit the bandits who threatened their lives and livelihood.

Even the boom of distant thunder didn't prevent them from sinking into deep sleep.

Linklater let the men sleep extra the next morning. The sunlight finally stirred most of them and as they straggled out of their bedrolls some started checking horses and harnesses knowing that the strain of the day before was sure to have left some weaknesses if not actual damages. The cook's bell brought the latest sleepers to their feet.

The setting was idyllic. There were in a natural mountain meadow in which the horses and mules were grazing contentedly. There was a bubbling stream winding along the bottom. The morning sun was brilliant. Birds raised a symphony of music. It would be easy to ignore the reality that somewhere there was a gang that would rip this apart with deadly gunfire.

TWENTY-FIVE

Mid-morning the crew that had been sent to close off the trail they had travelled yesterday cantered in. Matt, the foreman of that group, rode up to Linklater with a grin on his face.

"All taken care of, sir!"

"Why the grin, Matt? You look like the cat that ate the canary!" replied John.

"Well sir, seems Mother Nature is on our side! I can see that you didn't get any rain here."

"We heard the boomers."

Matt continued, "That was a vicious thunder storm that tracked right up the Kootenay Valley. We had to take shelter for the night in a shallow cave. This morning I hiked back along that rock ridge on the north side of the trail to where I could get a good look. We did our part to hide that entrance, but let me tell you, Mother Nature did a far better job. That downpour completely wiped out our tracks and everyone else's. As we came back here this morning we could see where the rain petered out. The storm never pushed over this low range. Doesn't get much better than that, sir!"

Matt loped off to join his crew at the chuck wagon where they polished off the remnants of the breakfast the cook was putting away.

Even though the caravan moved out much later than the first day, they made great progress. The advance work that Linklater had had his hunters, herders and wood-cutters do was paying off big time.

Over the next several days the migration north took on a regular rhythm and pace that the animals did well on.

The Pards rode in a cluster part of the time so they could chat even while they were trailing their pack horses.

"Hard to understand why people would live in a place like Montreal when all of this is just sitting here waiting for people to enjoy!" offered Cody.

Darcy grinned, "Yeah, but then it would be spoiled for people like us that love wilderness!"

Jed commented, "If it was just people like this crew with a leader like Linklater, it would probably be OK. I've got to admit that some of these guys sure know a thing or two about horses and mules. It even makes it a lot of fun harnessing up this herd when there's people to work with that don't have to be told what to do and they just go ahead and get it done."

"Listen guys," said Cody on their second full day moving north, "I've been thinking about our mission to bring Leblanc and Lagasse to justice. With the Chief Trader at Kootenay House in cahoots with them we've got a big problem in bringing them in. Seems to me that we've found a straight-shooter in Linklater. Even under this new Colonial government, all the Hudson Bay Factors are given the powers of police and junior judges until a full judge can come and hear the case if it is needed. The Chief Trader can't hang anybody, but he can hold a prisoner any length of time while they wait for the Chief Justice to come."

"Seems to me that we could trust John with the information about our real mission here. In fact, he can probably be a big help with all his experience. What do you think?"

There was a pause while this suggestion was worked over in their minds.

Quinn was the first to speak up. "Well I agree that Linklater is a good guy. Right from the first he's treated me as an equal who can carry his own load. I never got that back in Montreal. I think he would care about what we care about and he would keep our secrets just because we ask him to."

Darcy added, "It would be great to have his backing from the start. He would be able to tell us if he thinks we have enough evidence plus we would be way ahead if he would help us out with his crew – at least the ones he knows he can trust. A few more guns on our side – great!"

"OK," Cody nodded, "we'll talk to him after supper tonight."

Meanwhile, Newt James was glad to be away from the suffocating presence of so many people at the Fort. Riding on his own in the quiet of the breaking dawn was the closest he came to finding peace inside. He was still tortured by all the gruesome deaths he had seen and had caused in the Union Army. Newt wondered if he would ever be able to out-ride the nightmares that had chased him into this wilderness. Well this would be the last time he would let himself get caught up in a scheme that would cause horror for other people. One favour to Joe Morgan so Morgan wouldn't have any claim on him to do anything in the future and then he would push farther into the mountains of the north west. He could change his name and work a trap line where he would only have to deal with Indians and a fur trader and that contact would only have to happen a couple of times a year.

With that resolve settled in his mind, Newt started looking for a ford where he could cross to the west side of the Kootenay without getting very wet. It would be a long day's ride to get to the Stone Gulch hideout of Morgan's Border Patrol gang so he knew a shallow ford would eventually show up. He also took a slower pace than normal figuring that if he didn't push his mount too hard he could keep moving longer. He reasoned that if it was getting dark when he made it to Stone Gulch the gang wouldn't be able to leave until the next day and he would have done Linklater a favour by delaying the chase at least by a few hours. Little did he realize the riding he would be doing in the days ahead.

Darkness overtook the messenger before he found the hideout and he was forced to make camp for the night rather than risk his horse stepping in a gopher hole and breaking a leg. He also decided that having a fire was too big a risk because for all he knew he might be within sight of a look out of Morgan's desperadoes. They would probably come in with guns blazing rather than asking after his health. No matter how much he craved some steaming hot coffee he made himself content with jerky and water. As he settled down for his night's sleep he wondered if his story would hold together when it was given to Joe Morgan. Would Morgan figure out that he hadn't pushed as hard as he could have? Would the gang leader blame him for not pushing on in the dark?

Newt spent a restless night with the nightmares plaguing him over and over. With dawn's arrival he was on his way. A couple of hours later he was suddenly braced by two rugged, rifle-toting men.

"Hold up! Border Patrol needs your name and your business!" one of them demanded. Newt gritted his teeth at being accosted like this but quickly realized that they were saving him from having to search for their hideout based on the skimpy directions he had been given.

"I've got a message for Joe Morgan and the Border Patrol."

The armed lookouts laughed at him, "Likely story! Get down off your horse and keep your hands where we can see them." They raised their guns to enforce what they had said.

"Look, my name is Newt James and it's urgent that I deliver a message in person to Morgan."

When they heard Newt's name the guns were lowered. "Morgan said you might be coming but he didn't expect you till just before the big party Linklater is throwing."

"Take me to him. There's been some changes, he'll want to hear this right away."

"Hope they didn't cancel that party and the free whiskey. I've been thirsty ever since I heard about it. But there's a bit of a problem, you talking to Morgan."

"What can be the problem? Just get moving so I can see him!"

"He ain't here. He heard about a shipment of gold being put together in Rock Creek and going through Libby. He figured it was his government duty to collect some taxes on that package and that he could take care of that and be back in time for the rendezvous. He'll be right twisted though if he doesn't get those Trading Post goods. He figures that booty will put us on easy street for the whole of the coming winter."

"You're using up time with all your yakking mister! Show me the trail to Libby. I've got to catch Morgan." Newt growled.

Back at the caravan, the day was finishing with a late supper.

When everyone had eaten and dusk was settling in, Cody approached John and asked. "Could we have a private talk with you?"

"Sure," Linklater responded, somewhat surprised, "Have you run into a problem?"

"No problem, but we have something to deal with when we get this move over and we could use your advice on the matter."

The five men found a spot a little away from the rest of the camp and settled on the ground, because the Pards obviously wanted to be out of earshot of everyone else.

Linklater was surprised as he realized that such a dangerous mission had been put in the hands of men so young. Yet,
as he listened to their collection of evidence along with their
assessments of people's actions, he began to be convinced that
they had a serious case against the pair of Hudson Bay rogues.
He had heard of the suspicions about Leblanc and Lagasse for
a number of years but had dismissed some of the accounts as
bitter gossip by those who didn't have the wilderness skills to
do well in these vast mountains and valleys. John had even pri-
vately thought that the Hudson Bay was sending out bumbling
idiots because all the previous agents that came to look into the
rumours seemed to have accidents that either kept them from
learning very much or even got them killed! Now he was hearing
information from these young men that there was indeed a very
serious problem and he felt a wave of regret for not having given
more help to previous investigators. That would change now, he
resolved, as he continued to listen to the accumulating evidence
that showed the evil of the reign of terror carried on by the two
former Hudson Bay employees.

The Pards began their story rather hesitantly, starting with
the theft of their horses. They went on to the series of events that
pointed to Leblanc and Lagasse being the men behind the whole
network of crimes committed in the region of Kootenay House.
As they saw that Linklater was truly interested they began to
add even the smaller details. John's questions spurred them on as
well and actually caused them to put connections between some
of their experiences that they hadn't considered before.

After spilling out all that they had been through they began
to mull over with him what they could do with their evidence
and what steps needed to be taken against the offenders.

"Assuming that we are going to survive against the Border
Patrol, I'll be working with you from here on!" Linklater's voice
had taken on a new tone of authority. "Since everything north of
the 49th parallel was made into a British Colony in '58, all the

Chief Hudson Bay Traders were given the authority to uphold law and order in their territory in the name of Queen Victoria. The regional head of the Hudson Bay at the time was James Douglas in Fort Victoria. When he saw what was happening in the gold rush on the Fraser River...thousands of people suddenly trying to grab the same claims sometimes by killing one another, it looked like there could be a climate of lawlessness where no one was safe from harm. Plus Americans were taking their gold south out of the territory without the British administration getting anything as taxes...he begged England to make this all a Crown Colony, and, of course, with him as Governor! The Hudson Bay was the only organization that covered these mountains so we were made officials of the Crown.

Quinn threw in a question. "So, will you hang these gangsters when we take them down?"

Linklater chuckled, "Well, I'm not supposed to. Governor Douglas asked for a judge to come from England to keep things civilized. His name is Judge Begbie and I hear he's getting a reputation for hanging! I can do everything but hanging and I can hold someone until the Judge comes through then he gets to make that decision. Anyway, by us working together on this, Leblanc and Lagasse will surely face a day of reckoning to pay for their crimes!"

Cody was too excited to sleep much that night. He had never admitted to any one his niggling fear that he and his young friends might not be up to bringing these two scoundrels to justice. Now his mind kept churning over all that had happened on their mission and what was yet to happen. John Linklater was a godsend for the developments that still needed to come. It looked straightforward from here but Cody was learning that the path to success often had some big twists and turns. Now he was anxious to get back to Kootenay House so they could track down their quarry and bring them to justice with Linklater's help.

TWENTY-SIX

Newt James felt the cold hand of fear clench his gut when he realized that Joe Morgan had gone the opposite direction from Fort Kokanee. His dawdling the previous day was coming back to haunt him and could put Morgan out of reach of the caravan moving north by the time James found him and the gang doubled back. There would be no dawdling now. He would have to push his horse to the limit.

It seemed he would never find the few log structures where Libby Creek joined the Kootenay River. Newt had been told by the lookouts at Stone Gulch that there wasn't much to the settlement but he still expected more than the couple of shacks that looked in danger of falling into the creek and one or two lodges that showed dimly back of the cabins in the evening gloom.

Newt cautiously walked his tired horse toward the one building that showed faint light through the cracks between the logs. The sound of voices reached him as he got a little closer. Then he noticed the red glow of a cigarette as a man in dark clothes emerged from the shadows beside the structure.

"Hold up, stranger!" The man cradled a rifle in his arms as he came towards Newt. "What's your business here?"

Newt, feeling very tired and edgy, didn't feel like explaining himself over and over to lookouts who over-estimated their authority when they had a gun in their hands.

"Get out of my way," he growled, "I need a drink and then my business is with Joe Morgan, not with you!"

"Now, that's no way to speak to Mr. Morgan's Border Patrol Deputy,"

The guard started to move to his right so that he would be broadside to the horse and have a clear line of fire to the rider. He had to look down to be sure of his footing on the rocky ground and in that moment Newt drew his gun and fired into the air. The shocked "deputy" stumbled on a rock and landed painfully on his back-side as his rifle clattered away from him. The gunshot immediately brought several men spilling out of the cabin with guns in their hands. They drew up short when they made out the horse and rider in the deepening dusk. The pistol Newt James held aimed at them brought them all to a standstill.

"I'm tired and thirsty and I have business with Joe Morgan – no one else. Where's Morgan?" Newt's tiredness gave him a boldness beyond himself.

A man at the front of the cluster of men spoke up. "Morgan's inside but it might not be a good time to try to do business with him. He's mad as a mother bear just out of her den when her young'ns are threatened."

"What's the bur under his saddle?" Impatience rasped out in Newt's question.

"The big gold shipment we were after turned out to be the bragging of an old prospector from Rock Creek. He panned a small poke out of that creek, enough to get him through a winter in the south. He got liquored up one night and called his travel south a gold shipment. The rumour built from there. Morgan's trying to wash the memory of that out with booze. He ain't nice right now!!

"My news won't wait. I've got to talk to him now!"

"It's your neck mister. Be warned, there'll be guns on you all the time. Don't make any dumb moves!"

Newt swung down off his mount and the men parted to make a path into the combined trading post and saloon. It wasn't hard to pick out Joe Morgan. He was sitting by himself in the middle of the dimly lit room. His table had several empty bottles along with a couple that hadn't been opened yet. He was obviously planning a long evening of drinking. A couple men stood back against a trading counter that doubled as a bar. Each had a hand on a pistol as James brushed through the door along with the others crowding through behind him. They were eager to see the excitement that was likely to come when Morgan was drunk and brooding like a gathering thunder storm and then was braced by this newcomer.

Morgan didn't even look up as Newt James approached.

"Morgan, I need to talk to you.!" Newt spoke with a raised voice, hoping to pierce the drunken cloud in Morgan's head.

Joe slowly raised his head and looked over his shoulder at his two guards. His words were slurred.

"Why haven't you shot this loud mouth?"

"It's about Linklater and Fort Kokanee!" Newt blurted out quickly.

Newt could see Morgan straighten a little. He turned his head back and raised his eyes to try to register who was pushing in through his fog.

"Newt James! I do believe that's you." Morgan's words were very slurred. "Sit down and have a drink with me and tell me about Fort Linklater and how we're going to wipe them off the earth."

"It's not good news, Joe! Linklater's pulled out and he's got a whole caravan headed north across the Border."

Morgan's eyes narrowed and focused in on Newt as he leaned in close. His whiskey breath over-powering!

"What do you mean, Newt? You were going to let me know when they were going to pull out. We were just going to meet up with them and take over their caravan!"

Morgan's face was turning a bright red as his anger burned hot. Now he was yelling...."I've been duped by a dumb old gold-panner and now you tell me you've messed up and you're making a fool out of me as well!"

The gang leader was pushing himself up off his chair and reaching for Newt's neck.

Newt, fearing for his life, spluttered, "We can still catch them Joe! They can't move very fast with their waggons loaded down. I came as fast as I could once Linklater told everybody just on the same day they pulled out. He's trying to trick you Joe. He should have to pay for that." Newt was desperate to deflect Morgan's anger away from himself.

Morgan let go of Newt's shirt and sat down again. He was mumbling about everybody trying to make a fool out of him. How he needed to make Linklater an example so people would know better than to jerk him around. So that people would respect him!!

The room stayed very quiet for a time. Then Morgan lifted his head and locked eyes with James.

"Newt, I saved your life and you've been beholden to me. Help me make good this time so that I can take that caravan and you'll have no more obligation to me! Is that a deal?!"

Newt wasn't about to say "no" with all those gun hands stand-ing around itching for action. Newt nodded, "I'll do what I can, Joe."

Morgan smirked, "I thought you would. So, Newt, what do we do?"

"Well, I'd head straight north through Granite Canyon and take that Elk Pass. They say that Pass marks the British boundary. We should be able to get on the far side of them and we can turn south along the Kootenay River. That would make us meet them head on before they make the Border. That's two, maybe three days of hard riding."

"You heard him, boys!! We leave at dawn.

TWENTY-SEVEN

A noticeable change in the terrain began to slow the caravan's progress as they approached the north end of the valley. At first the meadows just seemed a little rockier but could still be navigated by simply turning around the bigger rocks. Then boulders began to block the way and the scouts had to stay ahead to find a path that wasn't blocked after going around a first outcrop of rock.

On top of that, the mountains were closing in to make the valley much narrower. The small river that had been such a lifeline on the valley floor was narrowing and twisting through a cut in the cliffs that wouldn't even allow a sure-footed saddle horse to get through. It was the talk of the camp that evening.

Linklater was challenged by the mule team drivers. "Linklater, did you just send us up this valley to dash our hopes at the end? It's looking beyond impossible up yonder!"

Pretty much everyone turned their attention to John as the same question had been in all their minds.

"I'll admit it's going to be tough to get through but I've been all the way up through the pass that's ahead and we can make it.

It's going to be slow. Just past the top of the trail, we'll have to winch the waggons down, but only in one spot. The good thing is that if the Border Patrol gang does find us the pass will be the ideal place to hold them off. It's narrow with lot's of cliffs to shoot down from."

"Sounds like you're leading us right into a trap, Linklater! Why didn't you tell us about this before we left and give us a chance to go our own way? Look's like a fool's errand to me!" It was one of the mule team drivers, Slocum, spewing the anger. It had become obvious over the past few evenings that he was drinking heavily.

It brought murmurs from the rest of the men, some supporting the driver, but most telling him to back off. He wasn't through.

"If my wagon breaks a wheel or if it's crashed when you're winching it you'll pay up!! I'll take it out of your hide if I have to!!" His liquor-fuelled anger was boiling over as he yelled, to the point he was on his feet and menacingly moving toward John.

In one quick movement, Quinn stepped in front of Slocum and blocked his path. He towered over the angry man so that Slocum could see nothing else. He took a wild swing which Quinn blocked and with the other hand Quinn grabbed the front of the man's shirt, lifting him to where only his toes touched the ground.

"That's drunk talk that could get you into a whole lot of trouble mister!! Why don't you go sleep it off before you make things worse for yourself." Quinn gave the man a shove backwards which almost landed him on his back. Slocum slouched away muttering under his breath. His swamper went with him promising that he would make sure Slocum didn't have any more to drink that night.

Another voice spoke up. This time it was Oscar, one of the hunters who kept the supply of fresh meat coming in to the cook. The hunters doubled as scouts both ahead and behind the caravan.

"Linklater! What about the Border Patrol? Seems like we're going so slow we're kinda inviting them to find us. The hair on the back of my neck is prickling when I'm out scouting." This brought some murmurs of support.

Cody, feeling like John was under attack, spoke up to support their plan. "We can only go at the pace of the waggons. If we don't clear the way enough we'll end up with a broken down unit. John says that now it'll only be a couple days until we're in the pass and there it's so narrow we can easily hold off the gang."

There were lots of comments back and forth among the men as they mulled over their situation. Linklater got their attention again. "We knew we would have to deal with the Border guys somewhere on this gamble. Not knowing where they are is harder on our nerves than what the battle itself will be. Here's what we do. We'll double our night guards, two up ahead and two behind but spread out. From now on keep a weapon with you. If you've got a pistol in your kit, wear it from now here on. Keep a rifle within reach. We're going to need to tie the pack-horses in longer lines so some of the wranglers can work on clearing trail."

Once again John's leadership brought the men around to agreement with the steps they were taking. All of them knew that there were no guarantees on this expedition and now they felt they were wresting control back to themselves. They would willingly take on the Border Patrol as long as they felt they were doing everything they could to come out victorious. Cody and Darcy volunteered to be the additional guards on the first watch. Quinn and Jed volunteered for the second watch.

Cody and Darcy walked to lookout positions that would watch over their back trail as dusk was turning to dark. Darcy wondered out loud if they would make it through the inevitable clash with the Border Patrol gang.

"We won't be able to do much about Leblanc and Lagasse will we if we let down our guard here and get blown to bits by these marauders."

"Yeah, there are no sure things about this mission," Cody responded. "I sure hadn't thought about having to outsmart a murderous bunch of thieves just to move this trading post north."

Darcy's voice was quiet as he asked, "Do you think we'll make it, Cody?"

Cody was a little taken aback by the slight quaver in Darcy's voice. After a little thought he said, "Yep, I really do think we'll make it. Linklater's been real smart and if we'll stick with his plan we have everything we need to succeed."

"Alright then, if you are sold on the plan, that's good enough for me!"

"One more thing, Darcy."

"Yeah, what's that?"

"While you're putting in those hours watching for bad guys... it's a good time to pray!"

Darcy didn't offer any comment. The boys separated to their agreed lookouts and to their own thoughts. As Cody settled in, he let the vastness of the canopy of stars capture his sense of connection with this pristine wilderness. There was no moon so the stars sparkled brilliantly. His grandfather Tompson's explanations of the reliability of the stars came back to him. He had treasured the times the two of them had gone out at night to track the positions of the planets. Grandpa had said if you learned about the stars you never needed to be lost in the wilderness. Those lessons gave Cody an anchor tonight as he pondered the planning behind the stars. There was someone and/or something over all of this vastness. And if that "one" could create and track all those stars, Cody was sure that "one" could track him and care about him as well.

As he let his mind idle through the past days the image of Sophie came to him. He didn't push it away this time knowing that he had hours to mull through his feelings for her. He acknowledged to himself that there had never been a girl like her in his life before. She was wonderful company and life felt full of energy when she was near. It would be easy to think that they were meant to be together from now on. Sophie was already older than his Gramma Charlotte had been when she married David Thompson at age fourteen. However Cody knew that he had no idea of where he might want to settle down or what kind of work he might want to do. It would be unfair to give Sophie any false impressions about these things. He certainly didn't want to end up doing what so many Hudson Bay traders and trappers had done by taking what they called a "country wife" - living with an Indian woman while in the west but when it came time to return east or back to Great Britain they simply abandoned the woman and any children they may have had together. No, Sophie would be a very close friend he hoped, but marriage was not in sight for Cody in the near future.

As the end of his time to stand guard approached, Cody let out a tired sigh, looked up at the starlit sky once more and simply said "Thank you!" Then he gave out the coyote howl plus three "yips" that would bring Darcy to meet him as they headed to their bedrolls for their half night's sleep.

It was a subdued crew that went about the work of the new day. Most stood around to eat their breakfast quickly and then many cleaned and oiled guns before strapping them on. Hunters added pick axes and crowbars to their long guns as their equipment for the day. Mule drivers checked their equipment closely minus the banter that usually went on with the other wranglers. Earlier than usual, the caravan started its slow crawl for the day to the sound of sledge hammers breaking up rock.

TWENTY-EIGHT

Joe Morgan cursed as darkness dropped a curtain across their increasingly rocky path that finally forced them to make camp for the night. The Border Patrol gang had pushed their horses to the point of exhaustion hoping to make the junction with the main Kootenay River trail by day's end. It was there that they hoped to cut off the Linklater caravan before they crossed into British territory which was just a few more miles north of where the two trails joined. As ruthless as Morgan was he still knew that if they ruined their horses, either by exhaustion or by lameness, their prize was certainly lost. But he had pushed both man and beast since leaving Libby giving little opportunity for sleep or food so this break forced itself on them regardless.

Newt James was hoping that they would make that cut off before the Trading Post crew got there given the threat that Morgan had hung over him. So now instead of holding back as he had done at first when he had wanted to let Linklater escape, his innate selfishness took over so that his only thought was doing whatever he had to for self-preservation. Newt cringed deeply as they stripped saddles off their mounts. His doubts of their ability to capture the caravan grew ever larger and fear for his life twisted his insides.

That night even Morgan slept through dawn until sun up. His foul mood was evident to everyone as he roared at them to get up and started kicking those that didn't instantly scramble out of their bedroll. He kept yelling all the time it took to water the horses and get them saddled, raving that they were all trying to hold him back from the loot he deserved.

It was mid-day by the time they came to the Kootenay River and found a ford that would let them cross to the side that had the main north south trail. Newt wasn't sure what they were expecting by simply crossing this wagon road but whatever they may have thought might be there - wasn't. It was eerily still. Not a person or animal in sight. No tracks of a large group of horses passing through. No wagon ruts which would have cut in to the softer spots given the load they would be carrying. The gang milled around on their horses waiting for direction. Finally Morgan told them to take a break for whatever lunch they had which for most of them was jerky washed down with water. Someone started a fire and boiled some coffee which made everyone hungrier as the aroma drifted past them. The horses, though, got a much needed chance to graze in the narrow meadow that separated the river from the forest.

Morgan found Newt and growled, "Well, smart guy, what do we do now? Do we go north or south?"

"How the heck can I know? Look, I do know that the waggons they were using were heavy enough to cut some big ruts in soft ground and crush bushes along the trail. Maybe if we send scouts both directions for half an hour they would be sure to cut some sign."

Newt was scratching for anything that would keep Joe thinking about something other than his vow to kill Newt if they missed the caravan.

"If there's no tracks in that much distance then something's happened that they haven't made it this far."

Joe was about to remind Newt of his death sentence if this raid failed when the sound of children's voices cut through the murmur of men talking and horses grazing. The sounds were such a huge contrast that everyone, including the horses, froze while they determined what was going on. All the men turned towards the musical laughter of children obviously at play.

In moments a family emerged from the forest, a father and mother with three children. The adults were carrying what looked like huge reed baskets and long poles. They stopped when they saw the Border Patrol gang. The mother called the children to her. The family looked like they wished they could disappear but being on foot had no chance. The Border Patrol gang members slowly surrounded the Kootenay Indian family like wolves slavering over anything worth stealing. The eight year old boy started to cry. Morgan reached out and grabbed him by the arm yelling at him, "Shut Up!"

The mother begged for the boy's safety in rapid Kootenay language. Morgan raised a hand as if to strike her. Her husband spoke up obviously defending her but the meaning of his words were lost. Morgan looked around at his men and asked, "Anyone here understand their jabber?"

A hard case half breed by the name of Slash was the only one who spoke up.

"My Dad lived with a Kootenay woman but didn't have much to do with her band. I picked up enough that I can make my way in their language."

"Slash, you tell them that if they don't tell me what I want to know this pup is going to hurt real bad!"

After he told them what Morgan had said the Mother responded with a stream of talk, holding a buckskin bag out to him while the Father nodded his support.

"They say they'll answer all that they know just so the boy will be alright and they're offering you their lunch as well."

"Ask them if they've seen the caravan or any unusual activity."

After several exchanges back and forth Slash reported that they had seen people walking, mostly going north but no waggons. Morgan wrenched the boys arm up between his shoulder blades making him scream with pain. The Mother fell to her knees begging for her son.

"Ask them again," Morgan spit out.

Again Slash talked back and forth then said to Morgan, "They swear there have only been people passing on foot with maybe three or four mules on this trail in the last four days. But not one wagon, maybe a travois or two. Looked like trappers or prospectors. They can see this road from their camp. Seems like what happened." Slash added this last bit because as hard as he was he didn't like a kid being hurt.

Morgan shoved the kid down making him cry out again.

"Let 'em go. They're useless to us."

The men stepped back letting the family continue on their way to the river with their fishing equipment.

"Well Newt, looks like you're going escape with your hide in one piece!" Morgan grinned at him. "That caravan hasn't come by here and I've been up and down this trail enough times to know that it would have to fly over top of us for us not to have it trapped somewhere south of here."

Newt felt a rush of relief, yet he was puzzled. From what he knew of this trail, that pack train should have already passed this place. There was something out of place which wouldn't let him rest easy yet. He didn't want Joe Morgan more worked up than what he had been so he didn't voice his doubts to him.

TWENTY-NINE

Tension was growing to the boiling point among members of the Linklater caravan. Everyone was conscious of the slow crawl up this hidden valley knowing that by this time the Border Patrol Gang had to be closing in on them. No one knew for sure how much time they had to work through the narrow mountain pass that lay immediately ahead of them. What was known was that no wagon had ever gone through this narrow defile. It looked impossible but Linklater kept assuring them that he had checked it out and that they would get through even though it would be hard.

The wranglers blamed the waggons for the slow pace. The drivers blamed everyone else for not clearing a road fast enough. Darcy commented to his buddies about what he had inadvertently overheard from the drivers.

"Slocum is stirring up trouble. He's talking to other drivers and saying he's going to bloody some noses if people keep trying to tell him how to drive his rig."

Jed added, "He was talking big last night when we were taking harnesses off. He was also drinking more than anyone else. He's

174

blaming you, Cody. Saying you're too big for your britches – you know – young whelp and all that. 'What do you know about what kind of clearing should be done so a wagon can move without getting broken down.' That kind of thing! I think you need to watch your back."

"Cody, let me do an attitude correction on him?" Quinn was red in the face angry that Slocum was bad mouthing his friend. "He can't get away with stuff like that!"

"I sure wish this kind of thing wouldn't get in the way but I think it's inevitable. And I think it will have to be just him and me to get it settled. So as long as you help by keeping others from interfering... between his anger and his liquor, the odds are in my favour."

Cody was right. The inevitable happened mid-morning. In reality it happened because of the booze haze Slocum was living in and he failed to see the small jog in the path that skirted a low sharp outcrop of rock. The rear left wheel crumbled with a loud crack. Instantly Slocum was shouting curses into the air. As he climbed down to see the damage, a crowd gathered to see for themselves what was happening.

"See, this is what happens when we have snot-nosed kids trying to tell us how to operate the freight business! If Cody McVeigh had a brain, this road would be decently cleared. Instead their freeloading laziness makes us freighters pay with broken down waggons. Things have to change. People are going to have to listen to me once I take care of McVeigh!"

Cody stepped forward, "Slocum, you're the one who's going to have to change. You can't be stirring up trouble all the time."

Slocum spit towards Cody, "I suppose you're going to be the one to make me change!? Listen youngster, you better run back to your Mama!"

With that, Slocum made a sudden charge at Cody, catching him by surprise, and his momentum carried them into the crowd and down onto the hard ground. The air whooshed out of

Cody's lungs momentarily stunning him. Slocum got in a couple glancing blows to Cody's face while squirming to get up to his knees so he could get more power behind his punches. Those punches were enough to alert Cody to defend himself. Just as Slocum loaded up for a hammer blow, Cody jerked to the side causing Slocum's fist to drive into the gravel. That gave Cody the moment he needed to spill his adversary to the side and to spring to his feet. The men crowding around yelled advice to the fighters with almost everyone cheering Cody on.

Slocum lumbered to his feet and both men went into a fighting stance face off. "This is your chance to run away before you get hurt, pup!" Slocum goaded. Cody stayed still, waiting for Slocum to make a move.

Cody saw his eyes twitch and readied for the punch that was coming. Slocum moved to his right and swung a roundhouse right fist at the same time. Cody leaned back, blocked the punch with his left arm and made a lightening right hand jab to Slocum's nose. Blood sprayed out as Slocum roared with pain and shook his head. He charged Cody again. This time Cody side-stepped his rush but stuck his foot into Slocum's path. The enraged driver spilled face first on the ground. As he struggled to his feet Cody was ready. The combination left and right blows to Slocum's jaw turned his legs to rubber and he wilted down in a heap and stayed still.

The murmurs of the crowd grew in volume as it became evident that Slocum was out cold. The Pards had worked their way to the front of the crowd and now turned to watch for anyone who might want to take advantage of Cody while he was getting his breath back. But the murmurs turned to comments that they were glad that Slocum was put in his place as well as admiration for the quick and thorough job Cody had done.

Linklater raised his voice, "Look, we are really close to the pass. Now that this trouble is out of the way, we can mostly cross the pass tomorrow. Let's get at it so we can be in a good place if we need to fight the Border gang. Where's Gunnar?"

Gunnar Larson was a big broad-shouldered Swede who had been the blacksmith for the Linklater Trading Post. He had chosen to stick with Linklater and had equipped his own wagon as a mobile shop.

"Over here boss! I started coming as soon as I heard the wheel snap but your little commotion there held me up. I fix it pretty quick. Give me three or four helpers and we be on our way in a couple hours."

The Pards were delegated to be Gunnar's helpers. He quickly had them working like beavers. He sent Quinn to cut a sturdy fifteen foot tree trunk. Darcy and Jed got to fill a tub that Gunnar pulled out of his wagon with water. Cody helped Gunnar lift down a forge and an anvil. Next he brought out the coal that was tucked near the front of the wagon. Cody couldn't believe his eyes (rather his "eye" because the other one had swollen almost shut) as he glanced over all the specialized tools Gunnar had brought with him. Gunnar soon had a fire started under the coal. He put the bellows in Cody's hands and showed him how to bring the fire to its hottest temperature.

Before long Quinn was back with a log on his shoulder. He, Darcy and Jed found a couple of flat boulders they could wrestle into place as a fulcrum and, using the log, pried the corner of the wagon so the damaged wheel was off the ground. The freight wagon was so heavy it took all of Quinn's weight plus Darcy's to raise it. Jed quickly had the wheel off and the corner braced with no difficulty.

Once Gunnar assessed the damage on the wheel, he set Jed and Darcy to carving duplicate spokes for the two that had broken. Quinn got the task of carving a curved piece to replace the wood rim that the heavy metal rim circled. Cody stayed on the bellows as Gunnar bent to the task of straightening the rim. Soon the very foreign sound for this hidden valley of a hammer pounding on metal on an anvil filled the air. All the Pards admired the amazing skill that soon had the new spokes in place, the new section of wood rim spliced together and the restored metal rim ready for mounting. None of them would want that kind of work but they recognized and appreciated the craft that Gunnar showed.

Now with giant tongs holding the rim, the blacksmith heated the whole rim by turning it repeatedly in the cherry glow of the forge. Gunnar kept urging Cody to pump the bellows harder. Then, under the blacksmith's instructions, Quinn held the wheel ready as the hot rim was placed over the wood rim causing smoke to immediately furl out. He then plunged it into the tub of water, spinning it to immediately cool the whole wheel. When it was lifted out,the iron had shrunk to a perfect size to lock the wood parts of the wheel solidly together. It didn't take long for the wheel to be back on the freighter. The boys did let the weight come back on the repaired wheel rather gingerly, each hoping that the part they had whittled would hold. It was as good as new. Cody helped Gunnar cool the forge and repack his equipment in his wagon. As Cody bent to lift the unused coal into the wagon, he straightened up to find himself face to face with Slocum. At least he was pretty sure that the bruised and swollen face belonged to Slocum.

After a moment's pause, he spoke up, "Lad, I owe you an apology. The liquor got hold of me far more than I realized. You've beaten some sense back into my thick head. And here you are repairing my wagon. I didn't expect you would do me favours after the way I treated you. You may be young but you're a better man than me. Would you accept my hand?"

Cody took the proffered hand and said, "Yes, I would. We need each other to get all the way through this tight spot. Thank you for clearing this up right away."

The waggons moved out and were soon caught up to the progress the rest of the caravan had made.

THIRTY

The Border Patrol Gang rode confidently south along the Kootenay River anticipating an easy conquest of the caravan from Fort Linklater. Only Newt James harboured a sense of unease but he kept it to himself. He knew that something was out of order if the wagon train had not reached this point of their journey north.

The gang loped along at an easy pace, double checking their firearms as they went. Each one was savouring the loot they would scoop up. It would be like taking candy from a baby so that they would have a winter of eating, drinking and making merry.

Others besides Newt began to question what was happening when they still hadn't come upon the caravan by the next afternoon. Men glowered at Newt. Others threw questions at Morgan.

"Looks like we're chasing a fairy tale, Morgan!" "Where's these easy pickin's?" "How much riding we gonna do for nothing?" "Whose side is Newt James on?"

By this time Joe Morgan looked like a thunder storm about to burst. He pulled up his mount without any explanation, walked over to where Newt James sat his horse, reached up to grab James by his shirt and dragged him down to the ground. As his feet hit the ground Morgan's fist hit Newt's face. The pent up fury over not finding the Linklater wagon train funnelled itself into a devastating beating that left Newt crumpled on the ground.

Morgan, exhausted from his attack, stood panting to catch his breath.

"Get him up," he rasped between sucking gasps. A couple men hurried to lift James to his feet. Another poured water from a canteen over his head. Morgan again grabbed him by his shirt and held him just inches from his own face.

"You better come clean, James, or you're dead right here and now! Have you led us on a wild goose chase?"

Newt tried to focus in the midst of pain and through eyes that were rapidly swelling shut. His first words were mumbles that couldn't be understood. Morgan shook him and yelled at him to answer him. With huge effort Newt managed to look right at Morgan and spit out that he had not betrayed him in any way. He repeated what he had seen and heard just before he had left Fort Linklater. Beyond that he had no explanation for not finding any trace of their quarry.

Morgan threw James backward against his horse where he crumpled to the ground. The other men either stood around or sat their horses trying to avoid Morgan's glare. This was the way Morgan kept his men in line because they never knew when his fury would be suddenly directed at any one of them for no good reason. Beyond that his sheer size and physical strength intimidated the best of them.

After stomping around for a few minutes Morgan seemed to come to a decision.

"Listen, we've come this far we might as well ride on to the Fort. We'll at least get some hootch there and maybe find out something that makes sense about this caravan."

The Border Patrol Gang made sure everyone at the Fort knew that they had arrived. For some it was the ground trembling, for others it was the sound of pounding hooves. Some were so drunk that they didn't know the gang had arrived until the shooting started. They were only shooting into the air but by the time they had galloped a couple times around the Fort enclosure, scattering people in all directions, they had everyone's attention. The whole Fort area had taken on the atmosphere of an old fashioned "Rendezvous" at the peak of the fur trading era. Clusters of people were engaged in all kinds of entertainment from card games to axe throwing competitions to bare knuckle fights with lots of others betting on the outcomes. Linklater's farewell party was well underway!

"Listen up!" Morgan shouted, "We're tracking down some illegal border activities. Linklater has violated border regulations and he needs to be brought into line. Anyone who has information about his attempt to escape responsibility is required to bring it to us."

Off to one side, a cluster of men started laughing and one of them shouted, "you mean you want help robbing them!" Morgan immediately fired over their heads which put a full stop to any joshing.

"Now, where do we find something to cut the dust in our throats?"

Several men pointed toward a woodshed where free liquor was being doled out a cup at a time. As Morgan and his men moved in that direction the crowd parted like Moses going through the Red Sea. The man behind the chopping block held out a tin cup of whiskey to Morgan, which Morgan promptly slapped aside.

"Give me the jug!" Morgan demanded! "I'm not wasting time on tin cups!"

"But, but, but..... That's that's not f f f fair," The server spluttered!

Morgan bent down, pulled a knife from the top of his boot, and put it to the throat of the hapless man.

"I'll decide what's fair! Go ahead men," he roared, "this fair gentleman has saved a jug for each one of you!"

As the Border Patrol gangsters rushed to grab their jugs some murmurs of slurred complaint bubbled from the men who were close enough to know what was happening. Morgan turned and glared in the direction of the comments which was enough to bring a nervous silence over the onlookers.

An hour or so later, Newt James came walking up to where the gang was lounging around.

"James, you look like dog vomit! I should have killed you so I wouldn't have to look at your mangled face."

Morgan was obviously way into his liquor.

"Well, Joe, you'll be mighty glad you didn't do that." Newt spoke with a definite slur because of his swollen lips. "I was down at the river getting some cold water on my face and this old timer came wandering out of the bush. After some jawing back and forth, about how he's nervous around people and whether I would trade the pelts he has over his shoulder, he claims he knows how Linklater disappeared! He says that for the right price he'll show you."

Morgan squinted against the sun. "Does he have any idea what a mistake it is for him to make a fool out of me? Any old idiot can claim he has information and try to get something for nothing!"

"I warned him real good. I told him to just look at my face and to think carefully before I would come and talk to you. He says he would swear on a stack of Bibles and on his mother's grave! It might be the break we've been looking for."

"Well, bring him here. If his story doesn't hold up we'll make him dance for us! A few gunshots at his feet will give us all a good laugh!"

"Joe, I know this isn't what you want to hear, but he says his throat closes up if there are more than one or two people. He wants you to go to him!"

Morgan cursed, took another swig from his jug, and got to his feet after the third attempt. The old timer's name was Clint. With Morgan pushing him to speak faster, he got his story out.

He had been fishing in the area of the clay banks (hoodoos, he called them) when he heard the rumble of what turned out to be the Linklater caravan. It wasn't anything out of the ordinary to Clint at first. Over the years he had seen freight traffic increase on the Kootenay trail. It was his standard practice to stay out of sight and watch from a hideout. But this was no ordinary group of travellers. The noise and dust showed Clint that it was a huge collection of travellers, and well worth watching! To his amazement, the head of the caravan turned into one of the draws between a couple of the hoodoos. He knew this was a big catastrophe because all those ravines came to an end a little ways in. But this one kept swallowing the pack train very slowly but surely. The head of it never re-appeared. Clint had taken special note of the location of this ravine so that he could go back some day and see where it went.

Morgan scratched his head as he mentally searched for the holes in Clint's story.

"How come no one else has been talking about this cut in the clay banks and the traffic going in to it? Those waggons would leave some deep ruts in the clay that you would see if you were going by at a gallop!"

"Well I just couldn't believe that that caravan wouldn't be coming back out so I settled into a cave I knew of that was within sight of that entrance. At dusk a couple men came to the entrance and tried to scratch out their tracks. I knew it wouldn't be very good cover-up because of how deep those wheels had cut in. It didn't matter because that night there was a thunder storm to beat all thunder storms. A real gully-washer! God's honest truth, I've never seen so much rain come down in that amount of time. Water poured out of that ravine like the whole Kootenay River was coming through there. Next morning I walked over that ground and I could not pick out even one clue that a whole pack train had gone through there just the day before. God's honest truth!!!!"

Morgan scratched his head vigorously! Dust flew. His eyes came into focus. He stared at Clint.

"I would not want to be in your skin if you can't find that passage through the clay banks! But it's the only lead we have right now. Newt, he'll ride double with you."

The Border Patrol gang were a sorry looking collection of humanity as they drunkenly saddled up. Some took three or four attempts before they could get their saddles on their horses. Others fell over to the far side of their horses once they were saddled. Yet, with saddlebags replenished with free food at the Fort, they managed to be on their way, struggling to sit upright in their saddles, in half an hour. Morgan had fire in his eyes and hatred in his gut as he lashed his mount into a gallop. Linklater's outfit was making him look bad in his men's eyes so this had become a personal vendetta, to destroy Linklater and grab those valuable supplies.

Eventually Clint waved his arm to signal a stop. He pointed to a sharp ravine and declared that to be the secret entrance. Morgan pulled his horse around a second time, scanning the landscape.

"Doesn't look any different than a hundred others, mister! What makes this the one?"

"There's the cave I huddled in during that cloudburst!" pointing back to the right, "if you go inside there, you can only see that one hoodoo as you look out. They went in on this side of the column."

"Let's go see!"

The Border Patrol reined their horses toward the cut in the bank. The horses were nervous about the narrow passage and several shied. They turned the first corner and showed their surprise that, in fact, it opened to the left. Several more twists and they all started to believe that this was a passage through. Clint was breathing quieter. Another corner and curses sounded from the lead riders. A jumble of fallen trees blocked the path. Morgan immediately yelled at Clint that nobody, not even a single horse let alone a large pack-train with waggons, had gotten through on this path.

Clint felt panic rise up as he stared at the scene before him. But then he saw the answer.

"Mr. Morgan, those chips haven't weathered yet, They are all freshly fallen. Linklater's outfit must have brought them down to block you."

Morgan turned slowly to survey the downed trees once again. The logic of Clint's comments and the evidence before him settled in to overcome the rage that also boiled in him. Another block!! Would the frustrations never be over?

"Does anyone have an axe? Of course not! But we need axes. Newt, you take a couple of other riders with you and bring back axes and saws so we can clean this out. Go!!"

Newt wheeled his horse around and nodded to a couple of men at the back of the pack to come with him as he galloped past them. They turned and followed Newt as they made the fastest time through the twists and turns that they could.

"Hey!" Clint yelled in Newt's ear, "what about my payment for showing you the trail. Turn around so I can collect!

Without slowing at all, Newt yelled back at him, "You're alive! That's a big reward because Morgan never lets someone like you survive. He planned on killing you once you pointed out the trail. But it looked like he was so frustrated by the trees across the trail that he forgot about you. You're a lucky man!"

THRITY-ONE

The Linklater caravan had finally come to the last obstacle blocking their way back onto the Kootenay River trail. Almost everyone shook their heads in disbelief that they could possibly conquer this last challenge as they got their first detailed glimpses of what was ahead. It looked like this north end of Hidden Valley was completely blocked by mountain ridges and cliffs. There was a continuous stretch of sheer rock face about half way up the mountain in front of them that appeared to have no break at all.

"This is not looking good!" Darcy blurted to Cody as they rode side by side. "Looks like we're completely blocked. It's too bad to come this far and now have to abandon everything."

"Welllllll! Yeah! Unhuh!" Cody stumbled over his words as he looked at the scene ahead, but still didn't want to give in to Darcy's pessimism. He searched his mind for any glimmer of hope that he could use to counter what looked like disaster for their plan. "The creek is still running north so there must be some way out. Linklater hasn't let us down so far. Guess we'll have to wait till we get right up to that ridge."

Cody was thinking out loud as their mounts kept walking closer and closer. "Things often look more difficult than they really are when you get up to them. There's probably an easy route up here that only Linklater knows"

Darcy scoffed, "Cody, you are a dreamer and one of these times your dreams are going to get us into big trouble.!!"

"This isn't my dream, it's Linklater's!" Cody said defensively.

As they rounded a last twist in the trail that threaded through some sizable boulders they came out to the edge of a small meadow. The final challenge of Hidden Valley stood out in bold relief like a painting designed to give every detail of beauty and of impassibility. On the left was the last mountain of the range that separated Hidden Valley from the Kootenay Valley. It sloped east toward their location, but ended in a sharp and deep cleavage to the valley floor that provided the outlet for the creek. Everyone could see the water racing toward the crevice where it disappeared into a cloud of spray. The spray and the rushing sounds signalled a considerable waterfall that cut off any possible trail along the waterway. Cliffs on the right side of the river channel rose sharply from the water for at least a hundred feet. From there a ridge continued east. It showed a saddle formation at about two o'clock before it continued to elevate sharply joining into the mountain range that had framed the east side of Hidden Valley.

Linklater signalled for everyone to make camp and then, once the animals were loose to graze the meadow, to come together for a meeting.

Cody was expecting a lot of complaining when the whole crew was assembled in the shadow of their mountain obstacle. Surprisingly, there was a sense of expectation. Someone said it for all the others.

"Well Linklater, what surprise do you have for us this time?"

John blew air out of his lungs and started into his plan. "It sure feels like we're running out of time. But......by this time tomorrow we should be on the other side of that saddle. From there we can hold off the Border Patrol as long as we need to. We need to have guards watching our back trail all day as well as all night."

Linklater continued, "See these cliffs? They jut out from the main mountain and behind them we've found a switch back opening that will take us right up to that swayback ridge. There's a few trees and a few boulders to be cleared out."

"What about the waggons, John?" It was Slocum calling out the question. Cody wondered what would come next."

"Do we have to unload them or can we double team them and make it to the top?

It was a very reasonable question that included some alternatives. Slocum had really come through with a new attitude.

One of the men who had scouted the route with Linklater responded that double teaming the waggons was worth a try. Everyone knew that having to unload, pack the goods onto horses and people for several trips up and down and then reload the waggons on the other side would multiply the work and the time into a mammoth job.

Linklater got everyone's attention again, "Let's try to get one waggon to the top by nightfall. So, everyone grab a crowbar, an axe, a pick, a shovel. We'll make that route passable by the time the teamsters get harnessed and rolling up to us!"

There was a surprising chorus of shouts and enthusiasm. The prize of success was just one last mountain away and Linklater's assurance that there was, in fact, a way over the ridge was good enough for everyone there.

Jed had slipped away from his buddies while they were getting some tools from Gunnar. He showed up with a big grin on his face just as they were getting back on their horses to head to the slope.

Quinn scowled at him, "Jed, quit trying to get out of a little honest labour on these rocks! I saw another sledgehammer in Gunnar's wagon just waiting for you."

Jed teased back, "I feel sorry for you and your slave labour. I've been recruited for a much more important job!! Slocum asked me to help with harnessing the mules and then to ride the front left one to steer. Can you even imagine what we can haul with twelve mules at once?!"

With that Jed skipped away leaving his buddies staring after him.

"How does he do that?" Quinn wondered out loud. "He's just going to ride to the top while we break up rocks with sledgehammers!"

The Pards moved out to join the rest of the crew headed toward the base of the trail that would be their route to British territory and beyond the clutches of the Border Patrol gang. Everyone not involved with the mules and waggons divided into crews of five or six men with each group working on a short section of the trail. The air was filled with sounds of metal on stone, axes on trees and voices barking as the boys moved to the front of the work parties. Quinn had the biggest sledgehammer and started whaling on an outcrop of rock that jutted into the path. Cody and Darcy bent their efforts to rolling several boulders to the side of the path with crowbars.

A sudden sharp yell from Quinn got everyone looking up to where he was working. His sledgehammer blows had brought results. But once the outcrop gave way it started a slide of boulders that had been balanced on top. Cody and Darcy jumped out of the path of several huge rocks that rolled directly across the trail and crashed into the bushes below. One sizable boulder took a crazy bounce and started rolling downhill right at the men working there. People yelled warnings, dropped their tools and scattered in all directions. Finally the boulder veered off to the outside of the trail with a huge bounce that gave it considerable air time and then a spectacular crash on the cliff below. The only damage was a sledgehammer handle that was splintered into a million pieces. After a few derogatory comments shouted up to the Pards, everyone got back to work.

It seemed like the progress slowed considerably when they had to do a switchback. The problem was that it had to be big enough to make the turn with twelve mules in front of the wagon. Once the turn was made everyone was surprised at the width and gradual slope of the natural trail, like a sloping chimney, hidden behind the cliffs which towered on both sides. The crews moved quickly through this deep crevice in the mountain with only a few rocks to be moved aside. When they emerged on the far side they could see that, while it was still quite steep, the rest of the way to the top was mainly an alpine meadow.

Some of the crews continued working their way up the slope chopping off an occasional bush or rolling stones to the side. The Pards and others were sent down to shadow the freight wagon and to offer whatever help might be needed as the first trip up was attempted.

The air was filled with excited sounds of wranglers tussling the mules into a formation that was unusual to the animals. Drovers yelled at them and pushed and pulled until the long line began to take shape. Still the mules danced and pranced, tossing their heads up and down. The harnesses jangled as Jed skipped up onto the lead mule and Slocum climbed up to the high seat on the wagon. He grabbed up his bull whip and made it give a sharp crack above the heads of the first few mules. Jed gave a loud "hurrah" and smacked the rump of his mount as soon as he heard the whip. All twelve mules lunged forward into their harness. The wagon creaked and groaned but yielded readily to the massive pull of the dozen sturdy animals all headed for the freshly carved mountain road.

Progress was rapid until the team reached the start of the rise. The mules leaned into the harness as their muscles rippled to keep the wagon climbing. Jed could feel the power of the one he was riding and felt a thrill at that strength multiplied twelve times. He shouted encouragement as did Slocum. Men walked beside the wagon kicking aside an occasional rock that was directly in the path of a wheel. After a good steady pull, the mules needed a first break. Slocum yelled out to Jed to pull up and he set the brake as Jed pulled on the reins bringing the whole team to a stop. The mules blew out their breath, pranced a little and then quieted.

Slocum asked the men walking with the wagon to give it a heave to get it started rolling when the rest time was over. A couple of men went to each wheel and got ready to pull on the spokes while a dozen more took hold of whatever would give leverage as well as pushing on the back of the vehicle.

This process was repeated several times until they approached the hair-pin turn. What had seemed like a very large turning area when the men were clearing and extending it, now looked rather small in light of the space taken up by twelve mules in harness. They gave the mules an extra long blow while Slocum and Jed got down to plan out where the sweep of the team could extend as well as take note of the hazards. They agreed that they needed every inch of turning circumference in order to get the wagon around and to do that, they would have to bring the mules as close to the edge of the hundred foot drop off as possible without going over.

Jed walked at the head of his mount rather than riding as they carefully started into the circle. Everything was going well with the right hand lead mule looking sure-footed and confident on the very edge of the built up path. At the very moment Jed went to turn his animal further to the left, away from the precipice, the edge began to crumble where some of the fill had not settled firmly. That right hand mule let out a frightened bray, and its hooves began to flail as it began to sink towards the right. Jed felt his mule begin to yield to the weight of the struggling animal and instantly knew that the whole team was in peril. Icy cold fear gripped him. Slocum yelled for Jed to pull his mule's head to the left as well as forward at the same time he grabbed up his bull whip. He yelled at his team to keep going forward. His whip touched the back of the sixth mule on the right hand side which caused a huge surge along that side as all the mules did everything they could to avoid the sting of the whip.

Jed reefed on the head harness of his mule while he kept his legs churning backwards. His yells were intended to keep the animals from total panic. The right hand mule kept its legs churning seeking something solid. The combined surge forward and the heaving to the left gradually pulled the right lead animal back to solid ground. They kept the surge going until they had completely finished the turn and were pointed uphill in a straight line.

Slocum set the brake and yelled for the wheels to be blocked. Jed sank to the ground as the adrenalin rush ebbed away. The thoughts of what almost happened...the mental replay of twelve animals and the whole freight wagon spilling over the edge and smashing down onto boulders a hundred feet below just because he led them too close to the drop, left him weak and shaken. Slocum and the Pards rushed over to Jed.

"Jed, are you hurt? Did the hooves of the mules get you?"

Jed slowly shook his head, "No, I'm not injured! But I can't believe I brought the whole outfit that close to disaster!"

"No, no lad," Slocum spoke up, "You had them on the path we had agreed on. The bank gave way where we thought it was solid. In fact, you saved the day! If you hadn't responded the right way we were goners!!"

Cody noticed that the wranglers who were trailing the saddle horses for the return trip back down the mountain had moved up to check on the excitement. He waved them over.

"Jed, I'll grab a little food from your saddlebags. Let's take some time to eat and we'll all feel better for the push to the top."

THIRTY-TWO

Half an hour later they were ready to move again. Slocum climbed to his high seat on the freight wagon and Jed mounted his lead mule. With a flourish of the bull whip and "get up" shout from both Slocum and Jed, the parade moved ahead.

The huge crevasse that provided the continuing road towered so high that it seemed like they were entering a tunnel. The mules balked at the shadowed trail. Slocum called for some of the wranglers leading the saddle horses to go ahead so the mules could simply follow. The rest of the way to the top was steady hard work. However, no major obstacles appeared to halt their progress. By late afternoon the wagon creaked to a stop as they came over the last hump to where the ridge provided a wider than expected stopping area. Although all hands breathed a sigh of relief, it seemed that the men were too spent to do much celebrating.

It was dusk by the time everyone was back to the bottom of the mountain with the animals turned out to graze. It was a quiet meal. Soon the bedrolls had been laid out and the air filled with snoring. That same trip up and down would need to happen several times in the next day.

Dawn seemed to come far too quickly. The smell of coffee drifted over the camp thanks to the cook being up ahead of daylight. The wranglers were already herding the animals closer to camp where the piles of harness waited for them. Lots of grumbling and complaining soon indicated that sleep was finished and all they could do was drag themselves to the chuck wagon.

Now that the trail was known to be passable, the crew threw themselves into getting everything ready to go up the mountain on this day. Pack horses were loaded up. Smaller waggons were hitched to four horse teams rather than two horses. Some of these remuda horses hadn't been in harness for weeks and didn't take kindly to it, but the wranglers muscled them into cooperating.

It seemed like the mountain was alive that day. Waggons of different shapes and sizes were crawling up, sometimes waiting for extra help to get over the steepest parts. Animals and people coming back down, had to find spots that they could step off the trail while a loaded pack train or wagon crept on up the incline.

All the camp was finally loaded and the last supplies gathered on to a hay wagon that would be the last vehicle up the slope except for the cook and his helpers and their chuck wagon. It was time for one last noon meal at this camp. Some of the food would be carried up to the top so the last crews of the day making the climb up would not have to come back down.

The Pards, minus Jed, and others were just bringing their tin plates so they could take care of their immense hunger when the sound of a hard galloping horse coming towards their camp from the south grabbed their attention.

Cody spoke up, "That doesn't sound good. Something's wrong!"

Shouts began to sound out louder than the hoof beats.

"Riders coming! Get your guns! Border Patrol gang is coming at us!"

Food was forgotten in an instant. Tin plates clattered to the ground as men ran for their guns. Some how the gang had caught up to them. This would be the big showdown that the Linklater caravan had expected. They had set guards throughout their journey knowing that eventually it would pay off. There was no fear striking their gut reactions this time, just a sense that this was one more challenge coming across their path. They had learned to trust each other and to work together. All of that would pay off now as they ran to meet their enemy.

Cody yelled at the messenger, "How far back are they?"

The guard tried to still his horse so he could look at Cody but the mount was prancing from the excitement he sensed in his rider.

"I was on a high point so I could see their dust probably a mile or mile and a half. They are moving fast!"

"We'll head out to intercept them as soon as possible so we can hold them back from the camp. Go tell the others coming back from the mountain! Go!"

The other two had their horses saddled and were holding Cody's horse as he grabbed up his saddle and threw it on his mount. Saddle bags loaded with ammunition supplies were thrown on as well. All their horses knew the urgency in the voices of their riders and sprang into a full gallop as soon as the reins were loosened.

"Watch for the first sign of them so we can get behind some boulders!" Cody yelled to his mates.

"Keep your heads down in case they get the first shot!" Darcy shouted out.

They could see the dust cloud of the approaching villains and knew they were also kicking up a dust cloud which was made larger by the others of their crew that were coming up behind them. There was nothing secretive about this. The two groups were heading straight into an all out battle. The Border Patrol gang was determined to eliminate anyone standing in their way of the riches of the Linklater trade goods. The Linklater crew was just as determined that they would not give any quarter to murderers and thieves.

The Pards raced to the lead of the crew members that had happened to be in camp at the time of the guard warning them. Their pulses were racing. They would have to take a strategic stand for the whole caravan. The excitement of the coming challenge retained only visions of glory in their young minds. In their anticipation there was no room for worry over the danger ahead. The terrain between them and the gang was well known to the Pards which gave a big advantage as they knew where the big boulders would give them great cover for repelling the coming attack.

The dust cloud of the onrushing gang loomed toward them until it seemed they would clash right on the trail. Cody watched intently, remembering a particular cluster of wagon size boulders that would give superior advantage. At seemingly the last minute he waved his arm vigorously and yelled out.

"This is it! Take both sides!"

Horses skidded to a stop as riders sawed back on the reins. Men bailed off their mounts and gave them a slap to send them back the way they had come which caused mayhem until the last horses freed of riders got turned around and led the herd back to the camp.

Guns bristled on top of huge rocks ready for the first appearance of the enemy. The first Border Patrol rider rounded a corner and immediately fired the pistol held in his hand at the same time he yanked his reins. His horse skidded to a stop and reared, tumbling the rider backwards onto the ground. Gunfire erupted from both sides as the hapless gangster scrambled on all fours behind a boulder and then got back to his mates.

After the first flurry of lead balls being shot indiscriminately, the gunfire exchange slowed down as long guns had to be reloaded. A black cloud of burnt gun powder replaced the cloud of dust and stung the eyes of the fighters. Linklater's men began to slip from one boulder to another to get to the sides of the enemy. Their firing from their new positions began to press the gang back. Quinn ducked as a lead ball pinged off a boulder beside him.

"Ouch!" He yelped as a shard of the rock clipped his cheek.

"Are you hit bad" Cody called to him.

"I'm not sure! Must not be bad if I'm talking to you, right?"

"Guess so. Where are you hit?"

"Just on my cheek. The slug just knocked some of the rock at me."

The shooting had settled down into a slower rhythm as rifles and six shooters had to be reloaded on both sides.

Darcy called from the far side of the trail, "I think they're falling back. Should we move forward?"

"Better wait till Linklater gets here. He'll know what has to happen up on the mountain before we can move one way or the other," Cody responded.

"Linklater!!" The voice boomed from the gangsters. "Where's Linklater? Probably hiding up on the mountain trying to think up another disappearing trick. Well you can't hide any more! You have to surrender to the Border Patrol."

The Pards answered with a volley of shots. The battle was at a stand off until one side or the other made a move. The sound of rapid hoof beats signalled the arrival of someone from the caravan. It was Linklater. He dismounted when he got to the first of the defenders. Then the men from his crew that were hunkered behind protection motioned him forward until he found Cody and Quinn. They quickly brought him up to date.

"Morgan! Is that you trying to act like you've got some kind of authority?" John yelled across.

"Linklater, our guns are our authority and you will surrender to me one way or the other. Just turn over your goods now and we might let you save yourself by hiking over the mountain. Other wise you'll all die here in the rocks!"

John called back, "Morgan you should check out your situation better before you make big claims. You and your men don't have a hope of taking anything from us. You're the ones who should surrender or just turn around and go back to your caves."

"If that's the way you want it," Joe Morgan replied, "Here we come! Let'em have it boys!"

A blizzard of shooting erupted and some of the gang started darting from boulder to boulder as they advanced toward their quarry. The caravan crew had come to full alert as they heard the exchange between the two leaders. They were zeroed in from good vantage points that gave them the means to take careful aim.

Once again the cloud of spent gun powder rose from the battlefield. Mixed in with the roar of gunfire were several screams and yells of pain from the gangsters. The shooting stopped almost as rapidly as it had begun. Voices calling out that they were hit and down told the tale that the gangsters had taken a big hit trying to over-power the Hudson Bay crew. The silence of a standoff settled back over the battlefield.

John huddled with the Pards to talk over their situation. Darcy spoke up, "We're holding them good for now but now they know they can't just roll over us they'll be looking for other ways to get the advantage."

"I agree that we can't just stay put and expect to keep the upper hand. We're pretty much packed up at the camp. Just the chuckwaggon and a hay wagon yet to go up the trail. As they go up, we can do a steady retreat. I'm thinking that where that cliff has split out from the mountain would be a good place for taking our big stand. There's great cover just beyond that spot and there is no other way except to come through that crevice. What do you think?"

Linklater looked to each of the Pards to get their nod of agreement with his plan.

As Cody added his final nod he said, "There will be a bright moon tonight so we'll be able to hold them at that gap all night and as long as we need tomorrow."

John shook his head, "I hope they give up once they see how narrow that gap is so we can have every one available to get the waggons down that steep far side tomorrow."

"I don't think those guys are going to quit for anything. They sound really mad that we've fooled them this far," commented Darcy.

The pull back went as planned. Linklater's men were able to hold the bandits at bay while the last waggons moved up the mountain trail. It irked the gangsters that they could see the vehicles but that they couldn't get within the range of their rifles. There was only sporadic firing, often as one or two of Morgan's crew would get impatient and would be briefly exposed as they scuttled to another position to try to find a way forward.

As the Linklater crew leapfrogged back by dividing into three groupings, the Morgan gang kept the pressure on them by moving up as soon as some space permitted. The gang, at first, assumed that they were gaining ground but soon realized that they were only moving as much as the caravaners gave them. When they backed their way through the campsite, Cody noticed that others of their crew had made sure there were some critical supplies waiting for them.

"Jed," Cody called softly to him, "Check that pile of things behind you. Looks like saddlebags that hopefully have powder and shot in them."

Jed quickly distributed the supplies so that everyone was well equipped for starting their backwards journey up the mountain. The planned retreat went more quickly as they began the steep ascent. Good places to take cover were not as plentiful so the relays had to be made in rapid and longer sprints.

Before long they were at the switchback and shooting down on the enemy. That kept the gang pinned allowing everyone to get around the switchback and through the split in the cliffs. This gave them time to settle in to great protection to blanket the exit from the narrow opening. The cook sent food and canteens down for them in case it turned into an all night stand.

Linklater cautiously crept up to the hideout where the Pards were ensconced. Just as he arrived, Quinn fired a shot at the first head that poked around the edge of the cliff. A couple more shots blitzed the opening sending a message that there was no way through the protection the caravan crew had established.

"This is great, really secure," said Linklater, "But we can't just sit here forever. Who knows how long they can hold out? It'll depend on what food they happened to bring with them. They will count on us being anxious to continue to move on, which I am."

Suddenly Quinn spoke up, "I've got an idea. John, can I borrow your horse?"

When he nodded agreement Quinn simply said, "I'll be back as soon as I can."

The Pards looked at each other with questioning looks. It wasn't like Quinn to have an idea all on his own without checking it out with the others and especially not like him to act on something with such speed. With no other ideas coming forward as to how to eliminate this stand off, everyone hunkered down to wait for Quinn to return.

Time dragged. It seemed a very long time and nothing was heard of Quinn. An occasional shot erupted as a body appeared around the cliff edge or the gangsters fired a shot towards the defence line, seemingly just out of frustration.

Like a sudden boom of thunder, Quinn's voice, from up above, roared out over the mountain side. "Get back from the cliff's or die! It's coming down!"

Everyone jumped. After a moment of shock, those closest to the opening in the cliffs started to run uphill. They kept in a crouch as they ran in case one of the bandits was foolish enough to still be in the pass looking for a desperation shot.

A huge flash and roar erupted from the precipice above the split in the cliff. It was as if a volcano had suddenly blown it's top! Black smoke billowed out from the source. A rumble started to grow as a rock slide started to follow the initial house size boulder ejected by the blast. Dust continued to blossom as a huge swath of mountain side tumbled down into the cleft where the trail was disappearing. It seemed the slide would never stop but gradually the deafening noise subsided and left the whole crew in awe at what they had just seen.

Jed was the first to move, "Where's Quinn? Can you see Quinn? We have to find him! Maybe the blast was bigger than he expected."

They all peered up at the thinning dust cloud. "What are you all expecting to see up there?"

An apparition called from behind them. All they could see was a totally black face with whites of his eyes almost glowing above a big white-toothed grin. His clothes showed a few rips and were covered in dust.

"It blew sideways a little more than I expected and tumbled me back a little. But wasn't that a great ka-boom?!!"

His laugh soon had everyone else that had gathered around him laughing. The realization was sinking in that his "bomb" had totally blocked the Border Patrol gang from any possibility of any further attack. The cleft in the mountain side was completely filled in with huge boulders and debris. His mates began clapping him on his back, congratulating him, giving him cheers. He finally had to admit that he was somewhat hurting and that it would be nice if they didn't get quite so physical in their excitement.

Cheering spread up the mountain side as the news was passed along that the Border Patrol Gang was completely blocked. It took some minutes for the realization to sink in that the pressure and tension of these past days having to function under the constant threat that a deadly attack could come at any time was wiped out.

"Quinn, where did you get the idea to start a rock slide," chuckled Cody, "I can't believe how well that worked."

Quinn was becoming more like his shy self as the adrenalin rush subsided and he stopped trembling.

"Ah, it just popped into my head. I didn't know if it would really work or not."

"Come on, Quinn, none of the rest of us had any ideas to solve the stalemate. You did it. Tell us about it."

"Well, once when my Dad was roaring drunk he was frustrated by a stump in our yard that he had been digging at for a long time. He got a cask of gunpowder and put it under that stump. Part of the stump went through the roof of our house! The roof leaked all winter so we could never forget what the gunpowder had done. Then when we were clearing the trail up here and that big boulder gave way and almost killed people, I looked a little more closely and could tell that there was a big overhang that was ready to give way if it had a little help."

"How did you know how much gunpowder to use?" Darcy asked.

"I didn't know how much to use," Quinn shrugged, "but I remembered seeing a pack-horse go by with a cask on it's load. When I got up to it, it was tied to another cask slung over the horse. I didn't want to take time to separate them so I just took them both. Do you think I wasted the extra cask?

Quinn looked quite concerned. The others erupted in laughter.

"Quinn, with the results you got for us you can have as much gunpowder as you ever want!!"

Quinn settled back with a contented smile. "It was a pretty great blast, wasn't it!!!"

As the day drew to a close, clusters of the Linklater crew lingered where they could see from the top of the mountain down to the valley floor where the Border Patrol gang were milling about. They couldn't believe that they were completely blocked from pursuing their quarry. While an individual might climb over the rock slide, it was impossible for a horse. And the Border Patrol were not about to become hikers. Every once in a while one of them, in frustration, would fire a gun in the direction of the spectators even though they were far out of range. Some of the gang were already riding south to get out of Hidden Valley.

THIRTY-THREE

Camp that night was a very happy place with lots of conversation. Men talked the events of the day over and over along with other stories triggered by all that had happened. Quinn was the undisputed hero and the tales of his exploits had grown considerably by the time everyone settled for the night. Linklater posted night watchmen although they didn't expect any intruders. They knew it was impossible for a horse to get over the rock slide and no gangster would climb over on foot just to get revenge. So the whole crew enjoyed settling down for the night pushing the problems of getting down the far side of the mountain off for the next day.

That night each of the Pards had dreamy thoughts tumble around their minds. With the pressure off from a murderous gang tracking them down, they once again turned their relaxing images to what life might be in the future.

Jed wondered what he might do with a remuda of fine thorough-breds and a few freight waggons. Riding up the mountain at the lead of a twelve mule team had given him a sense of what could be accomplished with the right animals and right equipment. He would have the finest outfit in the west. Merchants and contractors would know that they could count on "Jed's Freighting Company."

Quinn couldn't help revelling some more in the heroism he had been treated to that day and imagining what great exploits he would do in the future on the side of good rather than evil. He had never before experienced such a contrast from the derogatory slum of Montreal to the affirmation of these rugged peers in the wilderness. A new hunger was awakening in Quinn.

Darcy had never felt such pure relief. Being under threat for days on end had taken a big toll and now that the threat was removed he realized what a weight he had carried. His imagination carried him to a pleasant setting of good friends, laughter, food and music. A roadhouse! Yes, that would be ideal. He had some exotic recipes from his mixed parentage that would be sure to attract a wide clientele. Then another image of light-hearted loveliness floated into this vision. The laughter and spryness soon evolved into a grown up Maria and a smile stayed on Darcy's face as he drifted to sleep.

Cody knew that he was living life to the full. Everything he had experienced in this western wilderness brought a craving for more. There was nothing like working with a man like John Linklater. Together they had led this caravan through huge obstacles and had moulded a miscellaneous collection of men into a skilled crew working together to accomplish a great goal. Cody knew that he would do more in setting big goals and leading people to accomplish them. Then his sleepy mind brought up a pretty vision of a dark haired beauty. His heart responded with yearning as Sophie resolved out of the haze of sleepiness. Someday he would crave an intimate life-long union with this woman who seemed to understand him from the inside out. The twist that kept question marks over this dream was the very kind of future Cody was now anticipating. He wasn't ready to hold himself back by having to always consider a second person's welfare in every decision he made. Would he lose Sophie because he wouldn't settle down now? It was the only shadow on a very exciting future in this primitive, awakening paradise.

Breakfast brought about a relaxed buzz among the men. They were more than ready to start their descent onto the Kootenay trail and regain British territory.

Cody squatted beside John Linklater with their heaped plates and steaming coffee.

"John, what's ahead of us today," Cody asked conversationally. John's answer presented a new challenge that the Pards had never faced before.

"Once we get down through a stretch of scattered large trees, we're going to hit a patch of scree that will take a bit of manoeuvring. But beyond that it is open alpine meadows sloping down to the river. Should be all done in one day."

Cody nodded agreeably because Linklater had made it sound easy. "You've used a new word, John! What's scree?"

"Well, it's like a fairly steep rock slide but it's all small rocks mixed in with soil. For every step you take you slide another one."

Cody groaned, "John, you say those words easily but if I hear you right we're not going to just ride down that stuff you call scree."

"Just another new exciting part of learning to live in these mountains!!" Linklater laughed as he got up to get things started for the day.

It certainly was a new problem to be solved. The descent through the forest section went well. The process of clearing a trail was very familiar to the crew. So a path quickly developed with the men bending its course to take advantage of natural level spots for turns and finding the open avenues to minimize tree cutting. In fact the forest filled with the sounds of men carrying on conversations over the sounds of saws, axes, hammers, harness and animals. Everyone had the freedom to enjoy the good hard labour on a beautiful day in a spectacular setting with the pressure of the Border Patrol eliminated.

The mood changed noticeably as the path clearing crew reached the edge of the scree. One by one the first men to come to the last of the trees took a few hesitant steps onto the loose debris. Every step they took resulted in another foot or two slide nearly sending them off balance. Shaking their heads, they all wondered what would come next. An older member of that advance crew recalled hearing stories of horses and waggons tumbling down such steep loose mountain sides killing drivers and animals along with waggons being smashed to smithereens. Gloom was spreading back up the mountain as John and the Pards headed for the problem area.

"Alright, boys!" Linklater called out. "We'll walk some pack ponies down this little stretch to get the feel of it and then we'll do the waggons. Without any doubt all that rope we've brought along will be needed. Jed, you follow me with one of the mules. Maybe we'll learn something by seeing what a mule does compared to a horse."

Both the pack-horse and the mule gave loud protests as they were led out onto the loose footing. By careful angles and slow steps, scrambling with flailing hooves when the loose soil gave way, the animals made their way to the bottom and onto stable ground. The two men then found a footpath back up off to the side of the scree where there was a mix of rock outcroppings, and trees.

Cody walked over to Jed. "What is it like? Do you think we'll get everything down safely?"

"It's risky! There were a couple times my heart was in my throat cause I thought the hill side would keep giving way and the mule would be over the lip of the cliff on the right side of the slide." responded Jed. "Once you catch on that each step will only slide a foot or so you can make better progress."

"But what about the waggons?" Darcy asked. "Do you think we'll be able to get them down safe?"

Jed shook his head, "I'm glad I'm a pack horse guy and don't have to deal with that mess. You guys are on your own. At least the animals can scramble back up, whereas those waggons are just dead weight and that lip of the drop off gets scary close about half way down. Good luck!!"

Jed headed off to organize the guys available to load the pack-horses and work them down the hillside.

The rest of the Pards sought out Linklater to start working out the challenge of loaded waggons traversing the exact opposite of where waggons would follow the natural slope.

"Let's move all the waggons right up to the lip of the soft ground. Make sure you set the brake and block the wheels before you take the mules and horses out of the shafts." Linklater waved the mule drivers and wranglers onto that job.

"Cody, I need you to get a crew to tie off long lengths of rope to trees or rocks that we can pay out or snub as we need to, so the waggons will angle to the left to the flat bottom at the end of the scree."

"Quinn, we need a good size tree cut and tied to the back of each of the heaviest waggons to act as a drag brake just after they go over the edge and start down the steepest part. Take the men you need."

A flurry of activity followed these instructions. Men were glad to be assigned manual work towards getting the caravan down the mountain because it looked like an impossible task. They were glad to leave coming up with a successful plan to someone else.

An hour later the moment of truth arrived. The waggons were poised at the lip of the drop onto the scree. Men stood ready with the ropes so they could respond in an instant to commands from John. Stationed at every wheel on the first wagon was a crew member ready to pull the wheel blocks while Slocum was positioned to release the brake.

"Let'er roll!" called out Linklater.

The wagon creaked slowly forward as the brake and blocks were released and the ropes began to pay out. Its speed changed in an instant. The vehicle shot forward, the chain snapped taut as the drag tree catapulted over the lip and dug into the scree, causing the wagon to slew crazily from side to side. Dust billowed from all parts of the apparatus which looked to be speeding for a rock-face that would smash everything. Rope screamed through gloved hands and around the trees stripping bark in a flash. Linklater shouted for the ropes at the back to be snubbed. Even as that was being done , he yelled for the ropes to the front to be snubbed next. The wagon slowed and turned sideways but looked to be stretching rope to the breaking point. At a moment of truth the near side wheels of the conveyance left the ground and teetered....would the far wheels hold, would it tip or fall back . Time stood still, everyone paused to watch....then the wagon settled back on all four wheels, dust slowly settled to show that, in fact, it was pointed in just the right direction to be rolled ahead onto solid and relatively level ground. It took only a short time for the ropes to be manipulated, after the drag tree had been unchained, so that the wagon rolled to safe ground.

Lessons and experience gained from that first plummet down the stretch of scree turned the crew into an efficient work force for roping heavy waggons down the loose slope. None of the later waggons descended as quickly as the first. The task went from drama to simple hard work. At the late evening meal, as the men talked over their exploits of the day, great admiration for John Linklater's planning and leading could be heard in bits and pieces coming from the various clusters of workers. Including the group hanging around the chuckwaggon after the meal to get some bacon grease to soothe burns where ropes had worn right through gloves.

As everyone was settling down in the growing dusk, a rider who had been scouting ahead came back in a hurry.

"Hey, men!" he called out, excitement in his voice. "I saw campfires down below! It's the Kootenay Trail! We'll be on it tomorrow!"

Exclamations sounded from all parts of the camp. This was the target they had been working towards! Success was one day away.

Cody raised his voice with a question. "You said fires?"

"Yes, sir!!"

"How many?"

"Oh, probably half a dozen."

"Was it an Indian band, one of their temporary villages?"

"No, the fires were scattered. Spread out along the river."

"Hey John, doesn't that sound pretty strange. That many camps in this area?

Linklater mused, "Does sound strange. Guess we'll find out tomorrow. Let's double the lookouts for tonight. Going to be an interesting day coming up."

THIRTY-FOUR

It only took half a day to get the whole caravan the rest of the way down the mountain onto the Kootenay Trail. Everyone was experienced in their own role which made for great efficiency in moving the pack train along virgin road. Even so the Kootenay Trail looked like a broad highway to Linklater and his crew. They looked forward to the novelty of travelling on an existing road.

What the campfires had shown to them the previous night became evident as soon as they were within sight of the river and its companion trail. Several travellers could be seen at the same time. There were small knots of men walking together as well as solitary hikers. Some had a pack animal but most simply had a pack on their back.

The caravan was a novelty that drew a cluster of the curious as it emerged from the forest to join the main trail. The number of travellers was beyond anything ever seen in this wilderness setting. Questions flooded back and forth about who, what, where, and when, but nothing of substance came from the jumble of voices. Words like bonanza, gold, and claims floated to the surface grabbing the curiosity of the newcomers.

"What's going on? Where are you headed?" Called out Linklater as they came up to the first threesome.

"I should ask you," one of the men responded, "Where have you been hiding that you don't know the biggest news of all? Gold, man!! There's the biggest gold strike ever found up on the Kootenay River. Stud Creek is the place to go. There's nuggets just laying in the creeks waiting to be picked up. Everyone is going to get rich if we get there soon enough."

The Pards looked at each other in amazement. Their world had suddenly changed beyond their imagination. Riches waiting to be picked up out of creeks? Could it be? They could get there faster than all these men on foot. Should they make a dash for it? Get there early and fill their pockets? Linklater would understand wouldn't he? It was the chance of a lifetime!

They could feel the fever! They had heard of gold fever and scoffed at it. Right now it was a powerful force invading their minds. Heart beats went rapid.

Darcy spoke as if in a trance, his eyes unfocused, "I think it's a sign for our future! Here we are, at this precise moment in time, thousands of miles from where we ever expected, all our circumstances coming together so that we can race up there in a few days and make our fortune. We can be wealthy. No one will call me 'chink' again. I can be king of my own life."

"Yeah!" Quinn breathed out. "I could buy a big house right in Montreal that I would own so that no landlord could throw me out in the middle of winter. People would call me 'mister' instead of crossing the street, shaking their heads and talking behind their hands when they see me coming."

For a few minutes Cody's mental pictures rotated from expensive clothes, to Sophie in a mansion, to him as a politician....then he gave himself a shake and said, "Wait guys, we can't just run off on our own. We've got an obligation to John Linklater. We've got to get this caravan to Joseph's Prairie. We've got to bring those crooks at Kootenay House to account. That's what we're here for."

Darcy turned on Cody and blasted him, "There you go again telling us what we can and can't do. Well you can't stop us. You're not going to pull rank on us to make us do what you want regardless of what we want this time. It's a free country out here, Cody, so back off!"

"Yeah, Cody, back off!" Quinn parroted Darcy. "I'm with Darcy and we're going to be wealthy. You'll be sorry you don't jump at this chance."

"Hey guys, I just think there's more than one side to this kind of thing. We've worked everything out together all the way. Don't let some sudden wild goose chase rip up the Pards." Cody tried to pull their minds out of the fever.

"Pards! Pards! Pards! Come on Cody, that's for kids, we're men now and we can recognize a gift when it falls into our laps like this. This is when it's every man for himself!"

Darcy's words cut deep and were hurtful even as they showed the power of the glitter of gold. Cody's heart sank as Darcy and Quinn turned their backs and led their horses to the far side of the caravan seemingly determined to strike out to make their fortune. Cody alternated between anger and crushing sadness. Anger that an invader had come to destroy their comradeship and sadness that his best friends were showing their backs over an argument about money.

"What about you, Jed? You heard them. Are you going to go chasing gold that may or may not be there?" Cody's voice had a bitter edge to it.

Jed was quiet for a bit. His mind tumbled and churned with a lot of thoughts and feelings. The words came slowly when he spoke.

"I was simply seen as a problem when I was born. The thirteenth to feed and clothe. Nobody wanted me. Always told me to get out of the way. I found my gold when I found the Pards, when I found horses. Here I'm wanted. Here I'm good at something. It's too much to throw away. I'll not be going."

Linklater walked up to them, "I thought I heard yelling. Something going on?"

Cody brought him up to date. He continued, "I have to admit, my first thoughts were about making a dash for the glitter. We could pass a lot of these people when we're on horse back, but then I thought about how many other people are headed there from all directions. Then I thought about what we need to do here. About our commission from the Hudson Bay."

Cody paused, "But how could I lose two buddies that quick over something they don't even have yet?"

"I've seen it before, Cody," Linklater said. "Even more I've seen the results. Very few actually find gold, fewer keep what they find, and most leave with less than they had. It really does start as a fever but it chills out pretty fast. I think your friends will be back sooner or later and my guess is they'll have their tails between their legs!"

With a shrug Cody said, "I just hope they make it back."

Darcy and Quinn, having thrown a few things into their saddle bags, galloped away from the pack-train as if escaping from jail. Their excitement was at a fever pitch. All they could think about was dashing through the line of plodding prospectors to find the creeks that held the future of their dreams. As their horses settled into a steady lope, they kept reassuring one another that they were doing the right thing.

"Cody and Jed are sure going to be sorry they didn't come with us!" laughed Quinn.

"You better believe it! Oh, we can share a nugget or two with them out of our treasure chest!" chuckled Darcy. "I feel sorry for them – missing out like they are. Amazing that they didn't jump at a chance like this! Man, this is living!"

"Yeah, their fault now that they have a few extra pack horses to look after!" Quinn offered.

"Ah, don't worry about about them. After getting over that mountain pass they were going to have too easy a time. The extra horses will just keep them busy to make the days go faster."

They got mostly cheerful comments from the men they passed. It seemed that they were all living the same dream and that they assumed there would be enough gold for all of them. Occasionally someone would jokingly offer to trade a donkey for one of their horses - "better suited for packing out the gold!" There were a few offers to buy food from them when people saw their bulging saddle bags. It seemed that small game had already been thinned considerably and big game was beyond the reach of miners with pickaxes. Food was becoming a serious commodity to the travellers, some of whom had been hiking for a week and had only what they could carry on their backs by way of food and possessions.

Late afternoon Quinn was the first to mention food for themselves. "What do you think about making camp, Darcy? I'm getting pretty hungry!"

"Ah, Quinn, you're always hungry. Don't you think we should go a little farther – there's lot's of people picking up gold as we speak? We want to get there before it's all gone."

They pushed on until dusk was settling in. Finally Darcy agreed to stop in a grove of cottonwoods nicely set back from the trail. It was considerably darker under the trees so they came back out to the edge of the grove and picketed their mounts close to where they would build their fire.

"I'll go find firewood, if you want to get our meal ready." offered Quinn.

"Alright, I'll see what we have in our saddlebags." Darcy responded willingly.

Quinn discovered that the easy firewood had been picked pretty clear by other campers so he had to scour farther back into the forest. He finally had to break dead branches from the lower part of some pine trees to get enough wood to boil their coffee. His size allowed him to reach branches that were just out of the reach of the average person. It was almost fully dark when he got back to their camp.

Darcy was upset. Quinn could tell by his voice even through he couldn't see the expression on his face.

"What's the matter with you, Quinn? Don't you know enough to pack food when we're heading out on a long ride?"

"That wasn't my job?"

"Yes, it was."

"You never said so!"

"I didn't have to say so. I was busy getting the tools we brought so we can work the gravel."

Quinn paused. He slowly realized the implication of what Darcy was saying and Quinn, in turn, began to get riled. "You're telling me that we don't have any food?" Quinn's voice got louder as he started toward Darcy. "You didn't pack any either. And you're trying to blame me?"

Darcy backed down quickly as he heard the temper rising in Quinn. "Ok, Ok, we both should have thought about it. All we've got is a little pemmican and a little coffee in each of our bags. We'll have to settle for that for tonight and then see what we can scrounge tomorrow. Where's your lucifers so we can put some coffee to boil?

"Lucifers? I don't carry lucifers with me! Cook always has that kind of thing. Now, I suppose in your great excitement to get us on the trail to our gold bonanza you didn't even bring a flint with you? Aren't you a great leader!"

"Shut up! You chose to come. I didn't make you. It's as much up to you to have stuff as it is for me."

Angry with each other, they sat silent with a good distance between them, finishing off the pemmican and drinking cold water trying not to think about the fat from the pemmican coating the roof of their mouths. Neither of them had any plan for the next day.

Meanwhile, the pack-train had gotten underway again. It took some extra time to get ready to move while Cody and Jed checked over the horses Darcy and Quinn had been looking after. Cody kept up an internal argument with the two that had left. His anger at their desertion growing as he listed all the ways that what they were doing was wrong. But then he couldn't help thinking back over the years they had hung out together which just left him feeling empty that it had come to this kind of conclusion. He hoped John was right – that they would come back – even though he stored up some things he would have to say to them.

Jed handled his sense of anger and loss by chattering while checking the rigging on his extra horses. "Do you really think they're gone, Cody? Maybe they'll turn around and be back by supper. I can't believe they'd just take off like that, we always talk things over as a foursome."

Cody wished Jed would keep quiet and just let him stew in silence. Yet he had come to realize that Jed had to put things into words so he let him go on without feeling that he had to answer everything. When Jed seemed to be running out of steam, Cody responded to his questions as a whole.

"Seems like we've run into something brand new in this 'gold fever.' We'll just have to ride it out for now. I've been so sure that our friendship is stronger than anything that tries to rip us apart. Guess this is the big test."

What should have been a celebration stretch of travel because of escaping the Border Patrol Gang and being back on the Kootenay Trail inside British territory was definitely clouded over by the desertion of Darcy and Quinn. It was a gloomy bunch of trail riders that made camp that night as Cody's mood was so dark that it infected all the others.

THIRTY-FIVE

Much farther up the trail, as darkness was descending, Darcy and Quinn were trying to imagine themselves with full stomachs and a warm fire boiling a final pot of coffee for the night. The more they imagined and talked about it the worse they felt. Darkness had fully settled over them. And their stomachs growled as their hunger kept growing. Their voices became softer even though there was no one around to overhear them. It just seemed that the night was pressing down on them.

"Darcy!," Quinn was almost whispering. "Look off to the north east. Is that a campfire or are my eyes playing tricks?"

"I can't see any camp fire. Wait!" Darcy shifted to the side a little. "Yeah, I think you're right. Hey, we could get some coals from them and if nothing else be able to have our own fire to stay warm and make coffee. Do you think we should go check it out?"

"It would be something to do besides just sitting here feeling miserable. Do you think we might be able to get a little food from them? I'd give anything for some bacon and biscuits."

Darcy groaned, "Don't even mention food like that. I'd settle for some week old bread. Let's go!"

"What if they're bad guys?" Quinn's voice was a little hesitant. "Maybe we should creep up and watch them for a bit before we talk to them. There's enough of a moon tonight that we could make our way through the trees without letting them know we're there."

"The good thing is that we're down wind. Their horses won't be able to smell us. You'll have to be a lot quieter than what you usually are."

Quinn grimaced, "Just because I'm big doesn't mean I can't move quietly. Especially this time when there is food involved."

The two of them moved out. At first they crept along on tip toes but soon realized that the fire was much further off than they had thought. So they hiked along the trail until it was time to slip in among the scattered trees and then even further to the east until they were moving silently through some underbrush.

The boys slowed their progress to a crawl in their carefulness not to reveal their presence to whomever was at the camp. Then a new aroma caught their attention. In unison both of them lifted their noses to catch more of this very attractive smell. Roasting meat! Vivid images of roast chicken danced before their eyes. It was so compelling it took huge self-control not to stand and march right in begging to share their bounty.

About the same time the aroma had reached them the sound of voices also became clear. Rowdy voices that signalled that, indeed, caution would be advised. The men were obviously drunk. They were alternately arguing, laughing and singing. They were creating such a ruckus that Darcy and Quinn didn't need to be nearly so careful about their own sounds as they moved close enough to peer through the bushes into the camp site.

They could see three men, even though they had expected more given the noise they were generating. All of them were dressed in dark tattered buckskin clothes that looked covered with dirt and grease. Gear was strewn helterskelter. A jug was being passed around continuously as one after another would stand up and attempt to sing another verse of their nonsense song while staggering around the fire. Once in a while one of them would check the makeshift spit where two rabbits were being roasted. Darcy and Quinn cringed as they noticed parts of the rabbits charring while other spots were still rare. They wanted some of that rabbit meat but were very unsure about making themselves known to this unsavoury trio.

Their choice was suddenly taken away from them. Quinn shifted his position slightly and firelight reflected off the metal buttons of his coat. The drunk who was singing at the moment saw the glint of four buttons and yelled a warning. With amazing speed, given their level of intoxication, a musket and two knives were poised to do serious harm to the young men.

"Get yourselves in here, ya varmints! I'll blast you to smithereens if'n you make one wrong move!"

The man was weaving as he spat this out. He looked like he might pull the trigger at any moment whether he intended to or not. Darcy and Quinn threw their hands in the air and stepped into the firelight.

"Well aren't you two fine young gentlemen to be sneaking up on us poor fellas! People doing that kind of thing deserve to be shot, ya know."

"We mean no harm. We just weren't sure if you'd be friendly or not." Darcy sputtered out. "Besides we're kind of hungry and we smelled your nice roast rabbits.

"We ain't friendly and we ain't giving away our tiny bit of food to scoundrels like you." said the one holding the gun. The longer the men were standing the greater the difficulty they had staying steady.

A second man spoke up. "Hey Fred, lookee at them nice canvas coats. I sure could use a new coat."

"But there's only two coats and there's three of us!" Fred slurred back to him.

"Ah Fred, I'd share my coat with you. You have it one day and I'd have it the next!"

Darcy and Quinn looked at each other. The situation was so ludicrous that, except for the musket that menaced them, they could have dashed away with no harm coming to them. Darcy gave a slight nod to Quinn for him to move closer to the drunks. Darcy started slowly towards them as well, talking as he stepped forward.

"Looks like you get what you want. I really hate to lose this coat..."

Fred squinted at Darcy as he came into more of the fire-light. "Fellas I think we got a chink inside that nice coat. He shouldn't be..."

Quinn's left arm swept Fred's gun hand up and his right fist slammed into Fred's jaw. The musket discharged harmlessly into the air a split second before Fred pitched back onto the campfire, smashing the rabbits into the ashes. At the same moment Darcy whirled to hand chop the knife out of the coat stealing bandit's hand, and in the same spin, kicked the knife out of the third man's hand. Fred howled as he rolled on out of the fire while the other two tried to figure what had happened to them. Darcy and Quinn plunged back into the bushes they had come through and kept moving as fast as they could in the moonlight.

The two eventually paused to listen for sounds of pursuit. Even the quiet seemed threatening to them. They agreed to stick close to one another as they continued forward and attempted to locate their own camp. Nothing seemed to distinguish the direction they should go. It felt like they had gone plenty of distance as bewilderment settled over them.

"Do you think we're going in circles?" Quinn said in a soft voice.

"I really have no idea." Darcy whispered back. "Maybe we'll have to just sit and wait for dawn."

They had just settled down with their backs against a couple big cottonwoods when they heard a horse nicker. The sound came from the left and back of the direction they had been moving.

"Did you hear that?" Darcy whispered.

"Yeah, do you think it was one of our horses? If it is, we missed our camp by a long ways."

"We'll only know by heading over there. We hadn't noticed any other camps so it is probably ours."

"OK, but we don't want to stir up another snake pit so let's go real quiet," Quinn cautioned.

The two moved toward the sound with great caution. Every step seemed to crash through twigs and grass but nothing stirred. Another snuffle from a horse corrected their direction but brought no other disturbance. In a few minutes Quinn stumbled over a saddlebag and fell flat on his face with a huge crash. Darcy froze.

"Yep, this is our camp!" Quinn chortled. "I found my saddlebags! I can tell by the smell!"

With the combination of excitement and hunger there wasn't much chance of them sleeping so they packed up their camp, which didn't consist of very much, and moved out onto the Kootenay Trail in the dark.

"Do you think those guys will come after us?" wondered Quinn.

"Not likely," said Darcy. "Once they got to sleep the booze would knock them out for hours. Plus, I think each of them have some sore spots that they won't want to bump into anything too tough today. But I'm just as glad to be gaining some distance from them."

"I sure hated to see those rabbits crushed into the fire. My stomach knots up just thinking about them. I'm really hungry!"

"Quit thinking about it, Quinn. Something is bound to show up today!"

They kept moving north all day at a good pace but as the day wore on Darcy's confidence that something would show up began to wane. It was the first that any thoughts about turning back from their gold seeking began to creep in. They only passed a couple of solitary hikers who asked them if they had any food to spare before either Darcy or Quinn could get the same words out to them. They tried keeping a pebble in their mouths but it really didn't lessen the hunger.

Mid afternoon Quinn signalled to hold up. "I think I heard something kind of strange up ahead. Thought we should just listen a bit."

Nothing but quiet for a few moments. Then an ugly sound that they both identified immediately as a donkey. But it sounded like a donkey with a sore throat.

"Think maybe there's a donkey having a bad day up ahead." said Darcy. "Let's take a look."

They walked their horses forward with the donkey braying constantly. As they approached the location they could see three men just sitting on boulders with their heads in their hands. They were all dressed in rough coarse clothing. On their heads were slouch hats with wide brims that hid their faces. There was a dense brush area just behind them from which the horrendous noise kept coming.

Because of the constant noise and the three men all looking at the ground, Darcy and Quinn came close to the men before one of them looked up and with a start called the others to look.

"Looks like things aren't going too well today." Darcy offered in sympathy as they dismounted.

"You got that right, Sonny! Hey, haven't I seen you before?"

Recognition dawned on the boys at the same time. "You're Jocko! We met when we were going down to Linklater's! What on earth is going on here?" Darcy blurted out.

"We stopped for lunch and had Dumbo hitched to some branches. She got bad spooked by a cougar and charged straight into that brush area. She dragged a branch with her reins and that shifted a snag. One tree falling caused another to come down so that she's trapped under a mess of deadfall. We've been trying to chop her clear but one of the trees came right down on her and every chop hurts her more. Now we were just talking whether we should put her out of her misery."

"How bad is she injured?" Quinn queried.

"Well, best we can tell, not too bad. Looks like she laid down as the trees came down. Can't see anything broken. Just that she's pinned. Probably bruised some, probably got some heavy weight just sitting on her." one of the other prospectors said.

"Maybe you boys, big and strong, could take a look?" Jocko was shifting from one foot to the other as some hope filtered into his anxiety.

Indeed it was a tangled mess of downed trees that the boys saw even though the three men had cleared away some of the debris. The donkey was firmly trapped. It's eyes wide with the terror and pain. Quinn quickly saw what was needed.

"Do you have some rope?" One of the men scurried for rope.

Quinn picked the top log and tied the rope to the top end after throwing the other end of the rope over a sturdy branch nearby. Quinn had the three old timers ready to haul and snub that rope. He and Darcy moved to where they could get a shoulder under the trunk about three quarters along its length. With a count of three, Quinn and Darcy strained upwards. Quinn's massive strength made the difference and along with Darcy lifting they got good elevation. The other men reefed on the rope causing the whole tree to swing a few feet to the side and to hang just above the jumbled pile of branches. Quinn and Darcy shifted to stand beside this first tree's new location and repeated the process.

"Now we can get the tree that's hurting Dumbo!" Quinn called out.

Having seen Quinn's system once, everyone scrambled into place with the rope ready within minutes. Because the donkey was stressed even more with all the activity around her, her noise increased in intensity. It took strong concentration to shut out the animal's distress while preparing to relieve her pain.

Quinn and Darcy had to be careful where they stood because the donkey had some movement with one back leg and occasionally lashed backwards.

"Careful there boys! She's got a kick that could break your ankle." Jocko warned. "She hasn't figured out yet that you're on her side!"

"Looks like we're ready." Quinn called. "Make sure you don't pull to the side until Darcy and me have got this tree lifted clear of where it's gouging her. Let's try not do any more damage in setting her free."

The boys moved into position. Quinn gave the instructions. "Darcy, when we get this lifted up to our shoulders we are going to need to lift with our arms until it is well over our heads. That's the only way that broken stub is going to clear her eye. Let's just hope she doesn't lift her head while we're doing the arm lift.

"Ready everyone! One, two three, lift!... Now, arm's up!... Now, the rope!" Quinn called out the steps. The huge tree gradually responded to their efforts and finally swung clear. The prospectors tied off their end of the rope.

Dumbo's cries stopped immediately to everyone's great relief. All the men soaked in the silence for a few moments then attacked the brush pile with axes. Soon they had the donkey back to the open field happily grazing.

The prospectors clapped Quinn and Darcy on theirs backs telling them what great heroes they were. Even better, they invited them to help themselves to the coffee that was still hot at the side of their campfire.

THIRTY-SIX

 Boys, we surely are owing to you." Jocko shook his head. "That four legged friend cost us more gold than we wanted to part with but we figured she would be the only way we could take a full winter's grubstake for the three of us. We truly were at our wit's end. Listen, we got some bacon we were planning to cook up with some flapjacks for supper. It would be our pleasure if you would consider sharing that with us. We could tell stories and have a great evening. How about it?"

Both Quinn and Darcy tried not to be too eager as they agreed to Jocko's suggestion. But they both wondered if there was some way to hurry the preparation of the promised meal.

The prospectors were indeed generous with the young appetites of Quinn and Darcy.

"I can hardly move! You've stuffed so many pancakes into me," Darcy groaned.

Quinn didn't claim that there had been too much of anything. He just sat back against a rock with a smile on his face. But it was obvious that both of them were going to be quite content to listen to some good story telling for the rest of the evening.

Jocko held forth on behalf of the prospectors. He told how they had arrived just as news was breaking out that gold had been found on Stud Creek. The creek got renamed Wild Horse Creek so it wouldn't cause ladies to blush every time this location was mentioned. They did some very profitable panning for a stretch. It was never their intention to settle in to work a location for the long term. They let others do that kind of hard labour. So as people began to flood in who actually staked claims the trio would move on when the claim owner showed up.

Jocko continued, "We don't like being around a lot of people for very long. That's why we're prospectors and trappers, although we only trap when we have to. It's starting to get pretty crowded on those creeks. People are even starting to build sluice boxes for trying to make really big profits. Hiring people to work them. But there's always people trying to get something for nothing — just trying to take from others. Why there are even rumblings that a gang is trying to muscle in by saying they'll protect the business people for a fee. Trouble is, if they don't sign up, something bad happens. It's feeling pretty dangerous — you boys better be careful heading into all that multitude."

When Jocko started to wind down he turned his attention to his audience. "Now tell me — you were four and now you're only two travelling pretty light. There must be a story there."

Darcy became the storyteller as he briefly reviewed what had happened since meeting Jocko the first time. The prospectors cackled when they heard of the grand deception of the Border Patrol Gang but they were rather somber when they heard about Darcy and Quinn taking off so suddenly from their Pards.

"Well boys," Jocko scratched his beard as he slowly responded to this latest part. "Pards are probably the most valuable thing in the whole world. Why we've been looking out for one another longer than we care to count. You'll need to get back to them before too long. A little side adventure is OK once in a while but it wears thin if it means being on the outs with the main people."

He paused to let what he had said sink in. The boys didn't have anything to say out loud even though they were silently presenting arguments for what they were doing. Those arguments didn't seem quite so powerful as they had at first but they stubbornly determined to hold on to them.

Jocko went on. "We can spare a couple days worth of rations for you and that will get you to where you can make your way to earning your own supplies."

Quinn and Darcy got underway early in the morning. The awesome mountains in the brilliant sunshine chased the doubts of the night before. The new day brought a fresh excitement to them as they thought of the hustle and bustle they had grown up with in Montreal. The thought of crowds didn't intimidate them at all. What Jocko had described filled their imaginations with possibilities. Their eagerness communicated to their horses so that both men and animals pushed as fast as they could maintain for hours on end. When they passed the turnoff to Joseph's Prairie, Darcy imagined what Maria would think of him heading off to find his fortune. A hero that would return with gold spilling out of his pockets!! However, he was careful not to say anything like that out loud to Quinn.

A couple of days brought them into a lot of traffic. The whole area was transformed into a beehive of activity compared to when they had travelled south through here. Tents were scattered along the Kootenay River as well as dotting both sides of every creek they crossed. Wood smoke hung over every collection of camps. People were on the move. Some had backpacks whether they were coming or going from getting supplies. Others were just arriving, mostly on foot, eager to get their pans into the creeks. Yet others were walking away with heads down beaten by the cutthroat realities of a gold rush environment. As they approached what looked like a larger number of tents along with some rough lumber attempts at buildings, they passed a scrawled sigh that said "Welcome To Fisherville."

Darcy and Quinn kept asking questions as they rode by people. "Where are the people panning for gold?"

Some laughed in return. "These creeks have been panned several times over. You have to go upstream to get to any virgin gravel for panning. Most of the action is on Wild Horse and Findlay creeks where they are building the sluices."

Darcy shook his head, "I can't believe that this many people have jammed in here in just the few weeks since we first came through here. How can we ever find gold for ourselves?

"I've got a more important question," Quinn replied. "How are we going to get food for tomorrow now that we've eaten everything that Jocko gave us?"

Darcy shrugged and was about to comment when they were distracted by angry shouts up ahead. They moved closer to see what was going on. They dismounted and joined the crowd that seemed to be focused on a tent which had a rough sign hanging on its front cross poles dangling above the open flaps. The sign had just one word scrawled in charcoal "Supplies."

"That's mine!" spat out one rough looking miner. His clothes were spattered with mud and were in tatters at his cuffs. His face had as much mud on it as his clothes, making him look very fierce.

"I was here first so get out of my way!" shot back an equally rugged customer who was a head taller than his opponent.

"Yeah, but I've got more money than you so I'm claiming it" The two men were pulling back and forth on a bag of flour.

"Put that flour down and get out of the tent," shrieked the owner of the tent. "If you rip that bag you'll both pay me. It's the last that I have!"

With that both of the customers turned on the merchant, "You're trying to rob us blind. No flour is worth what you're trying to charge."

The owner reached in to take hold of the bag to reclaim it. The three way tussle didn't last long. One of the customers suddenly lost his grip and lurched backwards knocking one of the cross poles free of its tie down. The crowd gasped and yelled warnings as the whole tent slowly collapsed down enveloping most of the crowd plus all three men who were now cursing loudly as they flailed about trying to free themselves from the canvas. The crowd was laughing as they enjoyed some diversion from the desperation that so many were facing including the frustration that the store shelves were mostly bare even if you had money or gold to pay the exorbitant prices.

Darcy and Quinn joined the laughter and got back on their horses. As they continued through the jumble of tents, they saw every imaginable combination of canvas and tin and wood cobbled together to provide some shelter. Most had a fire pit of some description near the entrance. Most businesses were housed in a little more developed state but were obviously a work in progress.

"I'm really hungry and I don't see much prospect for looking after my stomach!" mumbled Quinn.

For once Darcy didn't complain about Quinn complaining. "I know what you mean, Quinn, and I'm not sure we should eat what's being sold as food from some of these tent restaurants even if we had any way of paying for it."

They continued along, twisting and turning their mounts around the helterskelter tents. People seemed to avoid them. No one met their eyes. No one offered friendly "hellos" which they had been used to on the Kootenay Trail. Instead most turned their backs to the two horsemen.

"Hey you!!" someone shouted. "Hey, you two riders!"

Darcy and Quinn waved, thinking at least there was one friendly person in this rough and tumble community.

"Got a minute??!!" the man continued. "Can you come over here!"

There was a strange note of pleading in his voice that got the boys attention as much as the words themselves. They reigned their horses around and cautiously walked towards the man. He was standing leaning against a loaded freight wagon which was pulled in beside one of the more substantial business buildings. A four horse team, looking the worse for wear, was hitched to the freighter. All the horses were standing with their heads down showing complete exhaustion.

As they walked their horses closer they could see that the man himself looked worn out to the point that it was taking effort just to stay standing. Closer inspection showed that he had one arm in a sling. Still cautious, Quinn and Darcy swung down to close the distance. There seemed to be no other threat as they walked up to the man. His clothes were good quality but somewhat scuffed and rumpled.

"What's up, Mister?" Darcy said. "You're not looking too good. Why don't you just sit down against that wheel and we'll talk a bit."

Quinn helped him slide down to a sitting position. Darcy got his canteen and gave him a drink.

"Thanks, boys," he rasped out. "You're showing some kindness. I have to trust you. You're coming from the south so you're not the gang. You're not muddy so you're not working a claim. You're not wearing guns so you're not looking for trouble."

That much talk seemed to exhaust him again. As Darcy gave him another drink, Quinn asked.

"What on earth happened to you to put you in this bad a condition."

"I had to make a supply run down to Walla Walla. My driver got gold fever and I couldn't find anyone else on short notice that I could trust. I was pretty much out of everything; the shelves were bare. So, I took a wagon instead of a pack train over a road that isn't meant for wheels. Coming back I was pushing hard. Kept going after sunset – even though it was too dark to see the road. I hit such a rock it threw me right off the high seat. I must have landed on a hundred rocks all at once. It was some time before I came to. I'm pretty sure it's my collar bone that's broken."

"How did you ever get back? What happened to your team?" Darcy queried.

"They didn't run far, they were already over-used. But it's hard to wrangle a team with only one arm."

The man was obviously fading with telling his story.

"Look man, we'll give you a hand. Is this your living place?" Darcy offered.

"Yep, I have a cot in the back. Have to stay right here to protect the place! Corral's out back. I'll treat you right if you treat me right. Where's my shotttt-ggguuunn?"

Quinn and Darcy helped him to his bed and heard nothing more from him as he either passed out or fell into a very sound sleep. The young men looked at each other and shrugged as they walked back to the wagon.

"This isn't getting us any gold!!" Darcy moaned. "What do we do now?"

Quinn shook his head. "We can't just leave him, can we?"

They locked eyes for a few heart beats. Each of them mulled over their dreams of picking up pockets full of gold nuggets. However they couldn't silence the inner voices that called them to help someone in trouble. All the help they had received that put them far from situations of despair or derision in their own lives raised an inner clamour now for them to help a man who had fallen into an impossible situation.

While the mental tug-of-war was going on something happened that made the decision for them. Voices came from the other side of the wagon.

"Look, no one's guarding the freighter." "We could roll that barrel down to our tent and hide it there." "It's kinda like they parked it there so we could help ourselves!"

The murmur of voices grew as a small crowd began to gather. Darcy and Quinn made eye contact again and in that moment of silent communication make their choice. They circled the wagon and stared at the men in the front of the group that had gathered. Quinn's size alone would have made the would-be thieves step back. When the fierce scowl from Darcy was added on, it caused the whole group to simply melt away. None of that group had a criminal mind-set. They were simply men down on their luck who had spotted what they thought was an opportunity.

"Looks like we're stuck with it!" observed Darcy, when the small crowd was all gone. "This stuff will be easier to guard if it is inside and it'll have to be carried in sometime anyway. Do you want to take care of the packing in or the horses?"

"I'll look after the horses. Maybe we should get the pistols out of our saddlebags."

Quinn found a surprisingly good supply of hay and oats in the corral. He took considerable time caring for the four from the wagon as well as their own saddle horses. Just finding the connections on the unfamiliar harness took up more time than what they would have expected. By the time all six horses were watered, groomed and fed, Darcy had made a pretty good dent in the supplies on the wagon.

"About time you showed up ! Did you find some nice soft hay back there and take a little nap!!?" Darcy prodded.

"What's the matter, can't take a little honest lifting and carrying?!" Quinn shot back.

"I can't believe how much cargo can go on one wagon. There must be four or five tons. The good thing is the amount of food that's on here. I'm sure the man won't begrudge us a meal after all this. Did you catch his name?

Quinn grunted as he lifted a barrel down to the ground. "Can't say as I did. Guess we'll find out when he wakes up. What kind of food have you spotted so far – I'm really hungry?!"

"Seems to me we better get all this stuff in before dark and then rustle up some..."

Before Darcy could finish, a harsh high pitched voice cut him off!!

"Hold it right there you varmits or I'll take you out with my peacemaker!"

Both Darcy and Quinn spun around to look directly into the business end of a shotgun being held by a large woman. She was an intimidating presence with or without the gun. The boys held their hands up without any argument.

"Where's Nels?" she barked out!

"I think we just found out the man's name," Darcy said under his breath.

"Shut up, answer me or I'll ventilate your hides!"

"Ma'am, he's in the back room, sleeping off a really bad fall that busted him up pretty bad. We're helping not stealing!"

"So you say! I don't know you from Adam and no reason to trust you. Show me Nels. Keep your hands up. Higher!

Quinn's face turned scarlet at being herded by a shotgun, and worse, held by a woman. Darcy noticed it and quickly said, "Sure, we've nothing to hide. We'll take you to the man. Come on, Quinn."

When she saw the bruised and cut face and tattered clothing of the man her expression changed. She lowered the gun and reasoned out loud.

"Well you could have done anything you wanted with him in bad condition like that. You've tended him and you were carrying in not out." Reasoned the woman, as she let the shotgun droop. "Okay, tell me who you are."

After Darcy and Quinn filled in some details for her she volunteered back that her name was Roberta, "call me Berty" and that she had a camp kitchen and eating tent a few camp spaces away. She and her husband had operated the same thing at the Fraser and Rock Creek rushes but he had died in an accident at Rock Creek. She had carried on and when some friends, Nels being one of them, were packing up to head for the Kootenay Rush she came too.

"These gold rushes can be brutal but they also bring a lot of opportunity for making a lot of money with out ever having to dip a pan in the creek. After this one I should be able to go find my paradise. A little house with white picket fence and a nice garden plot in a valley without much winter."

Berty had warmed up considerably towards Darcy and Quinn, sensing that they would do for Nels just what he needed in his condition.

"Look boys, if you'll go ahead and get his supplies carried in, I'll rustle up some grub and bring it over to you when you're done. How does beans, bacon and biscuits sound?"

Quinn groaned out loud! His stomach did a flip flop at her promise. He was horrified to see Darcy shaking his head in refusal of her offer.

"Berty, we're flat out of any way to pay you and we don't want to take advantage of you, do we Quinn?"

Darcy raised his voice with these last words to drown out Quinn's words of protest.

Berty chuckled as she watched the changing expressions that passed over Quinn's face.

"No, no! Nels has done so much for me, this is the least I can do. One of you come and get it when you're done here. This late in the day is my busy time when it gets too dark for panning but the men have got some glitter to pay for a full meal. Boy, the stories I hear about how they'll find the big nuggets tomorrow. Tomorrow doesn't pay my bills so they have to show me ahead of time that they have more than promises in their bag. My place is four tents farther on, you'll see my shingle "Berty's Kitchen!"

THIRTY-SEVEN

Oh does that feel good!" Quinn had stretched out on some sacks of supplies. He was patting his stomach and smiling from ear to ear. The supplies were all under cover and the generous heaps of food tucked away where they were intended.

"I didn't think I would ever be full again," murmured Darcy. "Berty sure took care of that!!"

"Darcy."

"What?"

"We didn't get any gold today. We didn't even get to where we could have staked a claim let alone start panning. Not a very good start on our fortune!"

"Quinn, feel your tummy! I think if we had ignored Nels and pushed out to where new claims are being staked we still wouldn't have had any food cause we don't have any supplies, to say nothing of the right kind of supplies and no way to buy any."

"When you think about it, it kinda seems like we were guided to Nels. Doesn't it?" "Darcy?!"

All Quinn got in response was a snore. He smiled, settled his pistol in his hand, wriggled a bit on the sacks to find the best spot and added his snores to the cadence of night sounds in the middle of a gold rush.

All too soon Berty's voice was penetrating their dreams.

"Rise and shine boys! Daylight is wasting! Those tons of supplies aren't going to jump onto the shelves by themselves! Coffee's here!"

The aroma of the coffee was like a magnet lifting them off their makeshift beds. Berty had brought a nice big pot for them that overcame their grunts and groans and complaints along with helping them to remind themselves where they were and how they had gotten there.

Berty's voice barked another order, "One of you needs to go and help Nels out to the privy so he can relieve himself. Then help him back in here so we can sort some things out. Some of these supplies are for my kitchen and I'm needing them yesterday!! Be quick about it cause I can't leave Swampy on his own in my kitchen for very long."

Darcy started a fire and found the makings for flapjacks while Quinn helped Nels.

Nels was barely able to support his own weight by the time Quinn got him back into the store. The coffee and food helped as well so that, even though he was in obvious pain, he could take his part in the conversation.

"Boys, I'm in your debt for coming to my rescue. I could sure use your help for a day or two until these supplies are sorted out. Then I can pay you with gear that you need."

"And I can sure use some help getting my part over to the kitchen," added Berty.

Even though the glitter of gold was still in their minds, Darcy and Quinn really had no alternative to being storekeepers for a bit. They felt somewhat chagrined as they actually thanked Nels for the opportunity.

Darcy commented to Quinn, "Can you imagine how Cody and Jed would laugh at us to see us tending store when we rode off crowing that we would fill our pockets with gold?"

"Maybe this is just a temporary setback," said Quinn. "Maybe our big bonanza is still waiting for us and we'll get to it in a few days!!"

Berty harrumphed, "Don't look down on store keeping. It's going to bail you out of your own head strong pickle!!"

Before the boys could argue, she turned to Nels, "By the way, Nels, I had a visitor yesterday offering to provide protection for my business for a fee. He said he would be back today and that I would be real smart to pay the fee."

Nels groaned, "Here we go again. Seems like every camp attracts some bullies that try to take something for nothing. They're just vultures."

"This guy looked like a hard case, so keep your eyes open." Berty said over her shoulder as she headed out the back for the morning rush at her kitchen.

Some pounding at the front startled Cody and Darcy and had them reaching for their pistols. Ned spoke up, "It's Okay! This time of day it will be some miners wanting some supplies. That's what I'm here for – to sell all this stuff and turn it into my own gold mine. I'll try to point out where certain goods are by knowing the crates or barrels they are in. What I can't spot will be a treasure hunt for the two of you."

The boys were soon immersed in a flurry of answering the demands of very impatient gold seekers. When they found something requested they held it up for Nels to name the price. That was usually met with howls of disbelief and claims that it was daylight robbery. Nels simply suggested that they go buy it elsewhere if they didn't like it. Next the gold poke came up from inside their trousers and Nels weighed out the named amount. The crowd of buyers began to thin out around midday. They had made little progress in getting goods on the shelves but there was certainly more floor space showing.

"I can't believe the amount you can sell, Nels. And the price you can get really does make this into its own kind of gold mine!! commented Darcy.

"Yeah, and I'm going to be out of goods in a few days. People are still swarming in here and there is no way I can get a pack train down to Walla Walla and back to take advantage of this market." groaned Nels, as he pictured the profits he could take but would never happen because of the distance and difficulties of the supply route.

"Well, I'm feeling a little better watching you boys do all that work along with feeling my own gold poke getting a little heavier. I think I can get myself out to the outhouse without a nursemaid this time."

With Nels gone it gave Darcy and Quinn a chance to talk about what they had seen during the morning.

"Whew, can you believe the prices Nels is charging??!! Quinn exclaimed to Darcy. "This gold rush sure changes things."

"I was noticing how heavy some of those pokes were. I think we saw some pretty rich people today. It gave me an idea though."

Quinn laughed, "I'm not sure I should listen to another of your ideas. This last one turned me into a storekeeper!"

"Listen to me! Before Nels gets back in. Quinn, think about all the supplies that that caravan from Fort Kokanee is carry-ing! That's a Hudson Bay gold mine on the move. If they came straight here, Linklater would be a hero for the company! Besides the caravan, we've got another stash at Joseph's Prairie that we can turn into huge profits."

Quinn's eyes had lit up as Darcy talked, "I think this is a good one! Idea, that is! How do we get them to come here though?"

"Well," Darcy said quietly, "By tomorrow Nels should be recovered enough to run this place by himself. We could leave

early tomorrow. I'm not sure where we'll find them. But hopefully it will be before they turn off on the Joseph's Prairie trail."

THIRTY-EIGHT

Cody shook his head as another knot of gold seekers came past the caravan during their noon break.

"John, where have all these people come from? How do they even know about a gold find?"

Linklater laughed, "It's the moccasin telegraph!! News can travel through the wilderness by word of mouth faster than you would ever expect. Especially gold rush news! I've talked to old prospectors who were part of the '49ers. Thousands and thousands piled into California. There are some very rich people that are set for life because they got there early and were lucky with their claims. But there were lots of tragedies as well. Fortunes were lost in gambling. Gangs robbed people who carried their gold with them. Some just drank themselves into poverty. From what I hear it was a wild and woolly time. Virtually lawless!"

"But California is a long long way from here. People couldn't get here that fast." countered Cody.

"Well, you see, there was the Fraser River rush in '58. Thousands of people who didn't make it big in California saw a new vision of riches and flocked north. That's what spurred the process of this whole area becoming a British Colony cause it looked like this flood of mostly Americans would turn the whole Fraser River region into lawless chaos. That's when Douglas asked for all this to be made into a British Colony (with him as Governor of course) but also that they send a chief judge to come from England to carry out British justice throughout all of this wilderness. Then, of course, the Rock Creek rush in 60 – while not as big – moved a lot of prospectors half way here who have since been shifting around waiting on the next rumour."

Cody shook his head some more, "I wouldn't have believed it if I hadn't seen it – this many people erupting out of this wilderness. I wonder how Darcy and Quinn are doing?"

"Yeah, I've kinda wondered about them too. Especially when they took off so fast. I know for a fact that they didn't take near what they needed for food for a day, let alone for what they would need to even start panning for gold. I'm surprised they're not back already." said John.

"You think they'll come back? I guess I'd really like that but I'm still mad at them every time it takes me so long to hitch up the animals with the pack saddles they should be looking after. I don't know if I'll hug them or punch them if they show up! I'm leaning toward punching them! How could I trust them again. Maybe something else will pop up that takes their fancy and off they go!"

Another thought occurred to Cody, "John, do you think these gold rush people change anything about Joseph's Prairie?"

"What do you mean?"

"Well, if everyone's panning for gold, will anybody be trapping and bringing their furs for trade? Besides that, I wonder if it will affect what we're needing to do to bring down Lagasse and Leblanc?"

"They are all good questions that we'll have to answer as we go. It does make you wonder if Lagasse and Leblanc could resist the lure of easy money in the wide open atmosphere of Camp life. If people are determined to be bullies there's not much to stop them in a gold rush."

Jed rode up with his string of horses, "Well, now that you two have solved all the problems in the world, maybe we could make use of this daylight and cover a few miles!!"

Cody was immediately apologetic, "Oh, sorry!! You shouldn't have had to look after all the animals on your own."

"Just ribbing you! The cinches just needed tightening."

Cody met Jed's eyes, "Things are looking a little different than when we first got here. I'm not sure how it is all going to shake out! Are you doing okay?"

"Yeah, but I'm worried about our buddies." said Jed. "They could be in way over their heads and we can't even help them. It doesn't feel right. We're Pards. That means four of us. It won't be right until there's four again. Working with the livestock gives me a way to get my mind off them but I keep coming back to it."

Cody nodded, "Maybe after we get this stuff to Joseph's Prairie we can track them down and then go on to settle the score with Leblanc and Legasse."

"Yeah man! I'm all for that! Besides if you get to see Sophie again maybe you'll be a little better company!" Jed whooped as he kicked his horse into motion at the head of the caravan.

At the same time another booming voice called, "Whoa up, pack train! Whoa up! Can you hold up for a minute?"

Jed pulled up on his reins and halted any forward motion that had started.

"I understand that you're a Hudson Bay outfit? There was a question in the voice that came from a tall, burly, brown hair and bearded, man riding a paint horse.

"I may have something that belongs to you," he called as he rode up to the head of the caravan. "Howdy, I'm Jeff Blaine. Are you in charge of this big outfit?"

He addressed the question to John Linklater who was obviously the oldest of the three.

"Yes," John said, "I'm John Linklater, the Hudson Bay Trader from Fort Kokanee. This is Cody and this is Jed. Pleased to meet you!"

Both Cody and Jed nodded a welcome to this open-faced, friendly newcomer.

"What can we do for you, Jeff?"

"Well, back a couple hours, I pulled off the trail to, uh, answer the call of nature. It just happened to be where an obviously big outfit had made camp last night. It wasn't hard to read the signs. As I caught up with my horse and was swinging up into the saddle I noticed a brown rectangle with a design on it behind some bushes. It looked pretty official so I got down and investigated. It was the logo of the Hudson Bay and it was a pouch with a clasp. So I figured I better find the owner."

As Jeff was telling his story, Cody's face had drained of colour! He had already leaned back to get his hand into his saddlebag and was frantically feeling for his leather pouch even though he knew he was looking at it in the stranger's hands. All their authorization for their secret mission along with proof for payment of expenses from Hudson Bay Traders was in that satchel. Surely he hadn't been so careless as to leave it in some bushes!

In a voice that was little better than a squeak, Cody said, "I'm afraid that I have to admit that that is my satchel."

He swung down from his horse and walked the few steps to take the pouch from Jeff. His knees were weak as he examined the outside and then opened the flap. As he examined the contents his heart slowed towards normal and his sense of total dismay drained away.

Cody looked at John Linklater and croaked out, "It's all here! Nothing is missing!

Relief washed over him as he looked directly at Jed, "We're OK! We escaped disaster!"

It was as if time froze for Cody as a hundred scenes of disaster that might have happened to the Pards if this satchel hadn't come back to him flashed through his mind. While it took only moments it seemed as if he had to climb his way back to the present. He shuddered and then remembered his manners.

He walked with his right hand extended over to Jeff, who had dismounted by this time, "Sir, I owe you a huge debt beyond imagination. The loss of that pouch with its particular contents would have crushed the future for our crew and would have had repercussions all the way back to Montreal."

The two men shook hands with a firm and steady grip! "I am amazed that you brought that find back to us. Usually people think that whatever they find is simply their good luck and they make no effort to find the true owner." Cody continued to process out loud the thoughts that swirled in his mind. "What caused you to bring it to us? Not even open it to see what was inside?!! No one does that!"

Jeff laughed at Cody's muddled expressions of relief and disbelief. "Well, it did look important and, I admit, I had some moments of thinking maybe I'd found some treasure to help me on my pilgrimage. Doesn't everyone have daydreams like that? Then the thought came,

'What if that were my pouch and it was important to me? What would I wish would happen?' After all, the second commandment is to love your neighbour as you love yourself. I figured my neighbour was somewhere up ahead. Once that stuck in my mind I only did what was right."

"Well, thanks! Gosh!" Cody spluttered out. "A reward! Something like that deserves a reward, doesn't it Jed!?"

Jed was nodding in the affirmative, but Jeff spoke up quickly, "No, no. I didn't do this for a benefit to myself. A reward would take away from the pleasure of making your day better than what it was even though you didn't know how bad it was!"

Jeff chuckled at his own jumble of words. His laughter was infectious and drew the others in so that they were all softly laughing along with him. The humour provided an emotional release that lifted the atmosphere of their situation and made a connection for all of them to this unusual but winsome newcomer.

"Well, sir! Would you at least ride along with us and tell us the news from where you have been." Cody asked, sensing that there was a depth behind Jeff's pleasant exterior that was a magnet to him. "We can share our hospitality while we benefit from your stories!"

"That sounds like a great offer. I'd be glad to do just that."Once again, Jed got the caravan underway.

THIRTY-NINE

As Darcy and Quinn chatted and filled shelves they realized that Nels had taken a long time at the outhouse.

Darcy laughed, "I think maybe Nels has fallen asleep out there. Poor guy! He's still pretty sore."

Quinn chuckled, "You've got to be in bad shape to snooze in there. I'll go see that he gets back in."

When Quinn got through the back room, past the cot, he heard voices before he stepped outside. He paused, not wanting to intrude on a private conversation. Right away he heard strain and anger in Nels' voice even though he couldn't distinguish the words. Then he heard a second voice which was louder so he could make out the brief threatening words...

"Pay or else!"

That galvanized Quinn to burst out the back door with a loud crash. It took a moment to spot Nels and the second person because they were behind a jumble of equipment and a few bushes. The noise of Quinn coming out the door had ended the conversation and the second person was spinning away as Quinn located him. However he did a quick look back over his shoulder as he swung up onto his horse. It was enough that Quinn recognized the face and it sent chills up his back as he watched the man pull himself up onto his horse with his right hand. There was no doubt left in Quinn's mind that Nels had been accosted by Panther, the Kootenay Indian that had pulled a knife on the dock at Kootenay House and Darcy had kicked it out of his grip.

Nels had settled down unto a small stack of firewood. He looked shaken. Quinn went to help him up. Nels accepted his help as they slowly got back into the store. Darcy's eyebrows went up with an unspoken question to Quinn.

"What was going on out here?" Quinn asked even though he was pretty sure he already knew.

"He was waiting for me when I came out of the outhouse. Right in broad daylight! Demanded protection money so he and his friends could look after me. I told him to get lost and not come back."

Quinn said, "I head him say "pay or else!"

Nels added, "That was just after he said that there were some bad accidents just waiting to happen and that his bosses weren't people who would wait around for me to get smart!"

Quinn said, "I recognized him! It was Panther from Kootenay House."

To Nels he added, "We had a fight with the gang he belongs to when we first got to Kootenay House. Panther was the one who pulled a knife but Darcy kicked it out of his hand and broke his wrist at the same time."

To both of them Quinn added, "When he ran off to his horse, he was awkward mounting it and I noticed that where he would usually grab the saddle with his left hand he had to use the right hand and his left wrist is still bandaged."

Darcy asked Nels, "Did he actually use the word 'Bosses' cause that's what they called the gang leaders up north?"

Nels confirmed that he did.

Some customers banged in through the front door and for the next while they were busy trying to fill the shouted orders. Nels directed the boys to the most likely keg or box where they would find the needed goods if they weren't out on the shelves yet. There were the usual complaints about the high prices but Darcy and Quinn were getting more aggressive in defending the prices as they were realizing how unavailable these items were apart from this one source. Nels seemed to continue to gain strength from his bad fall, especially as gold payments for the purchases mounted up.

Around midday the traffic of shoppers dropped right off as it seemed everyone was taking a lunch break. It gave Darcy and Quinn a chance to broach Nels with their ideas.

It didn't take Nels long to realize that a bonanza of goods was just days away compared to the extended time for a trip to Walla Walla. Of course Linklater would have to agree to some kind of profit sharing.

Darcy said, "How could he not agree when it would work out for far greater profits for the Hudson Bay than he had ever dreamed of? Besides, Nels, it would bring our buddies here so the four of us could help you deal with this protection scam."

They agreed that Darcy and Quinn would leave at first light on the following morning. The rest of the day was a blur of serving customers and planning for the quick trip the boys would make. Nels was able to recruit a couple of men to take on guarding the store overnight. He had to offer an exorbitant wage given the rumours of trouble that businesses were facing.

Berty dropped by during the afternoon lull at her kitchen. She seemed agitated as she came in through the back door.

"Those thugs were back trying to collect money from me. I gave them an earful!"

"Berty, are you saying there was more than one? What did they look like?" Darcy queried.

"There were three this time. A couple of them hung back so I didn't get a good look at them. I think they were just there to look threatening."

Then she went on to describe the spokesman of the group which confirmed that it was the man they knew to be Panther. Darcy and Quinn told her a little of their past encounters with this gang. They also filled her in on the plans they had come up with.

"Well, I can't disagree with any of those plans. I hope your mates will be as enthusiastic about it as you are. There are a couple of regular customers at the kitchen that look like they could stand guard for a few nights. So between Nels and me, we'll make arrangements to hold off these cowards that sneak around the back of our places and threaten women. I'm going to be keeping my shotgun pretty handy. Nels, you do the same!!"

Berty had worked herself up into a lather! She stomped out the back way, calling over her shoulder. "I'll have coffee for you at dawn!"

Late that evening as they gathered their kit for early morning, Darcy and Quinn couldn't resist some chuckles over how well provisioned they were for the trip back to the caravan compared to how sparse their saddlebags were when they had arrived at Fisherville.

"I guess we kinda struck gold in our own way, right Darcy??! Quinn said.

"Even more so when we get the caravan and the Joseph's Prairie supplies up here. Imagine Linklater's shock when he finds out how much he can make. We should all get a good bonus out of this!!" Darcy chortled.

After they had finished organizing their saddle bags, Darcy and Quinn set a few pots and pans in front of the doors so that anyone trying to sneak in couldn't help but create a big clatter. They still slept fitfully dreaming about the excitement of the caravan crew when they learned the great prospects that awaited them in Fisherville. A noisy flock of crows squabbling over some garbage disturbed their sleep and notified them of the arrival of daylight. They had just cleared the doorways when Berty rushed in with the promised coffee.

"Dear o'dear, o'dear!" She exclaimed. "I can't believe they would do this! Pick on someone so helpless, so defenceless. Bullies like that deserve to be shot!! I'll do it myself, if no one else will."

"Berty, slow down. Who you going to shoot?" Darcy broke in to her tirade. Nels rolled out of his cot and pulled up his suspenders as he stumbled into the big room.

"It's Swampy!" She said.

"You aren't going to shoot Swampy, are you?" a horrified Quinn gasped.

"No, no, you dunderheads! The bullies, the gang, they beat Swampy half to death late last night. I just discovered him when I made coffee this morning. This can't go on. Why pick on him? They sent a message through Swampy that he managed to mumble out to me. They told him to tell me to pay or it would be my fault that more people would be getting hurt! One week, then they will collect. Have the gold ready he said."

"We've got to get going," said Darcy, "We'll do our best to be back in a week!"

Quinn nodded to them, "Do whatever you have to to stay safe till we get back. When we have extra help we'll take those bullies down. You can count on us!"

With that they threw their saddlebags on their horses, mounted and dashed south full of resolve to rescue these new friends once they had the rest of the Pards to back them up. There was not even a whisper of a thought in their minds that there would be anything but a wholehearted support for the plans that were foremost in their minds. To them this fit what the foursome were dedicated to do. They had helped someone in obvious need and would restore fairness to those being abused.

In one way or another this is what they had all done for each other. There was nothing but excitement beating in their hearts as their horses ate up the miles back to their partners.

It was late afternoon on the day they found the caravan. Things were settling in for the night and the evening meal just finishing up. It would be the last camp before the Joseph's Prairie junction. As they rode in, Darcy and Quinn called greetings to some of the Linklater men who were on the edge of the camp. There was a ripple of voices as the news that Darcy and Quinn were back skipped from person to person. Lots of people stopped what they were doing to see what the excitement was. Some of them called for the boys to show them the gold that must be spilling out of their saddlebags.

Cody, Jed, John and Jeff had gathered in a knot at the centre of the camp as the returning members reined their horses through the waggons and gear to where they were standing. Darcy and Quinn had grins from ear to ear as they said hello to the group. There was a general response, plus John Linklater introduced Jeff as a new friend.

Darcy was hardly off his horse when he began to rapidly announce what was most prominent on his mind.

"Listen, we've got to get this caravan north right away! We can sell everything and make a pile of money. People need help standing off the gang that's wrecking their lives. We can go back later and get the supplies at Joseph's Prairie. The Hudson Bay is going to think you're the best money maker ever, John. There's gold there that we don't have to dig out of the ground! I'm sure glad we caught you before you turned to Joseph's Prairie. Isn't that right, Quinn!!?? We think the Bosses from Kootenay House have set themselves up in Fisherville."

In the excitement and chatter of the greetings, and Darcy's jumbled words of the future as he saw it, no one noticed that Cody didn't enter in. A scowl had replaced the initial smile when the boys had arrived. Now he stood stiff as a log at the back of the cluster. His face was growing redder and redder as Darcy prattled on. He looked like he would erupt and he did.

"Aren't you the great heroes of the hour!" he said through gritted teeth. There was ice in his tone that cut through all the other conversation even though his voice wasn't particularly loud. All the chatter stopped instantly. Everyone turned to look at Cody and immediately stepped back when they saw the thundercloud look on his face. Jeff, sensing what was coming, backed away and left the group.

Cody continued, "You come riding back in here after deserting this whole crew, deserting your promises, deserting your obligations and deserting your friends. You simply broke the code we've lived by. Without any word that you have thought of anyone but yourselves you come riding in here and start trying to tell us what WE should be doing. You have no right to do that! How do you know that you are still part of this team after you ran out on us? You've got some cheek trying to boss us! Maybe you better get down off your high horse and check some things out first of all."

Darcy and Quinn stood with their mouths open, clearly shocked by the verbal barrage that Cody was pouring out at them. They sputtered out some words trying to respond to Cody but Cody wasn't at all finished. He stepped towards them, fists clenched. His voice becoming shrill.

"You think you're something grand when all you are are selfish renegades. Away on a lark, even though it meant others had to do your jobs. Was loyalty so cheap you could just discard it. You ran out on family! You broke the bond that no one has a right to break." Cody was beyond reason in his fury as he shouted, "A good whipping is what you deserve!"

He cocked his right fist and lashed it straight for Darcy's jaw. Darcy flinched but the blow never landed. A firm hand had suddenly gripped Cody's wrist and stopped his swing. Cody's eyes went wide as he looked into the determined, up close, face of John Linklater.

"No, Cody!" John's firm, calm voice commanded, "Not this way, it will just add wrong on wrong! Better go for a walk and get yourself together."

Cody spun on his heel and stalked away, pushing through the little crowd that had gathered to hear news from Darcy and Quinn.

The pent up energy of his outburst drove him to a fast pace. He didn't know where he was going while his mind kept churning over and over the thoughts and words and reactions that had boiled out in response to two of his very best friends crossing some invisible line. He should have handled it better. Yet they had hit some nerve that took control. How close he had come to causing even greater damage if John hadn't stopped him. He hated being out of control, hated that buried anger being brought to the surface. Those feelings had always been with him but how could he explain it. He didn't understand himself in all of this. It surely couldn't justify how he had reacted to Darcy and Quinn.

FOURTY

As his fury subsided and his mind began to slow, Cody found himself on the far side of the meadow and going uphill. The steep incline had been a big help in burning up the emotional overload. As he looked around he saw that he was part way up a knoll that overlooked the camp. It seemed like a natural site as an objective for his hike. When he came out on top he discovered Jeff sitting on the lip of the cliff looking down on the caravan circled for the night.

"What are you doing here?" Cody asked gruffly, feeling a little resentful that he had to interact with anyone just then.

"Well... actually... Cody... I was praying for you!"

"A lot of good that did! I haven't exactly been lifted up to paradise on the clouds."

"I thought it did a lot of good, considering you were kept from breaking Darcy's face."

"Aarrghhhh, I'm so mad at them I just boiled over." Cody groaned.

"Seems to me you're mad enough for a lot more than what Darcy and Quinn have done. Why don't you tell me about the pit this has opened up?"

Ordinarily this was forbidden territory for Cody no matter who he was talking to. Yet, something about Jeff's soft invitation felt like safe ground. Cody paced on the small patch of level ground beside Jeff. He frequently eyed the camp that was below them.

"I thought this was all behind me since crossing the mountains. This was instantly home and I felt peace like never before. Now I wonder if it was just an illusion. Do you know what I mean?"

Jeff nodded but said nothing, not wanting to get in the way of Cody's inner thinking.

"Don't get me wrong. I know I had a lot of good things in my life. Never hungry like some street kids. But I didn't belong. I just looked in the mirror and knew I didn't belong. Being a "breed" made it even more obvious. Oh, I had a grandfather through being adopted who was the best thing that ever happened to me until now. Trouble is I was always contrary at home. My parents just had different ways of thinking than me. When I found out I was adopted it explained a lot...in my mind anyway. When I found out my blood mother died when I was born I realized that I had been deprived of the nurture of my real Mom. Plus, I now knew that I came from a different way of looking at life. The big thing though was that my father didn't fight for me. He gave up and gave me away. He shouldn't have done that. I was his flesh and blood. Jeff, I've never seen a blood relative!! I've never looked at a face that has any blood connection to me."

"I'd never thought of that," Jeff offered. "It sounds like it is really important to you!"

"As we grew up, the four of us, our friendship really took on the place of family. We had chosen each other. We held together like family. Loyalty to one another grew and grew. We would never break the bond that became the Pards. Talking to one another was easy but when we went home it was really hard. This expedition has cemented our sense of family with one another. At least, I thought it had. But Darcy and Quinn broke something sacred. How dare they!!! They've destroyed a trust. I'm not sure it can ever be restored!"

There was sudden vehemence and bitterness in Cody's voice as his mind went back to the gold fever effect on two of the 'family.'

"I'm so angry with them. I want to thrash their weakness out of them. Maybe if they feel a lot of pain they'll learn how wrong they were and how much they've thrown away be being desert- ers. Jeff, I don't think I can ever look them in the eye again and feel like we're a true family. Something is lost forever. They've taken it from me, stolen it, left me powerless over the thing I cherished most. I don't know what to do."

Cody's fury was spent and he flopped to the ground beside Jeff.

"I know what it's like to have what you cherish most ripped away by other people." Jeff said quietly.

"Not as much as this!" Cody shot back. "This is about who I am, about where my very deepest connection exists. Look at you, you're obviously happy-go-lucky, at peace with the whole world. Wait till you have real pain about how you connect with people and then you'll know what I'm talking about."

"Cody, I've had the worst kind of pain and it was completely destroying me. I didn't have any peace at all. It came to the point that death looked mighty inviting. I felt like I couldn't ever go on. My reason for living had been crushed." Jeff's voice choked to a whisper.

They were both quiet for a few moments. Cody still nursing his bitterness but Jeff's emotion had grabbed a little of his attention so that he realized this was touching a deep wound in this new friend. Jeff, in the quiet space, was struggling with the difficulty of talking about such personal pain with a young man who, in his present self focus, might trivialize what was now sacred ground. Yet, by sharing it in these moments of Cody's soul searching, it could be what would give him a whole new view of his direction even a whole new view of his purpose in life. As painful as it was, Jeff knew this was his mission, this was a step in his pilgrimage.

In a quiet halting voice, Jeff started to tell his story. "I had it all once. It was my hard work that gave it to me, I thought. I was king of my own farm, my family, my life! I had a beautiful wife, a beautiful daughter. The war in the east caused the army units in our area to be pulled back there. Local militias were supposed to be our law and order. But most of them were raiders living on the edge of the law to begin with. This gave them cover to steal and pillage. Some of the gangs became very bold. None of them had come close to our little valley and I thought we would escape. Even if they came I assumed we could hold them off. Foolish! I should have moved my family into town. I should never have gone for supplies that day. Should never have left my family on their own. If only I could take those choices back! If only I had died with them....I felt dead inside. When I finally threw those first shovels of dirt onto the bodies of my flesh and blood everything inside me collapsed. I raged at God, I screamed at the brutes who had destroyed my world. I despised myself for not protecting them."

Jeff's voice had risen in intensity as the emotions stirred by relating the past events gripped his whole body. Neither said anything for some time. It was like a sacred silence as the enormity of what Jeff had been through settled into Cody's mind and heart.

Jeff spoke again. His voice had returned to it's usual quiet level. "I was in a stupor for two days planning revenge. It seemed to be the only coherent thoughts I could put together. Everything else was just dead inside me as I stared at the graves and the ashes of our house and barn hour after hour. I lived off the supplies in the wagon. I guess I would have done something when they ran out.....but what?"

"What happened to change you?" Cody asked quietly.

"Our travelling minister was just finishing his two week circuit and decided to take the extra time to swing by for lunch to see how we were doing. I could hardly talk, but he just sat with me and let me say a few words at a time until tears came. He didn't probe, he just was there and shed tears with me. Late in the day he made two small crosses – just tied sticks across each other – I knew it was all we could do. Then he simply said that we would come back the next day with better crosses and read and say prayers. His sense of what I needed was so true. There was no big discussion when he simply said let's go. And he and his wife took me into their home. I sat on their porch and stared at nothing for another day after the funeral. The wood pile saved me."

"How could a wood pile save you?" Cody asked, still feeling like he was staring into a man's soul.

"The minister's wife wondered if I would mind splitting enough wood for her to do some afternoon baking. After the first few swings of the axe, the blocks of wood became the brutes who had murdered my family. I chopped and chopped. There wasn't a knot that could stop my vicious swings. When I ran out of wood to be chopped I started in on the pile for the church next door. When I had done that I took the wagon out to the bush to cut trees. It'll be a coons age before they need more wood. When my rage started to burn down, the minister sat with me in the evenings on their porch and we talked and talked. He talked about the wrong done even to the Son of God....even to the point of crucifying a totally sinless man. Then he talked about forgiveness. It certainly wasn't what I wanted to deal with. The cutthroats that had murdered my family had simply gone beyond deserving any forgiveness. But Jesus had forgiven his murderers before he breathed his last. My friend told me that I would be a prisoner of hate until I received God's forgiveness and, in turn, forgave the men that didn't deserve it at all."

That's impossible!" Cody blurted out.

"My thoughts exactly. I sold my land, my horse and wagon. Bought a good saddle horse and started wandering, hoping to pick up some bit of information that would put me on the trail of the gang. Someone usually brags or gets drunk and spills enough to give a clue. My minister's words wouldn't leave me alone though. I went downhill pretty fast. I drank to hear what other drunks would say. Then I drank to dull the pain. Then I drank for no reason except to drink. All the time learning nothing about the villains that I hated so desperately. I was a prisoner of my hate."

"You sure wouldn't know that now!" Cody observed.

"It was a night like this. Crisp and clear. I climbed a ridge and looked out over a valley and the next mountain range. The stars couldn't have been closer. I gave into the truth of what my minister had said. Then, to use a phrase of some famous person, 'my heart was strangely warmed.' That's when this pilgrimage started. No more hate. No more self-destruction. Learning new things every day. I keep talking to ministers that I meet. Borrowing books. Helping where I can. Searching out what God wants me to do. Well, here I am. I don't know what lies ahead but this conversation was meant to be."

Jeff left Cody sitting on that knoll under the night sky. Cody's mind was tumbling from the horror of what Jeff had told of his family's tragedy, to the impossible forgiveness, to the majesty of the stars. His own resentment of what Darcy and Quinn had done diminished by comparison. The bigness and permanence of the constellations, still just like his Grampa Thompson had shown him way back in Montreal, spoke to Cody's inner person of a grand scheme of life that was drawing him forward. He felt a mystical connection that he couldn't explain even to himself.

Yet he didn't want to move away from it. Time seemed to stand still and minutes turned into hours as his inner turmoil gradually quietened. His issues with Darcy and Quinn came into perspective – small! His need to be in charge was exposed in the realization that huge forces beyond his control could and would change his direction. His response to those forces would make or break him.

It was a short night till the call to breakfast penetrated Cody's sleep-deprived head. His journey to wakefulness was slow at first but when he remembered his resolve from the time spent on the knoll he was quickly up to join in the line for food and coffee. When everyone had their grub Cody spoke up to get their attention.

"I need to say something this morning." Breakfast speeches were not common so Cody had full attention, especially in light of his eruption the day before. "I made a mistake yesterday. No one has to be part of this caravan, including Darcy and Quinn. It's the goals we share and the friends we make that are important. New circumstances will affect that and we'll have to adjust as we go, probably me more than anyone. Guys, I'm sorry I blew up at you. I'm aiming to do better in the future."

Cody walked to Darcy and Quinn offering his hand. They responded with a hand shake and a nod. It was a little stiff but accomplished the restoration that was so important.

"Now," Cody continued, "those that wish to should stay and hear what these two have to say to us. The rest can do your usual for moving out."

Over the next half hour Darcy and Quinn managed to get across a rather jumbled picture of what they had learned. Their excitement grew as they talked about the great opportunities for commerce. Everything was in short supply and prices were sky high. "You won't believe how much they're charging for everyday stuff." It didn't take long for John Linklater to be nodding his head vigorously as he realized that his caravan was a gold rush town gold mine for the Hudson Bay, for a pack horse train, and for everyone of their crew whose various skills could draw a fortune. Everything was in short supply and the caravan had the men and materials to fill those needs in exchange for a generous amount of gold. There were a few questions raised and quickly answered. There just didn't seem to be any reason not to head straight for Fisherville and then later to go back to Joseph's Prairie for the stashed supplies that had been left there before. With a few words of agreement back and forth the new destination was put into place. As word spread among the crew excitement grew that they would all have a chance to be part of a gold rush and make their fortune.

Darcy and Quinn felt greatly relieved that they had been restored to the Pards if not fully vindicated for their rash adventure up to the gold fields. However, they had more to share that was not for general consumption and they were sure this would put them back on good ground with Cody and Jed.

Darcy said quietly to them and to John Linklater, "Could we just walk a ways? There's some more that we would like to tell you.?"

Cody even managed a little chuckle, "What? Did you get some secret information about some gold nuggets that we can go and fill our pockets?"

"No, not that. But it is secret information," Quinn responded.

"Okay, we're all ears!" Jed chimed in, feeling very pleased that the Pards seemed fully back to easy interaction. It fit well with their years of learning to hassle things through, even to the extent of fist fights, and then to leave them behind and move on. This one had threatened on a deeper level as it could have meant going different directions into the future and that had rocked Jed much more than the others would have guessed. This was his family, his anchor, more than he had consciously thought about until it was threatened. Now he was eager to hear what else Darcy and Quinn had to share.

"Listen," Darcy said when they were certain no one else could hear their conversation. "We've found out that the Bosses have moved their gang into Fisherville and they aren't panning for gold. They are demanding payment from businesses, two that we know about for sure, for what they call 'protection' from harm or theft. But they are the danger themselves. They beat up on an old man who worked for a kitchen owner, beat him almost to death, just because she wouldn't pay."

Quinn jumped in on the story. "I kinda stumbled onto seeing the guy threatening our new friend Nels. It was definitely Panther from Kootenay House. The one Darcy took out with a kick. He didn't see me, but I got a clear view of his face."

Quinn couldn't help a chuckle, "He's still not using his left hand!!"

"So we're not going to have any trouble finding these guys and there are some people who will stand up to them with our help if we can actually bring in the Bosses." Darcy added.

John commented, "They just keep adding to the list of charges that will stand against them. I sure won't have any hesitation in putting them in lockup once we get established."

"I'm not sure we can let this go on until we are established," said Darcy. "They are so darned aggressive someone's going to end up dead before this is all settled."

A somber silence settled over them as the full gravity of the situation became apparent. "I think the Pards have a mission that will mean taking the mandate the Hudson Bay gave us to the limit. We can't let bullies run roughshod over innocent people. It was true on the school grounds in Montreal, right? And it is just as true for us in the Kootenay Valley seeing as we are here."

There were nods all around.

Jed was the first to jump into action. "Well, let's get'er done!" he called out as he swung into his saddle and waved the caravan forward. The excitement of their new destination and potential riches seemed to infuse the whole train with new energy. Even the animals moved at a quicker pace – or so it seemed as their handlers chatted with one another. The opportunities ahead were magnified as imaginations pictured what might be and crew members tossed out their ideas of how they could maximize these new possibilities.

FORTY-ONE

The next day around mid-morning, the Pards noted that they were passing the junction of the Joseph's Prairie road. They chatted about what their friends there might be doing and that they would be making a trip there in the future to pick up the supplies they had cached in the log cabin they had built. Cody was especially thinking of Sophie with very fond thoughts but also remembering the episode with Eagle Claw who had tried to claim Sophie as obligated to be his woman. Cody truly hoped Eagle Claw was abiding by his banishment and that Sophie felt no fear from him. Then Cody's mind went to the pure pleasure it had been to spend time with her, their walks, their sharing, her eagerness to learn all she could about Cody. Even the memories stirred his emotions.

"Cody...Cody...Cody!" The loud voice spoiled his reminiscing and he finally shook himself and looked around for the source of the intrusion.

"Boy, you were far away – probably in the arms of Sophie!!!" It was Jed laughing and goading Cody about his far away look. "Should we push on a bit before our quick noon stop? Quinn says there's a pretty good meadow over that next rise that will make a good place for a watering and graze."

"Sure, sure!" Cody responded, a little irritated that his day dream had been interrupted over something Jed could have decided on his own!

At the noon break, Cody led his horse a ways upstream so he could be by himself. While his mount drank it's fill, Cody mulled the overflow that had more than filled his life in the last couple of days. He had surprised and scared himself at the inner rage that had taken over his reaction to Darcy and Quinn. Where had that come from? Had he been so out of control that he would have seriously harmed a friend who was closer than a brother if someone hadn't stepped in? Then there was the conversation with Jeff on the mountain ridge. Somehow Jeff's beliefs were touching the deepest part of his life. He felt an inner yearning for what Jeff had, yet the fact that he had been "given away" as an infant still blocked his readiness to fully trust. It seemed opposite to God caring about him. However, forgiving Darcy and Quinn as Jeff had urged him to do, had certainly brought a relief and freedom that had been missing while they were off on their gold adventure. Now the caravan was heading to a new destination that brought a horde of new factors into their lives. There was the lure of great profits along with the dangers to their whole group of the gold rush environment. Having just passed the junction to Sophie's place added the pang of not being able to spend more time with her, but how could his life have room for the enticement of a love relationship that he knew could easily absorb all of his thoughts. On top of all this Cody knew that he couldn't let go of his commitment to bring Leblanc and Lagasse to justice. This was the bottom line task that had brought them these thousands of miles to be standing in this incredible wilderness setting of mountains and meadows and pristine rivers. Cody remembered Grampa David Thompson teaching him that if you ever felt lost in the wilderness there was one star out of the thousands to find and to lock onto. You could depend on the North Star to guide you. Right now Cody decided that he needed to lock onto their task of bringing in the Bosses as their North Star and let time take care of the rest of the confusion. He realized it wouldn't be easy but he felt like he had clarified a focus that could keep him on track. Little did he imagine how much that would be tested.

"Cody! Cody! Cody!" A new but familiar voice intruded in to his consciousness. Cody saw a figure running toward him with arms waving madly to get his attention.

"Pierre?" How could young Pierre be coming toward him from the north when they had expected him to be at their original destination of Joseph's Prairie? All kinds of thoughts tumbled around in Cody's head as Pierre approached. One thing for sure – Cody couldn't resist the enthusiasm and mile wide smile as Pierre rushed towards him. Even with all the questions that craved answers, Cody returned the smile.

"Pierre! What on earth are you doing here!! This is a big surprise!"

Pierre was dancing from foot to foot as he blurted out "We are going to get rich. All we have to do is get to the gold creeks and pick up some gold and trade for whatever we want!"

Cody cringed as he recognized the now familiar gold fever that had infected his young friend's head. Rather than argue some reality into Pierre's mind at the moment Cody jumped to some other obvious questions.

"How did you know we were here? Who are you with? Is your family alright?"

Pierre gradually got his story out. "Guys came by us this morning, hiking pretty fast to get to the gold. Said they had passed a big wagon train north of Joseph's Prairie road. Not sure it was you cause you should be going to Joseph's Prairie. Family agreed for me to come back and check you out. And it is you! Come on, Cody, we go fast and you see Sophie!!"

Cody's heart skipped a beat at the indication that Sophie was with the family up ahead. His first impulse was to gallop ahead and find them. But his second thought was to get the caravan moving so they could all catch up with Pierre's group as soon as possible. After a little more discussion with Pierre, Cody learned that there were two other families travelling with Broken Antler's family. Reassured that they were fairly secure as a larger group, it also seemed certain that they would be able to camp together by nightfall. Cody sent Pierre back with instructions for them to find a good stopping place for themselves and the wagon train.

Cody's mind was full of questions created by the presence of three Kootenay Indian families on their way to a gold rush town. Usually Indian families stayed away from any kind of collection of whites where there might be some conflict. Most of the time it was just men who ventured into places like trading posts until they were sure that women could come and go safely. From what Darcy and Quinn had described, this scrabbled together collection of humanity at Fisherville could offer only risk and insecurity. Cody's ray of hope, as he loped back to the wagon train, came from the fact that they had caught up with these folk before they were actually at the gold fields and could be persuaded to turn back.

The caravan had gotten underway by the time Cody got back to them. He circled around Jed's horses to pick up the lead rope for his own pack horses and then moved up so he could talk to the leaders as they moved.

"I had a young visitor while we were stopped!" The Pards and John Linklater looked at him waiting for him to go on. "It was Pierre! He's with three families heading for the gold rush. Broken Antler and two other families! I think gold fever has claimed them – at least it sure has Pierre firmly in its grip."

"That's crazy!" Darcy exploded. "Fisherville is the last place they should go! They'll end up in serious trouble. People will steal the buckskins right off their backs." Darcy took a breath and stared at Cody. "Is Sophie with them?" When he got a nod in return he went on, "Cody, you have to stop them. A girl like Sophie wouldn't be safe any time of day or night unless she's got an army with her."

"That's kinda what I was figuring as well. Look, we'll be able to turn them around tonight. They're going to wait for us up ahead at a good camp site."

The group chatted more as they rode along about what could have persuaded these peace loving native families to head into a gold rush. Cody emphasized that he only had Pierre's over-excited version to go by. John, the elder of the leaders, speculated that there were other factors that young Pierre had overlooked. Quinn had been quiet for some length of time and finally spoke up with an edge in his voice.

"I think you're forgetting that we've got some people in Fisherville counting on us getting back there as soon as possible. It's life and death for them – not just some kid's daydream about picking up nuggets in the creeks. Besides, it's the Leblanc and Legasse gang and that's what were supposed to be doing. Cody, I can see that your romance is going to get in the way!"

Cody's anger flared, his face coloured from the neck up. He was about to tell Quinn to shut up and to deny that his think-ing was weakened by "his" Indian Princess, but he swallowed the fighting words just in time as a sliver of possible truth in Quinn's accusation pierced his mind. The others in the group had grown quiet waiting for the explosion that was likely to come from Cody when someone first faced him with something he didn't like. The silence stretched out to where it was really uncomfortable. So everyone was surprised at the soft voice when he did respond.

"It would be wrong if we didn't get to Fisherville as soon as we can. Your promise to them has to be our promise. We'll stick to our regular pace even over this coming day," a day that held some nervous sparkle as Cody anticipated seeing Sophie. His eagerness was somehow even translated into a little faster step by his horse so that he periodically had to hold up for the rest of the caravan to catch up. Cody's thoughts tumbled as he mused on all that he had to tell Sophie about their adventures since they had said goodbye. He knew that he had faced some big questions about himself and he wondered how it would affect Sophie's view of him once he let her in on his inner thoughts.

It was a jovial reunion of the Pards with the Kootenay families. To meet up with people you already knew out in this huge wilderness provided a sense of connection unknown in most settings. Cody eagerly introduced John Linklater and Jeff Blaine. Broken Antler, in turn, introduced Yellow Bull and Winter Moon as heads of the other two families that were travelling together. The women and children stood back and nodded as each man indicated his family although no direct introductions were made. Pierre helped with translation when it was needed.

Cody struggled to keep attention on the introductions. His eyes kept darting to the cluster of women and children. Pierre had said that Sophie was with the travellers but she wasn't at the front of the onlookers. Darcy had to elbow Cody a couple times to get him to follow Darcy's lead in responding to the semi-official greetings that Broken Antler was giving.

Cody began to wonder if Sophie was avoiding him. Was she embarrassed to be associated with Cody? Had she decided that she didn't like this white boy after the Pards had left Joseph's Prairie? Cody's innards were feeling really weird. How could not seeing her at this moment cause all these doubts and sensations so quickly? Had he had something weird to drink or eat?

Then he caught a glimpse of her between two other women. Their eyes connected for a brief moment but then Sophie looked down almost immediately. Was there a promise in that glance? Did it say "I'll meet you later?" Cody wanted to believe that's what it meant but he was powerless to do anything about it without being rude and causing embarrassment all around. Another nudge from Darcy brought him back to the dialogue with Broken Antler. He heard Darcy speaking,

"Thank you for your offer of hospitality. We are well provisioned and our cook will already have food underway. However, perhaps we could have a campfire meeting tonight to tell each other about our journey and to discuss matters of the future?"

FORTY-TWO

With that plan in place, the caravaners turned their attention to their animals. Every one carried out their chores, removing saddles and packs, taking them to water, grooming done along with checking for sores that packs may have caused, hobbles tied to legs and turning the animals out to graze. Their food was ready by the time this familiar routine was accomplished. Cody didn't have much appetite and the time crawled by until they finally were seated around the fire.

Cody took the first turn in telling their story since building the storage cabin and then heading to Fort Kokanee. John Linklater took his turn and drew laughter from his audience as he told about the grand deception of the hidden valley. There was more cheerful murmuring at the account of Quinn's big explosion.

Cody took up the story to explain the new circumstances of the gold rush, Darcy and Quinn's experience of Fisherville, and the subsequent change of plans to establish business in the new tent city. There were lots of nods and grunts of agreement from the Kootenay men as the story unfolded.

Yellow Bull gave the story of their journey that had brought them to this camp with the wagon train.

"After the Pards had built the log storehouse, there seemed to be a lot more foot traffic going by our village. Gradually we learned more and more about this gold rush. But the thing that stood out to us was that the white men were running out of food by the time they got this far. They would barter for a meal, maybe trade a shirt for a bowl of stew. Trouble was that the prospectors didn't have much to trade from the packs on their backs. Gradually word filtered back that there was a shortage of food for the men out on their mine claims and they were afraid to go get food very often because of claim jumpers."

Yellow Bull chuckled, "Indians have perfect answer. Our food for this kind of thing has always been pemmican! Good nourishment! Dried meat, fat and berries all pounded together and made into cakes.

This has been a very good year for making pemmican and we are going to trade it for gold. Those two pack horses and their big sacks - - all pemmican! People will give us a new name. No longer Chief Joseph Band. We will be Gold Band of the Kootenay Indians."

A ripple of agreement and light laughter went through the cluster of Indians. Once the meaning of what Yellow Bull had said had been double checked with Pierre, the Pards glanced at one another as they were giving slight side to side motions with their heads. How could they politely tell their friends that this was a very bad idea without insulting them? Especially when they had brought along women and children who would be particularly vulnerable.

Surprisingly it was Quinn who spoke up first. "I would like to share my worries with you. When Darcy and I went to this tent city we found men so desperate that they were loco in the head. Some who do find gold think everyone is going to rob them so they carry a gun all the time. Many of them never find gold

274

and they are starving. Other men go there simply to steal from others. While it is true that some people get rich, it is a very dangerous place. I was looking over my shoulder all the time I was there because bad guys could show up at any moment. We think that it would be good if you didn't go to this place."

It was obvious that Quinn's words had a strong impact on the Chief Joseph men. Having watched him chop trees and lift logs, they viewed Quinn as too big and strong to be afraid of anything. So they talked among themselves in Kootenay for awhile as they considered what had been said.

Cody had been so intent on the campfire discussions he hadn't had opportunity to find Sophie in the group. The conversation among the Kootenay men gave him his chance to search her out with the hope they could make eye contact. She wasn't there. The only conclusion that came to mind in the brief moments before the men finished their parlay was that she must be deliberately avoiding him. He turned his attention back to the group but that didn't prevent a sinking feeling in his gut.

Yellow Bull spoke to give the thoughts of the men. "We are grateful for your information. Some of what you told us is new to us. Yet we are strong men and we can look after our families. Our band would be let down if we didn't trade our food for gold, just as we have traded our furs for supplies for many years. The Hudson Bay has stood up for fair dealing with us and we believe that John Linklater will carry that on. We will make one change. Because of what you have said we will camp out of sight of the city of tents and only go into it during daytime to conduct our trades with the miners."

The Pards would like to have argued with the men but Yellow Bull's response had made it clear they weren't going to budge. Darcy did add some comments about how spread out and disorganized the gold mining camp was so that they might have to be quite a distance from the centre of it. Cody lost interest as the discussions became casual and people began to wander away.

After a little wandering of his own he confirmed to himself that Sophie was not present and that she must be avoiding him.

Surprised that he was feeling Sophie's absence so keenly, Cody wanted to get away from people and be left alone so he could just process his thoughts. Surely he just needed to shake himself and get on with the mission he and his buddies were here to do. It was nice to have a female friend here and there but the really big things of life were the true motivations for him. At least that's what he was telling himself as he slipped out of the camp. He found himself turning up the rise of the meadow behind the camp and settling on a low ridge overlooking it.

He had just nicely hunkered down when a stirring in some brush nearby caught his attention. Flashes of possibilities started to go through his mind – animal, human? Big, small? Flee, fight? But in seconds Sophie materialized out of the bushes with a "Hi, Cody." His heart rate that had jumped when he first heard the rustling sounds, now continued to go up as she stepped near.

"I was afraid that I might not see you."

"I thought you were avoiding me," Cody replied, chagrined at the nervousness in his voice.

"My little sister was sick so I stayed with her until my aunt came back from the campfire. After, when I came, you were gone but Darcy guessed you would be at a lookout spot. He says you think big thoughts on a big hill!"

Cody chuckled. "Yeah, that sounds like Darcy."

Inside Cody marvelled at how easily he could pick up conversation with this beautiful young woman. Her manner and soft humour made him relax and let go of the questions that had worried him about Sophie's response to him.

"Are you thinking big thoughts tonight under thousands of stars? Isn't it hard to think big when we are so small under that sky and in these mountains?" Sophie queried.

"I don't understand a lot of what is inside me, Sophie, but I feel like something or some one is pulling me forward.

Everything was going good with the Pards. We were strong together. There were challenges, battles, and we met them and overcame them. Then this gold rush split up the Pards when Darcy and Quinn, without being reasonable, just took off to find gold. It shook me that there was something stronger than the ties we have with one another." Cody paused as he pictured in his mind watching his two friends gallop off to Fisherville.

"But Darcy and Quinn are here so you've overcome the gold rush, haven't you?" Sophie offered.

"I'm not as sure as I used to be. I almost became the problem when the two of them came back all excited about business we could do if we rushed to the tent city. I was so angry with them for breaking our code of partnership that I made it something worse than what it was. If it wasn't for Jeff helping me to see that forgiveness was stronger than bitterness we might have split apart. Jeff says that forgiveness is so strong because God set that as the basis for relationship with Him. I've got a lot of thinking to do about that but I saw how it healed the fracture in the Pards.

You know, Sophie, with all these people flooding in for gold, it's going to change life forever including you and your family. A place like Fisherville desperately needs people who will stand up for what's right and who will help overcome the chaos that Darcy and Quinn saw there. It's crazy, but I feel like the Pards and I can be part of life becoming good in a frontier town. In some ways it is an inheritance from my Grandfather Thompson; kind of like I'm carrying on something he started with Kootenay House. It's the next stage and I need to be part of it."

"Cody, you do think big thoughts. Those are thoughts that would never come to my mind but I can picture that you will take on big things. It is exciting to talk about them."

They talked about the journey to Fisherville and Cody did discover that Sophie was apprehensive about the trip. She shared a little of the discussions that had gone on before the decision was made to trade pemmican for gold. Before they returned to the camp, Cody urged her to continue to be cautious when the caravan arrived at its destination.

FORTY-THREE

Smoke hung stagnant in the valley signalling to the caravan that the gold rush camp was just ahead. Excitement and curiosity stirred every one of this wilderness band, some who hadn't been in a city for years, and some who had never seen much of a village let alone a tent city of hundreds perhaps even thousands of people. Even their horses were reacting to the mix of scents riding on the pall of smoke. Some of the horses were prancing sideways, others snorting and neighing, others tossing their heads causing a jangling of harness that, added to the usual creak and squeal of waggons and the shouts of wranglers, notifying residents that something unusual was coming into Fisherville.

It turned out to be as big an event as a county fair parade. Men crowded towards the slow-moving caravan waving their hats and yahooing. Those on the route could be heard yelling to others who were on other streets to come and see the spectacle. This only made the horses more difficult to handle and caused more dust and a general hullabaloo. Jed worked his way back along the pack-train helping drivers settle their horses, urging some to get down and walk with their lead horses to keep them from bolting.

Cody caught Darcy's eye and shrugged. "I guess we're not going to be able to sneak into town unannounced!"

"That's for sure, especially when Quinn is having so much fun." Darcy nodded for Cody to look over his shoulder.

Cody turned quickly just in time to see Quinn again causing his horse to rear to the cheers of onlookers who urged him to keep on doing it. To Cody and Darcy's amazement Quinn had also started whirling his lariat in a giant loop threatening to rope some of the bystanders bringing more laughter from the crowd. Quinn was grinning from ear to ear.

The Indian families showing up in the middle of the procession added a sparkle of variety that was cheered by most of the onlookers. The families themselves were gawking at the multitude of people and tents quite awed by all that was assaulting their senses.

At the head of it all rode the Pards and John Linklater. Men were shouting questions as they went along.

"Who are you? Where did you come from"

John Linklater called back, "We're Hudson Bay, come from Fort Kokanee."

"Are you going to trade? Have you got axe handles? What about blankets? Cooking pots?"

John chuckled, "Sure, we've got that and lots more. Bring your furs!"

That brought a loud guffaw from the questioner. "Nobody here bothers with furs!"

Linklater grinned at his own slip up in adjusting to his new environment. "Gold will do just fine!!"

At that moment Jeff rode up beside Cody and got his attention. He was looking stressed. "Thought you should know that the crowd is turning kinda mean towards the Native families. There's a few drunks shooting off their mouths. Some of them are making some pretty lewd comments toward Sophie!! Looks like it could turn in to a mob!"

"Is there anyone there to help her?" Cody was already reining his horse around.

"Jed is there but the others are having a hard time controlling their teams through these crooked lanes. I think we should get back there..."

A piercing scream cut Jeff's words off mid-sentence. Cody spurred his horse as he yelled for Darcy and Quinn to come now. Cody thundered back along the train of waggons bellowing for people to clear the way. He could see a roiling circle of men up ahead as he came around a slight bend in the road. He immediately picked out several rough appearing men in the middle holding onto females that they were mauling. In the same instant he was aware of others holding back the Indian men. With a huge roar for people to get out of the way, he forced his horse through the press of men who were mistakenly being entertained by these hoodlums. Several, who moved too slowly, were knocked flying by Cody's horse. Again Cody kicked the sides of his horse and it lunged toward the molester who was laughing after Sophie had violently pushed him back from trying to plant a slobbering kiss on her neck. Cody vaulted from the back of his running mount as the bleary-eyed man started to turn towards the source of the large roar. In that moment, Cody's full weight crashed against him carrying him backwards to the ground. The whole crowd heard the whoosh as all the air in his lungs evacuated in one large gasp. Cody scrambled up, grabbing the man by his shirt and hauling him to his feet. Although the drunk offered no resistance, Cody was in such a rage that he landed a round house right hand on the man's face bringing an immediate spurt of blood from his nose. Cody dropped him back to the ground and turned to gather up Sophie in his protective arms.

She yielded into his embrace with great sobs. While he was holding her and assuring her that she was safe, he took in the fact that Darcy and Quinn had followed him into the human arena and subdued the other two villains. They had mainly held a woman each to keep them from interfering in the first man's "fun" and had not assaulted them. The men of the band had been pushed around and prevented from coming to the aid of the women and now were freed up to gather their little clan back together. When Sophie had been somewhat restored, John Linklater, who had followed the others to this dust up, spoke up to the gathered crowd.

"Just so you know, my name is John Linklater. I am a Chief Trader of the Hudson Bay Company and under the authority of the English Colony of British Columbia have the obligation to keep reasonable law and order. We are now establishing the Hudson Bay Company here in Fisherville and will not tolerate this kind of behaviour of abusing another person, no matter their race or station in life. There is nothing more to see so break up this gathering and we look forward to trading with you."

Cody grinned his appreciation at John. "I like that, John! You just stuck your fist right into a hornet's nest didn't you?!"

"Why should we sit back and let stuff slide? At least people will know who to bring complaints to!"

"They sure will. I think you just drew a big target on your back though! Cody responded.

"Well, aren't you here to watch my back??! I wouldn't want you just sitting around with nothing to do." John jested.

"Having nothing to do is not what I was expecting! Now I'm real sure we'll have more than enough on our hands." Cody mused as his thoughts reviewed the varied threads that tangled around Legasse and Leblanc. "More than enough!!"

Cody shook himself out of his mental review and called to his buddies, "Hey, let's get this parade moving again. Darcy and Quinn you're going to have to show us to your friends' places. We better get a move on so we can get some things sorted out before dark."

Jed spoke up, "I'll stick with the Kootenays although I'm sure word is spreading all over that you risk your life if you mess with them!! Maybe Jeff can ride with me."

While they were mounting up Cody turned his attention back to Sophie who was still in his arms. Neither was in a hurry to break the embrace no matter what had been the occasion for it. "Sophie, I am so sorry that this happened to you. How bad are you hurt? Are you able to walk ?"

"I'm not bad hurt, just my wrists where he twisted my arms. He was punished enough. It will send a big message to anyone else so we'll be safe. Thank you." Sophie looked up and their eyes met and held as unspoken communication passed between them.

They slowly pulled apart, Cody saying, "I've got to get back to the front." Then added words that were probably unnecessary but needing to be said, "Make sure you stay with the group, and call for Jed or Jeff if anything is going wrong."

Cody swung up into his saddle and trotted up to the front. His mind, though, stayed with Sophie and her party. He had worried that something like this would happen. A lawless gold rush town held danger and risk for everyone. While a few would find riches beyond measure, most would find poverty which would lead them to desperation. Some would pan a fortune and lose it in the gambling tents or on the red lantern side of town. The men watching the caravan go by were largely on the losing side of their grand adventure. Just the fact that they were at their tents in the middle of the day showed that they were not finding any gold on their claims otherwise they would be working their diggings. Most looked filthy and hungry and men who were in that state were living on the border between civilized and lawless behaviour. Any newcomer, and there were scores of newcomers arriving everyday, was checked out as a source of income, legal or illegal, for those with fading dreams. Thus the caravan sent a thrill of anticipation through all of Fisherville for a multitude of different reasons.

FORTY-FOUR

As Cody regained his place among the leaders he heard Darcy and Quinn's names being called along with some vigorous waving. Those two were down from their horses as quick as a wink and shared some hearty handshakes with Nels and hugs and back slaps with Berty as if they were long lost family. The other leaders sat on their horses and watched the greetings with amusement. Amazing how friendships in the wilderness were formed quickly and deeply. Quinn asked after Nels' recovery from his accident and was assured that the healing was almost complete.

After a few moments Cody cleared his throat, "Hey guys, do you think we can get in on this little reunion party?"

"Oh gosh," Darcy chortled, "Nels, Berty, these dusty looking renegades are our outfit."

Darcy proceeded to give a short introduction of each one, as they dismounted, indicating not only the name but also a word of how they fit together. Cody, who gave a tug at his hat as a hello, Jed who was still with the Indian families as the fourth of the Pards, Jeff, and John Linklater. John stepped forward when he was named by Darcy as the Chief Hudson Bay Trader, extending a handshake to Nels and Berty.

"We've heard fine things about each of you. Thank you, on behalf of the Hudson Bay Company, for the help you extended to our fellows. We are grateful that we have connection with reliable people in the midst of this swirl of humanity. In talking with Darcy and Quinn, I'm under the impression that we can be of significant and pleasant benefit to one another."

Nels and Berty responded with enthusiasm and assured John that they welcomed the Hudson Bay as a reliable anchor for bringing civilization to Fisherville and welcomed the protection that Darcy and Quinn along with their friends brought to them.

Cody spoke up, "I hate to be pushy but we need your help with a few practical things. Some of the other details will have to wait till tomorrow."

"Surely," Nels quickly responded.

"With all this train of waggons and livestock, we need pasture and campground outside of this jumble of people. Didn't see any likely spots coming in here. Thought you might know something about the surrounding area. Besides that we've got three families of Kootenay Indians that need to camp somewhere safe."

Berty spoke up, "I've heard tell that there is an open area called Ponderosa Flats over the ridge to the east. Do you know about it Nels?"

"I've been there hunting the first week I was here, bout a mile or two east. It's a big bowl shaped grassland. Nobody is using it cause there's no gravel creeks that would have any gold. Just a pond fed by a spring that flows out as a mud bottomed stream. There's a wagon track follows a shallow ravine. It twists around some but it's not too steep. Come to think of it, Berty, probably the perfect place. Lots of graze."

It sounded right to Cody and John who were both anxious to get the people and equipment away from the attention of the motley crowd that had followed them through the dusty streets.

"Nels, Berty," John said, "If it is acceptable to you, we'll go and establish our camp and then come back this evening to talk business. I want to be sure we set up camp for a longer stay both for water and for security. Besides that, I've told the crew that I'll pay them off tomorrow morning and then they are free to follow their own course. Some of them are pretty itchy to get out from under the grind of the pack train. Some of them want to go pick up those nuggets of gold that are just laying there waiting on them! I think some will settle in and make this their home if they can find the right kind of employment."

"Fine, fine!" Berty exclaimed, "I'm just so pleased to meet the whole crew. Those two fine young men have not led us astray at all in what they said about your troop. I feel like I've been given a new lease on my future."

Darcy and Quinn both blushed at this praise, although it did show up much more on Quinn's freckled face than it did on Darcy with his darker complexion.

Ponderosa Flats was indeed an ideal setting for the caravan to set up for an extended stay. With the whole crew being wilderness savvy and having worked together for the length of their journey from Fort Kokanee, it took little interference from Linklater to establish the right setup. A little discussion put in place the means to protect their water supply from livestock with a plan for a secondary small pond catching the run off from the small spring-fed lake. With an eye to keeping a good distance from the tree line for security, the men also decided that it would be best to set the waggons in a loose circle in such a way that the camp could be defended from all directions. The Kootenays chose a location some little distance from the main camp but with equal access to the water, keeping in mind that theirs was intended to be a very temporary camp. The Hudson Bay crew threw up a rope corral where a scattering of small trees provided the posts and made for a generous enclosure for the sizable remuda.

While the setup was being completed, Jeff rode into the camp.

"Where have you been, Jeff?" Cody enquired to make conversation.

"Thought I'd do a little exploring of the Flats, you know, spot some game trails, see what kind of timber is close by. Saw more than I expected though!"

"What was that? Bear tracks?"

"No." Jeff's voice took on a serious tone. "I was riding just inside the tree line where there is hardly any underbrush but lots of soft needles. I guess I was pretty quiet. Came on a couple of men watching the camp. They jumped when I spoke to them. Asked them what they were doing although it was obvious. They mumbled something I couldn't understand. Native language I think. But they turned and walked deeper into the trees right away as if they had been caught doing something wrong. Probably had horses back there."

"Did they have any weapons?" Cody quizzed.

"None that showed and they weren't threatening towards me. They were dressed rough but I noticed today that most of the men in the gold rush look pretty rugged."

"Well, I had been wondering if we should keep posting guards at night like we have done on the trail. I guess you just decided that for us."

Nightfall found the Pards, Nels, Berty, and John Linklater gathered in the back room of Nels' store. As they were settling down with a cup of coffee provided by the thoughtful Berty, Darcy asked about Swampy.

"Berty, with all the rush of setting up camp I hadn't asked you about Swampy. Is he recovering?"

"It's just terrible, how bad they beat him. He wasn't very strong to begin with and now he's just a shell of a man. His body is healing but he doesn't want to step off my lot. I'm keeping this here shotgun within reach all the time partly just to reassure Swampy that they won't get to him again and partly for my own protection from these villains running roughshod over this camp." With that Berty reached behind the barrel that the coffee pot was on and produced her shotgun which she vigorously waved for all the men to see.

"We'll get a handle on the criminal element! I promise." declared Linklater. "But there's something I'd like to talk about first and then come to the matter of these self-proclaimed protectors."

With that John turned to address Nels.

"Nels, I have a proposal to offer you and you may want to take some days to think it over. The Hudson Bay has been all about the fur business in this vast wilderness. We've traded for everything a family or village could want, all purchased from us with furs. These gold rushes are changing things in a big way. With this move north of the Border that we've had to make, we have a whole trading post's supply of goods but no network of trappers to bring in furs. Besides, give a man a choice between working a trap-line for a winter or possibly finding a fortune in gold, most are going to choose gold so our prospects for building a business based on fur trading are meagre.

Now here you are already established, trading your goods for gold! Your business is so good you can't keep up with demand even though your prices are unbelievable to me. It sounds like you can't keep men on to run freight from your suppliers. It seems to me we can help each other. We have supplies sitting in waggons just a couple miles away and you have the knowledge and skill to turn supplies into way more gold than what it took to buy them in the first place.

"Nels, I can see a couple of possibilities as an offer to you. One would be a partnership in a Hudson Bay Trading Post. We could work out a percentage rate that would keep you in charge of the store as proprietor and us looking after all the related fur trading, building expansion and freighting and I guess we need to add security as well. A generous profit sharing could happen.

"Or – here's another possibility – we could offer you a fair price for your whole business and it would become a Hudson Bay Post. There's one condition on that offer that is very important. We would need your promise to stay on as an employee for at least a year at a generous salary. You obviously have a great instinct for knowing the market in a boom town which is simply foreign to me.

"What do you think, Nels? Do we have any hope of coming to an arrangement with you?"

A blanket of quiet settled over the group with everyone realizing that this was a significant direction setting decision that would affect all of them.

Nels seemed lost in his inner thoughts and the silence stretched out. Cody wondered if he was angry at being put on the spot by John's offers.

Finally, Nels cleared his throat and a brief smile crossed his face.

"John, you kindly suggested that I may want to think this over for a couple days. The reality is that I've been thinking about it for many days, ever since Darcy and Quinn helped me when I was very alone and desperate. It felt so good to be reinforced and supported by two strapping young men. I was going to broach this kind of possibility with you but I didn't want to seem too eager to change my circumstances. It might have seemed that there was something wrong with the business, and that I wanted to get rid of it."

Nels continued, "I am ready to take your second offer. If I can sell at a sufficient profit to put away a good nest egg for my senior years I will consider myself to have struck gold. As for continuing on as your employee, nothing would suit me better. I have great pleasure in the actual interaction with customers and to be relieved of the pressures beyond that part of the enterprise, especially now that these hoodlums are becoming vicious, will feel like a new start in life."

There was a general murmur of pleasure that came from the gathered friends. What could have been quite sticky was, in fact, fulfilling the goals of both sides in the agreement.

John stood to his feet and with his hand extended crossed to where Nels was seated. "Sir, I offer my hand as my seal that we have agreed to our proposal to buy your business and as my seal that we will work out all details to our mutual satisfaction!"

Nels stood to take the extended hand. "Thank you. It's indeed a pleasure." Nels continued around the circle of witnesses to this significant transaction. He shook hands with each one and added some words of appreciation that were appropriate to the individual. His excitement at having made the sale was evident. It was like a new lease on life as he savoured success in his business along with anticipation of continuing his skill, virtually a gift, of serving people's needs through the store.

Berty cleared her throat and everyone understood she was bringing them back to unfinished business.

"I'm glad for you Nels, but I'm going to have to face the reality of keeping the Kitchen going as the vultures are circling to rip away any profit I'm making. There are other business people coming to me for advice about this. I've been promising that things will change with your arrival. So far all I've heard is lovey-dovey deals for profit."

No one spoke for a moment or two. Cody broke the silence.

"You're right Berty. If we don't take these guys down, the Pards are failing their commission. Do these rascals have any kind of pattern so we can confront them? Do you know where they hang out?

"Look, they are like wild animals," Berty snorted, "they move around at dusk or later. But they slink around so you never know when they are going to pop up. Sometimes they say they will come back at a certain time to collect, otherwise there is no pattern."

Quinn growled, "I sure would like to get my hands on these bullies. Tell your friends to let you know if any specific appointments are made, then we can make plans of some kind to meet them."

FORTY-FIVE

As daylight stole over Ponderosa Flats, it unveiled an idyllic setting. The massive Rocky Mountains to the east showed in sharp silhouette against the lightening sky. The open meadows with scattered sentinel trees held the perfume of the pines along with the rich sent of earth disturbed by the arrival of the waggons and livestock the day before. The sun was just tinging the peaks of the mountains on the far side of the Kootenay valley with pink as the delicious aroma of frying bacon began to overtake the natural wilderness scents.

Men began to stir from their bedrolls, hungry for breakfast but also hungry for this day that would see them start a new chapter in their lives. Linklater had asked the cooks to serve up a super breakfast as an appreciation meal as well as a celebration for a successful arrival at Fisherville. A buzz of anticipation spread over the camp as the day brightened and the coffee brought these trail-hardened crew members alert. The aspirations of what might be ahead were as varied as the men themselves. Some were talking about heading out to home places far away, others spoke their dreams of finding their gold bonanza while still others thought they could find employment here and bring a sweetheart to marry.

Linklater had the boys carry a couple of barrels to the side of Linklater's own covered wagon where he kept his business affairs. Across the barrels he had them put the tailgate from the wagon so it could serve as a table. When the crew was finishing their breakfast John called out for everyone to get a coffee refill so he could start the wrap up in a few minutes. In those minutes he brought out ledgers that had the records of each man employed in this crew, a sturdy looking metal box secured with a padlock, as well as a stack of paper embossed with the letterhead of the Hudson Bay Company.

The Chief Trader jumped onto the temporary table and called for everyone's attention. The crew quietened immediately.

"Men, I won't take long. You've got new adventures ahead. This has been an amazing crew. You've each taken care of your own job as well as efficiently helping where we needed you to work together. We'll all tell stories about getting over the mountain at the north end of Hidden Valley and Quinn's big blast!!"

"Your good work has allowed this to be a successful business for the Hudson Bay Company so, in addition to the wage you signed on for, everyone will get a bonus!!"

That sent a ripple of exclamations through the gathered crowd. They nudged each other with their elbows and grins spread like an epidemic. Someone shouted out "Linklater for Governor!"

"So," Linklater continued, "Everyone is finished with the Hudson Bay Company today and you are all on your own. That is, unless you hire back on for a new position. Men, this is a boom town so there are a multitude of ways for you to make a living. I know some of you won't resist the lure of gold and you'll have to try your hand at prospecting. Have fun with that. But remember all those gaunt faces we saw yesterday. I encourage you to turn your payout into something lasting. For instance, the Hudson Bay has bought out Nels mercantile and we'll be expanding the building. We will be looking for carpenters, who will need whip-sawyers to supply the lumber, who will need loggers to supply the logs. A lot of other tent businesses will be wanting permanent buildings. Supplies will have to be packed or freighted in. Roads will have to be built. Hay put up for the winter. Well, you know what a town needs."

"I have three ways to pay you out, gold, scrip, or goods. I don't have enough gold to pay everything that way. Scrip is easy to carry and you can cash it at any Hudson Bay trading post in the future. It just might keep your nest-egg more secure than jingling gold in your pocket. Or you can take some of this equipment or horses instead of money. Let me know when you are called up."

So began a long morning of John paying out his employees. His meticulous record keeping payed great dividends. Occasionally one of the cowboys had taken an advance on his wage but had forgotten. The debt was claimed in the process but even though the crew member was disappointed that he ended up with less then he had dreamed about, no one could claim any unfairness.

Throughout the morning there was always a couple of the Pards standing by the table to assist Linklater, partly to call out the name of the next in line for payment and partly for security as the money box sat out on the table in view of all the men. However there was an easy atmosphere as this crew had bonded as friends more than work mates through the trials of the caravan. The Pards chatted with next ones in line and actually made some suggestions of businesses or employment that the men might consider. Several said that it was a new idea to him and that he probably would check out the possibilities.

Once the morning was well underway and assisting the payout was in the capable hands of his buddies Cody wandered over to the Kootenay camp. Pierre was doing something with a rope but he called out to Cody as soon as he saw his big friend approaching.

"What are you doing Pierre?"

"I'm practising to be a cowboy! My uncle says that when we get back I can have one of their colts for my own, but I have to be able to get a rope on it. I was just trying to rope that pack saddle."

Fortunately, Sophie joined them before Cody told Pierre how badly he was doing. "Cody, I'm glad you came. We are leaving for town in a few minutes to start trading our pemmican. But we are curious. There has been a lot of activity from very early over at your camp. I thought this was going to be a permanent camp."

"Well, for a lot of the crew that got us here, their job is done. So, they are collecting their wages and moving on. They are pretty excited."

Sophie's face clouded, "Does that mean that you are moving on and your friends?"

"Oh, no, not us!" Cody, noticing her sadness, spoke quickly to reassure her. "We actually work for the men who run the company back in Montreal. So they have told us to stay and help this part of the company do business. At least for the next while!"

"Cody, Cody!" Pierre was demanding some attention. "Show me how to rope! Please!"

Cody laughed, "I'm not a cowboy, Pierre, I'm not good at roping."

"But you've done it, haven't you?" Pierre insisted. "Just show me a little."

Cody took the rope, coiled it in his left hand, shook out the loop with his right hand and showed Pierre that he had to hit the front of the pack-saddle with the slip knot. Cody missed on his first try which brought giggles from Sophie which in turn made him determined to do it until he succeeded. Fortunately, he was lucky enough to get the loop around the saddle on the second attempt.

Pierre cheered and became absorbed in trying the technique for himself.

Cody and Sophie turned to walk into the camp and began discussing where in Fisherville they were most likely to find miners wanting pemmican. As they walked, Cody slipped his arm around Sophie's waist and she yielded to his embrace so that they were touching one another as they entered the camp.

Cody commented, "You know that I worry about you doing this kind of thing. Maybe you should just let the men do the trading."

Sophie pulled away from Cody, "I'm not going to be just a teepee Indian woman," she said in an angry voice. "The men get to do all the exciting things and I get upset at that. I want to feel the excitement of all those people crowded into each other. Maybe the miners would rather do their trading with a woman than a man!"

"Yeah, no doubt they would rather have the kindness of a female in their dealings, but you know what the excitement led to yesterday. You could have been seriously hurt."

"Oh Cody, that was just a one time problem. We're going in before noon today so things will be calmer and there won't be as much drunkenness this early. We'll be fine!"

With that Sophie went to join the two men who, with Sophie, made up the trading party for today. They each took a back pack of bricks of pemmican. Cody watched them start out with misgivings. He felt like he should go with them to guard Sophie from danger but he also needed to do his part with the Pards as they helped Linklater with the pay out of his crew. As Cody slowly walked back to the camp he mentally replayed his brief time with Sophie, how she welcomed his embrace and leaned into him while they walked and talked. He realized that he had a big appetite for more of that kind of closeness.

Meanwhile, the pay out of the crew was proceeding steadily. Every once in a while there was a loud "whoo-hoo!" and an excited "yahoo!" along with the beat of galloping hooves as one more wood chopper or hunter claimed his horse and rig for part of his salary plus the gold and scrip he was owed, then bolted for the allurements offered in a gold rush camp. For some of the men it felt like release from captivity as they had found the rigours of the caravan far more of a discipline than they had ever experienced before. They were ready to let loose.

Everyone gathered around the payout table would laugh and some would shout out a cheer in response to these exuberant departures. John, himself, would smile and shake his head as he remembered some of his own spit and vinegar when he first slipped the shackles of what seemed a restrictive home life. He had pushed the wild side for a time before being fortunate enough to find work chopping wood at a Hudson Bay Post when he had lost his last few coins in a poker game. He had taken an interest in the whole operation of the trading post, finding an unknown aptitude for pricing furs and negotiating the trade goods in exchange. He had worked his way up to Chief Trader in a surprisingly short time and was very satisfied to continue to invest his energies for the good of the company because that was abundantly good for him as well. So John's best wishes truly went with every young buck heading out to spend their earnings but he also wished them to land softly in transitioning to a more responsible stage of life.

As the process worked its way along, John had his eye out for certain key people for work he needed in developing the new Fisherville Hudson Bay Post. He had already talked to the Pards about the roles they could take so that their cover of being employees of the Hudson Bay would continue without any suspicion that their primary mission was to bring Leblanc and Lagasse to justice. So it had been agreed that Cody and Darcy would be designated Assistant Managers to work with John in coordinating the various arms of the Post so that food supplies, hardware, lumber, construction, livestock, pack trains, employees would all mesh together without one area being held up by a lack from another. At least, as much as that was possible given the isolation and great distances the location of Fisherville presented to the entrepreneurs of a gold rush boom town. For Quinn, John had recruited him to oversee the lumber operation. This was to include everything from falling the trees to delivering the boards and beams to the construction site. For Jed, he had already approached John about taking charge of their freighting business. His experience of working with the wranglers on the caravan had convinced him that this was his area of work for a lifetime. Jed's suggestion had been that if he could manage the transporting of goods for the Hudson Bay, using Hudson Bay horses and equipment, he would eventually buy that out and go into business for himself. Linklater had eagerly taken Jed up on his proposal.

To this point Jeff had been simply travelling as a friend with the Hudson Bay team. Jed approached him off to the side,

"Jeff, I'm wondering if you would work with me on my freighting business. Linklater is hiring me to handle the transportation and eventually I want to buy out the horses and waggons and make it my own. But I need someone to hire on with me for awhile to keep me calm when there is pressure. Certain kinds of situations get me too excited which leads to some bad decisions. What do you think?"

"Maybe for awhile," Jeff responded thoughtfully. "I really see my future as being a messenger from God letting people see His love for them in how I care for them. And then being able to talk to people about the true message that came through Jesus. But – I need some wages every once in a while to be able to carry on my calling. So - - - really Jed, your offer is an answer to my recent prayers. I'd be very glad to hire on with you."

A big grin lit up Jed's face. "Great! You're the first person I've ever hired. Besides, I've got lots of questions and I'm looking forward to some long conversations while we are on supply runs all the way to Walla Walla and back. I'm not sure that I've ever been an answer to prayer before!"

Jeff couldn't suppress his laughter. "So you're telling me that you're going to pay me to carry out my mission of talking to you about how God loves you."

"It works for me!! Let's go and get Linklater to sign you up."

As they approached the desk, John was talking with Slocum.

"Well Linklater, I've got to hand it to you. You've run a tight ship getting this convoy all the way here. I really thought your crew was too young and that we'd just be a trail of wreckage. Would have been a sight more pleasant if we'd had a little whiskey to fuel us up."

John replied, "Slocum, once we got things sorted out you've been a good teamster. You've earned your pay. What are you thinking about doing now?"

"I don't like the looks of this gold rush kind of town. Too many disagreeable looking people that I'd be sure to upset. No, I think I'll take my mules and my wagon and head down to the Flathead area. I've got some kin folk there. This whole country is pretty sure to open up a lot in coming years so there should be some freighting to be done."

"Good enough! Here's your pay. If you'll just unload at the Trading Post on your way through town we're all squared up. Best of luck, Slocum." The two shook hands as Linklater handed over the gold and scrip.

Jed stepped up just as Slocum left and had John sign on Jeff as an employee of the Hudson Bay with the assignment of working under Jed running supplies. They immediately set off to harness a couple teams to move waggons into town and get the supplies available to the store.

Next up was Gunnar who came to the table with a big smile. "Well, John, we made it, didn't we!!"

"Sure did, Gunnar. And because of you we didn't leave any wrecks along the trail. I still can't believe the repairs you made to keep us going. What are you thinking about your next move?"

John was writing out Gunnar's scrip as he answered thoughtfully. "This is looking pretty good here. There will probably be some actual mines that out last the boom time. I think I'd like to make a business here and next summer bring out my wife and children. So I'm just going to find a good place to park my wagon where miners will see it and start doing the blacksmith work that they will pay me for."

"Good luck, Gunnar! I couldn't think of a better guy to be part of building a real decent community out of all this mad grab for gold. By the way, I've got your first order. We are going to build a sturdy lock up storage room and we're going to need some heavy duty hinges and locks. Our second order will be Jed coming to you to check up the shoes on all our horses."

Gunnar grinned, "Yeah, Glad to have a rich customer like the Hudson Bay! See you soon."

Linklater worked through the whole crew by late morning. Some hired right back on for logging or carpentry. Some said they might look John up in a few days once they got the wrinkles out of their systems. Inwardly, the Trader cringed as he knew some were wanting to get to the gambling and drinking establishments, others to the red lantern side of the town. He had to let them chose their own route but hoped they didn't become big victims. He hated to think that a lot of the generous salary he had paid to the men would end up lining the pockets of shysters who fed off the lesser appetites of the young men.

FORTY-SIX

With the payout completed the men headed into town to get the work on the expansion of the store underway. It was urgent because of the large inventory that would have to sit in waggons until warehouse space was available. Fortunately Nels had claimed a large lot for the store premises providing abundant space for adding on to the existing building.

Quinn found the measuring rods where Nels had indicated. John said, "We'll build the main walls out of logs and just have dirt floors for now. That will give us quick and secure storage. Then we can use the whip-sawed boards for counters, shelves, doors and furniture."

With John's considerable experience with trading posts, it didn't take long to lay out the perimeter of the several rooms they would need. Quinn had them adjust the length of walls here and there to equate to a full length of the closest section of a rod which would save immense time for bucking the logs to the size needed.

Nels raised a question about the lumber they planned to use. "I'm not sure you will be able to get any sawn boards for quite awhile."

"Why would that be the case? With all the cut wood you've used on the store I just assumed it would be available," commented John.

"Well, there's only one saw pit going here and I was one of the first to line up an order. The word is that they can't keep up at all with the town growing every day and people wanting to move out of their tents. Especially before winter." said Nels.

John turned to Quinn, "Looks like we're going to need you to add another arm to the logging and building project that you took on. Do you know anything about saw pits?"

Quinn wrinkled his brow, "I know what they are but I've never bothered to look close up. It can't be that difficult to set up."

Nels chimed in, "Yeah, they are pretty basic but I watched these guys for a bit and there are definitely some tricks to the trade. You'll save yourself a lot of grief if you go see their set-up. They are on the north side of town."

"Sounds good to me. What do you think John?" Quinn asked.

"If you can learn from their experience it will pay off big time. Why don't you send out some of these guys that have shown up for work to get right in to cutting some logs."

Quinn stepped over to the cluster of men and took aside those that nodded that they were willing to do some logging. "Head over to the stand of pines just off the trail to Ponderosa Flats where the wagon track does a sharp turn to the left. We'll pay you per log ready for skidding out of the bush. Each log needs to be a rod long and good and straight. Oscar, will you keep a count for each man?"

Oscar nodded and Quinn pulled from a wagon enough double bitted axes to equip all of them. Before Quinn headed out to see the saw pit, he found Jed and put a request to him.

"We will be needing to skid the logs out of the bush as early as tomorrow afternoon. Can you fix us up with a horse and the right kind of harness?"

"Consider it done!" was Jed's straightforward reply.

Quinn found his saddle horse and headed out to find the saw pit. There was a good feeling in all of this for Quinn. As he trotted along, he felt important and trusted, so different than the treatment he had received growing up in Montreal. He wished his Dad could see him now. He was starting his own business. This was an opportunity beyond anything that could have happened in his former life. His big frame body would be an asset rather than something to be ridiculed as it had been on the school ground. He would be the one person to study the design of a saw pit and build one to serve the Hudson Bay's needs.

Quinn heard the saw pit before he laid eyes on it. The steady rhythm had a music of its own as the whip saw chewed through the log. As Quinn walked his nervous horse toward the contraption the sawyers were close to finishing a cut. The music of the saw belied the grunting work of the sawyers. The top sawyer was bare to the waist and his body glistened with sweat and his muscles bulged as he pulled the saw up and plunged it down again. The bottom sawyer was covered from head to toe but the sweat of his body was obvious through his shirt and the sawdust clung to him as it showered down with each stroke of the long two handled saw. He was giving no less effort than the top sawyer as they pressed the handles to make the saw bite as deep as their strength allowed. In a few minutes they finished their cut and a clean, smooth, straight plank laid down on the platform.

The top sawyer looked around as he traded off with the next man. When he saw Quinn his face darkened and the scowl on his face deepened as Quinn swung down from his horse. The sawyer started berating Quinn as he came closer.

"Why don't you guys leave us alone and let us get our work done. If you keep harassing honest businesses we'll all pull up and leave and then there'll be nothing even for bottom feeders like yourselves!"

Quinn was shocked at this reception by the glowering man who was now within arms reach and had his fists doubled. Quinn took an involuntary step back and raised his hands with palms out. "Sorry! I don't mean any harm. I was just wanting to see a saw pit in operation! If I'm interfering I will leave."

The expression on the sawyer's face relaxed and his fists opened slightly. "Who are you with?"

Quinn explained that he was part of the Hudson Bay caravan that arrived yesterday and that they had heard that there was a shortage of sawn lumber. "We thought maybe we could do our own without harming the market for the established sawyers."

"Oh, I'm sorry," the big man responded. "I thought you were one of them. Certainly you are welcome to have a look around. In fact, let me show you around while my partner takes over the top. I'm Orville, by the way!" This time he stuck out his wide open hand for a very firm handshake.

Much relieved, Quinn shook the proffered hand, "I'm Quinn and I'm running the lumber operations for the Hudson Bay. By the way, we've bought out Nels at the store and he's working with us as we expand it to a full Trading Post."

"Glad you boys have come," said Orville as they walked toward the saw pit. "This town is booming so nobody can keep up with supplies or demand. The Bay will help."

Here Orville started pointing out the essentials of a saw pit. "The log has to be high enough for a man to work the saw underneath so your main uprights need to be very sturdy. The more you can find a spot for a natural ramp so the log will roll onto the frame without much effort, the better you are." He went on to show how they held the log in place with a saddle and wedges; how they marked the cut with a chalk line.

The two men chatted easily as they moved around the operation. Quinn's eyes were taking in more than what was spoken and he was already forming some improvements he could incorporate for his own saw pit.

"Say!" Orville broke in. "Why don't I take a ride over to your site with you and maybe I can offer some suggestions. I think there is a natural site there. It was just too far out of the town when we were setting up. Now it's not far at all with all the growth out that way."

Quinn gladly accepted his offer. As they were skirting the edge of the hodgepodge of tents Quinn raised a question he had been puzzling over since his arrival at the saw pit.

"Orville, I have a question and I hope you don't mind me bringing it up."

"It's probably about the rude greeting I gave you. I'm sorry about that."

"Do you mind telling me about it?" Quinn pressed gently.

"It seems some thugs have decided to take a little cream off the milk of the gold rush. They showed up suggesting that a little fee would provide protection for our business. Do we look like we can't protect our own place? Hooligans! They came a second time and I threw them off the property. That's when the threats started. As they were leaving they yelled back that we would be sorry, that we should watch our step!"

Orville had grown red in the face as his anger mounted in reciting what had happened.

Quinn asked, "Have you had any damage done?"

"Mostly things have just been strewn around. But last night they broke some axe handles and one of the saddles on the platform. Just wait till I get my hands on their scrawny necks!! I don't know what to do. And I'm not the only one being targeted."

"Have any of the businesses given in and paid them their demands?" Quinn wondered.

"Yeah, some have. They just shrug and say it's the price of making a fortune in a gold rush. Kinda like taxes! But it's not right. Listen Quinn, some of us are getting ready to take action. We figure there's enough of us that we could meet them with rifles and put an end to their goon tactics. There's talk of a meeting in a night or two. You might give some thought to joining us cause they're sure to come after you as well."

Quinn nodded and without revealing anything of the Pards interest in tracking down the king pins of the scam simply said, "I'll give it some thought."

Further talk of the problem came to an end as the two arrived at the general area for the logging operations. Quinn was pleased to hear the staccato rhythm of axes bringing down trees that would quickly put up walls of the big Bay operation. After they did a big circle on horse back Orville pointed them towards a small bluff that extended the down slope of the timbered area that backed the intended lumber enterprise."

"Now there is a great site for your pit!" Orville exuded. "Put the platform at the level where the bluff takes that steep drop and one man will be able to do the work that needs three men on my site. The logs will just roll down a gentle slope on the ramp you build. You've also got a great asset with the ground being mostly gravel. With all the traffic, all the log skidding, your site will hold up in the wet times. At my place we have to use all the sawdust to build up the mud trails. You'll find you can even sell the sawdust cause people use it for flooring and for their paths."

"Well, I'd best be getting back. They'll be looking for me to top that saw. We'll keep in touch about that meeting so you can come if you want." With that Orville reined his horse around and cantered towards his business.

Quinn was mulling over the implications of vigilantes taking matters into their own hands as he turned his mount up the slope towards the tree fallers. He would have to get back to the others with this new information as soon as possible. Obviously a crisis was building that could explode Fisherville into armed camps that would kill and maim many innocent people. The sound of the axes kept him on course to find his crew.

"I'm going to need some extra thick logs as a framework for a saw pit." As he continued to explain his plan, one of the axemen spoke up that he had seen such a construction in operation. He assured Quinn that he could get the right logs cut and skidded into place by the end of the next day. Also that he would be very willing to help build it.

Quinn was very content to get that project turned over to someone else. The knowledge he had received from Orville was weighing heavily on his mind and was spurring him to get back to the Trading Post. He wished he had gotten a description of the gang members from Orville. However, at the time, it would have seemed out of place to pursue that much detail when supposedly he was a new business man in town and hadn't yet encountered this pressure.

As Quinn circled around to the Trading Post his path intersected with a small knot of people on foot. Turned out it was the Kootenays. Quinn pulled up to chat with them.

"Hey, how was your trading day?"

They were all smiles and Antler showed off his empty carrying sack.

Sophie was enthusiastic, "We didn't run into any drunks at all. People were friendly and polite. We even have some orders that we will take to them tomorrow. Tell Cody he had nothing to worry about."

Quinn chuckled, "I'll be very glad to do that. Good bye for now."

Getting back to the store, Quinn found every one busy at getting the Trading Post up and running. John and Nels were working on the book keeping trying to evaluate what had been

Nels' inventory so they could eventually settle on the full price for buying the business. John would need to justify that price to his Hudson Bay superiors. Cody, Jeff and Darcy were trying to unload waggons as well as deal with customers. There were lots of interruptions, as the boys had to ask Nels what to charge for the items. They had looked after Slocum's wagon first which set him free to, in his words, "Look after a raging thirst that had been building for days and days."

Jed came looking for Quinn. They spent some time looking over the harness that Jed had rigged for skidding logs. The attaching end that gripped the log was only temporary as Gunnar was working on making some tongs that would be a quick hitch. Quinn was more than pleased with what Jed had accomplished.

FORTY-SEVEN

It was evening by the time everyone could break from their work and Quinn could get everyone's attention.

"I picked up some new information from the owner of the other saw pit. Seems this protection gang is getting bolder and bolder, doing damage at businesses, and demanding more from people. This guy, Orville, is mad enough he wants to push back at them. He's talking about a meeting in a day or two to see if they can figure a way to deal with them. He asked me to come to the meeting."

Cody asked, "You mean a vigilante kind of pushing back?"

"That's what Orville mentioned. He figured they had rifles so they should be able to eliminate this problem. Do you think I should be at that meeting?"

John responded, "This could really get ugly! Armed groups going after each other! I think you should go so we can know where we are at in bringing these guys down. Hopefully you can be a calming factor in what goes on so that we have more time to track down the king pins."

"I don't know how much calming down we can do. You should have seen how furious this Orville was towards me when he thought I was one of the gang riding up to spy on them and pressure them. I think people are boiling inside and are getting to the point that reasoning isn't going to stop them," said Quinn.

Everyone's attention was drawn to the front door where someone was banging on the door and calling out John's name. John went to open the door to find that it was Matt, one of the wranglers that had worked for Linklater for a couple of years.

" Matt. Good to see you. Come on in, we're just talking over our day and our plans."

Matt nodded to each one that was present and was introduced to Nels. The men exchanged pleasantries and reminisced a little. They especially enjoyed chatting about Matt's role in closing off the gap in the clay cliffs that provided access to Hidden Valley. Generally, Matt was a nice guy who did his work each day without complaint. He was a little shy around people most of the time and preferred working with animals. This day he was a little more outgoing than usual and his friends assumed correctly that he had been using a little of his pay on some alcohol.

Eventually Matt cleared his throat and said, "Just thought I should pass on something I heard today. Don't mean to stick my nose in where it don't belong. Seemed like a little beer and a few hands of poker would be a good celebration for me so I found a tent that had both of those. Your names came up in the conversation in a way that isn't right so that's why I'm here."

"Tell us more, Matt." Cody encouraged, as everyone present was giving full attention to what was to come.

"Well, I was at a table with three other guys. One was a prospector who had panned an extra good day yesterday so was blowing it all in one afternoon. The other two turned about to be enforcers for tax collecting. That's their words. The more they drank the more they started bragging about how good they were at their job. I wanted to punch them for the way they said they treated people. But I remembered how you cracked down on bad boys at Fort Kokanee, John, so it hit me that maybe I was getting some inside information that I might pass on to you. I pretended to get pretty drunk but in fact I was cutting back on how much I was drinking."

"You said they talked about us?" Darcy asked.

"Well, kinda," Matt continued. "The old gold panner laughed in their faces, his whiskey was giving him some liquid courage. He told them they had better watch out because the Hudson Bay had come to town and would soon put them out of business."

"That must have riled them pretty good," Quinn laughed! "What did they say?"

"Actually, it didn't even slow them down. They said their Bosses had the Hudson Bay wrapped around their little fingers. That the Hudson Bay didn't do anything without checking with the Bosses. I couldn't believe what I was hearing and I knew that they certainly weren't talking about John Linklater!"

"Matt, let me ask," Cody interjected, "they called the leaders 'The Bosses'? As if that's their title?"

When Matt nodded his head, the Pards looked at each other in amazement.

Darcy said what they were all thinking, "That certainly confirms what we had figured. That this is the same gang that was at Kootenay House."

Turning back to Matt, he asked, "Did they use any other names for these bosses at all?"

"Yeah, but I didn't get them. Sounded like French names, Le, Le,...."

"Leblanc and Lagasse?" Jed asked.

"Sounds like it could be, but I wouldn't swear to it. I can tell you what they look like more than I can pronounce their names."

"What do you mean?" Cody, with a look of disbelief, actually erupted from his perch on a sack of beans, "Are you telling us you actually saw The Bosses in public?"

Matt shrugged, "Yep, was that something special? They just walked into the gambling tent all dressed up fit to kill!"

"When we came through Kootenay House on our way south, those guys stayed completely out of sight and just told their henchmen what to do to cause us grief. They obviously have gained a lot of confidence through the time since." commented Darcy.

"Come to think of it, that makes sense out of something those guys said," Matt frowned as he remembered the words. "Something to the effect that the Bosses had told them just a few days ago that the operation was all in place. They had enough control of the town that nobody would be foolish enough to seriously go against them and now they could enjoy the fruit of their labour!"

"You said you could tell us what they look like?" John queried.

"They are both pretty big guys, both black hair down to their shoulders, short black beards. One has had his nose squashed. One had a scar just under his eye, but their clothes stand out a lot more. Both have fancy buckskin shirts with lots of bead work and both came in wearing stove pipe hats and smoking cigars! Imagine, wearing stove pipe hats in a gold rush camp! I was going to laugh but I saw how men were being very serious in greeting them. Then I got a look at their faces and they have a mean look. Made a chill run down my spine. I left pretty quick and made it look like I was staggering drunk so those guys wouldn't think anything of telling a drunk all that."

Everyone was quiet, thoughtful, for a few moments absorbing what Matt had brought to them. John was first to speak.

"Matt, I can't thank you enough for bringing this information. Believe me it is a huge help. What are you going to do? Do you have any plans?"

"Not sure, maybe ready just to ride the wind for a bit."

Quinn spoke up, "Well, if you want to do a little logging or building we can use as many hands as possible for a few days."

"Thanks, I'll give it some thought over night. Happy trails!" With that, Matt slipped out into the night.

The group sat quiet absorbing the implications of Matt's news.

Darcy broke the silence, "Can you believe it? It's like our mission has been packaged up and plopped right in our laps in Fisherville of all places."

"We certainly don't have to go searching the bad guys out in some wilderness stronghold." Jed added.

"Where do we stand in pursuing them, John. What do you think we need to do?" Cody asked, his mind whirling with the close proximity of their quarry.

"Well, first of all, we stay on course for the next few days as we sort out the evidence that we have. Think about it, most of what we have is either circumstantial or attached to one of their goons rather than to the Bosses themselves. Even if we did arrest them, we don't have a lock-up where we can keep them. Quinn, looks like we need to focus on getting that log storage shed to where it can be secured."

Cody stretched, realizing how uncomfortable his bean sack had become, "I'm exhausted. I'm headed for some shut eye!"

As he stood, the window behind Cody exploded with a huge crash! Everyone dropped to the floor. Darcy and Jed began to crawl to the door. Jed collecting the store rifle leaning against the end of the counter. After a moment Cody blew out the lamp. With no follow up crash, Darcy and Jed were quite sure it hadn't been a gunshot. They got to their feet on either side of the door. Darcy opened the door and Jed immediately had the muzzle of the rifle into the open space ready to defend all of them, They stood still for a few moments searching the darkness, listening to the sound of their own heart beats. Nothing stirred. There was only the background blend of the sound of camp life.

"It's clear out here," Jed declared as he turned back to the room. "Is anyone hurt? Cody, are you alright? It happened right behind you.

"I'm not even cut, but something heavy came through the window. A rock maybe."

"I'll get a lamp so we can see what it was," Nels offered and quickly did just that.

A few moments of searching discovered the fist-size missile that had rolled under a chair. John let out an exclamation as he picked it up.

"There is something wrapped around it! Looks like a message."

All heads leaned in to a tight circle to watch as John carefully pulled back the string and the edges of the paper. Except for Jed, who kept a nervous grip on the rifle and an uneasy eye out the undamaged panes of the window.

"I can't make out the writing in this light. Let's move into Nels' room and get a brighter light."

Nels' living quarters were definitely bachelor accommodation. It was small with just one small table and only one window whose bottom was shoulder height. It assured that the group was safe from prying eyes while they investigated this mysterious message.

John carefully lifted the folded edges until he had the paper flat and turned to the side of the writing. Pulling the lamp even closer, he slowly read out words that were of inconsistent darkness from whatever instrument had been used to do the writing. It looked like the words had been scratched on the paper as much as drawn.

" 'John Linklater' Well it's definitely intended for here." He turned the paper to get a better angle from the lamp. Then he continued stating the words out loud.

"Meet tomorrow night, an hour after dark, behind Berty's Kitchen, Urgent"

It was when John read the name at the bottom, that there was a collective murmur of surprise.

"Sam Ogilvie!"

Cody blew out a big breath. "This day just gets stranger and stranger! Vigilantes! The Bosses themselves! And now our corrupt Hudson Bay Trader from Kootenay House!"

After a pause, Darcy asked, "John, will you meet him like it says?

"Definitely! I can't imagine what he wants to say to me given how completely differently we've conducted our commissions, but I'm curious as well as obligated. There is no other way for me to contact him so tomorrow night it is! In the meantime we've got business to run and construction to get done. Let's get some sleep!"

"Oh yeah, Cody!" Quinn said, "I crossed paths with Sophie this afternoon. She said to tell you they did good today and that they have some orders to fill tomorrow. She was pretty pleased and thought you worried too much."

"I just hope they get out of here soon so they can be safe! That adds one more thing that's going to keep sleep pretty much at bay tonight."

FORTY-EIGHT

By the time the sun had cleared the eastern mountains the next morning, the valley was alive with activity. Miners and prospectors were heading out of town. Newcomers were bumping into them trying to get inside information to guide them to their bonanza. Business people were preparing their inventory for a profitable day. The Hudson Bay of Fisherville was a veritable beehive of activity that added to the energy of the valley. The loggers were divided into crews falling new trees or trimming out the ones already down. They were further divided as to whether their logs were for the building or for the saw pit.

Quinn and Jed happened to meet on the way up to see where they could help the most. Angry voices came to their ears before they got to the men. When Quinn hailed them, the two red faced men turned to Quinn as if they would tackle him.

"It's your fault!" "You've got to sort this out!"

Quinn held his hands up, palms out. "Whoa, tell me. One at a time."

The first man, the wrangler with the skidding horse, said, "Cody told me to get logs down to the store first thing!"

"But I've got to have logs at the saw pit site so they can start on their job there." clamoured the other foreman. "We'll lose half a day if we don't get these skidded right now."

Jed spoke up, "Looks like we've got more crew than what we first thought. Give me an hour and I'll have another horse rigged to skid logs. Then there can be a horse pulling to both locations."

Quinn nodded and took some of his saw pit men down to the site to dig holes for setting the upright log frame. Jed fell into step with Quinn for a stretch of the path they both had to pass along. Quinn let out a chuckle and commented to Jed, "Can you believe this? Could you have ever imagined from our days back in Montreal that I would ever be in charge of a crew of men... that there would be people who would look to me for answers to a problem? I feel......Alive. This wilderness, these people! I belong, Jed. This is home."

Quinn blushed as he realized how much he had opened to Jed.

As he turned to the corral, Jed simply said, "I hear you, Quinn! I hear you!"

As the first logs arrived at the building site, men were ready with broad axes to take off knots so the first logs would lay firm and square on the shallow trenches dug to provide a level base. Several men had experience in using the broad axes for notching the logs for the corners. Good corners were key for the tightness of the logs so that little chinking would be needed to make the building strong and weather proof.

The day passed quickly with more than enough tasks for everyone. At the midday break, the Pards, Nels, John and Jeff gathered to give each other progress reports. At the store they had been managing to serve a steady stream of customers while unpacking waggons and stocking shelves.

John addressed Jed, "Looks like we are going to need certain staples that we apparently don't have in the cabin at Joseph's Prairie. That means we'll need them from Walla Walla. How do you and Jeff feel about handling a sizable pack train there and back? We'll have you take the furs that we do have on hand as well. You'll be gone long enough that a pack train will also collect the goods at Joseph's Prairie. My guess is that I can find a volunteer to lead that little expedition!! Right Cody?!!"

Jed didn't hesitate. "Yes, sir! We can handle that. It may take a couple days to check out all the pack saddles and double check all the tack we'll need before we can leave. Nels can give us the route and we can ask along the way. Yes, sir!! We'll look after it, won't we Jeff?"

Jeff merely nodded his agreement, although Cody sensed a degree of hesitation. Cody, himself, was amazed but a little concerned at Jed's self-confidence over leading this big a task. At the same time, Cody couldn't have been more pleased with Jed's personal development in stepping up to lead.

Quinn reported on saw pit progress and suggested they would have some planks to use for shelving and counters by the next afternoon.

Their impromptu meeting broke up quickly once they had wolfed down some lunch. They were all working in areas that they enjoyed and could see the progress they were making. It served to put energy into their steps.

It was early afternoon when the saw pit was ready for the first cuts of the whip-saw. The first cuts were slow and wandering so that the first couple of planks varied in thickness. While the crew was experimenting on the best ways to improve, Quinn's friend, Orville, came by to check on their progress. He offered to make some suggestions and Quinn was more than happy for the help. A few suggestions for marking the cut and for technique on the whip saw along with actual demonstrations made a huge difference for the crew. Soon they had a steady rhythm singing from the saw that promised useable lumber to fill their orders.

Quinn was more than grateful to his new friend. When he extended his hand to thank him, Orville nodded for them to step away from the pit.

"I had a second purpose to my visit this afternoon. There have been more assaults on people who resisted paying the 'tax' and anger is definitely building in the town. One Indian in particular has been noticed in all this business who particularly inspires dread. I'm not completely sure but I think I saw him and another of their gang up by those trees as I came here. They moved back into the bush once they spotted me. I think you'll be getting a visit before long."

"Anyway, the meeting I've talked about is on for tomorrow evening. We could sure use you there, Quinn!"

"I'm not sure. You've been good to me so there is a pull to attend. But......what's it going to be.....Guns and Booze and Torches?"

"No, no! Tomorrow night is just talk and planning. No guns and no booze if I have my way. People know you're with Hudson Bay so what you say will carry big weight. Meet just at dark at my pit."

Quinn shrugged as they parted. It wasn't a full commitment to be there but it wasn't a refusal either and Orville left feeling quite sure that Quinn would come.

"Quinn! Quinn!" A youthful voice pulled him out of his mental processing of his conversation. Pierre was coming across the meadow with his usual big grin.

"Pierre! How goes the pemmican business?"

"All sold out, big Quinn!" Pierre laughed. "Indians got a gold poke now! Heap big wampum!"

"That's great, but I wouldn't be bragging too loud about it. Not everybody has found gold and they'd love to take a short cut to get yours."

"Naw, just telling you cause you're bigger than all the bad guys. By the way, Sophie told me to tell you guys that we'll be heading back to Joseph's Prairie tomorrow."

"Thanks for letting us know. You keep safe Pierre! And say goodbye to your family for us."

"Bye Big Quinn!"

Quinn walked back to the saw pit. It was time for him to take a turn as the top sawyer. It was a great outlet for the pent up doubts and worries he had about the planned meeting. So many things could go wrong. Pull. He doubted that everyone would stay away from liquor before the meeting. Pull. The saw took a deep bite. He doubted that everyone would leave their guns behind. Pull. What if the gang knew of the meeting? Pull. What if?......Pull. What if?...Pull.

Suddenly he was at the end of the cut. The bottom sawyer called up that that had certainly been a record speed for cutting a plank so far. Quinn grinned, his emotions spent, his resolve for the meeting established. From there on the crew, Quinn taking his turn, had a very productive afternoon.

As regular as the setting sun, the men gathered for their evening meal. As much as the food was important, it also served the important function of everyone keeping up to date with developments around them. It helped them adjust their plans for the coming days as they monitored their progress. On this particular day it seemed that everything was doing well if not even getting ahead of expectations.

The obvious focus this evening was the pending meeting between John and Sam Ogilvie. They hadn't been able to talk about it during the day with other hired workers being around them all the time. Cody broached the subject.

"John, have you any further guesses about what Ogilvie wants? I can't imagine it being very good considering what we saw of him at Kootenay House."

John's reply was pensive. "It's been on my mind all day. Is he upset with me? Maybe he feels like I've moved into his territory by coming here rather than settling at Joseph's Prairie. But he has been an officious snob towards me in the past so putting a message on a rock through the window doesn't fit with that. I would have expected him to just come and confront me. From what you've said about his involvement with the Bosses, would he come and warn me? Maybe he is in trouble with the gang and is looking for a way out? I really don't know so I'm trying to keep an open mind rather than prejudge him."

"Well, skulking around in the dark says quite a bit about him, I think," said Darcy. "Should it be one or two of us that goes with you?"

"No, no!" John replied. "That could scare him off. I don't feel that kind of threat from him. I'll go on my own and I'll be fine."

With that settled, conversation moved on to other things. The secure storage building was moving along well and that brought a reminder to order window bars, hinges and a padlock clasp from Gunnar.

Quinn added his new information from his conversation with Orville. "Even though I'm still pretty negative about this kind of meeting, I've made up my mind to attend. I guess it's like Sam Ogilvie. We'll be better off knowing what's going on than to not know. Orville claims there won't be a lot of drunkenness but I'm worried about it."

"By the way," Quinn continued. "Pierre came over to the pit this afternoon. He says the Kootenays are leaving tomorrow."

Cody, who had been lost in thoughts about John's meeting with Sam Ogilvie, suddenly came to attention and turned to Quinn demanding he repeat what he had said. Smiles crossed most faces in the group at Cody's sharp reaction.

Quinn slowly replied, "Well I thought John's safety was maybe more important to discuss right now than your romance.

By the way, how come I'm the messenger in the middle of your heart throb?"

As Cody was on his feet headed to the door, he couldn't resist one sarcastic comment "So good of you to finally mention something that important!"

In moments, they could hear Cody's horse galloping out of town.

FORTY-NINE

As Cody cleared the lip of the Flats, his emotional energy had somewhat burned off, and his attention was grabbed by the beauty of the setting. The sun was close to setting on the range of mountains to the west. It was lighting up the scattered clouds with incredible colours from deep purple to fiery oranges and reds. The peaks ahead of him to the east were glowing pink. It was breathtaking and Cody wanted to share it with Sophie. The brilliance of the sky display was dimming as Cody rode up to the Kootenay camp. He had been so caught up in the sunset and how he longed to share it, he hadn't noticed strident voices that were now becoming unavoidable to his attention. The argument was taking place in Kootenay language so he had no idea of what it was about. He could tell that there was plenty of anger involved.

A woman's voice cut into the argument and silence was immediate. Then Sophie stepped around one of the lodges and came to meet Cody. She smiled up at Cody although she was a little strained. Cody swung down off his horse and greeted her with a brief hug. She was noticeably tense and Cody didn't pursue the matter although it seemed obvious that the argument, what ever it was about, was causing her distress.

She immediately took Cody's hand and pulled him away from their camp. "Let's walk over here to the water."

Cody tied his horse to a small tree and walked with her. Nothing was said for a time and the waning sunset that was constantly changing the hues of the whole landscape did it's magic on Sophie as well. Cody could tell that she was calming down.

"Do you want to talk about what was happening at the camp? I'm ready to listen."

"Oh Cody, this group of Indians doesn't seem to do well when it comes to money. When we don't have money and we do everything by trade, things go better. The men are arguing about how to keep the money safe. We had agreed that each of the men would carry a third so it wasn't at risk of all being lost or stolen from one person. Now Winter Moon says he is youngest and strongest of the men and he should look after all of it. It's a silly argument but he gets angry when he is told that."

"Maybe he has got a touch of gold fever now that he has seen some of it," suggested Cody.

Sophie sighed, "Well, let's not have our evening spoiled by them," as she leaned into Cody and his arm went around her shoulders.

This felt so right to Cody. He wanted to shield her from conflict yet he sensed that she was a very capable person in dealing with life issues within her world and even beyond. Even though he knew that he hadn't spent extensive time with Sophie, he felt he knew her in his heart and that went way beyond actual shared experience. It was almost scary but at the same time it was exhilarating. He felt like two different people at the same time. On one hand he wanted to let Sophie know how much he felt alive in her presence and how he wanted that into the future. At the same time there was a voice within reminding him of how young he really was and how much of life was pulling him into adventures beyond this part of the Kootenay valley, reminding him of how little he knew of what life might hold in days to come. There came a settledness that he wasn't ready to make any commitments for the future and that this evening was for enjoyment and deepening friendship.

Time went by far too quickly for this couple as they talked and shared each others' past experiences. Each one learning and probing as they described the impact on their own lives. The rising moon had turned Ponderosa Flats into a magical landscape by the time they needed to say goodbye. Cody held the reins of his horse in one hand as he slipped his other hand around Sophie's waist, drawing her to him as they shared a lingering, tender kiss. How Cody wanted to say more of how he felt towards her! Yet as he cantered away from her, he knew it was better that he hadn't said anything rash to mislead the tender heart of the woman he so cherished. He wondered if and when they would ever cross paths again.

By the time Cody pulled himself away from Sophie, John Linklater was standing in the cover of bushes and trees behind Berty's kitchen. He was growing impatient, feeling rather foolish as he began to wonder if this had simply been a hoax. It was well past the hour after dark that the message tied to the rock had stated. However, with no way of knowing what may have delayed Ogilvie, John was determined to stick to his post as long as there was any possibility of him showing up.

It was just a whisper at first. Then it repeated. Yes, it was a faint voice calling his name. He cautiously took a step out from his secluded spot. The voice repeated, calling him a little more to his left than he had been expecting.

Not much above a whisper John responded, "Ogilvie, Sam Ogilvie, is that you?"

"Come over here, let's just get back in the trees a bit."

John stayed on high alert. He still wasn't sure but that he was being led into an ambush of some kind.

Ogilvie urged him to come. "There's no one but me. Come so we can step back into these dark shadows!"

The renegade trader was obviously agitated. He kept making urgent waving motions with his hand to get John to the right place. Ogilvie's breath was coming in short, quick little gasps. He was rocking sideways from foot to foot. He spoke in an urgent whisper.

"John, thank you for coming. Do you think we'll be discovered? I have some things to do. Let me do them before I go to jail. Oh, John! I've created such a mess. I'm sure there is no salvation for me. There have been too many wrong things. This wasn't going to be my future. If only there was a road back. It's too late, it's too late!!"

The man was clearly distraught and looked like he might bolt at any moment. John was taken aback as he realized how irrational Ogilvie's words were. He didn't smell liquor on his breath that would explain his jumbled thinking. Apparently this was the outpouring of an over wrought and stricken conscience.

"Sam, slow down. I'm not going to do anything tonight but listen. Tell me what's gotten you so riled up."

"At first the two Frenchmen just included me in small price adjustments for them. Oh my, it seemed so little to start with. They charged me a lot less for their initial trade goods. But then later they held that over my head for kick backs on new supplies. Then they started stealing from other people and forced me to direct suspicions away from them. They even got into beating people who got in their way. I was horrified, at first, then when God didn't strike me with lightning I kinda got used to it. But it has blackened my heart. I need to cleanse my soul, John! I need to be cleansed. I go for days on end with out sleeping. I kept quiet about some Hudson Bay agents that mysteriously disappeared. Oh, I'm beyond forgiveness. There's no penance big enough to save me. The souls of those who were killed visit me in the night and they stand pointing their bony fingers at me chanting 'guilty' 'guilty.' And I am, John, I am guilty!"

Sam Ogilvie, had began to sob, with tears streaming down his face, and was rocking back and forth. His voice had never gone beyond a ghostly whisper which added to the surreal atmosphere of this confession. John's mind was spinning with all that he had heard. He really didn't have words to say to this wreck of a man standing in front of him. The crimes he had committed were truly terrible and were made worse by the entrustment of a Hudson Bay Trader to represent decency and law and order. His actions reflected on Linklater and all other agents of the Hudson Bay. Yet there was also a small level of compassion for Sam in that it was tragic for any human to be so crushed by circumstances that had gone far beyond his control.

Finally John felt he had to say something. "Sam, we will try to..."

"No, don't say anything to try to alleviate what is beyond any conciliation. Please give me some days as you promised just to listen tonight. I have yet a chore, an obligation, that comes from what little bit of soul is left in me that I must carry out. Once it is done I will submit myself to you for the punishment of my crimes. One thing more, John..." He reached inside his vest and brought out a rolled sheaf of papers and extended them to John. "Here is a written confession of all that I have said to you plus more. No matter what happens to me I want there to be justice served for all others who have so trampled on the goodness and decency of innocent people. Guard that for the law, please."

Before John could look up from the papers and respond, Sam Ogilvie was gone. He had melted back into the deep shadow of the forest and vanished. The meeting was over!

When Cody got back to the store, he found John pouring over some paper's by lamp light. He was so intent on them that he started when Cody spoke to him.

"Did the meeting with Ogilvie happen? Are those papers from him?"

"Yes and yes. Sit down. I could use your thoughts here. I've already briefed the others on what happened. It was so weird that I have to shake my head that it really happened."

With that, John reviewed again the actual events of the meeting.

"Cody, it was like he wanted me to be some kind of priest to him to hear his personal confession and to tell him he was forgiven. At the same time he declared that he was beyond forgiveness yet he had some kind of penance to perform."

"Any idea what he might be planning as penance," asked Cody.

"None whatsoever! His mind is so frayed there is no telling what kinds of ideas he might lump together. I just hope he doesn't hurt anyone. If his behaviour is too bizarre we may have to take him into some kind of custody to protect him from himself."

After a moment, Cody asked, "What are the papers about?"

"It's an amazingly detailed account of what he calls his sins. It's not only what he did but a lot of detail about the Bosses and their gang. There is enough here, as I read it, to put those criminals away for a long time."

Both men were silent for a few moments. It was Cody who broke the silence, "This is an awkward situation, isn't it? We know who the criminals are. We even know where they are. We have proof of their crimes. Yet, we really don't have the resources to do anything about it. There are no constables and no jail. They actually could just disappear at this point and get off completely. Then the Pards have failed in our mission from the Company. I shouldn't even say it, but it's tempting to turn the vigilantes loose on them."

"We haven't lost them yet!" John responded slowly as if he was thinking out loud and unravelling the dilemma as he spoke. "Think about what they know and don't know. They are so cocksure that they are kings of Fisherville that they have become public figures. They don't know the evidence we have. So they have no reason to not continue on with just what they have been doing. Their henchmen can keep intimidating people and they can just carry on bragging about how they have everything under their control. That should give us enough days to finish a lock up where they can be held for trial. I guess if we had to we could get some chains from Gunnar and have someone standing guard over them day and night. What do you think?"

"Sounds right. But we can't waste any time, can we?"

FIFTY

The next morning the men spent just a short time together to let each one know the course to follow. They all knew of the meeting with the deranged Ogilvie and that John had the confession papers. Darcy raised the most objection to waiting before bringing the Bosses in but after more discussion he could see the reasoning. For Quinn, it meant trying to inject some reasonable caution into the vigilante meeting he would be attending that evening.

"One more thing," Linklater paused as if wrestling with an important decision. "I've turned this over and over in my mind for what seemed all night. I think we have enough evidence,... probably more than enough...to send for Judge Begbie."

"Wow! The hanging judge!" Jed exclaimed. "Will he really come here?"

"He will if he isn't committed to some other place where they have court waiting for him. We've got Jed and Jeff heading west and we can have them catch up with the Judge before they swing down to Walla Walla. I'll write out an official request that you boys will carry with you. I understand the Judge has his own pack train so you won't have to worry about his outfit. Just deliver the letter and then get down to get the supplies. What do you think?"

"Does that mean that you are gambling on the Bosses being at hand whenever we want to arrest them?" asked Cody.

"Yep, that's my gamble. We'll keep some feelers out and if it seems they're getting spooked we'll take them in. I personally feel they are too arrogant to feel any concern."

There was a murmur of agreement that had a touch of excitement in it that they were drawing a circle around these crime bosses.

John continued, "Jed, Jeff, are you going to be ready tomorrow? Your first destination will need to be Rock Creek where you can ask after the Judge. Hopefully he isn't all the way out at the coast."

Jed and Jeff looked at each other for confirmation. "John, we can leave at dawn!"

As the meeting broke up and the men headed outside, one of the crew that had already been at work with a broad axe that was in his hands was standing off to one side facing down two rough looking men. The crew man called out to John.

"John, these two henchmen claim that they should talk to you. I think they should just vamoose."

He was waving the broad axe as he spoke. John went over to them. A couple of others backed John as he went toward them. The hooligans' eyes began to shift from side to side as if checking out the best escape route.

"What's your business?" John growled.

"Letting you know that your outfit is under protection. You haven't had any problems so far. Of course for this to continue we need a contribution from you. We'll be back in a few days. All we need is $100 and that will clear off what is owed from the previous owner as well as what you owe."

John raised his voice so that loud and clear he declared, "You are simply thieves and you'll never get money out of me. Get out of here and don't come back – ever!"

"You'll be sorry you take that route!"

The man with the axe started toward them and they left quickly.

John turned to his crew. "Well, that puts a line in the sand, doesn't it? I think we are heading into a big confrontation. From now on someone should have a rifle or pistol handy while you are working. Not likely they would do any damage during the daylight. We may have to have a night watchman."

It was early afternoon when Cody heard his name being called. He finished lifting his end of a log into place and turned to see Pierre waving him over. Cody called another crew member to come and take over the notching of the log. He was unsettled by seeing Pierre who should be travelling with his family group by this time of the day.

"Come with me, Cody. Sophie wants to talk to you and she was too shy to come and call you in front of the men."

"What's up, Pierre? You should be on your way to Joseph's Prairie."

"Sophie wants to explain it herself. She's just by the chicken coop over there."

The distress on Sophie's face made Cody's heart beat faster. As he reached out to take her in his arms he said, "Sophie, what is it? What has gone wrong?"

"Oh Cody, it's Winter Moon. He has disappeared since late last night. Somehow he heard of some gamblers getting together behind one of the saloons. He went crazy. You heard part of the argument last night. He wanted to take all the money from the pemmican so he could make it into a lot more. He was sure that he had a big run of luck just waiting for him. Of course the other men refused and they had a big row. He left after everyone else had gone to sleep. He even took the little bit of gold that had been given to both Pierre and me. Fortunately, the men kept their share tied around their waists."

As Sophie was telling Cody this news, his mind went back to something his Grandfather Thompson had told him about the Kootenays at Kootenay House. He complained that they were addicted to gambling. They gambled on everything. Once they started on some kind of game, they couldn't tear themselves away. It actually cut into the profits of the fur trade because they didn't get out to look after their trap lines in trapping season even though Thompson had berated them over and over. So Cody realized that this present day issue was deep seated and could turn out to be a catastrophe.

"Sophie, did Winter Moon say where the game was?"

"No, the only thing he said was that it was a roaming den. You know, they meet at a different location each night so that the gang can't move in on them and take all their money. Somehow, in talking with people yesterday he was told where to meet. That was part of his argument that if he didn't go last night he wouldn't know where to find them today. That's what we hoped for, that he wouldn't go last night and then the danger would be over. He's probably sleeping it off now somewhere, maybe just from exhaustion or, worse, if someone had some booze."

"We can't just leave him here, Cody." Sophie wailed. "Part of Band life is that we take care of each other. So we have to find him and take him home. Broken Antler and Yellow Bull are out looking for him now."

Anger welled up in Cody. He had already been very concerned for Sophie's safety – a young attractive Indian maiden in a frontier camp. So far there had only been that initial drunken rough house episode when they had first arrived. Now with this delay that would keep them at least another night and day Cody felt like their luck was being stretched too far. He was torn between his obligation to the construction crew and his need to watch out for Sophie. He had to make a quick decision.

"Darcy," he called out. "I'm going to be gone for a bit. Not sure when I'll be back."

With that he picked up his rifle and collected Sophie and Pierre and headed into the jumble of tents and half buildings close to the river. Pierre was excited to be allowed to come with them. Cody felt that he could provide an extra set of eyes that might spot their man.

"I can take the rest of the afternoon for us to look for Winter Moon, but, if we haven't found him by sunset we'll have to break off. It is simply too dangerous for you to be out here after dark."

The afternoon was fairly quiet and even though gamblers tended to gamble at night Cody asked over and over if anyone knew of the migrant game of chance. They were an unlikely trio to be searching for some back alley gamblers. However, in spite of the questioning looks that came their way they pressed on hoping they would come across some clue. Nothing surfaced.

Finally Cody called a halt to their search as dusk was settling down. "We have to leave. Maybe Broken Antler and Yellow Bull will have better results than us."

"But what if they don't, Cody? I don't know what I'm going to do?" Sophie cried.

Cody stopped and put his arm around Sophie's shoulders. "Some times we just have to ride things out. You can't make Winter Moon's choices for him and you've got the rest of your group to think about. It's Winter Moon that has broken the Tribal code, not you, and he has to live with the consequences. You can't let him destroy your whole band by his decisions. If he doesn't surface by tomorrow, I think you have to head back to Joseph's Prairie anyway."

It was well after dark by the time Cody had seen Sophie and Pierre to their camp and returned to the store. The evening meeting, which looked as though it would be a pattern for the Pards, John, Jeff and Nels, was just breaking up. They were all relieved to see Cody striding in. He gave a brief update on the situation for the Kootenays.

Cody had a question for them. "What about Ogilvie? Has there been anything more from him?"

Everyone shook their head in response. Darcy added, "We've talked about that but there doesn't seem to be any action on our part that would accomplish any good. Looks like we have to just wait and see."

Quinn was ready to leave for the vigilante meeting. "I think either Darcy or Cody should come with me. You are better talkers than me and might be better at keeping this from turning real ugly."

"Quinn, you're the one who gained Orville's confidence," Darcy said. "Besides, if they don't agree with you, just stand up while you're talking. You're big enough that they'll say 'yes sir' right away!"

That produced the desired effect of lightening the mood. Jeff followed Quinn out to where he had his horse saddled ready to go.

"Quinn," Jeff said. "I could tell in there that you really are concerned about this meeting. Just wanted to let you know that I'm going to go off by myself and pray for you while you're gone."

Quinn was quiet for a moment, digesting these unusual words from Jeff. Coming from anyone else Quinn might have scoffed at such a statement, but Jeff had proved himself to be a square shooter.

"That's real decent of you. I can use all the help I can get."

With that, Quinn mounted and headed off for Orville's saw pit. He really was unsure of what this next hour or so would bring and he was unsure of his own ability to talk and to adjust to what would be said. He had always been the strong silent type who would gladly let others do the talking for him. The Pards had been ideal for him because the other three were all outgoing. One of them would often answer for him when they saw him struggling to get words out. He had always been grateful for their support. This journey since Montreal had brought big changes to his life. Here a man was judged by what he did rather than by his family or by his wealth and Quinn had noticed that it had made him more willing to spit out the thoughts that he had. Now tonight he knew that his own opinion was just as important as anyone else's and would be given as much weight. In addition to that, he had the backing of the Pards even though they weren't physically with him. He would stand up for what was right whether the majority agreed with him or not.

As he approached Orville's saw pit, he noticed that a small knot of others had already arrived. Several lanterns gave a ghostly effect as the men milled about. Orville was pleased to see Quinn arrive. Quinn tied the reins of his horse to a nearby rail that divided the edge of the ramp from the access to the pit.

Orville introduced the newcomer to each of the men. It seemed that most knew each other. The host made sure everyone realized that Quinn represented the Hudson Bay.

"I really expected a lot more men to come," Orville said. "but I guess we better get started."

Orville outlined the problems that brought them together which prompted lot's of head nodding.

"If we don't do anything, it's only going to get worse. We're men not mice and we need to stand up for ourselves. I dare say that everyone here owns a rifle. By taking a united stand we can eliminate this problem from our town!"

This last statement brought one or two "Yes, sir!" responses but then just silence. Orville was visibly taken aback by the muted level of agreement. He tried again to whip up some outrage.

"Well, shouldn't we do something. Do we just let these hoodlums walk over us? Come on, men, what are you thinking?"

This brought a few murmurs and then finally one man spoke up.

"We're not much for being an armed gang! Aren't we going to end up just like the bad guys? That's why a lot of men didn't come tonight. We don't want gun battles in our streets."

"But we've got the right on our side." Orville pleaded.

"Doesn't the Hudson Bay represent the law? Now that they are here they should look after this gang."

Another man spoke up, "But I hear that the Bosses claim that they have the Hudson Bay in their pockets. Is that true? That's what I came to find out. It will make a difference in what I support."

"Well, Quinn. Sounds like we need to hear from you." Orville responded.

"The Hudson Bay does represent the Government in places where there is no other enforcement from the Crown. And whatever the Bosses may imagine about controlling the Hudson Bay it is not true of the Company here under John Linklater. We will deal with this problem. Give us a little time and you'll see."

With that, some of the men began to leave. There was obviously no appetite for what Orville had been proposing.

"Well, Quinn," he said. "I thought you were going to back me on what I was suggesting. But it looks like they weren't ready for action. This is a wrong direction but you guys have a chance to prove yourselves."

Quinn held out his hand, "No hard feelings I hope. Who knows what we might need each other for in the future. You certainly gave me good help on the saw pit."

Orville shook his hand. "No hard feelings."

Quinn was glad for the handshake even though he thought it was given with a little reluctance. The ride back to the store gave Quinn a chance to savour a good outcome. He knew his mates would be pleased with what had transpired. It did add weight to the need to bring the Bosses down in the near future.

Only John Linklater was still in the store when Quinn got back. The rest had retired in order to be up in time to help Jed and Jeff with their early departure in the morning. John gave a big sigh of relief when he heard that there was no appetite for an armed gang response to the criminals.

"It seems like the Hudson Bay Company has a good enough reputation through the years that people trust us to settle things down. People would just rather get on with their business." said Quinn. "Orville was kinda frustrated about it."

"Do you think he will do anything foolish on his own, like get his crew to bring rifles and go after the gang?" John asked.

"Well, we shook hands at the end of the meeting. To me it meant that he would support our approach to the problem."

"Good," replied John. "Now I can finish my letter to Judge Begbie with the outcome of your meeting. See you in the morning."

FIFTY-ONE

By the time the sky had a tinge of light most of the pack horses were harnessed and all of the Pards had turned out. Each one trying to be helpful. Darcy, who came to the corral grumbling, was the last to show up.

"If I'd known that you had this much help, I could have stayed in bed. Whose idea was it to leave at dawn when there are much better times in a day to get started."

Berty arrived with a pot of coffee so Jed and Jeff could have a quick cup of a hot drink before they started off. She even agreed that Darcy could have some in spite of his "bad attitude"! In fact Berty had brought enough tin mugs so everyone could have a drink. Although there weren't a lot of words exchanged, sharing that pot of coffee after all the rigging was in place took on an almost religious significance. Almost like a communion or a last supper environment.

Quinn had brought them all up to date on his meeting of the previous evening and that had emphasized the responsibility building on their shoulders. Everyone was conscious that a crisis was building and that circumstances would probably be quite different by the time Jed and Jeff returned.

The final act, once the two had mounted their horses, was John giving Jed a pouch containing a sealed letter to be delivered into Judge Begbie's hands. He shook hands with Jeff and Jed in turn adding the words, "God go with you!"

Jed nodded in response and Jeff said to everyone in general "God give you wisdom and protection in the steps you take here!"

With it being so early someone suggested they all go to Berty's Kitchen for a hearty breakfast. As they turned toward her establishment, Cody nudged Darcy.

"Look to the ridge north east."

A lone figure was silhouetted against the brightening sky. As Darcy and Cody looked the person turned so that the increasing light showed his features. There was no mistaking that it was Wolfleg.

"Wonder what he is up to? Should we circle around to intercept him and see what we can learn?" Darcy queried.

"I'm not sure we could gain enough to make it worth the effort. It's a reminder though, we should have a weapon with us all the time." said Cody as they entered the Kitchen.

Over breakfast they sketched out their day. They had the new storage room closed in and Gunnar was going to bring the hardware this morning. Cody said he would check in on the Kootenays later to see if they had located Winter Moon. Berty spoke up with a business order for Quinn.

"I have to think about winter coming before too long. Looks like I'll be able to get through by making this place a tabin."

"A what?" Chortled Darcy. "I've never heard of a tabin."

"That just shows that you haven't lived in a gold rush town before, Darcy. A tabin just adds board side walls to a tent. It's cheap but it cuts the wind in the winter. Most miners that come for something hot aren't going to take off their heavy blanket coats so the cool atmosphere suits them just fine. Then maybe next year I can put a solid roof over it. But...if the gold rush goes bust I won't lose too much by over building."

Quinn cut in, "Berty, you'll be next on my list of customers. You'll need to get your posts set in the ground before freeze up."

The morning flew by. Quinn actually enjoyed the physical demands of his turn on the whip saw. He felt so free today now that the issue of the vigilantes had been settled. Cody took an occasional turn skidding logs down to the construction. Gunnar came with his hardware to make this room secure whether for storage or as a lock up. The window was eight feet off the ground. It was a series of upright bars set in a metal frame. That frame was set in a channel cut and chiseled into the log at the eight foot level. A log on top of that with it's own channel locked the two foot by four foot set of bars in place. This design provided both fresh air and daylight for the enclosure. Equally sturdy hardware was installed on the door which was made out of some of the first planks cut at Quinn's saw pit. Both Darcy and Cody marvelled at what Gunnar had been able to manufacture.

Close to noon, Cody announced that he was going to take some time away to look up the Kootenays. They had been on his mind throughout the morning. He felt it was time to strongly pressure them to head back to Joseph's Prairie whether Winter Moon had surfaced or not. With no idea where any of the band might be, he reined his horse towards the trail out to Ponderosa Flats. Before long he spotted a little knot of people moving slowly toward the flats. As he approached, he could see that one of them was Sophie. It looked as though she was helping someone move forward.

They didn't seem to notice Cody coming close to them so he called out before he would be so near that it would startle them. When their faces turned toward him, he saw that it was Sophie and Broken Antler helping the person between them. Cody assumed that this man who looked in rough condition would be Winter Moon.

Cody dismounted where the trio had halted. He looked at Sophie and asked, "Winter Moon?"

Sophie nodded, "We had a message come to us this morning. I think it was the one you called Matt. He told us where he had seen a man from our band and said he'd probably be there for a while because he was in bad shape. It has taken us a long time to get this far."

"How bad is he?" Cody asked.

"Sick from too much alcohol and beaten badly. He hasn't been able to tell us about the beating. I don't know if he will even remember anything about it. And he has no money on him."

Cody took only a few moments to assess the situation. "Look, it's too far for the slow progress you're making. There's a wagon sitting by our corral. I'll go and get a team hitched real quick and then I can bring some water and blankets."

Sophie just nodded at him with a look of gratitude. Cody vaulted into his saddle and galloped back to the shop. He called out to Darcy as he got close enough to get his attention.

"Bring some water and a couple blankets. I'm going to hitch a team."

Cody sorted the harness with practised efficiency. His anger at Winter Moon made him work furiously. His reckless choices had not only brought disaster to him but had put the others of the band at risk as well. He wished Sophie had come to get him rather than going into the dregs of this gold rush camp with only Broken Antler. At least they had gotten outside of the town again without more harm coming to them.

Darcy helped with the final harnessing after throwing the blankets and canteen in the box. With a quick thanks for his help, Cody climbed up on the wagon seat, lashed the team into an immediate gallop and careened cross country to get back to the group.

They raised Winter Moon up to a sitting position and gave him a little water. He had difficulty swallowing and retched a little. After a few more minutes he was able to take a little more. Then they lifted him into the wagon. The blankets wouldn't be much cushion but better than nothing. Winter Moon revived a little by this time. He started saying how sorry he was.

Cody's anger flared at him, "Save it, Winter Moon! Your words don't mean anything right now. I doubt you even know all that you should be sorry for. So, I'm not interested in anything you say."

They got underway slowly, though it was much better than their laborious rescue trek had been so far. Winter Moon groaned and moaned with every jolt of the wagon. Cody really did try to avoid as many rocks and bumps as he could, but his anger was such that he felt little sympathy for Winter Moon, maybe even that he deserved the pain for what he had done to his family and band. Now it would be another day or two before they would be able to start back to Joseph's Prairie. Cody continued to worry that this gold rush town was no place for these Kootenays and especially Sophie. Their good fortune could run out at any time.

The afternoon was well on when Cody got the team and wagon back to the Hudson Bay corral. Winter Moon had revived better than first expected by the time Cody had left their camp giving some hope that they would be able to travel the next day.

Quinn showed up at the store at the same time. Darcy was sitting on a stump enjoying a nice break in the shade of the building they had put up in such a short time.

Quinn grinned at his buddies, "Listen, I need to look up my friend Orville to get some education about saw sharpening. Seeing as you two are not doing anything profitable at the present time why don't you come with me."

Darcy took Quinn's bait and fired back that they had more than earned a break. Darcy was ready with some more barbs that it was Quinn who was getting others to do all the hard work at the saw pit. But it was John's voice that cut off their verbal tussle.

"Go easy on one another, there! Look, you've all kept your noses to the grindstone in what we've accomplished so far. Take a break and go look around Fisherville together. Why don't you try out one of the Inns? See what kind of gourmet food this gold rush offers."

It was one of those ideas that didn't need a vote. Their youthful enthusiasm immediately put the suggestion into motion. Before long the three had their horses saddled and trotted off to do some exploring on their way to Orville's and later to a nice big meal and hopefully some apple pie.

The boys were relaxed as they circled through the jumble of crazy-quilt placed abodes. There was every kind of cobbled together tents, shacks and ramshackle shelters that made them shake their heads at what people were willing to put up with in the mad dash for gold. On one edge of town, a miner was working his diggings right up to the edge of a town tent. When the Pards remarked on it, the fellow leaned on his shovel and explained that he had bought out the owner of the tent because his vein of gold was continuing under it. He said the tent owner had been so glad of the generous offer that he had simply walked away and left everything behind.

"By the looks of it," said the miner, "This whole town may be on top of more than one vein of gold and could end up with everyone moving to make way for mining."

That left the Pards shaking their heads as they moved on. They took a good look at the sluice boxes that had sprouted along Wild Horse Creek. Some of the operations involved a considerable crew and were in various stages of development. Each of them were building so they could divert water from the creek over the bottom ribbed box. Some were already in operation and men were shovelling gravel onto the top of the sluice while others of the crew were rocking the box back and forth to encourage the gold to settle behind the crossways slats.

Quinn shook his head. "I'm glad that I got into logging and lumber. We may get a little sawdust down our necks but it's nothing compared to the muck and wet that they are slogging through all the time."

As they continued their tour, they were curious to see crude signs identifying new businesses. There was even a second hand business at a lot where those who had given up already could drop off almost anything and get a little cash for it. They got only a pittance but it would get them a meal down the road.

Cody commented, "That yard has a lot of sadness and disappointment in it. The people that owned that stuff would have come with the greatest optimism you could imagine and then they would have left with the bottom falling out of their world."

Their circle route to get to Orville's saw pit took them through the seedier side of town. The few saloons well supplied with gambling tables, houses of ill repute and inns generated business for each other and always managed to cluster together in their distinctively dark side of a new town. It was late enough in the afternoon that the activities of these operations were picking up. The bars and tables were filling up. The streets were alive with people looking for excitement to off set the drudgery of everyday mining. There were even some hawkers either offering some elixir or extolling the pleasures of one of the bars. With the lanes and streets so jammed with people as well as horse or mule drawn conveyances the Pards dismounted and walked their horses through the throng.

FIFTY-TWO

At first, they barely noticed a commotion coming from a knot of people ahead. As they got closer, they could hear one voice in particular over the responding shouts of others in the crowd. Once they sensed the direction of the loudest voice and zeroed in on it they also saw, standing higher than the average height of the press of people, two stove pipe hats.

Cody saw them first and immediately drew the attention of his friends to the unusual head gear. A strident voice had become clearer and seemed to be in the same space as the hat wearers. The Pards tied their horses at a hitch rail and wiggled their way through the crowd.

The words of the loud voice became distinct. "These men are the evil ones!" railed the voice. Their hearts are black and they will get the punishment due them. Beware they will ruin your soul."

The men in the stove pipe hats had stopped and had turned to the man haranguing them. "Go away Ogilvie. Go away before you get yourself into serious trouble."

The Pards were astounded to recognize Sam Ogilvie whom they hadn't seen since Kootenay House. He looked strange. There was a wildness in his eyes. A look of lunacy. The Bosses tried to ignore him and turned to continue their walk to the saloon where they played cards every day. The crowd kept pressing in which was agitating Leblanc and Lagasse.

Ogilvie continued, "These men have taken every good thing away from me. They are condemned to hell and they will take you with them. God's justice should be rained down on them. Who will act for God and shoot them down in the street like the dogs they are!!"

The Bosses were getting very angry. Their voices rose as they started to shout down their tormentor. "Stop it, Ogilvie!" Leblanc roared. "You can't get away with foolishness like this."

"Be quiet," Lagasse yelled. "or we will silence you."

"Oh just like you silenced those other Hudson Bay agents?" Ogilvie hissed. "That's right you murdered Hudson Bay agents who stood up to you. The devil take you. I know what you did. I've got evidence. I've written it all down. You're going to rot in jail! I'm the one who will testify and lock the jail on you for the rest of your lives. You thought you could use me any way you wanted."

The Bosses became enraged. They both decided at the same time that Ogilvie had gone over the line. In a flurry of action, both pulled pistols from under their jackets and fired point blank into the man standing pointing at them. A huge gasp went up from the stunned onlookers. Several cried out "Nooo!"

People had been watching, thinking it was nothing more than a little extra entertainment. But this!? A man gunned down in broad daylight!

The crowd was momentarily paralysed but then in shocked voices started calling "They shot him. Killed in cold blood. Get them!" Leblanc and Lagasse took advantage of that first slow response and started running up the street pushing people aside as they went and waving their pistols at anyone who looked as though they might step into their path. Cody and Darcy pushed through so they could get to Sam Ogilvie. They rolled him from his side to his back. The grim evidence was plain to see. One shot to his mid-section but the other one to his heart. Poor tortured Sam Ogilvie was dead. There was nothing to be done.

Quinn came up to his buddies. "Let's get after them!" he shouted. Cody and Darcy were immediately on their feet. Quinn had noticed the direction the Bosses had taken and led the way at a dead run. The crowd was still pressing in to get a glimpse of the murder victim. Quinn, with his big size, created a path for the other two to follow but they still were slowed by the press of people. So far they were simply able to follow the stove pipe hats which showed above the people walking on the street.

The hats came to a stop and the boys thought they were going to be able to close the gap that remained. But then Quinn, having glimpsed the reason for their halt, yelled over his shoulder, "Hurry, they're stealing some horses."

Cody and Darcy doubled their effort to catch up with Quinn and the shooters but only managed to be close enough to see them gallop out of town and to see them fling their hats away as they made a dash for freedom. The trio halted to catch their breath.

"We'll have to go back to the store," said Cody. "We don't even have any weapons with us!"

"Let's go then!" Darcy urged, "We saw what direction they headed out. We can scout out that way and maybe some other people will see them and let us know which way to follow them."

The Pards hustled back to their own horses. "What about Ogilvie's body," Quinn asked on the way.

"We'll get Nels to come with a wagon and collect the body."

As they went back past the murder scene, they asked a bystander if he could watch over the body until someone came. He promised he would make sure the dead man was treated with respect. It was all they could ask for as they rushed to get back to the Hudson Bay and not lose too much time pursuing the murderers.

The Pards had to swing around the jumble of tents and diggings. It took them north and then east before they could get a clear trail back to the store. It was also the most open route away from the crowd and the Bosses had naturally taken that direction as well. The boys stretched their horses to a gallop once they cleared the human traffic. As they went over a small ridge that gave them a long view of the east side of the valley, they spotted the fugitives heading south at a furious pace.

Darcy yelled, "I see them. Over towards the saw pit!"

Cody called back that he saw them. "Too bad we don't have guns with us, we could just keep going."

"Should one of us stay on their trail and someone else bring their guns?" asked Quinn.

"Too much risk, Quinn," called back Cody over the sound of their galloping horses. "They might take a trail that the followers wouldn't know about. Besides this could turn into a long hunt!"

They were still conflicted as they turned off the trail taken by the fugitives knowing that it put them further behind. Yet, their rational side knew they had to equip themselves for whatever might be ahead. Nels and John were startled by the way the boys stormed into the Trading Post. They all started talking at once, and at the same time, plucking ammunition off the shelves.

Cody took over the reporting and as the picture began to take shape John and Nels began hurriedly joining in the gathering of supplies the boys might need. Cody also told them that they would need to take a wagon to collect Sam's body.

John was amazed. "You're telling me that Sam Ogilvie confronted Leblanc and Lagasse right in the street? Right in front of a crowd of people? I didn't think he would ever have the courage to do something like that!"

"I think it was more madness than courage!" Darcy said.

"There's no doubt he was totally ripped up inside for all the evils he had been part of." John responded.

"How are you going to get back on their trail now?" asked Nels.

Cody paused in buckling his saddlebags. "Hopefully people will have noticed them on the run. The horses they stole are recognizable. One is real big and all black and the other is a buckskin. Definitely eye catching. Other than that, we saw the direction they were heading and we'll watch for fresh tracks turning off."

In short order, the Pards were back on their horses and well supplied for whatever this chase might involve. The shooting had taken away any ambivalence the boys might have had about the adequacy of their evidence against these gangsters in a court. They simply needed to track these guys down and bring them before the judge. Though they missed Jed as a team member on this chase, they knew he was doing his part by finding the Judge so they would be able to cap off their mission.

They headed for the saw pit at a gallop given that it was the last landmark they could positively connect to the Bosses. A few of Quinn's crew were still gathering tools from the day's work and making sure everything would be ready for the next day.

"Guys, did you notice a pair of riders go past here in a big hurry a bit ago?" Quinn asked them. The urgency of his question was obvious in his voice.

"Do you mean the fellas on the big black and the buckskin? Pretty hard to not notice them if you know anything about horses. I'd trade for one of those any day," one of the men answered.

"Those are the ones. They stole the horses, right after they shot a man in broad daylight!" Quinn informed them. "We're going after them. Did you see which way they went?"

Another man spoke up, "They headed for the Ponderosa Flats trail. But they're not going to get very far."

"Why do you say that?" Cody asked. "It's really important that we get them."

"The buckskin was starting to favour its right front leg. Looked like maybe it had picked up a stone." the man replied.

Another man spoke up, "Those guys aren't horsemen for sure! The rider should have noticed the limp by the time they went by here. Pretty soon that horse will be laid up and won't go any further."

"Much obliged!" Cody nodded to the crew and slapped his horse with the reins and yelled, "Let's go!" to his mates.

They didn't need any extra encouragement, and were kicking the sides of their mounts at the same time. The three charged off towards the Flats. Once they got to where the trail entered the ravine and began the twisting climb to the meadows, they reined in their horses.

"Depending on how lame that horse was, they could be anywhere ahead of us or they might have made it up to the Flats and then gone any direction." Cody was thinking out loud so they would all be reacting out of the same information. "I think that we should expect them to be holed up somewhere on this trail. There are a lot of good ambush sites and they could be at any one of them."

"Sounds right," offered Darcy. "What about weapons? We know they each have a pistol with one shot used in each one. They weren't carrying rifles."

Quinn spoke up, "I'm trying to remember if there were guns in the rifle boots of those saddles. I don't think there were, but I can't be totally sure. Of course we don't know what they might find in the saddle bags."

"Let's move on then," said Cody. "Go single file. I'll take the lead and watch for them straight ahead. Darcy watch for movement on the left, Quinn on the right. We'll go at a walking pace. Don't be a hero. If you think you see something, stop us and we'll check it out."

There was an immediate twist to the right in the trail. Surely the fugitives had gone beyond this spot but they had to treat it as a prime ambush spot. Once they rounded the corner they might be only yards from a potential gun shot. They were tight as a fiddle string as they kept their horses walking. Each one of them could hear their own heart beat and feel sweat break out on their faces. They rode with reins in one hand and the other hand on their handguns. It seemed quieter than usual but maybe is was just that they were straining to hear that telltale noise that would warn them of an attack.

"Looks like this spot is clear," Cody said over his shoulder.

They continued the twisting climb along the trail. Each one scanning every detail of the landscape, praying that they would spot the telltale movement, or reflection, or colour before a gunshot would reveal the ambush. The Pards hadn't realized how long the road was up to the lip of the flats. Now that they were seeing every deadfall and every boulder as a hideout, it seemed they would never make the top. The setting sun was becoming a threat to their pursuit. Darkness would be a definite disadvantage to bringing the murderers down. It took steely self-control to not push their pace because of the encroaching dusk.

Cody's horse suddenly moved its head to the left and swivelled its ears to point at a small grove of trees on top of a small bluff. A nicker whispered from the trees. Cody managed to call out, "Down guys! As he was rolling off his horse to the right, a gun shot shattered the evening stillness. A stinging sensation erupted on Cody's upper left arm.

Darcy and Quinn had landed close together on the lower side of the trail. They quickly assured one another that they were in one piece. The boom of the gunshot had turned their horses back down the trail and Quinn was able to gather them just below the last turn.

"Cody! Cody! Are you okay?" Darcy called in an urgent voice just above a whisper.

There was some shuffling noises from where Cody should be before a reply came.

"I had to get behind some cover. I'm okay. Got a little bite on my arm though."

"We're going to come up to you and take a look at your arm."

The ravine was narrow enough at this point that there wasn't even space to drop down to be completely out of sight. Darcy and Quinn crouched and darted from cover to cover.

"Did you see where they are shooting from?" Quinn asked.

"It came from the top of that small cliff. See the cluster of trees? I saw just a brief movement as soon as I could look up there after tumbling down. There has been nothing since so I think they are still there."

FIFTY-THREE

Once Darcy was sure they were all behind cover he moved to take a look at Cody's left arm. He took Cody's own bandana and with a little water from a canteen cleaned off the wound. The bullet had only grazed the arm but had caused enough bleeding to cause alarm. Darcy used his bandana to tie a patch over the wound which soon stopped the blood flow.

"Can you lift that arm?" Darcy asked.

Cody tried it out. Although he winced when he raised it, he was able to put the arm through a full range of motion.

"I'm fine," Cody declared. "Let's get back to running these outlaws to ground. There's two of them and only one horse so they can't get very far very fast if they stay on foot or if they ride double."

Quinn spoke, "It's dark enough now that I can work my way along the lower side of the trail to where I can get a shot at them. I can run from cover to cover."

"We'll give you about five minutes and then call them out. If they come out you'll be able to cover them from a different angle."

Quinn backed down further from the lip of the trail and then started working his way along the bottom of the ravine. He darted from trees to boulders to outcroppings of the land. Cody and Darcy could follow his progress although what they heard was nothing more than scraping sounds and what might have been a breeze in the trees. It sounded loud to them and they wondered if the fugitives could hear it. After a bit, Quinn stayed put and Cody knew that he had settled into as good a spot as he could find for a chance to bring down one of the pair.

"Leblanc!! Lagasse!!" Cody shouted. "Throw down your guns and come out with your hands up. We will get you, so you might as well give it up now!"

That brought a loud laugh back from the bluff. "You boys should go back to your Mammas. You will never get us and you will get hurt chasing us. So back off or we'll shoot you down just like that maniac Ogilvie."

In the quiet after that threat was issued, there was a flurry of shuffling noises from the location of the murderers. A snort from a horse and some muffled curses along with the sound of voices indicated something was changing. The three Pards tensed up ready to react to what ever was about to happen.

More scuffling noises and then a gun shot! Then the sound of a horse charging through some underbrush. As that sound diminished Cody called out.

"Quinn?! Are you alright?"

"I'm good!" The sound of Quinn's voice brought an immediate relief to his buddies. "Bring the horses quick."

As they came up to Quinn, he explained hurriedly, "They rode double out of here. There was one spot where they showed against the sky. That's when I got a shot at them. They're punishing that horse but we should be able to gain on them. They'll probably run the horse to death."

Quinn was mounting as he said this. The others were mounted by the time he finished. With a lash of their reins the trio bolted up the familiar trail. It was a reckless charge up that ravine trail but they accepted what Quinn said with one mind. There was no thought of an ambush now because no one could see into the dark shadows to pick a spot to hole up. The Pards had the scent strong and were not to be denied this chance to out run them.

As they came over the crest of the Flats trail, the clouds had just cleared allowing the moon to illuminate the meadows. It gave a bright reflection off the lower pond that the Hudson Bay crew had used to water stock. Although there were only a few waggons left of the Hudson Bay camp, it still stood out in the moonlight and showed a fair amount of activity around a campfire.

Suddenly shouting erupted from that camp, with numerous angry voices making demands and others refusing those demands. A shot rang out and the tone of the shouting changed. Someone was giving orders and the opposition was quieting.

"Let's get them!" shouted Cody. They were familiar enough with the terrain that they could gallop full speed even though it was night. As they pounded across the field, closing in on the camp, they saw two horses bolt out beyond the waggons on the far side of the scattered equipment.

"They've stolen fresh horses!" yelled Darcy.

The Pards had shortened the lead that the fugitives had because of the time it took them to steal the still saddled horses. Then the campers reacting with threats and a brief chase required the attention of the thieves which further slowed them. However, from where they mounted the horses, they could see a clear swath of field straight ahead. That's where they took off at a dead run so that they regained some of the lost lead.

"We'll have to circle around the camp to the right!" shouted Cody. "Too much junk if we go straight."

They wheeled to the right, circling around the spread out paraphernalia that could trip up a horse in the dark. The trio were urging their horses on to their limit knowing that they were close to exhaustion having charged up the ravine trail and now running hard across the plain. The odds had lessened that they would be able to run the murderers to ground now that they had stolen the fresh horses of cowboys who had just arrived back at their camp.

The moonlight was bright enough that the murderers could see over their shoulders the path taken by the Pards. That caused them to improve their lead by gradually veering to their left which also brought them closer to the forest where they could better hope to lose their determined pursuers.

The boys saw the change in direction and had the sinking feeling grow in them that they were not going to capture their quarry. Their horses were slowing from the long run and the forest was definitely their enemy.

Cody's heart came into his throat as he saw another potential disaster in the making. The arc of the path the Bosses were on would take them right to the Kootenay's camp. They were a vulnerable group especially with Winter Moon being virtually disabled at this point. Cody prayed that they would stay out of sight, prayed that none of them would do anything foolish like trying to intercept the escaping criminals. It seemed there was nothing he could do to warn them. A yell from him would only bring someone out to the path to see what was happening. A gun shot would probably bring the same result.

The reality was that that had already happened. The commotion at the wagon train camp had gotten the attention and the curiosity of the Indian families. Assuming that the men were just celebrating with a little extra booze in them several of them wandered out to where they could see the wagon camp. Some loud voices and someone firing a gun would not be unusual for that kind of celebrating. They even assumed that galloping horses could be part of the fun so they stayed on the path to watch.

Nothing could have prepared them for what happened next. One of the horses skidded almost to a stop as the rider realized there were people standing and watching. It's front legs pawed the air as the rider sawed back on the reins. Then he swung the horse sideways knocking the first woman backwards. She screamed. Others shouted for the horseman to back off. Instead, he gave his horse a severe kick in its sides making it lunge forward. Leblanc leaned way over to the side, circled his arm around the second woman, and lifted her up across his lap as he again dug his heels into the horse. Another frightened scream, this time from Sophie as she was lifted into the air and slammed across the saddle. Leblanc plunged out of the gathering knot of people and headed into the bush with his prize screaming and flailing. Just before disappearing into the trees, Leblanc wheeled his horse around and called out, "Tell those Bay boys to back off or this girl get's hurt real bad." With that, he and his captive disappeared into the darkness of the forest right behind Lagasse.

Cody's gut clenched when he heard the screams. It was the worst possible outcome of this chase. Horrible images of what was happening up ahead coursed through his mind. And he was responsible. If they hadn't been pressuring the fugitives maybe they wouldn't have gone in the direction of the Indian camp.

He called to his mates riding close together. "Sounds really bad. I'm afraid we're too late!"

"It might not be as bad as you think." responded Darcy, knowing full well how deeply and personally Cody would take any kind of harm coming to any of the Kootenays, especially to Sophie.

Their labouring horses brought them up to the distressed group of people. All three jumped down and everyone was talking at once. Cody singled out Broken Antler and demanded his attention. He started talking rapidly but in Kootenay. Frustrated, Cody looked frantically around and grabbed Pierre, telling him to translate.

"We heard the commotion at the waggons. Thought maybe the boys were letting off steam, celebrating with their pay. We didn't even worry about the two horses pounding this direction. But then the first horse knocked Crocus over. The man was mean, talked mean. Then he lunged his horse at Sophie. Grabbed her. Put her across his saddle and then they raced out. It happened so fast!"

Darcy jumped down to check on Crocus. She was banged up but nothing broken.

Pierre spoke up, "Cody, the man yelled back before they went into the trees, he said 'tell the Bay boys to back off or this girl gets hurt real bad.' Then they were gone."

"Was that it Pierre? Any thing else?" Cody asked as he grabbed him by the shoulders and gave him a shake, his voice urgent. "Anything else at all?"

"Nothing else."

"Easy Cody," Quinn broke in. "He can only say what he heard!"

Cody was immediately apologetic. "Oh, sorry Pierre! Thanks for your help."

"It's OK Cody. You'll bring her back, won't you?!" Pierre pleaded.

"You can count on it, big guy! Sophie will be coming back!"

The boys walked their horses over to the tree line where Pierre had pointed but they could see nothing that distinguished a trail. Neither could they see any hoof prints or other sign that they could make out in the dark.

Frustrated, Cody got down from his horse and peered into the forest even though he knew he wouldn't be able to see anything more on foot. He hated being so helpless when he was so desperate to help Sophie. He hated to think of what she was going through. He prayed that she would cooperate enough with her captors so that she would survive at least.

"I hate to give in to this but it is too dark for us to do anything," Cody said to the others as he stepped into his stirrup and swung onto his horse. "We'll have to be back here at dawn." Cody's voice was choked from the pent up fury inside. He couldn't get the sound of Sophie's screams out of his mind. He had to do something. Suddenly he veered toward the Kootenay camp and jigged his horse into a run. The other two were taken by surprise but then kicked their horses to keep up.

Cody dashed right up beside the knot of folks still watching for whatever would happen. He was off his mount before they were fully stopped. The camp fire light showed the dark fury on his face. He took two steps and was nose to nose with Winter Moon. He grabbed the front of Winter Moon's buckskin shirt and started to shake him.

"Damn you!" Cody hissed into his face. "You just had to drink, you just had to gamble. If you hadn't been totally selfish and, instead, thought of your band, this wouldn't have happened. Sophie would have been with her family on the trail back to Joseph's Prairie. I'm going to take it out of your hide."

While Cody was ranting at Winter Moon, Darcy recognized something he had seen a few times before. Cody was going over an edge. He was building towards an explosion. Darcy slipped down from his horse and quietly walked up beside Cody. As Cody said those last words, his right hand closed into a lethal fist. He started his punch but it never landed. Darcy, with his martial arts trained reflexes, caught Cody's arm in mid-swing. Then he blocked the left cross that Cody immediately threw.

Darcy blurted, "Not now Cody! It will only make things worse!" Cody stared daggers at Darcy for what seemed an eternity. Then he gave in and relaxed his stance.

"I'm just so frustrated!" Cody said through gritted teeth. "This didn't need to happen and now we can't do anything for hours. Poor Sophie, I can't imagine what she is going through.!"

Broken Antler spoke up, "Cody, we may be bad gamblers but Kootenays are very good trackers. We can help once there is daylight. We know where they entered the forest so we can pick up their tracks. We'll be able to stay right after them."

"Yeah, that will help," said Cody as he was coming down from his rage. "Come to think of it, Jeff told me about seeing some men just in the trees there watching the camps. Maybe there is a trail that these villains use. Alright, back here at first light."

FIFTY-FOUR

Sophie couldn't believe that her feet were leaving the ground. She had seen Crocus knocked over and heard her scream in the moment before the horse plunged forward at her. She thought she would be knocked over but the rider's arm went around her, his hand under her right arm. She screamed as he painfully lifted her and slammed her stomach down across the front of the western saddle. The horn gored into her causing her to scream louder. The rider cursed her, shouting at her to quiet down. She began to berate him but to him it was just noise as she was tongue lashing him in Kootenay. After a moment he grabbed her right arm and cruelly twisted it behind her back, yelling at her to quiet down or he would break it.

Sophie quieted to a whimper. The branches of the low brush in the forest were lashing and scratching her face as the horses continued plunging deeper into the wilderness. She covered her face with her one free hand. As the realization seared into her brain that she was captive to this man and his companion, she began to focus on her situation. Over and over she repeated to herself, "Survive, survive!"

After what seemed a very long time to Sophie with the saddle horn gouging into her side, the riders pulled up. The quiet of the forest settled over them and over the horses. There was no sound of pursuit. Lagasse said, "They wouldn't dare come in the dark. They haven't been over this trail so they have no idea what it is like."

Leblanc responded, "They'll wait for daylight. We'll be up to the cabin well before then. We can fort up and make our plans."

Leblanc lifted Sophie down after making her promise to stay quiet. He gave an extra twist to her arm that was still behind her back to remind her that she was helpless and that he could inflict any amount of pain at a moment's notice. When Leblanc turned to get his rope off his saddle he needed both hands for a moment. As soon as he took his hand off Sophie's wrist she darted away. Leblanc lunged after her and grabbed her hair. He swung her around and viciously backhanded her across her mouth. She gave a muffled cry and fell sideways to the ground. Leblanc pulled her back to her feet. Sophie daubed at the blood coming from her split lip with her free hand.

"You are very stupid to try to run. I'll always catch you and make you hurt worse. I was going to tie your hands in front but now, no way. Put your hands behind your back."

Leblanc tied her securely, mounted his horse and then pulled Sophie up to ride behind him. It was much easier than being belly down in front of the saddle but she was whimpering because of being a hostage and because of hurting from the rough ride and the blow to her face.

"Be quiet or I'll hit you again only worse. You're our ticket to freedom so get used to it. You're going to be with us until we've got our way clear out of here."

Lagasse spoke up, "All of this because of that worthless Ogilvie. We were on a gravy train until he messed into things. He sure got what was coming to him!!"

"We'll get out of this area," Leblanc said. "People owe us and we can collect for years to come. This is just a little prod to get us to cash in and move to greener pastures. Maybe even to New Westminster where there is green grass all year long!!"

They picked their way along a rarely used trail, although they had gotten familiar with part of it because of their occasional emergency rendezvous with some of their henchmen. So they were able to navigate even in the faint moonlight that filtered through the trees. The horses helped as they turned by instinct on the path that was free from underbrush. Sophie began to take notice of her surroundings and the major turns the party made. She heard the two kidnappers comment when they made a turn to the right that the fork to the left was the other one they took into town. After a time they turned their horses up a shallow ravine that took them up to a mountain bench that would be hidden from casual view. Once on the bench, Lagasse led them to the far side where the terrain took a sharp up-turn. The cabin appeared rather suddenly in a heavily forested area backed up against a cliff face. In this kind of location it had to be a trappers cabin that was only used in winter.

Leblanc dismounted and pulled Sophie off the horse as well. She twisted and squirmed trying to get out of his grasp as her feet touched the ground. He roughly pulled her toward the cabin. Lagasse was laughing at them.

"Hey partner! You need some help handling that little tart?! She is one fine piece of young female that you happened to pick up. I could maybe teach both you and her a few things, eh??"

"Shut up, Lagasse! She is our big advantage. But we need to bargain for our escape and if she shows too much injury those Bay boys won't let go."

Sophie hissed at them, "You've already gone too far! You'll never be free from someone on your trail. They'll track you down."

"Little girl, you don't know how good Leblanc and Lagasse are in the wilderness." Lagasse boasted. "Once we get some provisions and a head start no one will ever find us."

"Come on, let's get settled in so we can wait for Wolfleg to come. You take care of the horses. I'll get the girl tied down and a fire started," Leblanc said.

When they went from the porch of the cabin, which was faintly lit by the moon, to the inside of the cabin they were in total dark. Not wanting to let go of Sophie in the blackness, Leblanc called for his partner to come inside until they could get some kind of light. Lagasse took out his tin of lucifers and struck one. It flared so bright they could hardly see anything but it did show a candle on a shelf before it went out. A second lucifer was sufficient to light the candle. Then Sophie was tied to a rough, one piece chair cut out of a short log. Her legs were tied to the bottom of the chair and a rope around her waist which went around the back of the stump. With Sophie securely bound, both men went outside to care for the horses.

Sophie scolded herself for the terror that was in her heart. The candle light had revealed the sinister faces of her captors. She wanted to be brave, wanted to live up to the courage her people had shown through generations. But right now there seemed to be nothing that would let her get out of this very frightening kidnapping and out of the hands of these desperate criminals. So Sophie looked around to familiarize herself with her prison so she would know everything about it if a chance came to escape. It was one room with low ceiling beams. Probably built to shoulder height so that one man by himself could lift the logs to form the walls. But this must have been a shorter than average trapper because the walls were not very high. The French Canadians could only stand fully upright between the beams. There was a stove, which Leblanc was now lighting, at the back of the cabin. It seemed to be putting as much smoke inside the cabin as out the chimney. A bunk, which had some old furs on it, took up most of one side. There were several blankets tossed on the bunk from previous visits the Bosses had made here. A rustic sideboard made out of split cedar logs doubled as a table along the opposite side. One window space showed above the sideboard. It had a tattered animal skin serving as a covering to slow the insects. There were a couple more stump chairs scattered on the dirt floor. The door creaked on rusted hinges whenever it was moved.

Lagasse was laughing as they came back in, "What good fortune that those cowboys had not taken any of their gear off their horses! Now we can each have a bedroll for the night. Even the little tart can use the blankets!"

"Please," Sophie spoke up. "I need to relieve myself."

"Hah! Think we'll fall for that! Forget it!" Leblanc declared.

"No, please, you don't want me to soil the blankets. You can tie a rope to me so I can have a little privacy!"

"Probably should," Lagasse shrugged, looking at his partner.

Sophie carefully looked around in the moon light while she was outside, particularly noticing how tight the back of the cabin was to the cliff face. She also took note that there was a narrow yard on two sides of the cabin. In her mind she was thinking of how close rescuers could come to the building and still be hidden from view. That rescuers would come, she had no doubt. That assurance gave her a determination that she would find any way possible to foil her kidnappers.

FIFTY-FIVE

Cody spent a restless night. Dawn could not come soon enough. He was up and stirring the others so that they would have their coffee and breakfast finished before daylight came. Cody managed a little coffee but knew the knot in his gut would not accept any food.

As they talked over the coffee, they made sure that all three of them were taking full saddle gear so that they could be ready for every situation that might arise, extra ropes and ammunition, pistols either in a holster or settled in a belt, a rifle in each of the gun sheaths, a knife on each one's belt.

He was gratified to see that the Kootenays were finished their breakfast and ready for the day when the Pards arrived. They were eager to do their part to make up for the disaster created by Winter Moon. In the predawn, the party moved to the start of the trail they would follow because they had taken note the night before of just where the kidnappers had entered the forest.

Yellow Bull was the chief tracker for his band and he took the lead. Broken Antler was right behind him bringing a second set of eyes to watch for clues. Pierre came primarily to interpret but also to learn the tracking skills of his uncle. The signs were obvious at first. The two trackers showed the Pards the imprints of the shod horses. They were the freshest of all tracks and, as they pointed out to the three non Indians, easy to follow in the soft forest floor.

The Pards stayed close to the trackers on the early part of the trail. They were confident that their quarry would have gone some distance before stopping so there was no fear that the sound of their horses would warn the kidnappers of their presence.

As they progressed along the trail, Broken Antler began to scout ahead of the other five. No one knew what the fugitives might do in their flight. The pursuers couldn't risk bumping into an ambush or even accidentally letting them know they had a search party that close. As time progressed the Pards dismounted and led their horses on a short rein so they could hopefully stifle a neigh or a snort if they smelled other horses close by.

Broken Antler came back to them at a trot. He spoke rapidly in Kootenay and Pierre had to step forward to translate. "This trail divides in two about half a mile ahead. One trail continues then quickly turns up a narrow ravine. Not a good area for observing someone. The other trail veers to the left, possibly toward the town. There is a man slowly walking from town toward where the trail divides. He is looking over his shoulder and all around."

Cody blew out his breath. "Probably the contact person for the Bosses. They probably have an arrangement for a meeting place somewhere out here if there was any trouble. What did this man look like?"

"He is Indian but has a dark look. His hair is stringy and dirty, not in a proper braid."

"Sounds like it could be Wolfleg, which would make sense because of his connection with the Bosses." Quinn commented.

"Why don't we take him down now, because we want to arrest him for what he has done anyway. Besides, the judge is going to be here soon!"

"On the other hand," said Cody thoughtfully. "Maybe he can actually help us without knowing it. I'm sure he is just a courier. If Broken Antler can shadow him right to the hideout we can take him down on his way back when he is thinking about doing whatever the Bosses have told him to do. Is that possible Broken Antler? Can you follow him without him knowing you are there?"

When Broken Antler listened to Pierre's translation and understood the implication of what Cody was asking him a glimmer of a smile crossed his face. If Cody was not mistaken he also stood a little taller. This was calling on his special abilities. The stories around the Kootenay campfires made a legend out of Broken Antler's skill to be within arm's reach of deer before they knew he was there.

Once Broken Antler had agreed, Cody continued. "Their camp or hideout is probably up on that next bench and the messenger will have to come back down the same trail. What if we position a couple people on each fork? Darcy and Quinn cover the one he is coming up now and Yellow Bull, Pierre and I will set up an ambush on this leg of the trail. As long as it works out this way, Broken Antler, don't worry about getting back to us before Wolfleg comes back. We'll need your information after we have captured him and then we can give full attention to the Bosses."

"Understood?" Cody got a nod back from each one. "If we're guessing right this may get us to Sophie sooner than what we could hope for. Yellow Bull, you go with Broken Antler, and come back to let us know that he has actually taken the trail up the mountain side. After that we'll just settle into our positions and wait."

The two Kootenays melted into the forest. They were gone without even a whisper of noise. All three of the Pards looked at each other with wonder because to them there was no passage other than the trail. Broken Antler and Yellow Bull had not bothered with the trail.

Time crawled by. It was especially hard to do nothing when they knew that Sophie was helpless and that she could not know that they were pursuing every possibility that they could. Certainly she would know in her head that rescue was being attempted but she had to put in hours just going on faith that the Bosses would be captured and she would be set free. Cody agonized over what kind of treatment she might be suffering and what they might have done differently that could have prevented this from happening.

The tension of not knowing what was developing kept building for the Pards. It crossed each one's mind that the two scouts may have been spotted.

Finally Yellow Bull materialized from the trees. "Yes, the man they assumed was Wolfleg, had turned up the ravine trail." He reported through Pierre's translation. "Once he started up the slope he was more focused on the path ahead rather than looking around. Seemed like he was more confident that he couldn't be spotted. After he had gone by me, I was able to double check that the horses we were tracking had definitely gone up that path as well."

"Good work, Yellow Bull. Let's find our ambush spots and settle in. This might be a long wait."

FIFTY-SIX

Sophie spent a restless night with her hands and feet bound. She must have drifted off to sleep eventually because she was startled by the door on the front of the stove clanging shut. Both men were up. One was looking after the fire, the other checking out an old coffee pot. Sophie didn't stir immediately hoping to get some idea of their plans by listening to their conversation.

Leblanc and Lagasse used such a mixture of French and English that it was hard to pick out any meaning to what they were saying. She did manage to pick out the word "ransom" which seemed to be associated with her. It dawned on her that it must mean some kind of exchange in order for them to set her free. The two men argued over this, which made Sophie wonder if she might cause them to argue over her as well and distract them at the right moment.

She also heard the name "Wolfleg" over and over. As the morning wore on they became agitated whenever the name came up. They went to the door of the cabin over and over looking out for someone to come. When there was no one in sight they would let out an oath along with the name. Again, Sophie was able to discern that they were waiting on the person called by this name and were increasingly impatient that he wasn't there.

Sophie pleaded for another visit to the bushes which they cared for without any grumbling or hesitation. Her thought was that by showing no inclination to struggle she would lull them into carelessness. When they got back inside Sophie went to the rustic chair rather than the bunk and again the men didn't question her choice. She offered her hands in front to be tied rather than waiting for them to tell her to put them behind her back. Then they tied her feet to the bottom of the log made into a chair.

When it was getting late in the morning, there was a clear whistle from the edge of the forest. That galvanized Leblanc and Lagasse into action. Both grabbed a rifle and Leblanc stepped out of the cabin door. He looked around and then gave a shrill whistle. Wolfleg stepped out into the clear. Both men relaxed their guns and waved the newcomer across the clear space.

Leblanc started scolding Wolfleg in English. "What took you so long!? Didn't you think maybe we were really hungry here?"

"I had to get some things together to bring to you." replied Wolfleg defensively.

"Bah! To be this late you were sleeping off a drunk!!" Lagasse spat out at him. "Do you have some coffee in that pack?"

Wolfleg put down his backpack and began bringing out its contents. Lagasse immediately grabbed up the large canteen and coffee and began to fix a pot. He also took out some bacon, some beans and a couple bottles of liquor. Lagasse began spewing out curses as he rattled the stove door. It again seemed to be belching more smoke than heat from the damp wood and his efforts only seemed to make it worse. After a bit the wood seemed to catch better and gradually the aroma of coffee overcame the putrid body odours and the smoke of the cabin.

Leblanc and Wolfleg spent some time talking about the supplies they would need depending on how long they would be located at this cabin. Wolfleg was eager to fill them in on the sensation the broad daylight murder of Ogilvie had created. From his point of view they were big celebrities and their story would become known far and wide. Now that they had kidnapped the girl their legend would only grow. Wolfleg was clearly pleased to be one of their associates. Leblanc had to keep bringing him back to the plans they had to make. Once the coffee had boiled, Lagasse found something for each of them to use for drinking. As he was passing out the coffee and the jerky, Leblanc opened one of the bottles of whiskey and put a generous ration into his and Lagasse's coffees.

Leblanc leaned forward so that he was in Wolfleg's face. "Now listen carefully. We have decided on some terms that the Bay people have to carry out for the girl to go free."

Wolfleg laughed, "You're not actually going to let her go are you?!"

Sophie turned to ice inside when she heard those words. She held her breath waiting for the answer.

"We haven't decided yet. It will depend on how well this new Trader carries out our demands." Leblanc responded. "Anyway, here is what we want and you are to get this message to Linklater. The ransom starts with ten thousand dollars in gold. Then we need another horse with saddle for the girl to ride on. We have to have a pack horse with a grubstake on it for the winter and it better be generous! We'll go south into the United States territory. If everyone behaves, the girl will be left at the International Boundary. If there is any attempt to arrest us, any ambush, the girl dies first."

Lagasse spoke up, "You got that Wolfleg? Don't forget any of it. Make sure you have everything and be back here by noon tomorrow. Got it? Noon tomorrow. If they think they can delay us let them know that we will start to take it out on this little tart. Her screams will be music to our ears!!"

Wolfleg slipped out of the cabin without any more words. The Bosses looked at each other and grinned at the thought of the ransom that would come. "We will be on easy street, my friend. Let's drink to our future!" Leblanc said as he lifted his cup which he had refilled with straight liquor.

"Ah, yes. We have enough liquid to make it easy to wait for our wealth to arrive."

FIFTY-SEVEN

Darcy and Quinn immediately mounted up to get to their area of the trail that they were to cover. They took note of the fork as they passed it and from there began to watch for the best possible site for taking this messenger down. Yellow Bull had assured them that, although he had not laid eyes on the hideout of the Bosses, the ravine extended far enough up the mountain side that they could get into position without fear of being heard.

Darcy pulled up when they were four or five hundred yards beyond the fork, "This looks like the right kind of location. See the turn in the trail and the dense brush for one of us and just up there a large tree trunk that would fully cover someone."

"Looks good," Quinn responded. "I'll take the horses on down the trail so they don't give us away."

The boys settled in.

Cody, Pierre and Yellow Bull did the same on their leg of the trail. A fallen tree beside the trail provided one nest and a couple of cedars side by side on the opposite side served for the other. Pierre took the horses back along the trail out of earshot to where he could tie them to branches. They had all agreed that they would do their best to capture Wolfleg without using guns. While they were confident that they wouldn't be heard in normal moving around, a gun shot might well carry to the fugitives and put them on guard. Of even greater concern was taking the messenger alive so they could interrogate him. Their success in rescuing Sophie might well depend on what they could learn from him.

The minutes crawled by with each one nervous, each one wondering if they were in the right location, each one asking himself if he could carry this off without using the gun that he was fingering. Would the rescuers know the moment when they had to shoot? Could they counter whatever weapons Wolfleg might be carrying? Yellow Bull had said that he didn't have a rifle. Yet they knew he would have a knife and possibly a pistol.

Waiting in ambush gave too much time for thinking, but each one was alert to every sound from their surroundings. This was their mission. They had been working towards this for months. Excitement coursed through their veins. Even though this confrontation had been initiated by the Bosses themselves killing Ogilvie, they were more than ready to seize this opportunity. Then, when they kidnapped Sophie, it became very personal and elevated the drive inside each of the rescuing party so that they would face down whatever may occur in these next hours.

Quinn heard the squirrel scolding first and knew something or someone was on the move. He signalled to Darcy with a low whistle and Darcy waved back. Quinn spotted movement through the screen of brush and readied himself. Wolfleg rounded the turn in the trail. He seemed to be deep in thought. Quinn recognized him from Kootenay House. Now, Quinn had to hold back and let him pass according to the plan. Twelve, thirteen, fourteen, fifteen steps and Quinn stepped out into the trail.

"Hey!" Quinn called loudly.

Wolfleg spun around, a sneer instantly on his face!

"We need to talk to you Wolfleg and we need to talk to you now!" Quinn was talking in a loud voice to cover any noise Darcy may make.

Wolfleg's hand went to his hip where his knife flashed into his hand. "Come here and my knife will do my talking!"

Suddenly Wolfleg was choking as Darcy's right arm was tightening against his throat from behind. Wolfleg thrashed and twisted against the grip of the arm. Darcy's left hand grabbed the villains jaw and gave a menacing pull to the left.

"Stop, quiet, or I'll break your neck!" hissed Darcy.

Wolfleg felt the immediate effects of the choke hold and the twist Darcy was applying and knew he had no way out. The knife dropped from his hand and he surrendered. Darcy, maintaining his hold, took Wolfleg down to the ground face down.

"Hands behind your back!"

Quinn grabbed the hands and twisted Wolfleg's arms up so far that the pain stopped any struggle. As well Quinn had planted his knee in the middle of the captive's back. As Darcy stood and looked down on the capture he had a fleeting image of an insect pinned to a display board that he had seen once in Montreal. Darcy retrieved a rope he had cached at his ambush spot and soon had Wolfleg's hands securely tied behind his back. They had him sit on the ground while Quinn retrieved the horses.

Once Wolfleg saw that he wasn't going to be killed immediately, he began to protest his innocence and to berate these "young pups" for being so foolish as to mess with him.

"After all I have very powerful friends. You will be very sorry."

Darcy hushed him and debated with Quinn as to whether to let him walk or should they tie his feet and put him belly down over one of the horses along with a gag in his mouth. Their captive promised to not talk if he could stay on his feet. They decided on a tether rope around his neck and kept him walking ahead.

As they got well past the fork in the trail, they made enough noise so they wouldn't be mistaken for an enemy. There was great relief for the trio at this site to see the captive in bonds and to see that both captors were without injury.

"What have you learned from him?" Cody asked. "Has he talked!"

"Nothing," Darcy responded. "He still thinks he can tell us what is going to happen."

Cody saw red as his anger flashed hot. He grabbed the front of Wolfleg's shirt and twisted it up under his chin, almost lifting him off his feet. "Listen, you scum, we don't need you but you can help your own cause by cooperating. Now tell us where the girl is and what is happening to her."

"I don't have to tell you nothing! You are the ones who are going to do as we say!" Wolfleg spat out at them. "We have demands that have to be met by noon tomorrow or else that girl is going to be in more pain than you can imagine!"

Cody's fist exploded into Wolfleg's face with a sledge hammer force that would have thrown him to the ground if Darcy and Quinn hadn't been there to catch him.

" You hooligan! In case you haven't noticed, you're the one that is tied up. Now start telling us where Sophie is."

Wolfleg smirked, "The Bosses will get me free. They run this whole town. Their power will put you in your place and you better get busy on getting their demands met."

Cody blew out an exasperated breath. "Let me paint a picture for you. The Bosses have already sacrificed you. They are only using you to look after themselves so they can escape. They heard enough from Ogilvie before they gunned him down to know that they will hang if they are caught. Ogilvie told them that he had written everything down and the Judge will have it all. I've seen what he wrote. You're in there Wolfleg. If you don't help us and those two get away, it will be you that will hang.

Don't fool yourself, they aren't providing any escape for you, just for themselves."

Wolfleg looked wildly from one to another of his captors. Looking for some sign that this wasn't true. He was met with steely expressions on all the faces. His growing realization that there was no way out of this showed in his changing expressions.

"Are you going to take the fall for them? If you hold us back now and that woman is tortured and killed you will hang for sure." Wolfleg's eyes changed to fear as Cody rammed these words at him.

"I'm not going to take the fall for them. You'll make sure I don't hang?" Wolfleg was pleading.

"We can't promise, but we will tell the judge what happens now." Cody said.

Darcy and Quinn relaxed their grip on their captive's arms. Although they still had his hands tied behind his back and the loop around his neck.

"You saw Sophie?" Cody asked and Wolfleg nodded that he had.

"What condition is she in? Have they hurt her?

"She's tied up. But only a cut on her lip shows anything. Otherwise, she's fine."

Cody couldn't help but pursue this further. "They haven't... er,..gone so far as to...er...molest her?"

"Naw, their saving that for later on" The smirk crept back on Wolfleg's face. Cody clenched his fist and took a step toward him but held back when he saw the cockiness drain from him.

Darcy spoke up, "Tell us what their hideout is like."

"It's an old trapper's cabin hidden back across this next bench up." Wolfleg went on to gradually reveal a full picture of the cabin's situation. The details got filled in under persistent questioning from the Pards. They even found out about the two bottles of whiskey and that the murderers were not in the habit of drinking it sparingly for the sake of having some tomorrow.

The men were gathering their gear even while Wolfleg was talking. They debated what to do with their prisoner. Taking him in to town would take too much time.

Quinn suggested, "Lets just tie his hands to his feet behind his back and leave him by the trail until we came back for him."

Darcy shook his head, "Even though this trail is hardly used someone might come along and let him go. I think we should take him into the trees a bit, gag him and tie him to a tree."

Cody nodded, "Preferably a tree with an ant hill at its base!"

Wolfleg squirmed and squeaked, "You can't do that. You might get shot and never come back to...."

Quinn had decided that the gag should be applied first. Then he and Pierre took him into the trees far enough that he couldn't be seen from the trail. By the time Quinn had sat their prisoner at the base of a tree and tied his hands behind the trunk and tied his feet, Pierre was open-mouthed at the impossibility of Wolfleg ever squirming free.

Quinn looked down at him as they were about to leave, "Is there anything else you'd like to tell us to make sure we're successful so we can come back for you?

Wolfleg glared daggers at him but shook his head that he had anymore to say.

FIFTY-EIGHT

The men checked all of their equipment, making sure guns were loaded and free to be drawn and that knives were in their belts. Each one had a canteen and filled it in a stream they crossed in case it developed into a stand off.

There was lots of nervous energy. They were closing in on deadly enemies. Sophie had to be set free without being caught in any cross fire. Justice for so many people harmed and even killed by these men hung on the success of this operation. This was the climax of the mission that powerful men in Montreal had declared these men too young to carry out.

They mounted up and moved out with firm determination. They had understood that they could ride to the top of the ravine without being detected by the kidnappers. Once they gained the top they all got down and began to walk in the direction Wolfleg had told them. This mountain bench was heavily treed so they proceeded quietly and cautiously.

Suddenly Broken Antler appeared from among the trees. He had come noiselessly as an apparition so it gave everyone a start. Their reaction put a big grin on his face.

"I have been all around their cabin but staying back in the trees so they couldn't see me. We can get very close on two sides. It looks like they are getting quite drunk. They have come outside occasionally to take a leak and they have argued back and forth. It looks like they are feeling over-confident, obviously helped by the booze."

Cody was re-assured by having this kind of information from one of their own. It confirmed what Wolfleg had told them but they hadn't been sure whether Wolfleg might have been deceiving them to lead them into disaster.

"Great help, Broken Antler! I don't know how you do it."

"You should leave your horses here so their horses don't react and warn them that we are near. Once you have looked things over and decided what we are going to do, we'll let Sophie know that we are here."

Darcy's head snapped around to look at Broken Antler. "What do you mean about letting Sophie know?! How can we do that without letting Leblanc and Lagasse know as well?"

"We do crow talk. Our band at Joseph's Prairie learned to use crow talk when we were hunting. Deer and elk don't worry about crows and we could tell each other what to do with different crow caws. Sophie learned it, too."

"Well, that's good," said Cody with a frown on his face. "But don't forget, Sophie is tied up in there at the hands of murderers who have guns and are getting drunk. Anything could set them off. Let's hope we can take them down without any bullets flying!"

They tied their horses to branches and loaded themselves with gear. Guns, ammunition, ropes, knives, canteens, and a couple of hatchets had them equipped for whatever they might face. Broken Antler led them through the trees. As they neared the cabin, he signalled for them to be extra cautious and quiet. Finally he motioned for them to get right down on hands and knees. This allowed them to crawl up to a cluster of willows where they could peer through to scan the cabin and its setting.

After quietly watching for a while, they moved back a little to discuss what they might be able to do. Any kind of frontal assault was out of the question. So they considered how they might separate the two villains. If they waited long enough they would have to relieve themselves and that would mean one out with one in. That might mean a long wait while in position and then what would they do to get the one left inside before he hurt Sophie.

Darcy had an idea. "What if we smoked them out?

That got everyone's attention. Darcy continued, "They've got a fire going even though it's the middle of the day. From what I could see, the back of the cabin is so snugged up to the flat face of the bluff behind it that with a long branch I could lay a flat piece of bark on top of the chimney. They wouldn't know anything was happening until the smoke was building up inside. Even then they might think that it was just a bird's nest falling down to block the chimney."

"One of them would be sure to come out to investigate the cause or just to get out of the smoke," Cody added. "Quinn and I could be at the corner that is close to the trees and tackle them from behind as they come out."

Quinn nodded in agreement, "Cody, what if you have your rope ready and lasso the first one out and then I could take care of the second one?"

Cody asked a question of Broken Antler, "How do you think Sophie will react to the smoke? Will she panic?"

"She is used to the smoke from our fire in the floor of our lodge. In fact, she seems to tolerate it better than any of the other women. She'll know to get down close to the ground as soon as she can."

Darcy took some time finding just the right branch for reaching from the knoll to the chimney. He finally settled on using a whole aspen tree. It's main trunk had been forced tall in the thick cluster where Darcy got it. Yet it was still sturdy enough near its top that the fork provided by one of the branches would bear the weight of a piece of bark. He then left the hatchet with the Indians so that it wouldn't clank against something that would warn the cabin occupants that someone was nearby.

Cody had been checking his rope and the loop so that it would perform smoothly at the critical moment. They agreed that they could be in position within half an hour. Cody and Quinn would have eye contact with Broken Antler who would have eye contact with Darcy. Broken Antler said that he could signal Sophie to sit still and wait in crow sounds just like they would do if the men were stalking a deer or elk. Then at the half hour, Darcy would signal to Broken Antler to give another crow call that the take down was starting and Darcy would place the bark over the chimney.

FIFTY-NINE

Inside the cabin Leblanc and Lagasse were treating themselves generously with the whiskey. Sophie was worried about it because her experience with drunks was that they got abusive and aggressive. Fortunately for her, these two got aggressive with each other and quarrelled over little things such as what they might do in the future with all the wealth that was coming into their hands. They seemed to give no concern about pursuers trying to find them. Wolfleg had sworn to them that no one had seen him on the trail and no one had even seen him leave town. They knew that this cabin was so secluded that the odds of someone just happening on it were virtually nil.

Just when the kidnappers were tiring of their arguing and were starting to throw in occasional lewd comments to Sophie, she heard something that set her heart racing. It was the faint cawing of a crow. What got her full attention was the distinctive pattern of the bird's call. The men of her band used their ability to imitate a crow's cawing to signal each other when hunting. As a young girl Sophie had begged and begged her father to teach her how to do it and what the different sounds and patterns meant. If what she had heard was indeed sounded by a human from her band, it would have a follow up pattern of caws. She held her breath, hoping, willing her ears to hear the second half of a signal.

There is was! So realistic that no one would give it a second thought except to note that crows are in the area. Sophie let out a big exhale, trying not to change her expression or her manner at all. Huge relief flooded over her to know that she had been found and that rescue was under way. Her heart was racing as she began to ponder what would have to happen. If these brutes caught on that their pursuers were close by, she was in mortal danger.

Was there anything she could do to help? The signal from the crow calls was the one that meant stay put. So the men coming for her were not expecting her to do anything except to stay the same and to not cause any alarm or crisis to the captors. Probably it would be helpful if there was some way to keep their focus inside the cabin rather than outside. She had an idea.

"I'm really hungry!" Sophie spoke up. She had been so quiet that it surprised the men when she blurted this out. "Please! You have the bacon and beans that that man brought. I'll be getting weak if you don't give me some."

At first the men just scoffed at her. "You think we are your cooks? Close your yap. We have important drinking to do!"

After a bit she risked it again. "It's not fair. I'd get it myself if you let me. You can watch me, just untie me. I'll even cook for you and save you from having to do it."

"What's made you so helpful?" Leblanc growled. "You think we've had too much whiskey and that you could escape? We're too smart for that!"

Sophie quietened for a time because she thought she had pushed as much as she could. After a bit it was Lagasse that came back to the thought of food.

"You know what? Talking about bacon is making my stomach growl for something more than drink. I think I'll cook up some and heat those beans up as well. No use saving them when we'll get all those supplies tomorrow."

Lagasse stood up and weaved his way over to the stove. Having to duck under the low crossbeams made his stagger more exaggerated. Then, once again, he began to do battle with the stove. The handle on the front stuck so he tried to open it by kicking which almost landed him on his backside. When he took a firmer hold on the handle he pulled his hand back immediately because of the heat still left from the earlier fire. He added several sticks from the wood supply and their dampness brought a curl of smoke out of various holes in the stove. Curses flowed freely and loudly. Next he started rummaging through the remains of metal things that may have been pots or may have been gold panning pans. Sophie was satisfied that the idea of food had stirred up lots of cover noise while whatever needed to be happening outside was going ahead.

Darcy took a wide circle deeper back into the trees and then scrambled up a broken rock incline to get above and behind the cabin. Then with great caution, placing each step where it would cause no noise, he made his way to the lip of the small cliff backing the cabin. He had to get to the very edge in order for his pole to be long enough to reach the stove pipe. A few pebbles fell and Darcy froze. Fortunately there was some metallic noises coming from the cabin at the same time. Obviously those inside were stirring about which would cover inadvertent small sounds from outside. Darcy got himself set with footholds that would give him a good base when he made the critical reach with the chimney cover. He signalled Broken Antler that he was ready.

While Darcy was finding his way, Cody and Quinn had also melted back into the trees and had circled the opposite direction. The trees were so thick that there was little underbrush which allowed them to move quickly. Their side of the cabin was opposite to the window side. As they neared the cabin they slowed their progress and began to watch where each step would land. Once at the side of the cabin they peered cautiously around the corner. The entrance area was clear so both men showed themselves to Broken Antler and signalled that they were ready simply waiting for Darcy and the crow call.

With each one in position Broken Antler crossed his arms on his chest. He looked to Darcy first and Darcy responded with crossed arms. Then he looked to Cody and Quinn. They also made the sign of crossed arms back.

Broken Antler raised his head and gave an incredibly realistic series of caws. He waited a few moments and gave a different series of caws. Sophie registered the significance of that signal and her heart rate went up. Darcy raised his aspen pole and stretched to get the patch of bark centred over the stove pipe. The pipe looked rusty and fragile to Darcy and it actually settled a little to one side. Darcy tensed wondering if he needed to lift the bark up. It held after its bit of movement.

Smoke started billowing from the stove and was quickly filling the small cabin. The two men stared stupidly at the stove. Their inebriated minds sluggishly processing this new phenomena. Leblanc yelled at Lagasse.

"Can't you even get a fire going without burning down the cabin, you idiot?"

"It's not my fault. Must be a squirrel's nest blocking the flue."

Sophie started to scream as loud as she could hoping it would give their heads too much to handle.

"Help! Help! Fire! Help me, I don't want to get burned up. Please help me, Lagasse! You wouldn't leave me here would you?"

Leblanc yelled "I'm leaving. You look after her, Lagasse!"

Leblanc swayed as he headed for the door. He picked up his rifle leaning against the doorpost and cradled it in one arm.

Sophie grabbed at Lagasse and caught his sleeve as he weaved away from the stove. The smoke was causing their eyes to sting!

She tugged him towards her, and, in a pleading voice said, "Just untie my feet from the chair and I'll get myself out!"

He hesitated a moment, staring at her with his bleary eyes. Then he knelt down to pull the slip knot that held her legs and feet. As he was kneeling to do that Leblanc stepped through the door into the fresh air. Now was the moment Cody was waiting for. He took one step away from the cabin, gave one swirl of his lariat and the loop flew through the air. It settled nicely over its target but the loop was too big. Cody's heart skipped a beat as the loop fell to the ground. However he recovered quickly and began hauling back on the rope. To his great relief the loop caught on Leblanc's ankles and with one extra big pull the fugitive was flat on his side gasping to fill his lungs with air. Quinn pounced and grabbed the rifle away from under him.

Lagasse had nicely loosened the ropes at Sophie's ankles when the commotion happened outside. Lagasse, wondering what was happening to his partner, reacted to the noise by slightly raising his head to listen for sounds. At that moment, Sophie saw her opportunity. She swiftly brought her bound hands up and drove her thumb into the man's eye. The pain was instant and devastating. He roared and jerked to his feet only to collide full force with one of the crossbeams. He was knocked out instantly and crumpled to the floor.

Sophie immediately freed her feet from the tangle of rope and fled to the fresh air. "It's me!" she cried out as she got to the door. She ran directly into Cody who was drawing his pistol and expecting to confront Lagasse. His mouth fell open as he saw her come out of the smoke. He took her into his free arm, kept the pistol aimed at the door and asked, "Lagasse?!"

She shook her head, "Knocked out, on the floor!"

Again Cody looked at her with amazement, shook his head, called Darcy to lift the bark, and started into the cabin. He crouched down to be under the thickest smoke, took a big breath and plunged into the murky interior. He quickly found

Lagasse who was beginning to moan with pain, holstered his pistol and dragged the man backwards out the door.

Quinn took over from there and quickly had him hog tied just like his partner in crime. They frisked the two criminals thoroughly relieving them of two knives each. When the prisoners were secure, everyone sat on the ground getting over the shakiness that set in after the intensity of the capture and freeing of the hostage. Each one related their experience from their perspective. Darcy told how precarious his spot was when he reached the pole over to the chimney. Sophie told what incredible relief it was to hear the crow calls. But the biggest reaction was caused by her account of the eye gouge and the knock out by Lagasse jerking upright and colliding with the cross beam.

Finally Cody brought them to consider their next steps. "We have to get these guys into jail in our new storeroom. I think our best security is to tie them onto their horses. We can pick up the other one when we get our rides."

He turned to Broken Antler and Yellow Bull, "I'd look forward to partnering with you any time. Your tracking, scouting and crow calls were amazing."

Broken Antler responded, "You boys work as a team with us very good. You are always welcome to our band."

Darcy asked, "Think you'll head home soon?"

"Pack today, leave when sun comes up. We've had enough gold rush!" Yellow Bull said with a big grin.

SIXTY

Cody asked Darcy and Quinn to get the prisoners tied onto the horses. He took Sophie's hand and they walked to the far side of the small clearing so they could have a few minutes to themselves.

"Cody, I knew you would come for me so I never lost hope even though the night was so very long."

"I couldn't think about anything else, knowing you were in the hands of two of the most ruthless men I've ever known. I am so glad that you weren't harmed."

"Cody." Sophie paused, obviously searching for words to express her inner feelings in English. "You tried to warn me that your world was full of bad things, especially for an Indian girl. I had no idea. If everyone was like you it wouldn't be a problem. Now I've seen the worst and all I can think about is getting back to my family, my band, where I've been safe for all these years. I love you, but I'm not ready for your world."

Cody was quiet as they came to the edge of the forest. Inside he was churning as he tried to process all his feelings along with

Sophie's words. Finally he turned to face her, taking both her hands in his.

"Sophie, I know there is a connection between us that I've never experienced with anyone before. I hear your words and my head says they are right, but my heart is arguing against them. You will always be very very special to me. I don't know what is ahead for me and for my partners. I guess Jeff's words have influenced me, so I can say this, we'll leave the future in God's hands and see what happens. I love you and I'll think of you always."

Their hands released and their arms slid around each other. The world seemed to stand still as their lips met. The kiss was tender and seared into the memory of each of them. Then they turned to walk back to the others, hand in hand, although each tried to find a way to wipe a tear away without the rest noticing.

Quinn and Darcy had saddled the stolen horses. Then,very carefully, with Darcy holding a pistol on them, Quinn untied the feet of Lagasse, virtually lifted him into the saddle with his hands still tied behind his back. The next step was to tie his feet together under the belly of the horse. Amid loud protests, they performed the same actions with Leblanc.

They made their way back to the fork in the trail. This location carried much more significance than simply where they retrieved their third prisoner. The Indians would turn south to their camp and the rest would turn northwest toward the town. Cody and Sophie had said their farewells back at the cabin and there was nothing more to say. Yet, each of them wondered if this was the last they would ever see of each other. Should they break from the course they were on which would take them many miles apart and declare a promise to see more of each other? In the end their reserve held and they parted with a nod along with the general words of farewell that the rest of the group shared with one another.

Once the Indians had departed, the Pards debated how best to transport the prisoners back into town and to prison.

They retrieved Wolfleg while they were figuring the best way to handle three desperadoes. Once they had retrieved Wolfleg and he stumbled back to the trail, the French Canadians began a verbal lashing, blaming him for being stupid enough to get ambushed and bring about their downfall. They threatened that if they could ever get their hands on him, he would be finished permanently.

Wolfleg responded with a sneer, "You've made me do your dirty work for so long it's about time you paid for it." With that Wolfleg spat in their direction.

Quinn had a suggestion. "The two Bosses didn't mind riding double last night so they can do that again! Then we can all ride."

Darcy jested, "Maybe one of them would like to have Wolfleg double with him. They seem pretty cozy!"

That brought a string of curses so that Darcy just shrugged and laughed. With the day moving on, Quinn did just what Darcy said to save the time of getting one of the already mounted ones moved to another horse. Soon the Indian was tied behind Lagasse and both of them were complaining.

The boys retrieved their mounts and with Cody leading the horse with Leblanc, Quinn leading the double mounted one and Darcy riding drag, they headed for town. They had no idea what a sensation it would cause when they got to the edge of town. Word spread faster than a wildfire that the Bosses were coming into town as prisoners. The route became crowded. People jeered the men who had threatened so many of the town people. Some spat at them. Others were just curious to see the men with the stove pipe hats cut down to size. When the jeering got a little rough, Cody assured the crowd that these men would face justice. The Crown Colony Judge would come and hold a proper trial, and he also assured them that the judge had already been sent for.

Someone farther back in the crowd yelled out, "Is that the Hanging Judge that's coming?"

Cody didn't answer that question but the question itself settled over the crowd as they pondered that they might be looking on men who would pay the ultimate price for what they had done. Soon the little parade moved through the crowd to where they hadn't heard the question about the Hanging Judge and the jeers and cheers regained volume. Leblanc and Lagasse sneered out at the ones who yelled that they would get what they deserved. In fact, they yelled back at them to watch out for when they would get free.

The question about hanging stayed with Cody as they gigged their horses forward. Even though he had no hesitation that the murders these men had committed deserved hanging, there was something different about it now that he knew the criminals personally. A life was a very precious thing. Something beyond a price tag. Something unique in each and every soul. Cody reflected that he was glad he was in a place to uphold the value of life through the civilized justice that the judge would bring into this far-flung corner of the Colony. An additional thought came that he had reason to be grateful for every influence that had pushed him to this side of the law when he could easily have ended up on the wrong side in his youthful anger at life. The image of his Grandfather Thompson came to mind; that elderly man who had always cared for him and who would share words from the Bible that had always been so important to him. Cody recognized an anchor there more clearly than ever before.

A shout from Darcy jarred Cody out of his reverie! Cody turned his head to his left to try to see what had caused Darcy's reaction.

"No! Look right! There's a gun!"

Cody swivelled his head the opposite way and spotted a wizened hunched man lurching his way through the crowd. He was waving an old pistol back and forth in front of him as he limped toward the riders. About three steps behind came Berty widening the wake created by the gunman.

"Swampy! Swampy!" Berty was huffing out as they came closer. "You come right back here! You're only going to get yourself shot. Hold up, right this minute!!"

Cody vaulted off his horse landing directly in front of the man. At the moment Cody's feet touched the ground, he swept his left arm up under the hand holding the gun. His right fist clenched to knock the man off his feet. But in the brief contact of the up-sweep of his arm, there was so little resistance that the right fist never moved. There was an audible click when the gun was pointing to the sky but nothing more. It was not loaded!

"Dear, oh dear, oh dear!" Berty was saying as she chugged up to the man she called Swampy.

"Those are dirty, mean, rotten scum of the earth!" Swampy had found his scratchy voice. He was trembling as he pointed his finger at the prisoners. "They beat me up and now I've got a limp and only one eye. They have to pay for their crimes!"

"Now Swampy," Berty sounded like a mother, "These fine young men will see to that! Won't you Cody? Now you come back with me and I'll get you some tea."

"I promise Swampy," said Cody, "These guys will pay for what they've done to you and to a whole lot of other people."

As Berty shepherded Swampy limping back through the crowd, Cody's anger swelled. The evil that these men had carried out by victimizing weaker people could never be fully paid for. But there was a big satisfaction in putting a stop to it where he and his buddies could.

They moved forward with their prisoners. The crowd thinned out as they neared the Hudson Bay facility. John Linklater came out to meet them. He was grinning from ear to ear.

"We had heard that you had these scoundrels in custody. The news swept through here like a forest fire. This is a great sight. Even better that you have three arrested. I was expecting only two, but this takes care of a number of crimes that Ogilvie had written down."

Cody couldn't help grinning back. This had been their objective since that first morning by the Columbia River when they read their secret commission from the Bay directors. There was a sweet sense of satisfaction for the Pards in delivering these men into Linklater's custody.

"We've got a little problem though," Cody said. "These guys are desperate and they blame the Indian for their capture. They'll do anything to escape and likely kill Wolfleg if they ever get their hands on him."

Again Linklater chuckled, "We're ahead of you on that! Figured you'd bring these guys in so had a couple men use some of the lumber Quinn's sawyers have cut and put in some dividing walls. Gunnar's coming to do some chains. We'll have these fellas real cozy while we wait for the Judge."

"I sure hope Jed and Jeff will be able to track down Judge Begbie." Darcy said, as he pulled Wolfleg down from the horse.

SIXTY-ONE

Jed's mind couldn't stay off the fact that he was entrusted with a message to the top Judge of the Colony of British Columbia. It energized him so that all he could think about was eating up the miles as fast as the pack horses could move. Jeff had to whistle for a halt before the first morning was half gone.

"I think you gulped a little too much of Berty's coffee this morning, my friend!"

Jed seemed puzzled by his comment.

"OK, I'll spell it out. Everything you're doing is at a fast pace. The horses won't last two days at this rate. We have to slow down or we'll end up having to lay over an extra day for them to recover."

Jed stared at Jeff for a few seconds and then a sheepish grin crept over his face. "I was just going over in my mind the last few miles, and I guess you are right. I'm just wanting to get this message to the Judge as soon as I can! But it would be terrible to have to hold up for a whole day because we pushed too hard."

Once they had established the speed the horses could handle, the journey became very enjoyable. Both men were content on horseback as the scenery was constantly changing. The beauty of nature was on lavish display in these mountains and valleys. The map and directions that Nels had given them was easy to follow, so they could relax and drink in their surroundings.

The campfire at night was a natural time for telling stories. As the days passed the fireside stories became more personal. It was fertile ground for a growing friendship.

They marked their progress by talking to the occasional prospector, trapper, government agent or wanderer. From such people they learned that Judge Begbie had been in Rock Creek recently and that someone there would know which direction he'd headed when he had departed that dying town. Also, from stopping to share the latest news from one another they were assured that they were only a couple of long days from Rock Creek which was good because Sasquatch had been destroying campsites in the area.

"Really??!!" Jed laughed at the story assuming that some story teller had gotten a little tipsy and let his imagination run wild.

"Be very careful. He's at least eight feet tall, and covered with shaggy hair. You can smell him a mile away but he always manages to crash through the brush and get away before men recover from the fright and go after him. The worst thing is how spooked horses get when he comes anywhere near!"

They celebrated that evening by dipping into their supplies to share a tin of peaches. The atmosphere of their trip so far had been nothing but peaceful and congenial. Jed and Jeff had agreed that there was no need for them to stand watch at all and they would wake at daylight as was their custom.

As dawn came, the two were sleeping soundly, when a ruckus broke out at the picket line. Suddenly there was total turmoil. Horses were neighing, snorting, stomping. There was a sound of terror in the shrill tone of their whinnies. Both men were instantly awake and on their feet. Rifles were retrieved from saddle scabbards and cocked. Several horses had pulled free of the picket rope but were just milling around. The whites of their eyes were huge and showing obvious fear.

The two men, scanning the forest, couldn't see any obvious threat as they got to their horses and began talking to them to calm them. It was dangerous work because the horses were so agitated that they continued to rear and twist even though Jed and Jeff moved among them.

As they settled Jed called softly to Jeff, "Can you smell that?!"

Jeff replied, "I sure can. It's horrible. Not like anything I've ever smelled before! Something is out there!"

"No wonder the horses reacted. We might as well saddle them up. It will calm them to have us working around them."

"Sounds like no coffee this morning! It would smell so much better than the Sasquatch's breath!" Jeff grinned.

The horses were skittish to the point that it took more time and more patience than what the men wanted to give. After a while Jed queried, "You think that story could be true? An eight foot tall hairy monster?"

"Have you got a better explanation for the horses going crazy and that horrible smell?" Jeff responded. "Maybe we should go look for tracks."

Jed was quick to respond and there was just a little nervousness in his voice. "Not today! We have to find the judge as soon as we can, don't we?"

Both men mounted. Again it took extra time for each of them to get their string of six pack horses all going in the same direction. Finally they got them settled and it looked like they were going to make up some of the time lost. The trail divided a narrow meadow with a river off to the right bordered by a jumble of trees and brush. To the left was a narrow open strip ending with clay banks that had numerous narrow ravines eroded into them.

Suddenly Jed's horse whinnied and reared. Jed struggled to stay in the saddle. At the same time he heard a very strange sound like an animal roaring in great pain. Distress spread down the string of horses with each animal wanting to go its own direction. Jed made an instant decision and yelled to Jeff.

"Head them into that closest ravine. We'll lose them if we don't get them there!"

The men kicked their horses into a gallop and turned them to the ravine. Their mounts fought their bits with every step but turning away from the noise and accelerating into a run suited the animals and they followed the pull of the ropes. The horrible smell caught up with them as Jeff and Jed pulled to the side of the gulch to let the horses go by them to enter the small box canyon. The two grabbed their rifles, vaulted off their horses to let them join the rest of the herd in the ravine and and raced to take positions behind some boulders and bushes. The weird sounds and awful smell kept gaining in intensity.

Something was out there. This was nothing imaginary. Panic rose up in both men making it seem like their stomachs were in their throats. Jed pushed down the urge to turn and run realizing there was no where reasonable to go. He felt a tingle spread over his whole body. Jeff fought paralysis. It was like everything had disconnected from his head. He had to give himself a shake to get his firearm ready for whatever was crashing through the tall brush on the river side of the trail.

Something brown with shaggy hair showed through the thinning screen of bushes.

"Did you see that?!" Jed gave a forced whisper to Jeff.

"Yeah, big, hairy and tall! Isn't that what that guy told us? It's moving our way!!" Jeff's voice barely squeaked. He wiped his hands on his pants to dry the sweat. "Are there two of them!?"

"Get ready! It's going to come out of the bushes just past the big pine."

Both men tightened their grip on their rifles, trigger fingers tensed, ready to pull!

There was another glimpse of brown just before the tree and then...

Neither man could believe his eyes. Their jaws dropped, their rifles lowered. Standing in plain view was a two hump camel. It stopped and tested the scents on the air. The horses went into a frenzy. Jed and Jeff stood fully upright.

"I don't believe my eyes," Jed breathed out. "Are you seeing what I'm seeing?"

Jeff was standing shaking his head. "I've seen a picture but camels are in deserts across oceans!" He tried to make sense of what was undoubtedly standing a few yards from them.

The camel gave a big shake of its head, along with a snort, turned and lumbered up the trail in the direction from which the pack-train had just come. Jed and Jeff hadn't moved by the time it faded out of site around the first corner in the trail.

Then they looked at each other with wonder and questions on their faces. Finally, Jed just had to say something for the sake of something normal.

"Wow, that was weird. Do you think that it's some kind of sign from God that you and I see a camel on the trail to Rock Creek? What could it mean?"

That brought a release of laughter from Jeff that undid his tension. "I don't think it is any kind of sign from God. I think it means that someone lost a camel, maybe from a circus, and we happened to see it."

"Well," Jed responded, his voice a little more normal now, "we're sure a long way from any circus but there it was! It's a pretty rare event for it not to be some kind of sign, at least in my mind."

SIXTY-TWO

When they arrived in Rock Creek, Jed and Jeff learned that they had missed the Judge by a week. However, fearing that they may have to follow him all the way to New Westminster, they kept asking around while picking up fresh supplies. The proprietor of the Mercantile responded to their questions by pointing out an Indian guide who had left with Judge Begbie. He assumed that the guide, Douglas Bone, was back after delivering the Judge to his next location.

When Jed and Jeff met him they found he was quite happy to tell them about the Judge.

"Yes sir, I know where the Judge went because I showed him how to get there. He wanted to get to Osoyoos. I told them they couldn't take the trail down the mountain on the east side of the Okanagan. He just has horses, no mules. Mules can go up and down that mountain pretty good but horses get into big trouble and have to leave their loads behind. That Judge sure does pack a heap of stuff so he had to take a better trail than that goat trail!"

"So!" Jed broke in when Douglas took a breath. "Mr. Begbie is at Osoyoos now?"

"Yeah! Haynes told him he had a number of cases that needed sorting out. So I figure he'll be there a bit considering how slow he was here."

Jeff cut in, "Now, who is Haynes?"

"Oh you don't know John Haynes? He's the gold commissioner and the customs agent. He tries to collect duty on all the gold and goods crossing the border. That's why there's getting to be lots of side trails around Osoyoos. Mr. Haynes has caught a few and they're the ones on the list for the Judge. I can't imagine anyone just walking into the customs house and handing over some of their hard earned money. Course I didn't tell the Judge about my opinion. He might not have paid me my fee!"

They spent the night at Rock Creek and got an early start for the several days journey to Osoyoos. Douglas Bone was persistent in offering his services as a guide "for a small fee, much less than he had charged the Judge!" But as they asked around Jed and Jeff became confident that the trail was busy enough that with the few landmarks they had been told about and the people they could ask along the way, they would have no problem finding their way to Osoyoos. They knew they were fortunate that the Judge being at this location had provided the least diversion from their Walla Walla destination compared to other possibilities that may have occurred.

Jed and Jeff couldn't believe the change from Rock Creek to Osoyoos. Rock Creek had abundant forest but now they were in what seemed like a desert. As they turned north in the valley bottom, they could see only barren hills and mountains on either side. There was a stream and a lake providing moisture for a line of trees and brush. They could see buildings further up the valley which was a welcome sight given how inhospitable the climate seemed at the moment. They tethered their pack horses on the edge of the village.

As they got into the village it seemed mostly deserted. Some chickens clucked and scratched close to the first buildings. A dog followed a scent across the street but they could only see one person further up. He was outside a building that had a sign proclaiming "Gold Commissioner."

"Good day," Jeff greeted the man who seemed to be guarding the building given the fact he was cradling a rifle and had brought it to a more ready position across his chest as the two rode up.

The guard kept a stern look on his face. He barely nodded in return. "What's your business here?"

"We understood we could find Judge Begbie here, so we came looking for him." Jed answered.

That caused the guard to stiffen and swing the rifle more in their direction. "Why are you looking for him? He's a busy man."

Jed responded, "The Hudson Bay Trader in Fisherville, John Linklater, sent us with a request for the Judge to come and hear a case of murder"

The guard visibly relaxed, "Oh, then you mean no harm to the Judge! Well, the trial is underway under that grove of cottonwoods." He nodded to some tall trees farther along. "I'm guarding the prisoner for tomorrow's trial. There had been some talk of this guy having some buddies that would try and help him escape."

"Thanks," Jed said. "Can we just go and listen to the trial?"

"You bet, it's quite a show with the judge in robes and a wig. People have come from all over. You don't want to mess with him though. He is called the Hanging Judge!!"

Jed and Jeff made their way over to the grove of trees. Even though there were lots of people, there was very little noise. A baby cried but was quickly shushed by the mother. One voice carried to them as they got closer and they assumed that was the Judge.

"Let's see if we can get close enough to hear." Jed found himself whispering even though they were still quite far from the proceedings.

KOOTENAY JUSTICE

They were in time to hear the Judge declare a guilty verdict. Then the Judge went on to lecture the man on the evil of drunkenness and insist that he change his ways. After delivering a sermon, the Judge fined the man two dollars to pay for the damages against the Trading Post where he was trying to take some cigars without payment. He had apparently broken some items when the clerk tried to collect.

At that the Judge declared a recess for two hours for everyone to get lunch.

The timing was perfect for Jed and Jeff. They made a beeline for Judge Begbie only to be stopped by an official looking guard asking their business.

Jed explained, "We have a letter for Mr. Begbie from John Linklater. It concerns criminal activities in the Kootenays."

The Judge had passed close to them and when he heard John Linklater's name he stopped and turned to address the two newcomers.

"I heard you refer to John Linklater. Has he moved north of the International Boundary yet?"

"Yes, sir," Jed responded. "He's now operating in Fisherville, right in the gold rush."

"Ah! I see. And you have a letter for me from him?"

"Yes, sir!" Jed couldn't help but be extra polite in the presence of this man he had heard so much about.

"Well join me for lunch, and we'll talk things over."

With that the Judge lead them further back in the trees to a sizable tent. A table and chairs were set up in front of the tent. The Judge disappeared into the tent while two more chairs were quickly unfolded and two more place settings were laid. When the Judge came out of the tent he was minus the wig and the robes. A cold lunch was momentarily set on the table and the two trailsmen invited to partake. Jeff and Jed were suddenly self conscious about their clothes and their manners. In their minds

405

they were awestruck at the polish and luxury of Judge Begbie's travel arrangements.

However, it didn't take long for the Judge to set them at ease. The lack of judicial garments made him much more approachable. He explained that this was the first time for him to visit Osoyoos and mentioned the potential he observed for this valley. He could imagine some great possibilities for gardens and orchards in the future.

Soon he was asking questions of his two guests. He seemed immensely interested in their journey and where they had come from. He especially enjoyed the fact that Jed was from Montreal and questioned him about the state of development of that burgeoning city. He commented that he loved to act in the theatre and wondered if he could ever take part in some productions that were giving Montreal a reputation as a cultural centre.

Jed and Jeff were certainly seeing a different side of the Judge than what they would have imagined. Once lunch was consumed, Judge Begbie took up the letter that had been delivered to him. He read in silence.

"You know about this?" Judge Begbie asked. The two nodded that they did."

"Are the ringleaders in custody?"

Jed responded, "They weren't when we left. Mr. Linklater said they seemed so self-assured that they would not leave Fisherville. They feel they have the town completely under their thumbs."

"Did you see this writing that Ogilvie has put on paper recording the crimes the men have done? Does it seem thorough?"

Again, the men responded affirmatively. "I'm sure not educated for legal things," Jed said, "But from what we saw on paper and what we experienced from these guys on a personal level it should show that what they did makes them guilty."

Jeff added, "Mr. Linklater said with the eye witnesses to their extortion and the evidence in hand he could have arrested them already. The concern was when you might be available to hear their cases."

Judge Begbie pondered his situation in light of this urgent request. After a few moments he said, "I've never been to the Kootenay region and this seems to provide the right opportunity. I should be able to accomplish the needed hearings there and return to the coast before snowfall. It will take me a few more days to wrap up here in Osoyoos."

Feeling very relieved that this part of his task was successful, Jed made a suggestion.

"From what I've learned from others, you would have a better journey by going a ways south from here before going east. That provides a more travelled route to the east and north until you get to Fisherville. Also, we might finish our business and be returning when you are travelling and we could travel with you."

The Judge liked that possibility and discussed the probable timing of concluding the judicial business. Jed and Jeff offered their speculations as to the length of time before they might cross paths with Judge Begbie.

"There is one thing that could change my route," the Judge mused. "We are wanting to have a pack trail all the way to Fisherville that is entirely within the Crown Colony. We are contracting with a Mr. Dewdney to build this four foot wide route. He claims there are great obstacles. It's possible that he is just driving up the price of the job by making these claims. I'd like to see for myself. If we can find a guide or get good enough information we'll possibly turn north in time to experience his problems. He says there is a great marsh that is a huge lake in runoff time."

SIXTY-THREE

The trip to Walla Walla proceeded according to plan. The young men were able to purchase all the needed supplies and get back on the return trail without delay. The hard work of running a pack train became a reality for Jed as he pondered this as his long term business. Their day had to start very early to allow for watering the animals and lifting a hundred and fifty pounds onto each side of the pack-saddle ensuring that the loads were balanced side to side. Then they had to prepare their own food before starting out. Next came the planning for good places to overnight with graze and water. Jed found the experienced wranglers they met along the way very friendly and very helpful with information for making the best of the long trail.

On the Judge's part, he too was able to complete his legal duties in the time estimated. For his part in bringing justice and civilization to the wild frontier, Judge Begbie did not travel light. So once his duties were finished his two staff members who doubled as wranglers along with being a court recorder and a bailiff began packing up the legal camp. The court wranglers were well organized, having done the set up and break down for the Judge numerous times. As was usual they hired a couple local men to help but it still took a full day to ready all their equipment for travel.

As Jed and Jeff's return trip brought them close to the international boundary, they expected to hear of the Judge from the occasional travellers they met. They assumed that the number of days it had taken them since parting from Mr. Begbie would have allowed him to be well ahead of the Hudson Bay pack train. Finally, about the time they did cross the border back into British Columbia they got word from a prospector that a bigger than average camp was set up on the Moyie River with someone sitting on a chair by the river's edge. Jed and Jeff grinned at each other as they both recognized the description of Mr. Begbie.

When the Bay pack train caught up to the Judge's camp late in the day, Jeff thought that the judge must have hooked up with another pack train to account for the number of animals. But they soon learned that the fourteen horses were indeed all carrying the kit of this frontier Justice. Sure enough, Mr. Begbie was sitting at a table with tea in a china cup enjoying the pristine wilderness in cultured style.

There was an atmosphere of reunion as the three greeted each other as good friends. Begbie seemed genuinely pleased that he could spend the evening in give and take dialogue with the young wranglers. Once they had cared for their animals, Jed and Jeff sat down to a very pleasant meal prepared by the Judge's hard working staff. During the course of the meal, they learned that the Judge planned to stay in that location for an extra day. There was good grazing for the animals which were showing considerable wear and tear and his crew had indicated that they needed to do some maintenance on their equipment. That suited Jed and Jeff just fine as they had been pushing hard as well. They would easily make use of a full day for the benefit of their own outfit.

What they hadn't seen but learned on subsequent evenings and mornings was that the Judge did in fact share the work of caring for the animals and the luggage. Typically the time of preparing and clearing the meal was time the Judge used for reading and planning for his work as Chief Justice of the British Columbia Crown Colony. But these evenings were given to chatting with his young friends. Begbie had a voracious appetite for knowledge and for sharing that knowledge so that their conversations ranged over a great variety of topics. Jed and Jeff realized that they had a special opportunity through this exposure to one of the leading men of British Columbia.

As that first evening came to a close the Judge picked up a book that was among his papers. One of his staff brought a lantern and both staff members found a place close to the fire. The book was the Anglican Book of Common Prayer. It was the Judge's habit to finish each day using the Book of Prayer as the guide for his evening reflection and he included anyone connected to his party.

The next day Jed raised the subject of the Prayer Book while they were finishing their noon meal.

"I hadn't figured that the work of law keeping and the Bible would go together. Some of the police that used to chase us in the alleys in Montreal certainly weren't church goers, even though they used religious names as curses."

The Judge chuckled, "And you probably weren't heading into the church yourselves!"

Jed had to laugh at himself as he agreed.

"In reality," the Judge continued, "Doing the work of the law properly is the work of the Bible. There is a Bible verse that I repeat to myself often. It comes from the Psalms and it says, 'Righteousness and justice are the foundation of your throne; love and faithfulness go before you'. Those are four very big words — righteousness, justice, love, faithfulness. If they could be kept in balance we'd have a great society. Jesus showed some very religious people that they had overbalanced on religion and lost sight of justice. It gives us a goal to always keep in front of us.

Jeff spoke hesitantly, "So, if I get this right, in my own case there is nothing wrong with me wanting justice for my family. Praying that the murderers would be caught and tried in court."

"Life is precious and sacred and the only payment that can measure up to taking a life is another life – the life of the murderer. And, according to the Bible, only the government appointed judges have the right to decide that. I know that people are calling me the Hanging Judge, but, believe me I look for any bit of evidence that can keep someone from having to pay with his life. If there isn't any doubt at all, then ultimate justice has to be applied."

The Judge had grown very somber as he talked this through with his young friends.

"Well lads," said Begbie, "As you can tell, the weight of my job is never far from the surface. It's part of the reason I enjoy nature and wilderness travel so much. It gets me away from the sadness and tragedies that plague our society and remind me of the basic and simple pleasures of God's gifts to us. This evening let's plan to tell humorous stories. That will lift our spirits beyond these morbid topics that are part of my life."

During the afternoon, the focus was on repairing and strengthening harness and pack-saddles. But they were working close enough that Jeff and Jed could ask the Judge about the route he had taken.

"Well you know I wanted to check out an all British Columbia route," the Judge said. "So we found our way to the Salmon River and then to the pass that would take us over to the valley with the big marsh. Oh my! That was a rugged, difficult climb. There is a kind of trail that we could follow but it certainly put the whole outfit in peril over and over. It will be impossible in the winter."

"We had amazing good fortune when we came down the east side. Not only was it a much easier trail, when we were almost to the bottom we met Mr. Dewdney himself coming the opposite way. He was most concerned for us heading out onto the marsh. Even though it is low water time, he was afraid we would get off the trail and bogged down in the muck that never dries up. I'm not sure he even has a route that he has confidence in. So he decided to turn around and be our guide. He was able to contact some of the local Kootenay Indians who had a couple of canoes and rafts that got us across the main channel of the Kootenay River. I sure feared for our supplies on that raft. The horses had to swim the river. Those marsh flats will certainly be a constant challenge."

"From there," the Judge continued, "Mr Dewdney got us started up the Goat River with directions to cross over to the Moyie river and here we are."

Jed and Jeff had picked up bits and pieces of news about Fisherville from people they met on the long Walla Walla trail. They came to realize that dramatic events had taken place since they had departed. But they weren't sure what they could believe. Late that afternoon a miner who had been successful in his search for gold and who also had the wisdom to sell out his claim at the peak of its production, rode up to their camp. He was on a very fine horse and was dressed above the average. He seemed to be particularly well informed and so the Judge invited him to share a tea break with them in exchange for news from the gold fields.

This miner knew John Linklater well and had very specific knowledge that a daylight street murder had taken place, that an Indian girl had been kidnapped and then rescued at the same time the murderers had been captured. He reported that the villains were in custody waiting for the Judge. So the need for the Judge to get to Fisherville as soon as possible was confirmed. For Jed and Jeff the news validated their pressure on the Judge to make his way to their town. Now a further murder had taken place in broad daylight and there were abundant witnesses that would seal the case against the desperadoes.

The news of the day actually made for a jovial evening as matters of their journey were settled. After the meal, the deepening dusk made for a pleasant atmosphere for sharing light-hearted stories over a small campfire.

Jeff started when it came around to his turn. "Have you ever heard of Sasquatch!"

"Oh, yes! Kind of like Big Foot and Yeti! I'm eager to collect stories of them," Judge Begbie responded.

"Well," Jeff continued, "We started hearing rumblings and warnings of Sasquatch as we were heading west. Stories of campsites being ransacked, horses run off, and a terrible stink left behind. The details were more specific than a myth should generate. Needless to say we were on our guard!"

Jeff and Jed alternately moved the story along. They did not spare themselves in describing the gut clenching fear that had them as tight as a fiddle string. As they described the creature moving closer and closer, Judge Begbie leaned forward, absorbing every detail. He was into the story in a big way.

When Jeff built to the climax, describing their fingers tightening on their triggers, and then exclaimed, "It was a two hump camel" Begbie erupted in laughter. He laughed until tears rolled down his cheeks.

"Oh my! Oh my!" chortled the Judge as his laughter subsided. "Imagine, a camel popping up in the middle of British Columbia! No wonder people were talking Sasquatch!"

The two young men had been laughing heartily as well as they saw the humour more clearly through the reaction of Mr. Begbie.

Finally, Jed asked, "Do you have any ideas about how a camel would be where we saw it?"

Begbie had calmed down to an occasional chuckle, "Actually, I do. Indeed I know how it came."

"Several years back the Fraser Canyon was a bottle neck for getting supplies up to the gold fields. Everything had to be packed in on narrow twisting trails. Feed for animals was scarce. Horses were falling down cliffs to their deaths with the supplies on their backs lost. A man by the name of Frank Laumeister came up with a harebrained scheme to use camels as pack animals. He thought they could go further than horses or mules without food or water. There were some for sale, twenty three in all, in Arizona where they had been brought in for a construction project."

"Wow, who would have guessed camels as pack animals around here!" exclaimed Jed.

"Well it didn't turn out very well," emphasized the Judge. "You saw how your horses reacted. Imagine coming around a corner on the narrow Fraser Canyon trail and coming face to face with an ugly camel that you've never seen before! Turned out they didn't like horses any better than the horses liked them. They bit and kicked other animals any time they got close enough. It created mayhem. It caused some horses to go over the cliff as they tried to turn around where it was too narrow. We got so many complaints that we had to outlaw camels within four months of them first coming. Actually, it turned out that their feet are made for soft ground - sand over in the deserts – rather than the rocky riverside trails in this country. So they were going lame as well."

"Whatever happened to them?" asked Jeff.

"Well, they weren't producing income but still eating hay. We think they were simply turned loose. The sad assumption is that they couldn't survive on their own and that they died off. One or two may have been taken in by farmers just to have the exotic animal to show off to visitors. But I am surprised that one of them got that far east and is still creating a stir, even as

a Sasquatch! Oh my! You've given me the best story of the year.
I'll be telling Sasquatch stories around a lot of campfires!"

SIXTY-FOUR

The moccasin telegraph had worked well to let the citizens of Fisherville know the Judge was arriving. There had been lots of talk in the community about the brand of justice that Mr. Begbie would bring to the frontier town. Rumours had swirled and grown until people were expecting thirty horses in his pack train. They were also expecting him to ride in wearing his wig and robes!

It turned into another parade giving entertainment for the locals. People actually cheered the Judge. With some calling out encouragement for the Judge to "hang 'em high!" Both Jed and Jeff took note that Begbie was enjoying this attention and the bantering with people along the street.

Jed gave the lead lines for the Hudson Bay pack train to Jeff and moved up to the front to guide Mr. Begbie to the Hudson Bay store. John Linklater was waiting on the steps to welcome their honoured guest and to offer him the services of the Hudson Bay.

"Judge Begbie, we are very glad that you have come to this edge of the wilderness. We offer every assistance you may require to the extent this village can provide it. I invite you to accommodate yourself in our quarters."

"Much appreciated, Mr. Linklater. I'm sure that I will call on you for some necessities. However, I have a very adequate camp kit with me that gives me work space as well as reasonable comfort," Begbie replied. "If you can suggest a convenient setting for my camp that will be excellent."

John Linklater had expected this desire for the temporary setting for their legal headquarters. He indicated the young man standing beside him.

"This is Cody McVeigh who headed up the team sent out from Montreal to bring these renegades to justice. He and his men will show you to a campsite and will be available to assist you in any way you need."

The Judge acknowledged Cody with a slight smile. "I've been hearing quite a bit about you and your crew from Jed. If what I've heard is to be believed, I'm sure this hearing will be moved along without a hitch. Lead on then, young sir!"

A campsite had been cleared a hundred yards back of the Store and a pole corral that enclosed some grassy meadow, some trees and a small creek had been set up another hundred yards beyond that site.

The Judge's men set to work with the volunteer help of Cody, Darcy and Quinn. The main tent that provided the living quarters for the Judge was placed at the far border of the prepared area.

Cody asked, "Wouldn't it be more convenient if the tent were on the side of the site closest to the store and other conveniences of the town?"

One of the Judge's men explained, "The tent also provides the resources for the trial. The front opens wide and has an awning that extends far enough to cover the witness stand as well as the Judge's table. Having it on the far side let's people come and go from town without interfering with the trial."

"Does the Judge want very many people coming to the trial? Won't they make too much noise?" queried Darcy.

The court clerk laughed in response. "The Judge would like everybody to come to see British justice at work. You'll see how he can keep a crowd quiet! I'm amazed every time I see it happen."

Jed and Jeff were left to themselves to off load their pack train. This was made more difficult because of the prisoners occupying the store room. Nels did come to their aid after he had assured himself that Linklater and Begbie had everything they needed for their legal work.

Once the work day was ended by darkness, the Hudson Bay crew and the Judge's crew were all invited to a meal in Berty's kitchen provided by Mr. Begbie. It was his appreciation of the help he was receiving. It was a great chance to catch up with one another on all the developments since Jed and Jeff had departed to find the Judge. It worked doubly well to give the Chief Justice an over view of the more recent villainy carried out by the Bosses and the people they controlled. Murder and kidnapping on top of all the crimes chronicled by Ogilvie, made for an obvious outcome for the trial.

As Jed and Jeff started detailing their journey to Osoyoos and Walla Walla, the Judge broke in and insisted that they jump right to the story about Sasquatch! That certainly got everyone's attention and the two had to share that experience. Mr. Begbie was chuckling all the way through the buildup as Jed and Jeff didn't spare themselves for the spine tingling fear they had each felt. The whole group erupted with side splitting laughter when they finally revealed that their Sasquatch was a two hump camel. Once again Judge Begbie had tears rolling down his cheeks.

"That's the best story I've heard all year! It was just as good the second time. It will make for some great story times as I work my circuit."

The next day was all business. Each of the prisoners was interviewed separately by the Judge. He explained that he was defence and prosecutor as well as Judge. That didn't move the Bosses at all. They remained surly claiming that everything was a set up and they were just protecting themselves. Judge Begbie shook his head as they went so far as claiming that Ogilvie really had a gun and that they had had to kidnap the girl otherwise the wild Bay boys would have just shot them down.

It was a different story when he interviewed Wolfleg. Wolfleg started spilling everything once he understood that the Judge was promising that he would not hang if he gave true testimony about his involvement with the Bosses. That was the step Begbie had been concerned about but once Wolfleg started to sing the Judge knew that this was not going to be a long trial.

He also interviewed Robert Scot the Assistant Trader from Kootenay House. When Robert had learned that Sam Ogilvie had been murdered and the Bosses arrested he was both relieved and distressed. He was glad that the abuses carried on by Leblanc and Lagasse were ended. His days as an assistant in the evil contrived by the Bosses and supported by his employer were finished. However, he knew that he would have to pay a price for his participation in it. Still it was better to face the music now and start over somewhere far from this Kootenay region.

Robert had packed up the affairs of Sam Ogilvie and in the process discovered a satchel full of secret records of the disappearances of a number of Hudson Bay agents sent to the area to look into thefts of Bay property. These documents had dates and details that Robert knew would be valuable in any trial that might come. When he heard that the Judge was on his way to Fisherville, Robert determined that he would attend and make this material available to the court. Judge Begbie briefly reviewed the material in the satchel and suggested that it was good backup material to what he already had from Ogilvie in case there was some question about details. He asked Robert to keep it in a safe place and be ready to produce it if needed.

By noon he announced that the trial would go ahead the next day. A ripple of excitement ran through Fisherville. People changed their plans to be able to attend the court of the vaunted Judge Begbie, the Hanging Judge. Conversations were charged with energy as neighbours speculated how the day would unfold.

Judge Begbie called together his bailiff, his clerk and all of the Hudson Bay team.

"Even though everything seems straightforward for this trial we will still follow proper protocol and security." the Judge said. "My bailiff and clerk know their jobs well and will keep the trial on a proper track. We need you to carry out security. I am deputizing each and everyone of you and you alone will be entitled to carry weapons in the vicinity of the court. Those inside the court will carry pistols and those outside the court are to have rifles as well as pistols.

Quinn asked, "Does that mean we'll take firearms from people if they show up with them?"

"Absolutely," the Judge responded. "Here's the assignments that I think will work best. John and Nels will shuttle the prisoners in and out of the court. Darcy and Jed will guard the prisoners while in court. Jeff will collect guns from people and watch over them while they are there. Quinn, I want you to be my guard while court is in session. Cody, you are to be the crew leader. If anything changes or someone needs some help you are to look after it. With everyone carrying out their assignment, I'll be able to concentrate on directing legal proceedings from the Bench."

"Sir," Jed spoke up, "Seems to me we should have some kind of seating for the visitors who will be closest to your bench. We could skid a few logs into place. Might be better crowd control."

Judge Begbie nodded his agreement. Jed and Quinn left the meeting to care for it.

SIXTY-FIVE

The trial day dawned bright and clear. People started arriving well before the planned time of nine o'clock. Jeff had to circulate through the early crowd to catch up with confiscating guns. Most of the men did not carry firearms and those that did were more surprised than angry when Jeff asked for their weapons. The excitement grew as the appointed time drew near. People were speculating on the evidence to be given and the appearance of the murderers. Jeff even heard some suggestions that there would be a hanging before the day was over. The volume of conversation rose as that rumour rumbled through the crowd. The deputies heard the rumours also and realized that good order was not to be taken for granted. Quinn moved into position at the back and side of the elevated table, while Darcy and Jed found seats at the front where the prisoners would come a little later.

Promptly at nine the clerk stood and called out in a loud clear voice. "Attention! Attention! By the authority of Her Majesty, Queen Victoria, ruler of the British Empire, this Court of the

Crown Colony of British Columbia is hereby called to Order. Judge Matthew Baillie Begbie presiding. All rise!"

There was a ripple of exclamations, some oh's and awe's, as Judge Begbie strode around the canvas partition towards his raised chair and table. His long black rode billowed out behind him. The carefully coiffed wig extended down to his shoulders. The grey of the wig making a startling contrast to the black of his robe. He smoothed his robe behind him and took his seat from which he could see over the heads of people standing. His gavel raised and smacked down as he proclaimed "Court is now in session. Be seated"

There was no doubt in anyone's mind as to who was in charge. With that call to order, the entrance of the Judge, the robe, the wig, the gavel and the booming voice, law and order and justice had come to the Kootenay's.

The first few minutes were used by Judge Begbie to lay down the rules of behaviour expected of everyone in attendance. He explained that the Hudson Bay people who had the empowerment to act on behalf of the Queen's Court when the Judge was not present had been duly deputized to provide security for the proceedings and thereby were the only men allowed to carry firearms.

The clerk immediately called for the first of four claim disputes that had been registered with the court. They were only brought before the judge because the people involved happened to know that Begbie was coming. Otherwise the issues might have been settled by fists or guns, certainly by threats of bodily harm. The Judge asked a few questions of each of the parties involved in the four cases and after a brief pause to consider the matter gave his ruling. After each judgement there was a general murmur of approval that fairness, if not happiness, had been served by Judge Begbie. People in attendance were seeing justice in action and the general attitude of respect for these court proceedings took a giant step forward as they experienced the justice process being exercised.

Once the claim disputes had been settled, Judge Begbie called for the prisoners to be brought into the court. He explained that because one of the three was a significant witness to the charges against the other two, they would need all three prisoners present. He declared a recess until the prisoners were in place.

Cody stepped away from the press of the onlookers and signalled across the open space to John and Nels. They had been waiting for this sign that they were to bring Leblanc, Lagasse and Wolfleg to the court.

"Alright," John said to the three whom they had had sitting with manacles on at the back of the Hudson Bay facility, "Time for you to get your justice for all those people you've denied justice to."

Leblanc growled as he struggled to his feet with the chains making it difficult. "You think this little side show of a court can hold us you've got another think coming. This ain't over Linklater. You'll pay for the treatment you've given us!"

"You've received a lot easier treatment than what you've deserved Leblanc. You boys better plead for mercy because that's your only chance for anything other than a rope!"

John and Nels got them shuffling towards the court. As their path took them close to Cody who was standing about halfway, John motioned him over.

"Listen, I don't think there's anything to it, but Leblanc did sneer that the court wouldn't be able to hold them. It's probably just empty words on his part."

"Well I don't see how there could be anyway someone would try to break them free. It would be pretty foolish. But, thanks for mentioning it. I'll stay back a bit from the crowd and keep a strong watch for anything unusual."

As the prisoners were led through the crowd a general rumble of reaction broke out, people cursing, some even spitting! Those who had been victimized in one way or another vented their anger. Wolfleg cringed at the level of rancour, but Leblanc and Legasse snarled back with amazing brass considering this was a major step to the gallows.

Once again the clerk called for order, and once again had everyone stand as he announced Judge Begbie presiding. The Judge strode to the elevated table, rang his gavel, and declared court in session. There was a sense of great respect that had been established by the earlier cases. People quieted quickly and the Judge had them seated where there was something to sit on. Most of the rest sat on the ground. Some simply stayed standing. No one had any difficulty hearing Mr. Begbie as his theatre experience had taught him well in projecting his voice.

The Judge took considerable time outlining the charges against the prisoners. He noted that he would depend on the eyewitnesses regarding the shooting death of Sam Ogilvie, and the written record that Sam Ogilvie had given to John Linklater for other charges regarding criminal activity these men had carried out. That written testimony also served as the basis for charging the prisoners with four more murders of Hudson Bay Agents, sent to investigate crimes connected to the Kootenay House trading post, who had been thought to have met with accidental deaths. He further explained that Wolfleg was charged with being an agent in many of these crimes and was present because he had agreed to testify against Leblanc and Lagasse.

Finally, as Judge Begbie finished his extensive list of charges against them, he looked at the two French Canadians and asked, "How do you respond to these charges?"

Leblanc and Lagasse had smirked all the way through the listing of charges. Now Leblanc spoke up and said, "Nah, Judge we are not guilty! Ogilvie was a crazy man. He was sick in his head and he just made up that stuff that he wrote down. Besides we shot him in self-defence. He had a gun and was going to shoot us!"

Wolfleg lunged enraged to his feet causing a great rattling noise. He shouted, "You're liars and you dragged us into all that stuff. You've ruined our lives as well as your own!"

Judge Begbie was pounding his gavel to bring order. Darcy was wrestling Wolfleg back down to his seat. Shouts were erupting in the crowd agreeing with Wolfleg.

"Quiet!" the Judge roared. "You'll have your chance to tell your story but not until you're asked, Wolfleg!"

Order was restored. Leblanc and Lagasse still smirked thinking that they could disrupt this court so that it would be left in a muddle. Wolfleg continued to do a death stare at the two that had entwined him in their guilt with promises that were never fulfilled.

The Judge asked for Robert Scot to step forward, which he did. "Robert, I didn't expect that I would need the contents of your satchel today, but it appears that some things need to be settled early. Those documents will accomplish it. Please bring them as soon as possible."

Robert turned to go to the Hudson Bay Store where he had been staying and where he had cached the satchel. The court proceedings resumed behind him. As he reached the edge of the onlookers, Cody saw he was on an errand for the Judge. He had not heard what had been said between Robert and the Judge. When he enquired and learned the nature of the task, that important evidence was being conveyed to the trial, Cody thought it best to accompany Robert. There was no objection on Robert's part.

It was a quick retrieval and the two men started back immediately knowing that the Judge could use the material right away. They walked past the store room that had served as a jail and were about to step outside when they heard an unusual noise. It was just a rumble in the distance. Could have been thunder from a distant storm but it was a clear day.

Cody held Robert back from going outside. He then slipped out the door and stepped immediately to his left where there was an alcove between buildings. His hand dropped to his pistol and he stiffened at the sound of charging horses. Those horses burst into sight at full gallop about three buildings over headed towards the court gathering. As soon as the dozen horses were clear of the building the Indian riders began a startling "Yip, Yip, Yip" and an occasional Indian war-hoop. The charging horses began to circle the court, the riders waving rifles in the air. With each circle the horses crowded a little closer, tightening their path towards the centre. There was a chorus of yells and shouts from the people attending the trial which added to the bedlam.

Quinn immediately pushed Begbie down to the floor and tipped the table forward onto its side. Quinn covered the Judge as best he could with his own body, while keeping his arm free to be able to use his gun. Darcy and Jed as well as John and Nels drew their pistols and pushed the prisoners to the ground.

Leblanc chortled, "Now you guys find out you shouldn't mess with Leblanc and Lagasse!

"Shut up!" Darcy hissed. Then at a shout he said, "Hold your fire! Everybody get down!"

Some one called out, "Give us our guns!"

"No!" responded Darcy. "No shooting unless they shoot first!"

Robert slipped out the door and huddled with Cody in the alcove. After a moment of seeing the riders on the horses he said to Cody, "Those aren't Kootenay Indians, they are Peigans from the plains. They are part of the ring that steals the Kootenay horses and sells them to the rest of the Blackfeet. I've seen some of them at Kootenay House!"

Suddenly Cody stiffened, "Well lookee here!"

A lone horse and rider had appeared through the same gap as the galloping horses. This one had taken a few steps out into the open but was now just standing, watching intently as the circle tightened around the court. Robert followed Cody's gaze and also stiffened.

"Cody! That's Big Plume! He bosses these Peigans!" He said in a forced whisper.

Big Plume started walking his horse forward, staring intently at the action as if he was closing in on the right time to snatch the prisoners.

"Right! I recognized him. Stay here!" Cody turned, drew his pistol and began sliding along the back wall of the buildings, keeping as deep into the shadow as possible. It seemed Big Plume would not notice him he was so focused on his warrior riders. Choosing his moment quickly and carefully, Cody quietly stepped up behind the now stationary horse and rider.

Planting the barrel of the gun firmly in Big Plume's back, Cody urgently commanded, "Freeze! Not a sound or you're dead! Hands up!" Big Plume jerked upright, but raised his hands.

"OK, now give the signal for them to retreat! Right now! They do anything else and it is you that's dead! Do it!!"

Big Plume put two fingers in his mouth and gave two sharp piercing whistles. The racing horses immediately pulled up. The riders all looked to the gap they had raced through. Big Plume crossed his arms above his head. Instantly every horse spun away from the court and fled directly away to disappear into some kind of cover until quiet fully descended over the area.

"Robert, get some rope!" Cody croaked out. "Now, Big Plume get down. Any wrong move and I will plug you."

Cody had moved along the side of the horse to pull the rifle out of the saddle boot. Robert came with rope and began tying Big Plume's hands behind his back. By this time a volume of chatter was rising from the court site as people were putting their nervousness into words, each one telling their own version of what had happened and how near to death they all were. John and Nels, who had spotted the action Cody was in, were running across the space to assist as they could.

Quinn had let Judge Begbie up once the danger was evidently over. He was astonished to see a pistol in the Judge's hand.

"Where did that come from?" Quinn asked.

Begbie grinned and said, "These robes are good for more than just appearances. You'd be surprised what can be hidden underneath! Now, what on earth was that all about?"

People were getting themselves sorted out. Most were dusting themselves off after being flat on the ground. Quinn saw Cody leading several people back into the court. He nodded in their direction and said to the Judge, "Looks like we're going to find out in just a few minutes."

Once court was reconvened, the Judge asked Cody to step up with his new prisoner.

"I expect you can shed some light on this escapade, Cody. Please let us in on what was going on."

"Sir, this is Big Plume. He operates a horse ranch that deals in stolen horses. Primarily he steals them from Kootenays and sells them to the Peigan Indians, part of the Blackfoot Confederation on the plains just east of the mountains. Today was an attempt to free these prisoners. He was directing that attack using Peigans. They intended to frighten everyone with that closing circle of horses and rifles, and lift the prisoners onto the horses and gallop off with them."

Leblanc sneered at Big Plume, "You idiot, couldn't you even do one operation right and get us out of here!!"

"Ah," said Begbie, after telling Leblanc to be quiet, "Looks like we have all the major players now. Wolfleg had kindly included sufficient information about Mr. Big Plume that we can simply add him to the people charged in this court hearing." Looking directly at Big Plume, he continued, "Mr. Big Plume, you have actually done us a great favour in showing up today. I believe that once we are finished today we will be able to declare that Kootenay justice has been done."

The court moved rapidly through the rest of the day. The Pards entered their evidence which corroborated Ogilvie's written testimony and Wolfleg's stories. The metal button, the fringes from the buckskin shirt and the partially cut hobble all sealed the doom of the four men.

As dusk was setting in, Judge Begbie asked Leblanc and Lagasse to stand to hear their sentence. With considerable rattling of chains they slouched to a standing position.

"By the powers vested in me as Chief Judge of the Crown Colony of British Columbia, I sentence each of you to death by hanging!"

Leblanc kept the sneer on his face but it was obviously forced and was simple bravado. Lagasse sagged and almost collapsed and was held up by John Linklater.

A great stirring rippled through the court. People looked at each other and nodded that this was due justice for the lives they had taken.

The Judge was continuing, "You will be transported to New Westminster and there be dealt capital punishment on the last day of November."

"Now, in the matter of Mr. Wolfleg. I do believe that he was controlled and manipulated by Leblanc and Lagasse. Still, he flagrantly broke the law and bears a significant level of responsibility. I sentence him to five years in custody in New Westminster."

"As to Mr. Big Plume, I find that the trade in stolen horses aided the continuing of the illegal operations that have been under scrutiny in this trial. However, there is no evidence of physical violence carried out by the horse ranching operations. The sentence therefore will be one year to be served in New Westminster.

SIXTY-SIX

The Judge hosted a thank you dinner at Berty's Kitchen for everyone who had assisted with the trial. It was a great way to celebrate. Stories were told that were greatly entertaining and mostly true! John Linklater turned out to be more of a story teller than the Pards had experienced on the trek from Fort Kokanee. However, no one could top Mr. Begbie who had the whole group laughing until their sides ached.

Late in the evening, John called for everyone's attention.

"This night brings to a significant conclusion a mission committed to four young men – the Pards - as they have come to call themselves. The Hudson Bay directors, thousands of miles from here, took a big risk and sent these men on a secret mission to bring these scoundrels to justice. I have to admit, when they showed up at Fort Kokanee I was alarmed at how young they were. But they proved themselves beyond what I could ever have predicted. So, I propose a toast to congratulate them on the completion of their mission."

Everyone raised their drinks and clunked their tin cups with one another. Then the Judge led off with a rousing rendition of "For They Are Jolly Good Fellows!"

"Well lads!" Judge Begbie broke the silence, "What will you be doing now that your commission is finished?"

This time it was Cody who broke the silence. "We haven't even talked about that. Jed has talked about doing freighting."

Jed spoke up saying "There is nothing like that long distance pack train experience if we're not on the trail together."

Quinn chimed in. "I've got all kinds of orders for lumber that can keep me going for a long time. But — I could leave that at a moments notice if we're needed somewhere else."

"Don't forget." John broke in. "We need to look after Kootenay House now that Sam Ogilvie is dead and Robert Scot released from the Hudson Bay. I'm not sure it can ever regain the trust of trappers again. So with the experience in closing down Fort Kokanee, I'm sure Cody and Darcy can look after one more Trading Post."

Cody and Darcy looked at each other and scowled. They hadn't signed on with the Bay to become storekeepers. It was too big a contrast with chasing down criminals. There was a big wide world out there that they hadn't experienced yet and, one way or another, they were determined to see more of it.

Cody said, "Yeah, I guess we'll do what we got to do. If that means Kootenay House, well what do you think Darcy?"

Judge Begbie laughed at the discomfort on the faces of Cody and Darcy. "It looks like you two were sentenced today given the look on your faces! Listen, the next big thing out here is going to be stern- wheelers and railroads. Mining is going to be big and the ore is going to float south on boats to connect with railroads to the smelters. There's even talk of laying a railway from the east all the way to the Pacific. Even talk of British Columbia joining the eastern provinces in a Confederation. This means huge dollars changing hands. It also means the likelihood of corruption stealing in. I'm going to need a crew like the Pards to keep those sailors and railroaders on the straight and narrow. Interested??!!"

The expression on Darcy and Cody's faces had changed from distaste to anticipation. The Pards all looked at each other and a smile crept up on each one as they imagined what the Judge might have for them in another valley in this incredible wilderness.

End

CPSIA information can be obtained at www.ICGtesting.com
Printed in the USA
LVOW12s2342180214

374233LV00001B/4/P

9 781460 230916